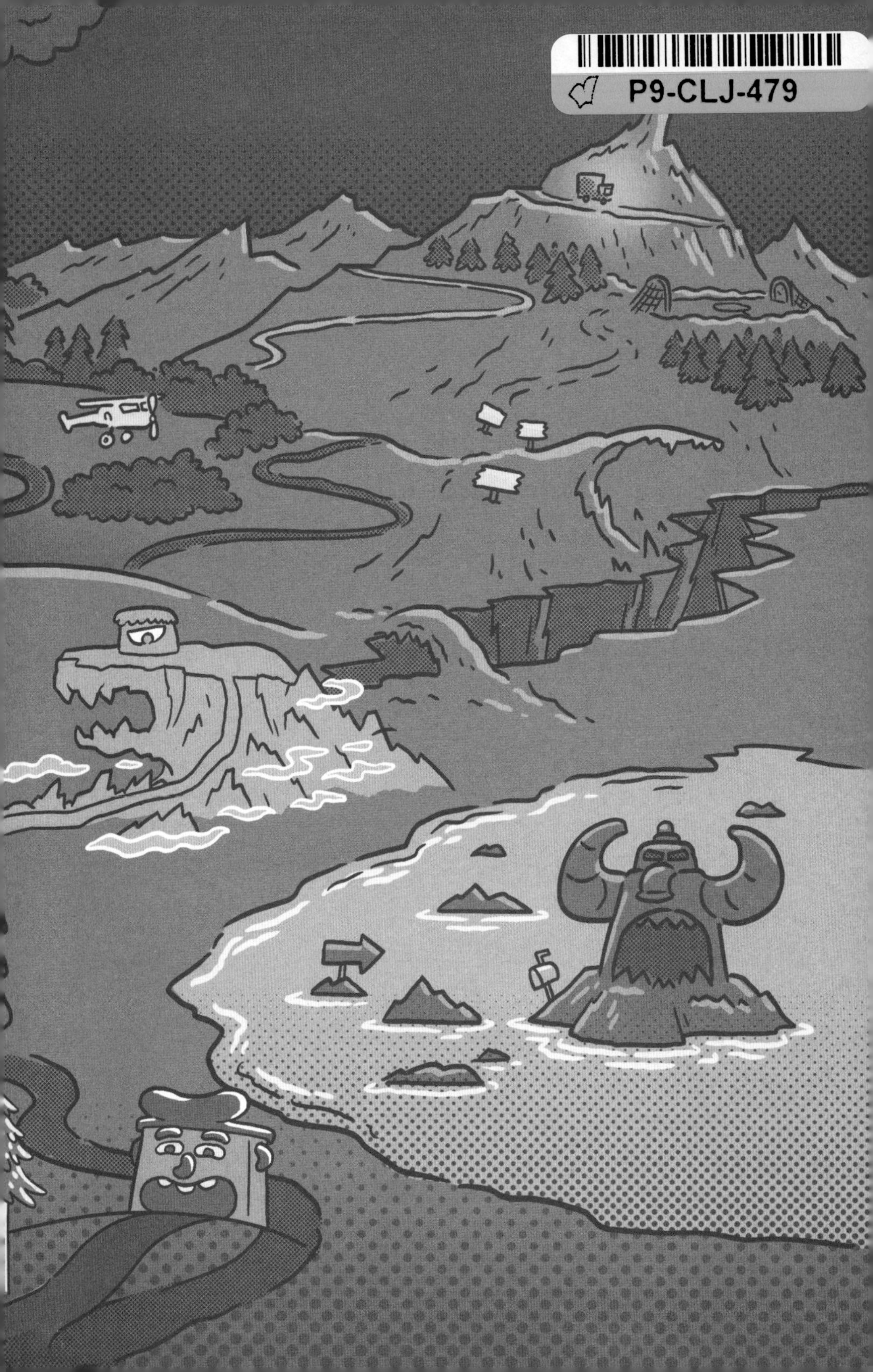

DINO MIGHTY!

LAW AND ODOR

BY **DOUG PALEO**

ILLUSTRATED BY **AARON BLECHA**

CLARION BOOKS
IMPRINTS OF HARPERCOLLINS PUBLISHERS

HARPER
alley

CLARION BOOKS IS AN IMPRINT OF HARPERCOLLINS PUBLISHERS.
HARPERALLEY IS AN IMPRINT OF HARPERCOLLINS PUBLISHERS.

LAW AND ODOR

LIBRARY OF CONGRESS CONTROL NUMBER: 2022937877
ISBN 978-0-35-862795-1

THE ILLUSTRATIONS IN THIS BOOK WERE SKETCHED IN PENCIL
AND THEN CREATED DIGITALLY.
TYPOGRAPHY BY PHIL CAMINITI

22 23 24 25 26   EP   10 9 8 7 6 5 4 3 2 1

❖

FIRST EDITION

CHAPTERS

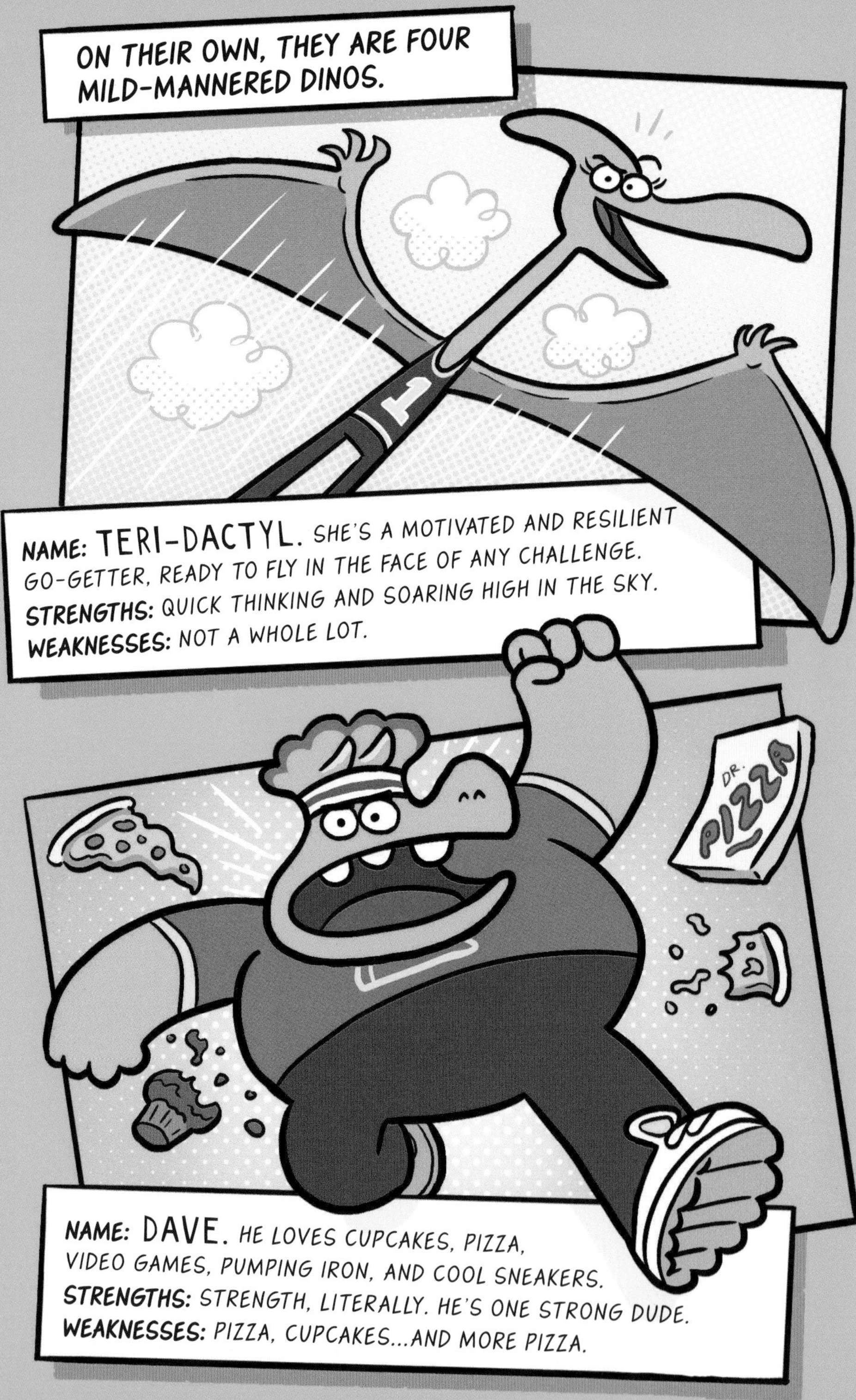
ON THEIR OWN, THEY ARE FOUR MILD-MANNERED DINOS.
1
NAME: TERI-DACTYL. SHE'S A MOTIVATED AND RESILIENT GO-GETTER, READY TO FLY IN THE FACE OF ANY CHALLENGE.
STRENGTHS: QUICK THINKING AND SOARING HIGH IN THE SKY.
WEAKNESSES: NOT A WHOLE LOT.
DR. PIZZA
NAME: DAVE. HE LOVES CUPCAKES, PIZZA, VIDEO GAMES, PUMPING IRON, AND COOL SNEAKERS.
STRENGTHS: STRENGTH, LITERALLY. HE'S ONE STRONG DUDE.
WEAKNESSES: PIZZA, CUPCAKES...AND MORE PIZZA.

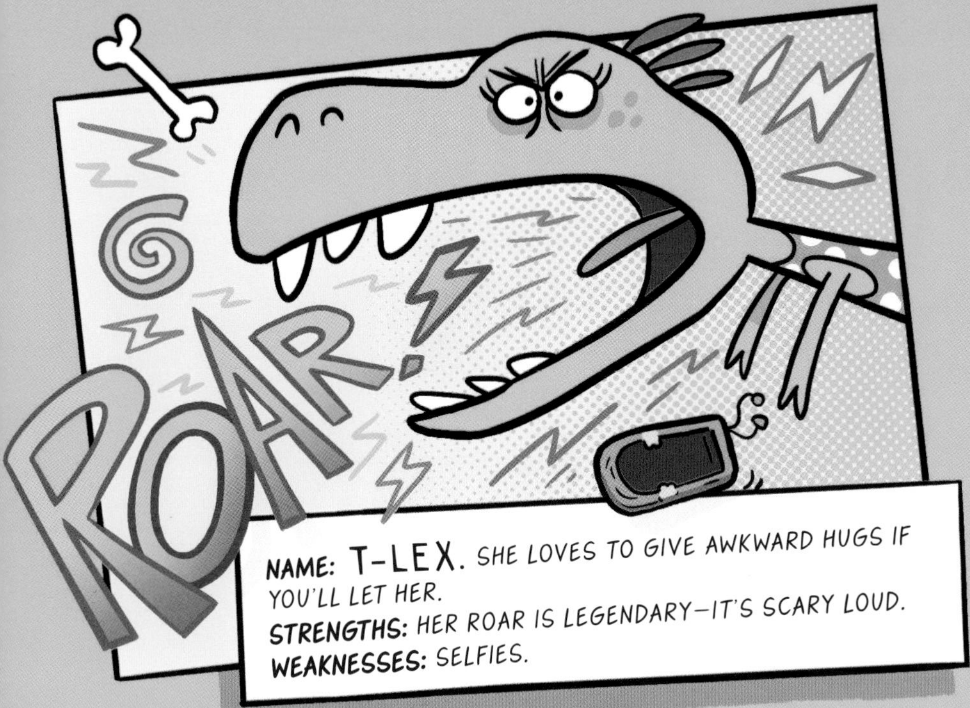
ROAR!
NAME: T-LEX. SHE LOVES TO GIVE AWKWARD HUGS IF YOU'LL LET HER.
STRENGTHS: HER ROAR IS LEGENDARY—IT'S SCARY LOUD.
WEAKNESSES: SELFIES.

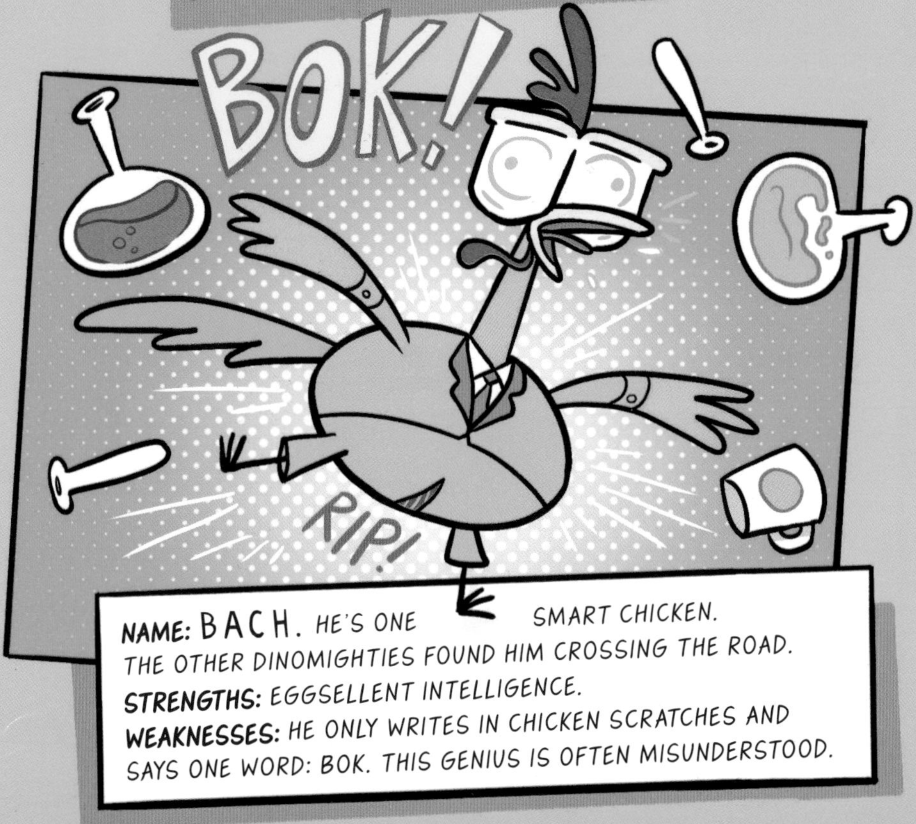
BOK!
RIP!
NAME: BACH. HE'S ONE SMART CHICKEN. THE OTHER DINOMIGHTIES FOUND HIM CROSSING THE ROAD.
STRENGTHS: EGGSELLENT INTELLIGENCE.
WEAKNESSES: HE ONLY WRITES IN CHICKEN SCRATCHES AND SAYS ONE WORD: BOK. THIS GENIUS IS OFTEN MISUNDERSTOOD.

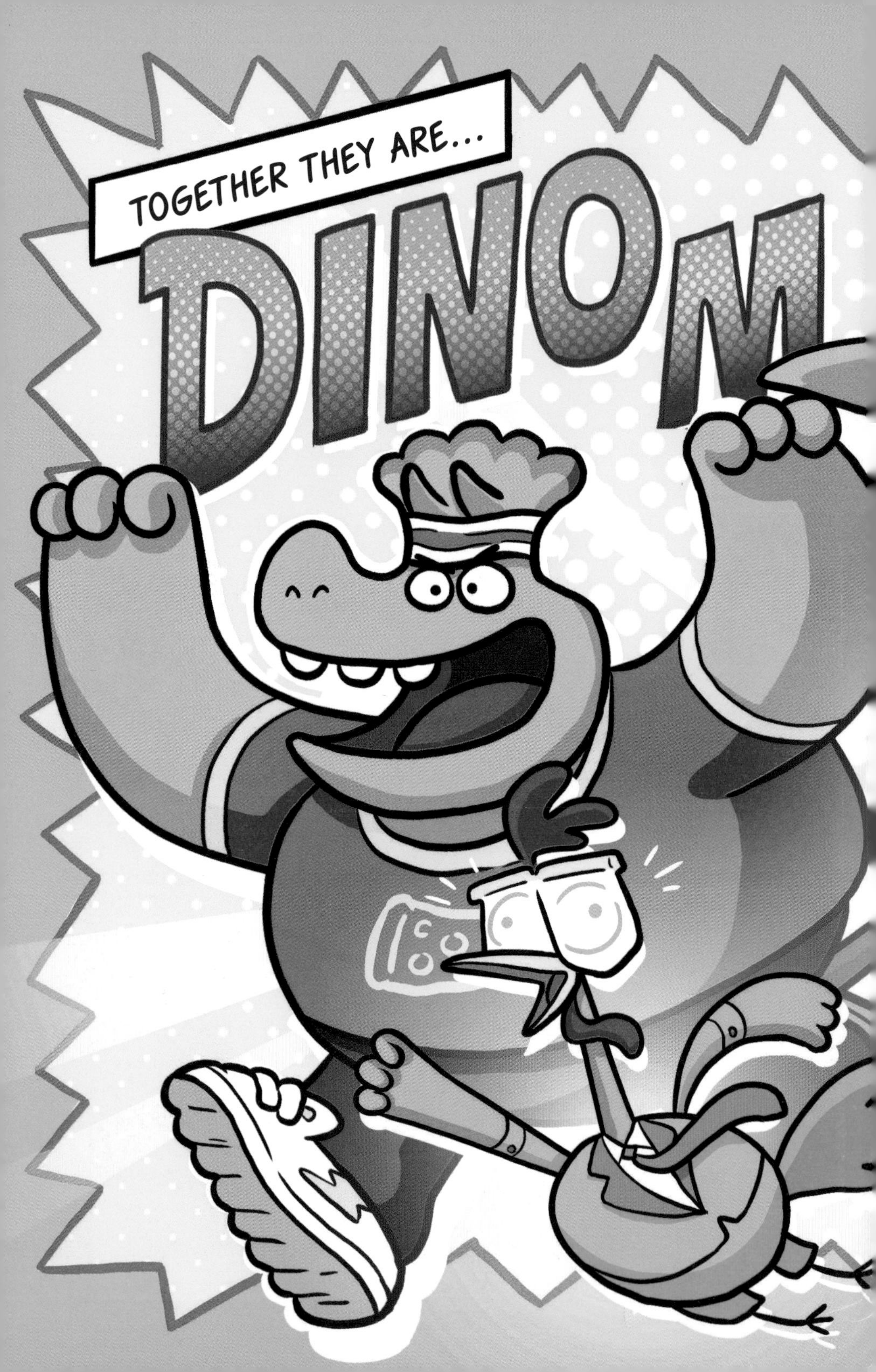
TOGETHER THEY ARE...
DINOM

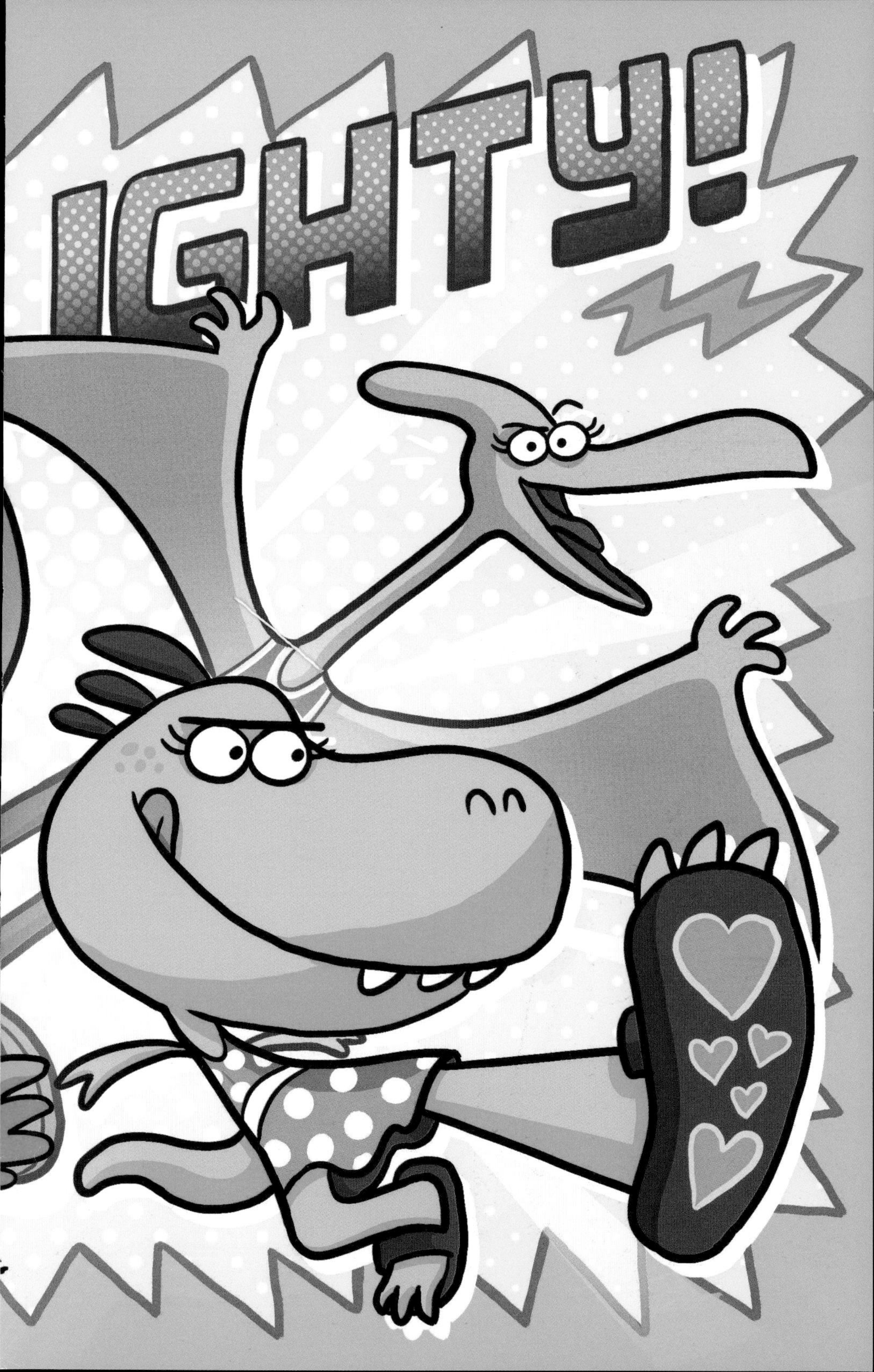
IGHTY!

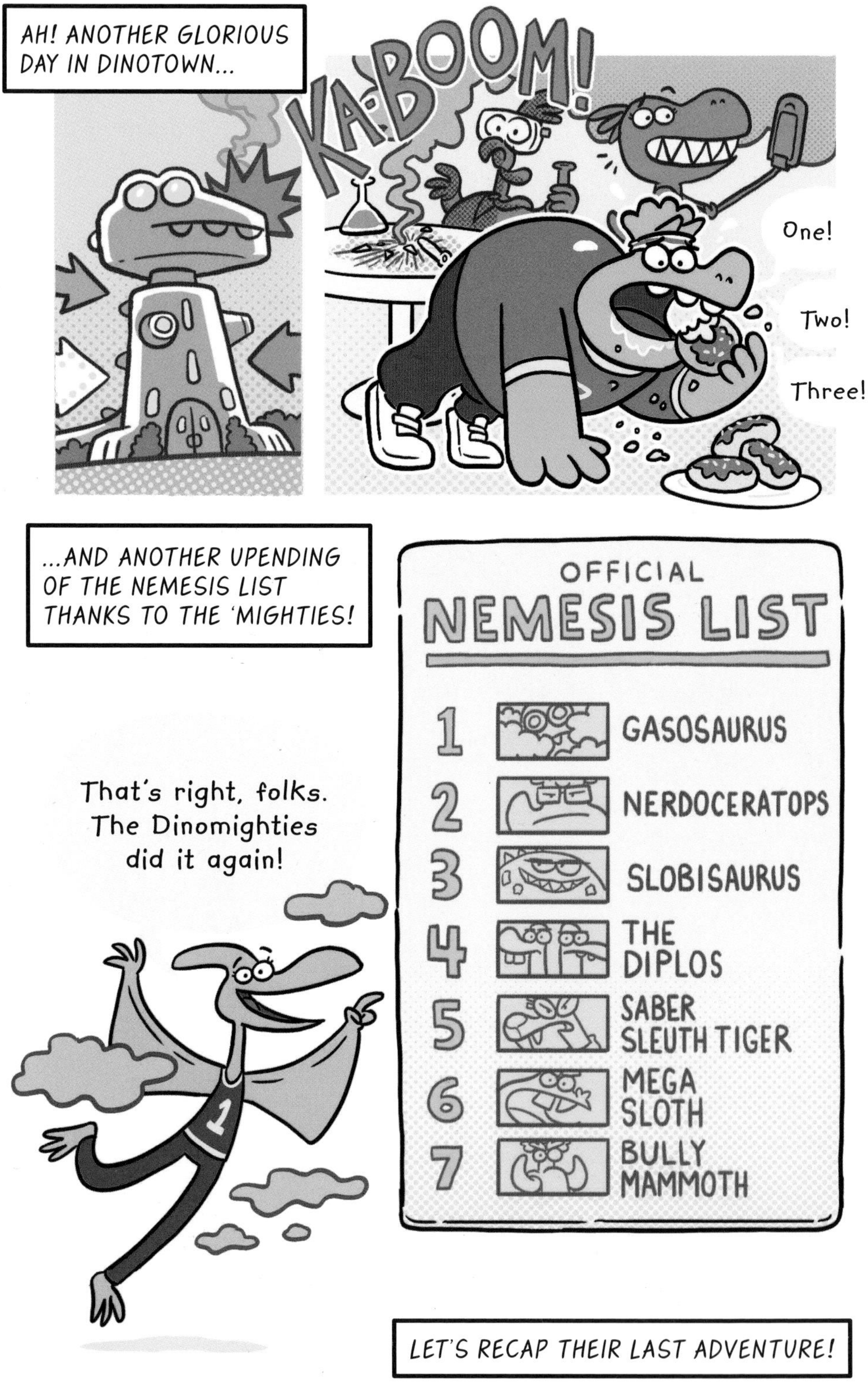
AH! ANOTHER GLORIOUS DAY IN DINOTOWN...
KA-BOOM!
One!
Two!
Three!
...AND ANOTHER UPENDING OF THE NEMESIS LIST THANKS TO THE 'MIGHTIES!
That's right, folks. The Dinomighties did it again!
OFFICIAL
NEMESIS LIST
1 GASOSAURUS
2 NERDOCERATOPS
3 SLOBISAURUS
4 THE DIPLOS
5 SABER SLEUTH TIGER
6 MEGA SLOTH
7 BULLY MAMMOTH
LET'S RECAP THEIR LAST ADVENTURE!

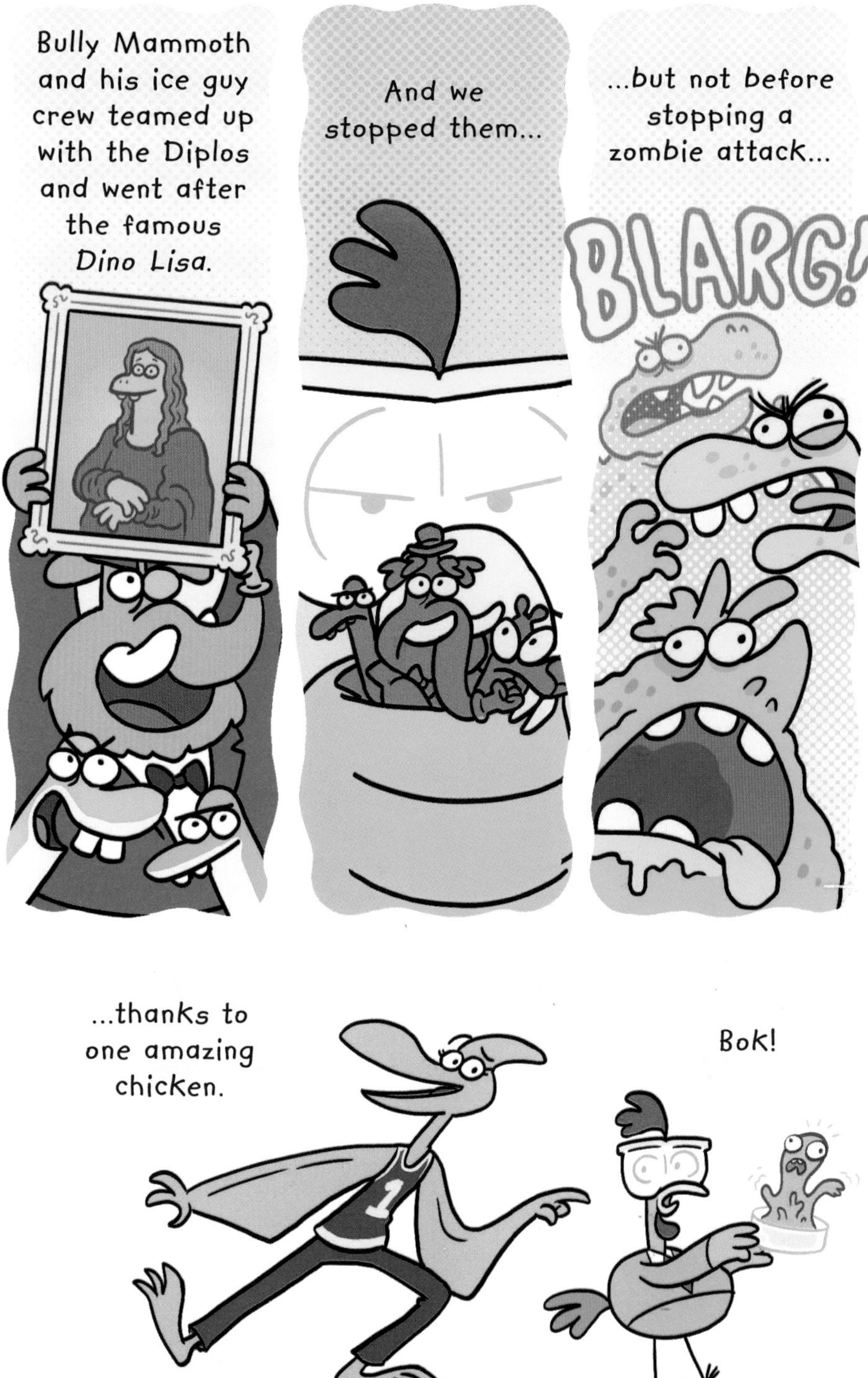
Bully Mammoth and his ice guy crew teamed up with the Diplos and went after the famous *Dino Lisa*.
And we stopped them...
...but not before stopping a zombie attack...
BLARG!
...thanks to one amazing chicken.
Bok!

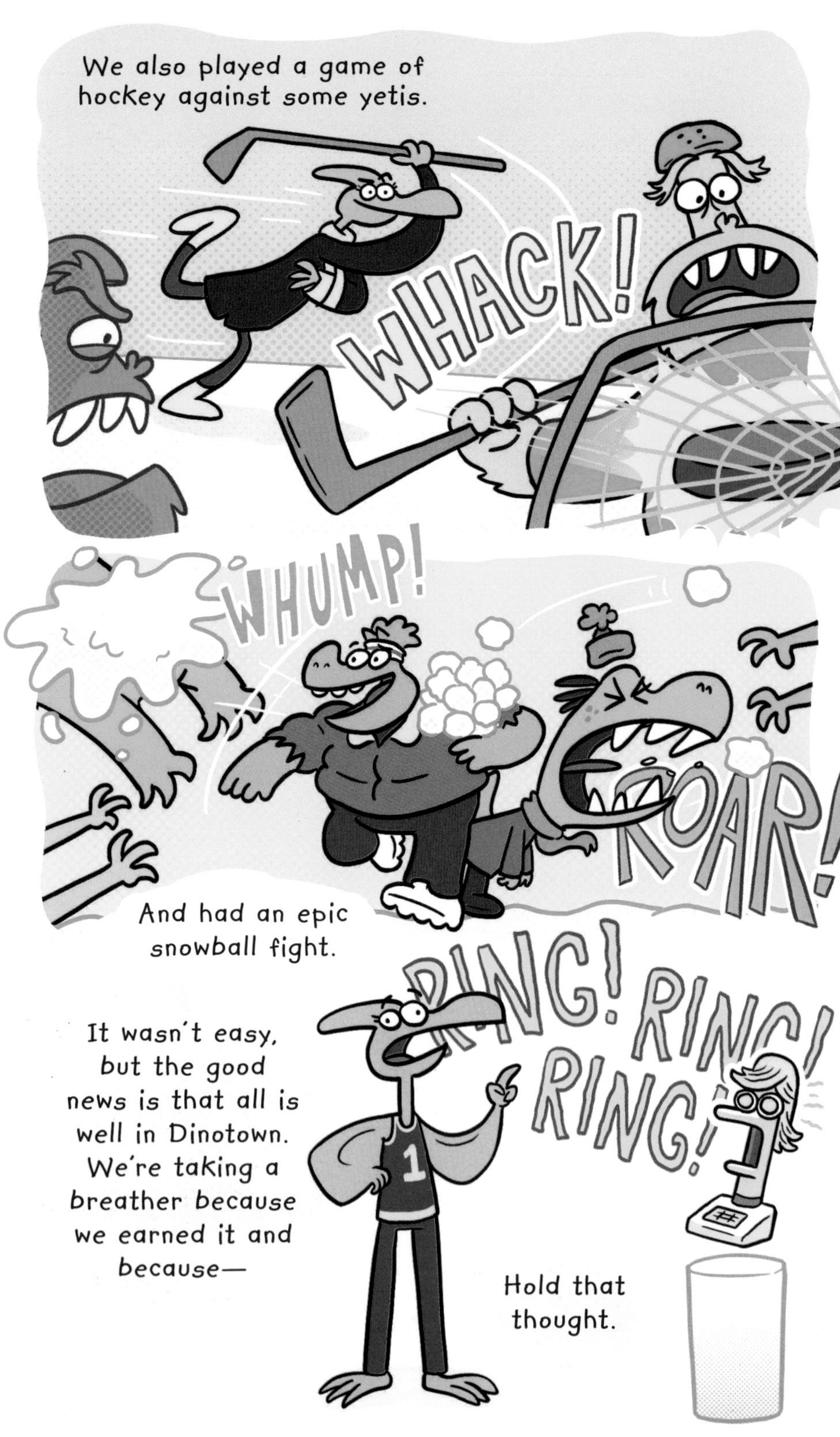
We also played a game of hockey against some yetis.
WHACK!
WHUMP!
ROAR!
And had an epic snowball fight.
RING!
It wasn't easy, but the good news is that all is well in Dinotown. We're taking a breather because we earned it and because—
Hold that thought.

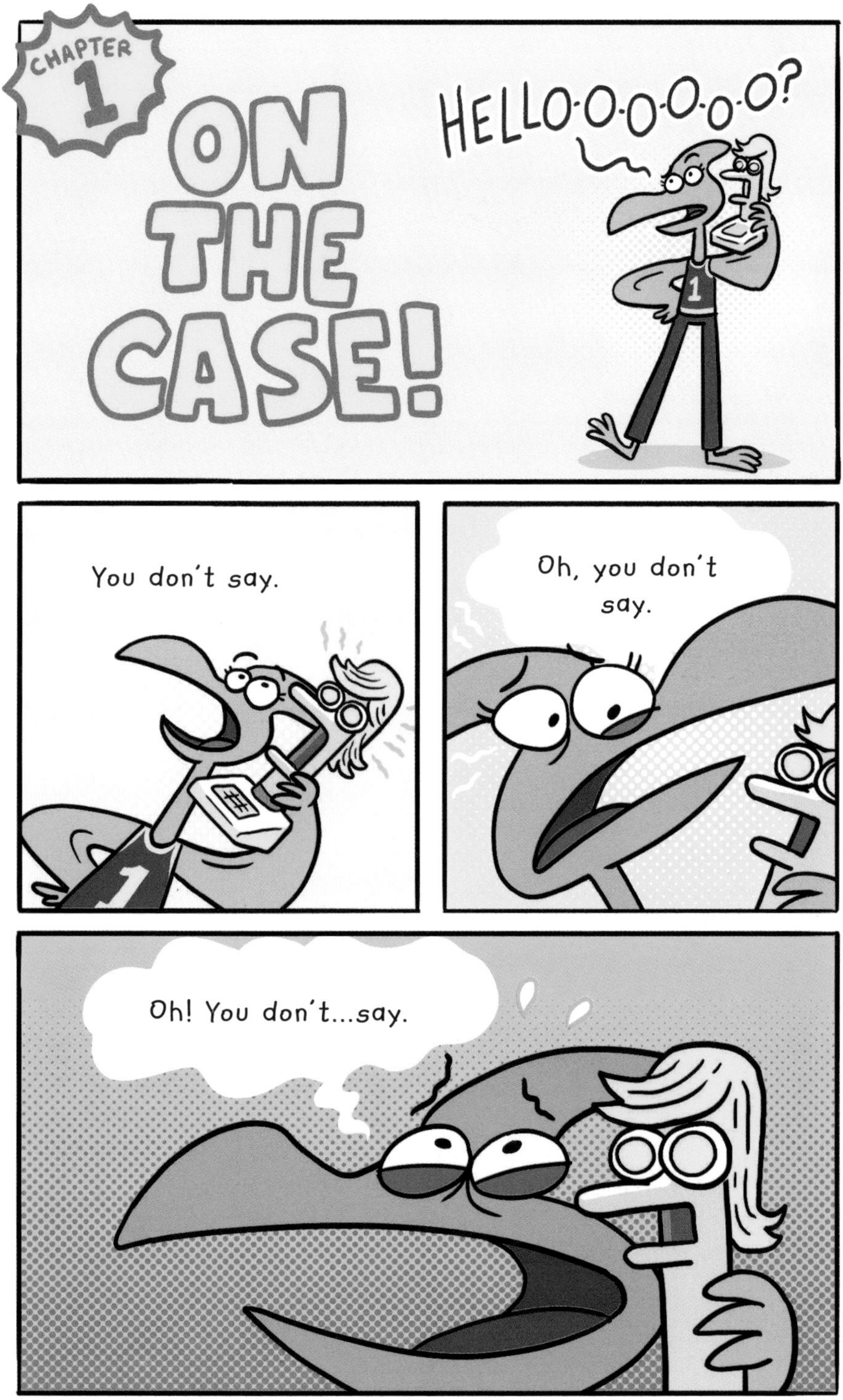
CHAPTER 1
ON THE CASE!
HELLO-O-O-O-O-O?
You don't say.
Oh, you don't say.
Oh! You don't...say.

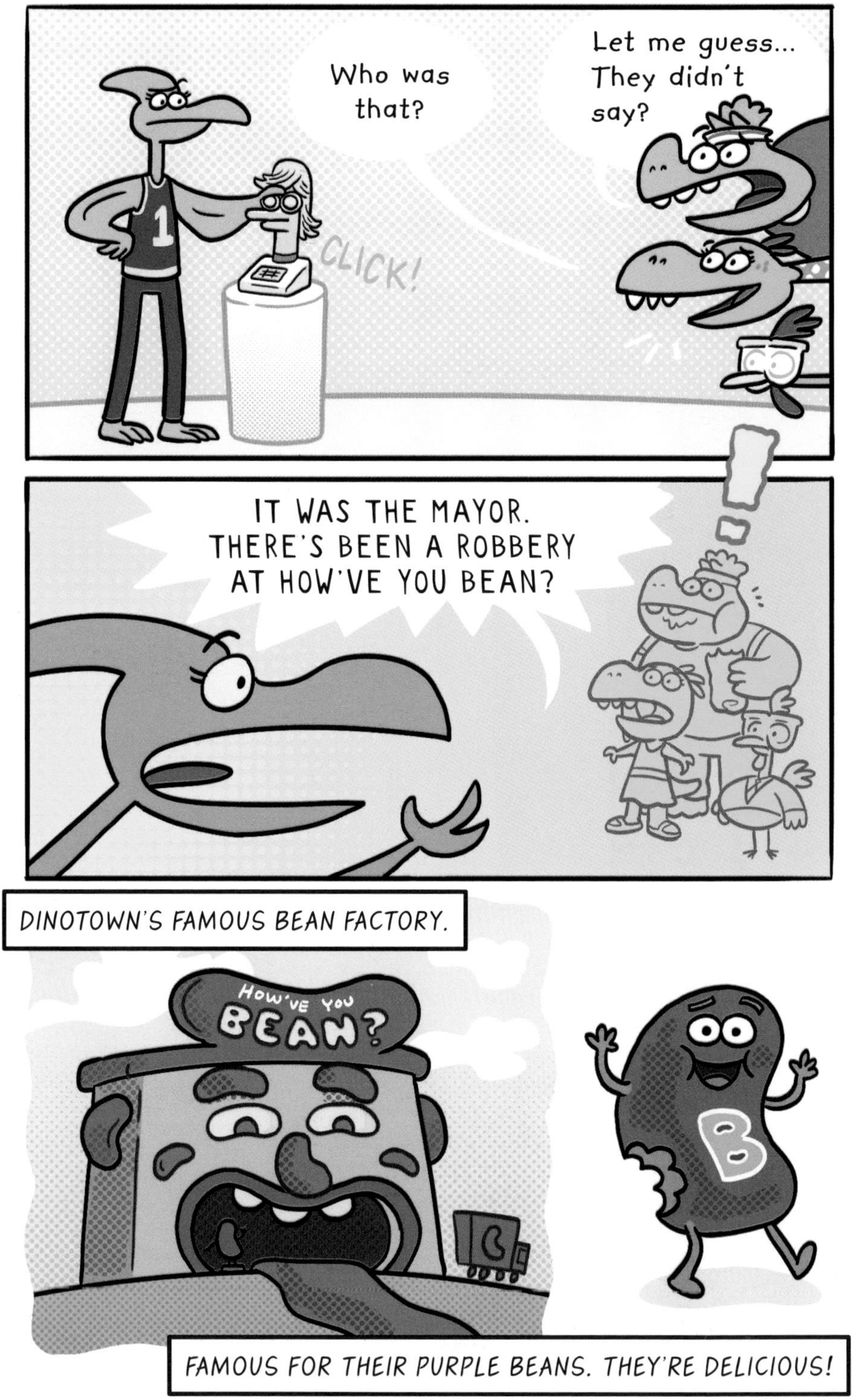
Who was that?
Let me guess... They didn't say?
CLICK!
IT WAS THE MAYOR. THERE'S BEEN A ROBBERY AT HOW'VE YOU BEAN?
!
DINOTOWN'S FAMOUS BEAN FACTORY.
HOW'VE YOU BEAN?
B
FAMOUS FOR THEIR PURPLE BEANS. THEY'RE DELICIOUS!

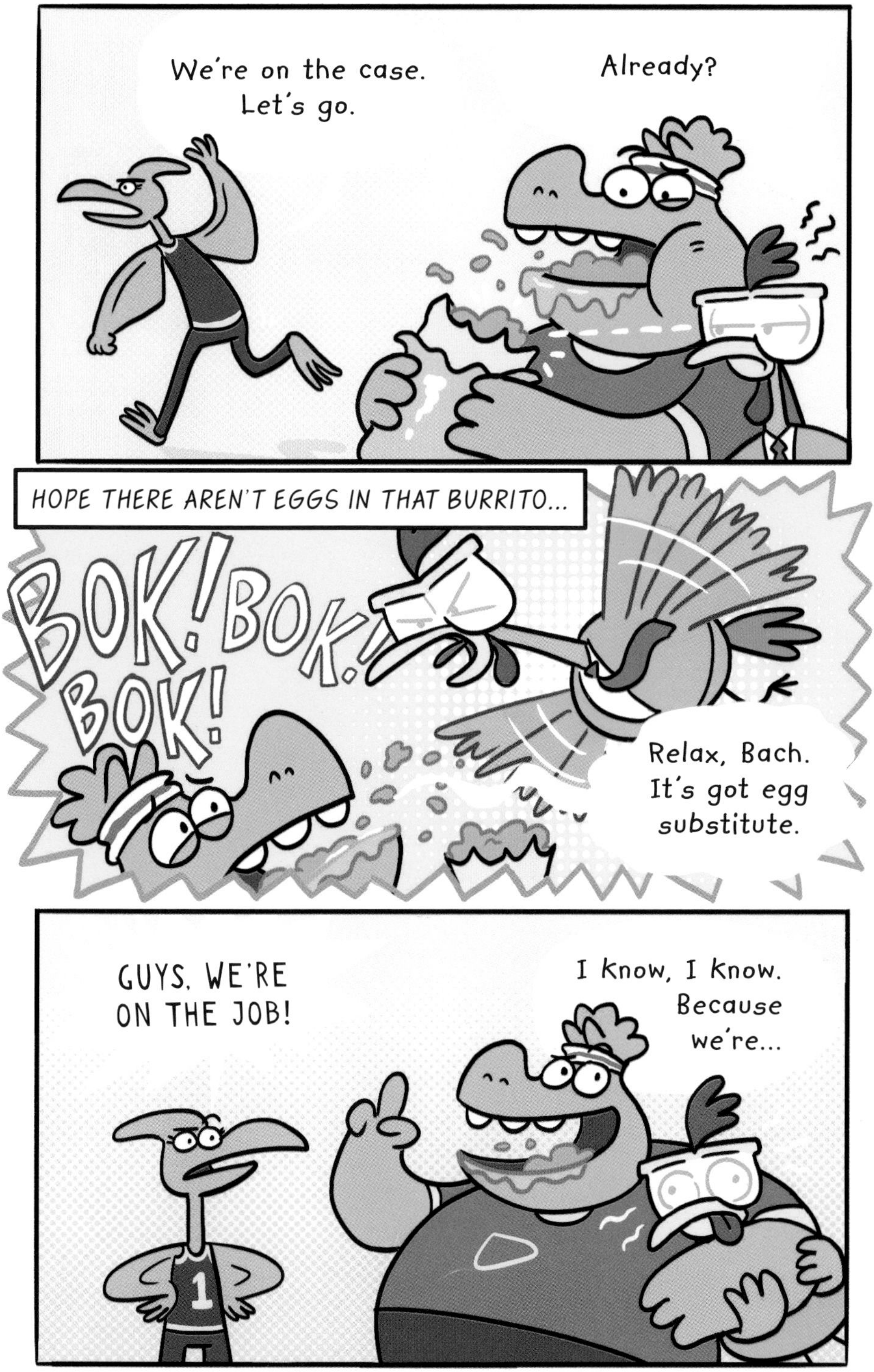

We're on the case. Let's go.
Already?
HOPE THERE AREN'T EGGS IN THAT BURRITO...
BOK! BOK! BOK!
Relax, Bach. It's got egg substitute.
GUYS, WE'RE ON THE JOB!
I know, I know. Because we're...

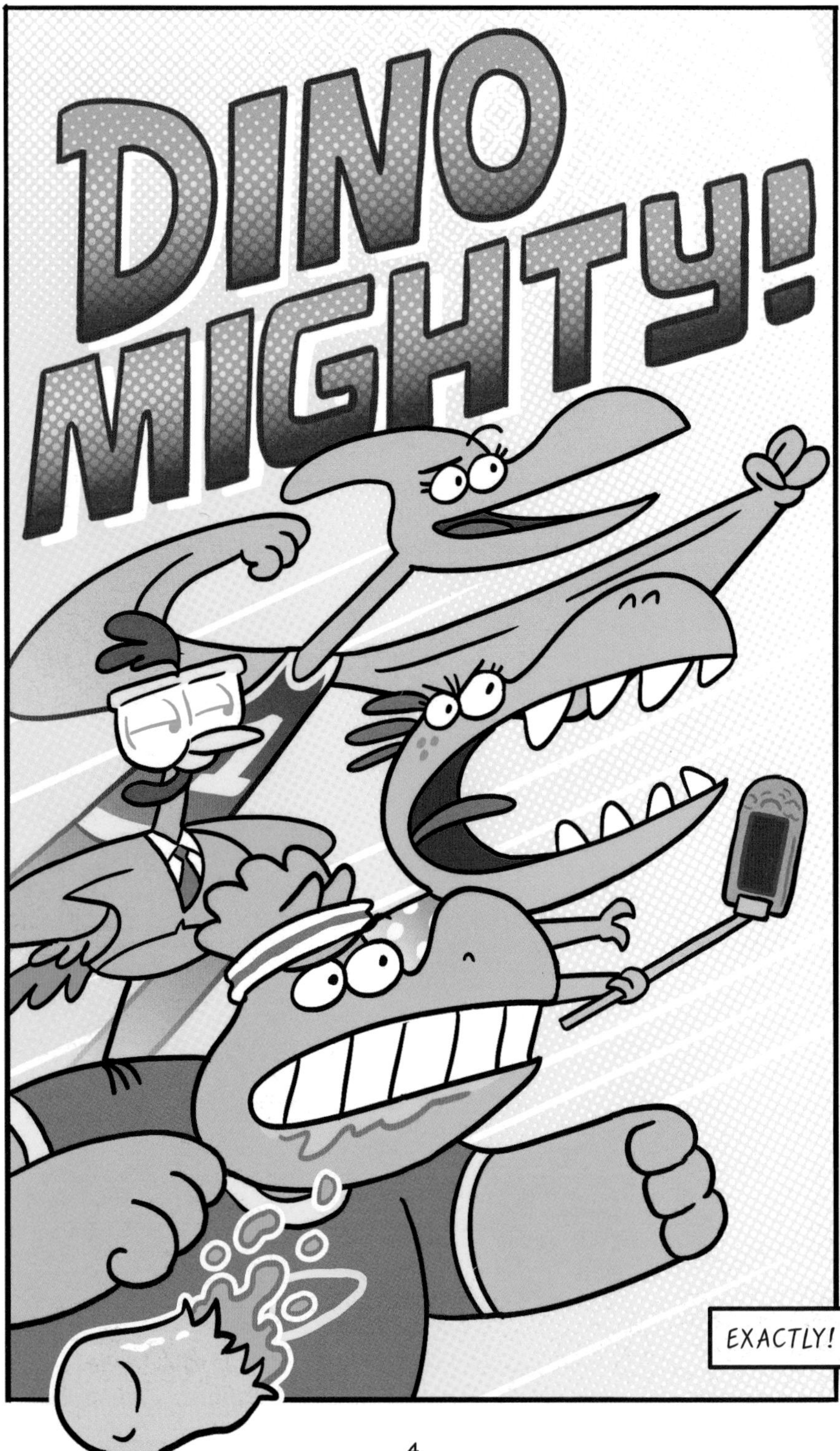
DINO MIGHTY!
EXACTLY!

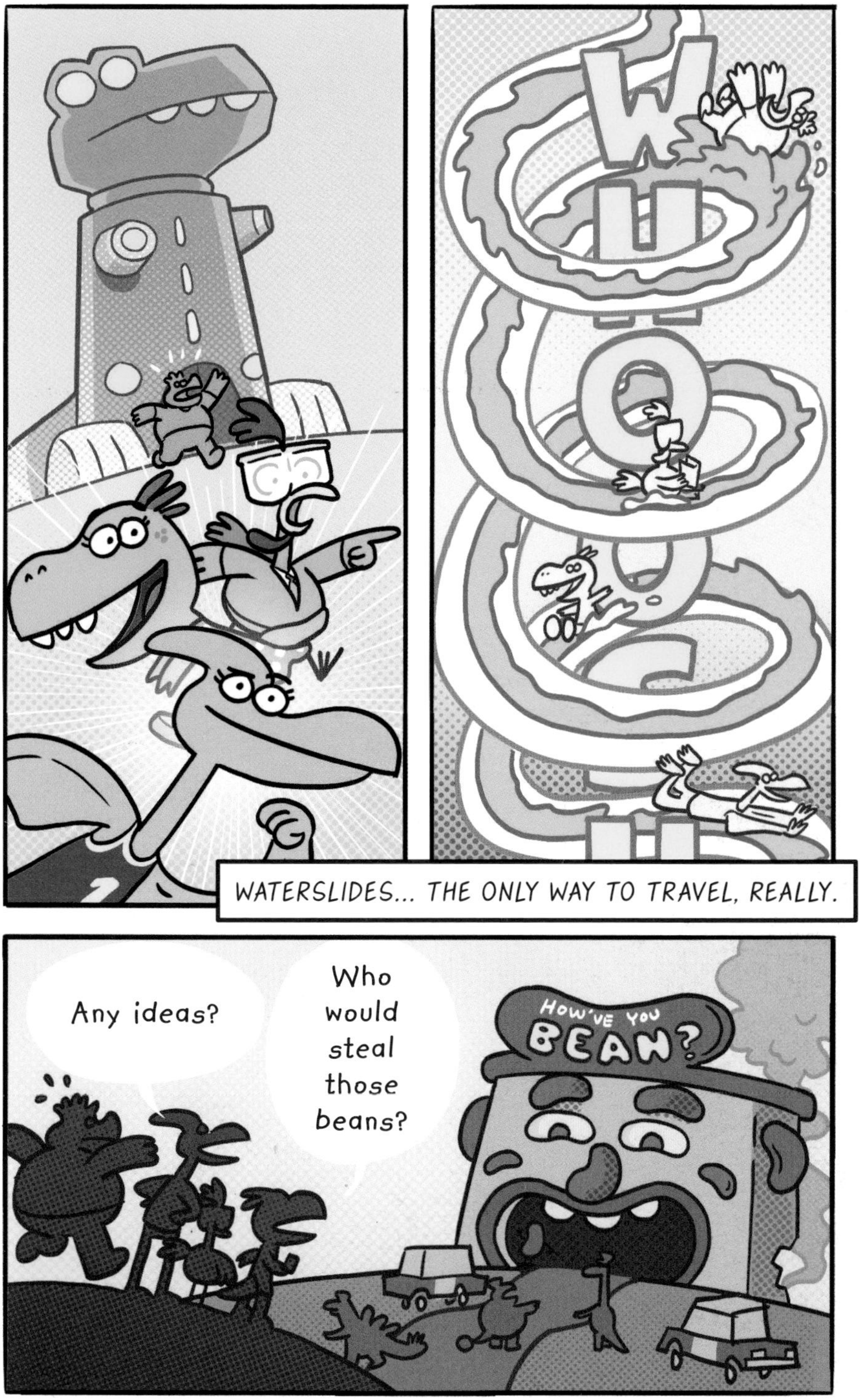
WATERSLIDES... THE ONLY WAY TO TRAVEL, REALLY.
Any ideas?
Who would steal those beans?
HOW'VE YOU BEAN?

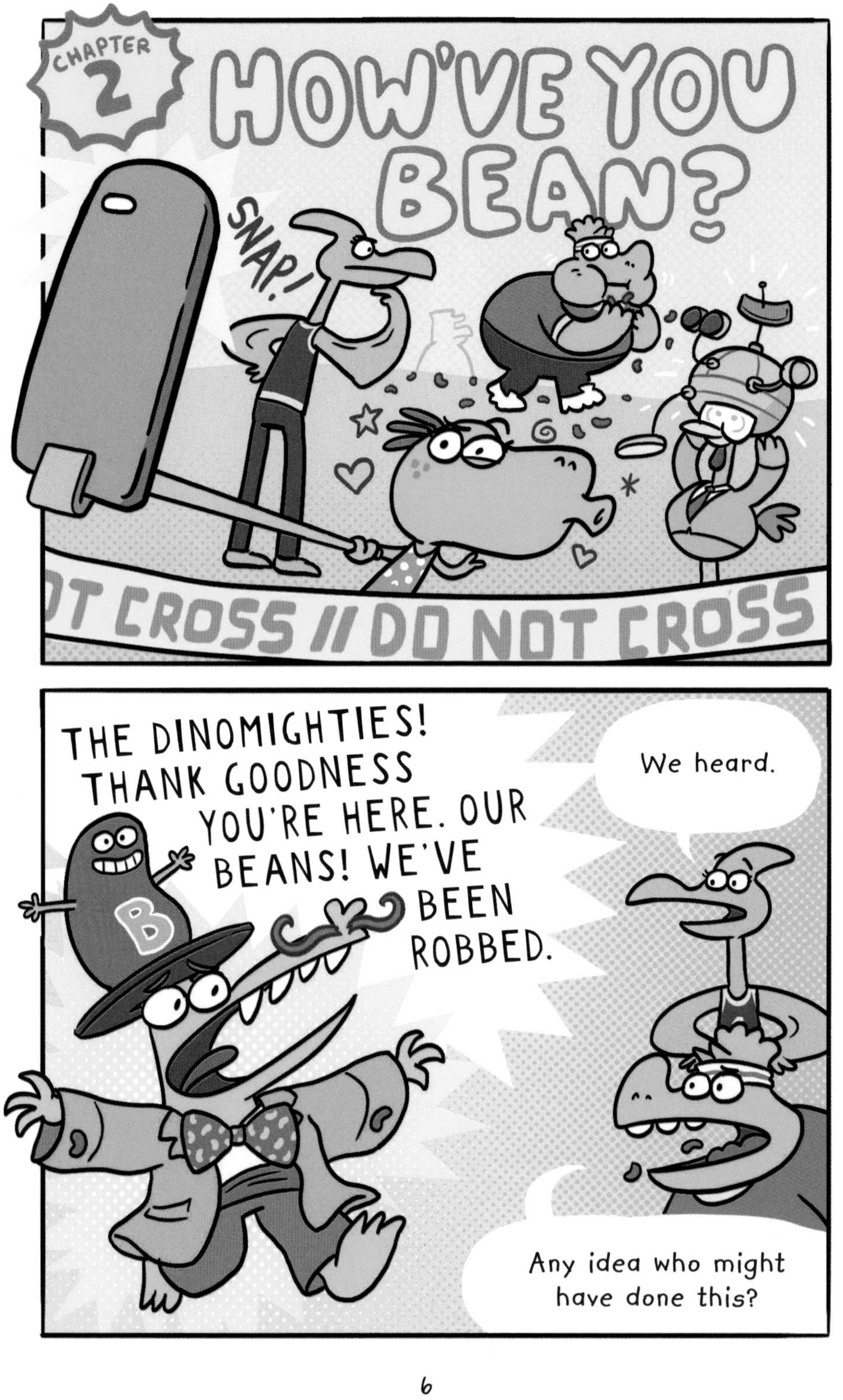
CHAPTER 2
HOW'VE YOU BEAN?
SNAP!
OT CROSS // DO NOT CROSS
THE DINOMIGHTIES! THANK GOODNESS YOU'RE HERE. OUR BEANS! WE'VE BEEN ROBBED.
B
We heard.
Any idea who might have done this?

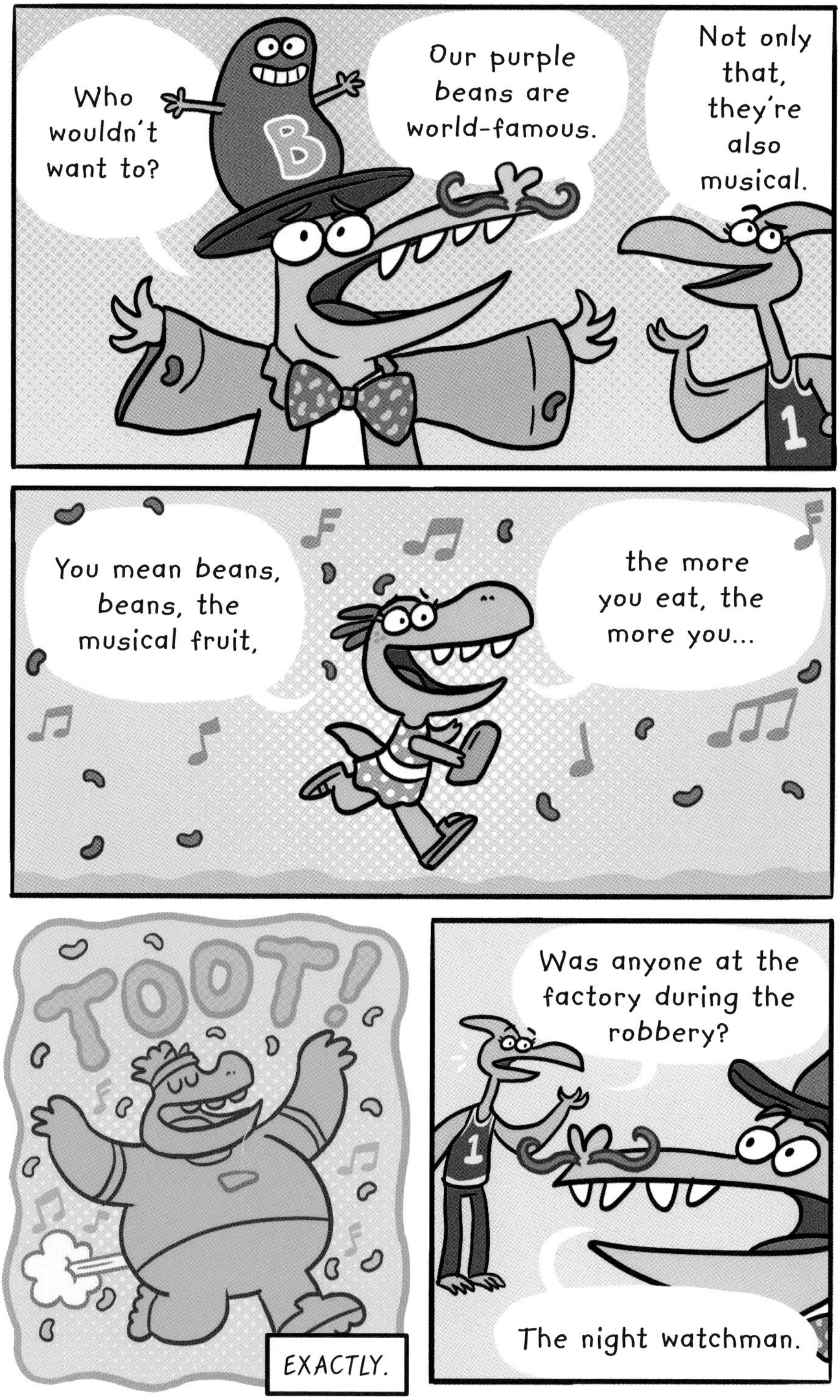
Who wouldn't want to?
Our purple beans are world-famous.
Not only that, they're also musical.
You mean beans, beans, the musical fruit,
the more you eat, the more you...
TOOT!
EXACTLY.
Was anyone at the factory during the robbery?
The night watchman.

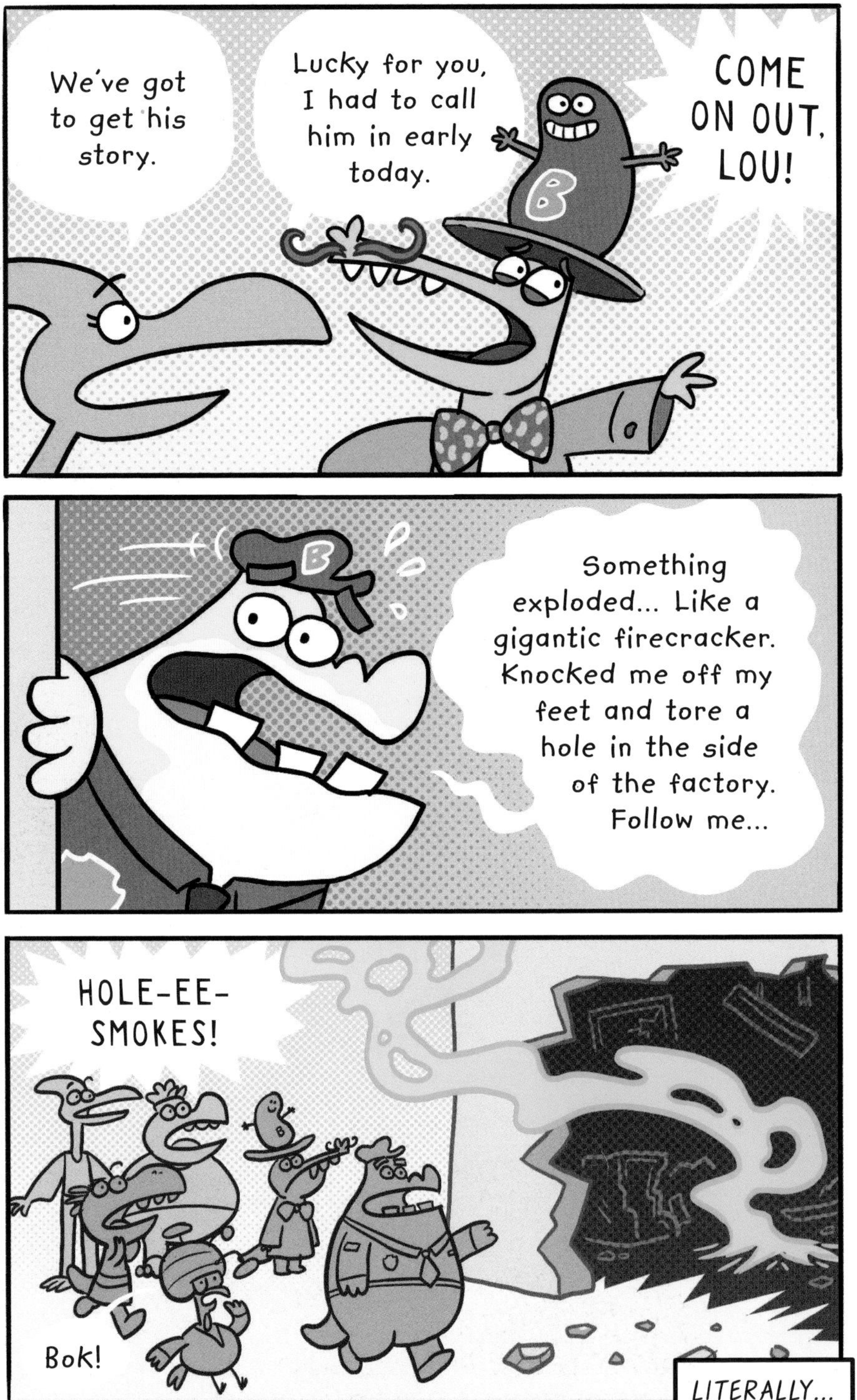
We've got to get his story.
Lucky for you, I had to call him in early today.
COME ON OUT, LOU!
Something exploded... Like a gigantic firecracker. Knocked me off my feet and tore a hole in the side of the factory. Follow me...
HOLE-EE-SMOKES!
Bok!
LITERALLY...

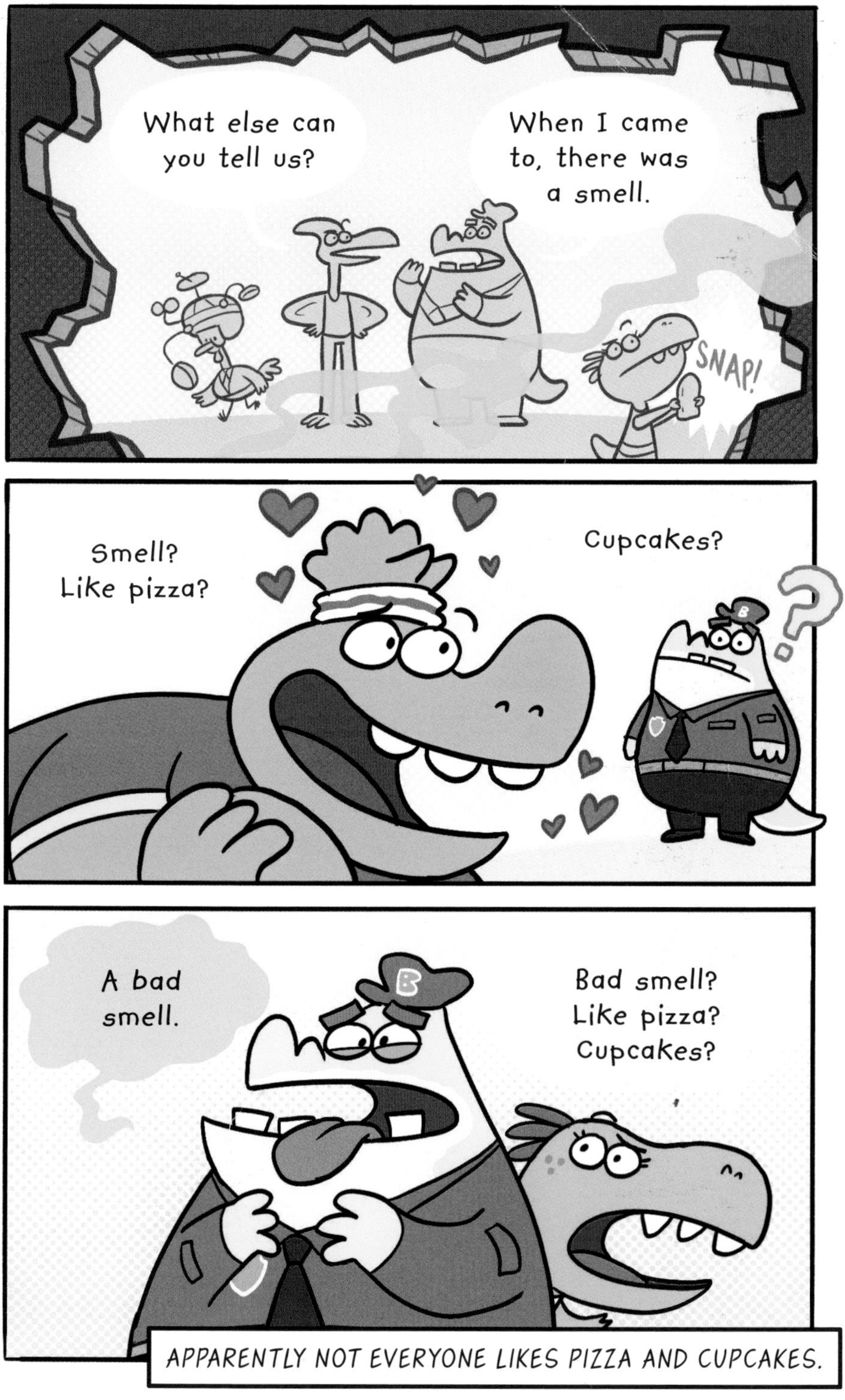
What else can you tell us?
When I came to, there was a smell.
SNAP!
Smell? Like pizza?
Cupcakes?
A bad smell.
Bad smell? Like pizza? Cupcakes?
APPARENTLY NOT EVERYONE LIKES PIZZA AND CUPCAKES.

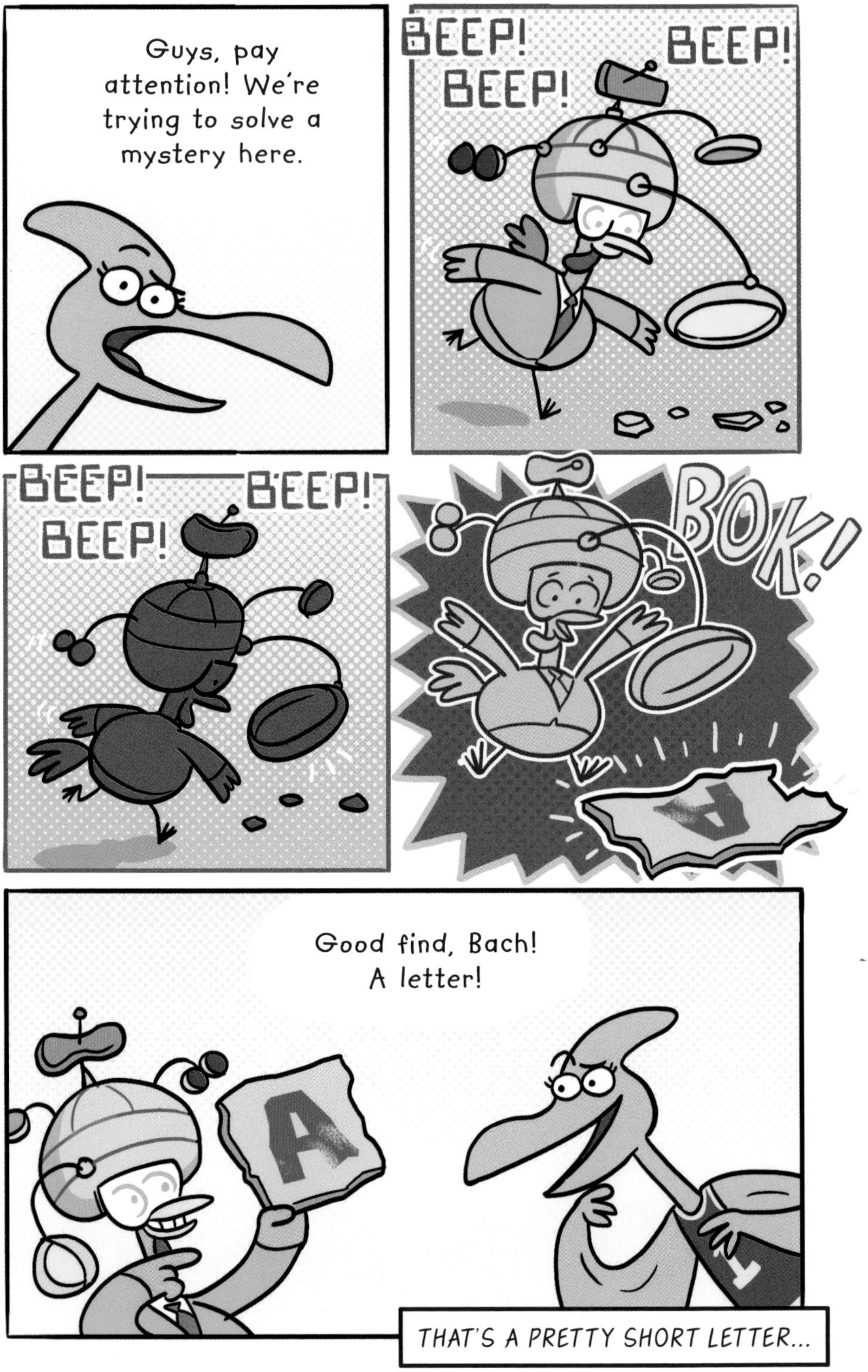

Guys, pay attention! We're trying to solve a mystery here.
BEEP!
BEEP!
BEEP!
BEEP!
BEEP!
BEEP!
BOK!
A
Good find, Bach! A letter!
A
THAT'S A PRETTY SHORT LETTER...

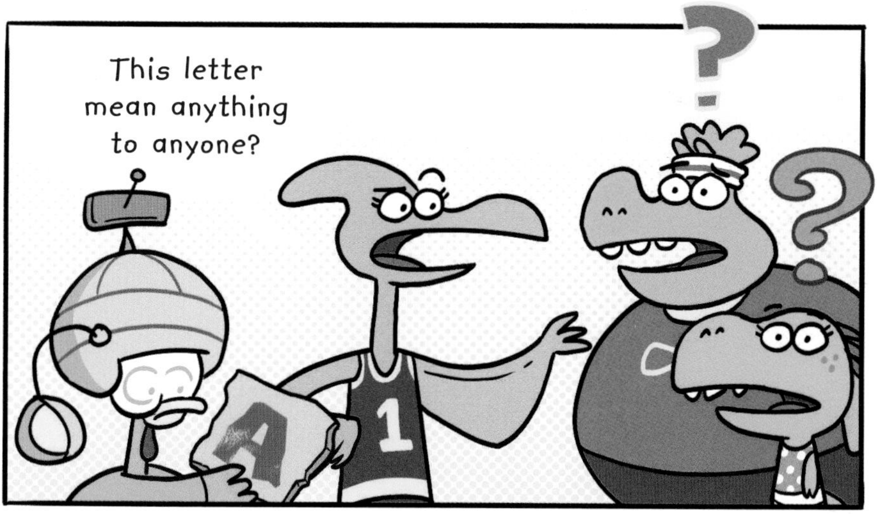
This letter mean anything to anyone?
?
?

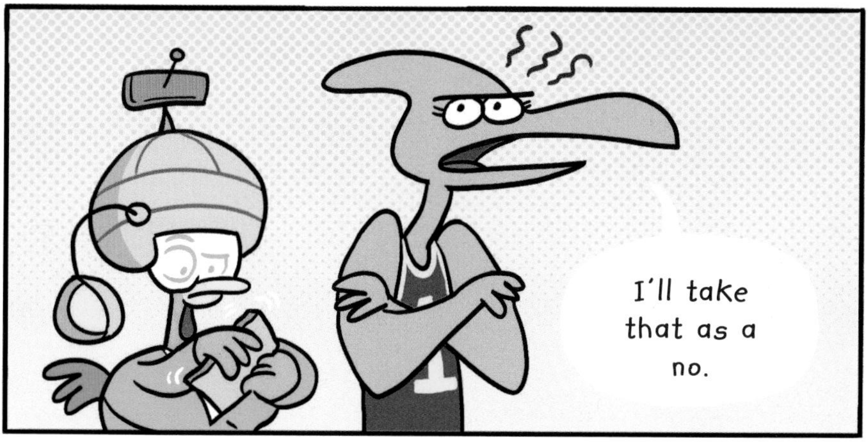
I'll take that as a no.

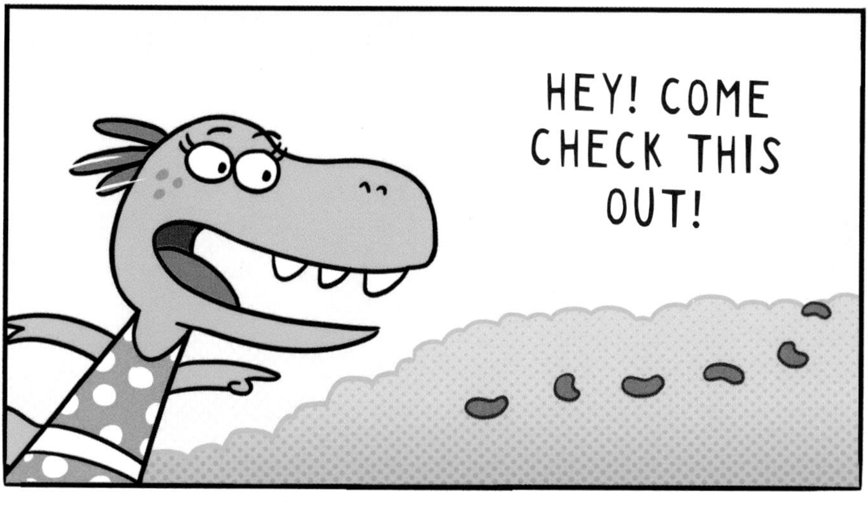
HEY! COME CHECK THIS OUT!

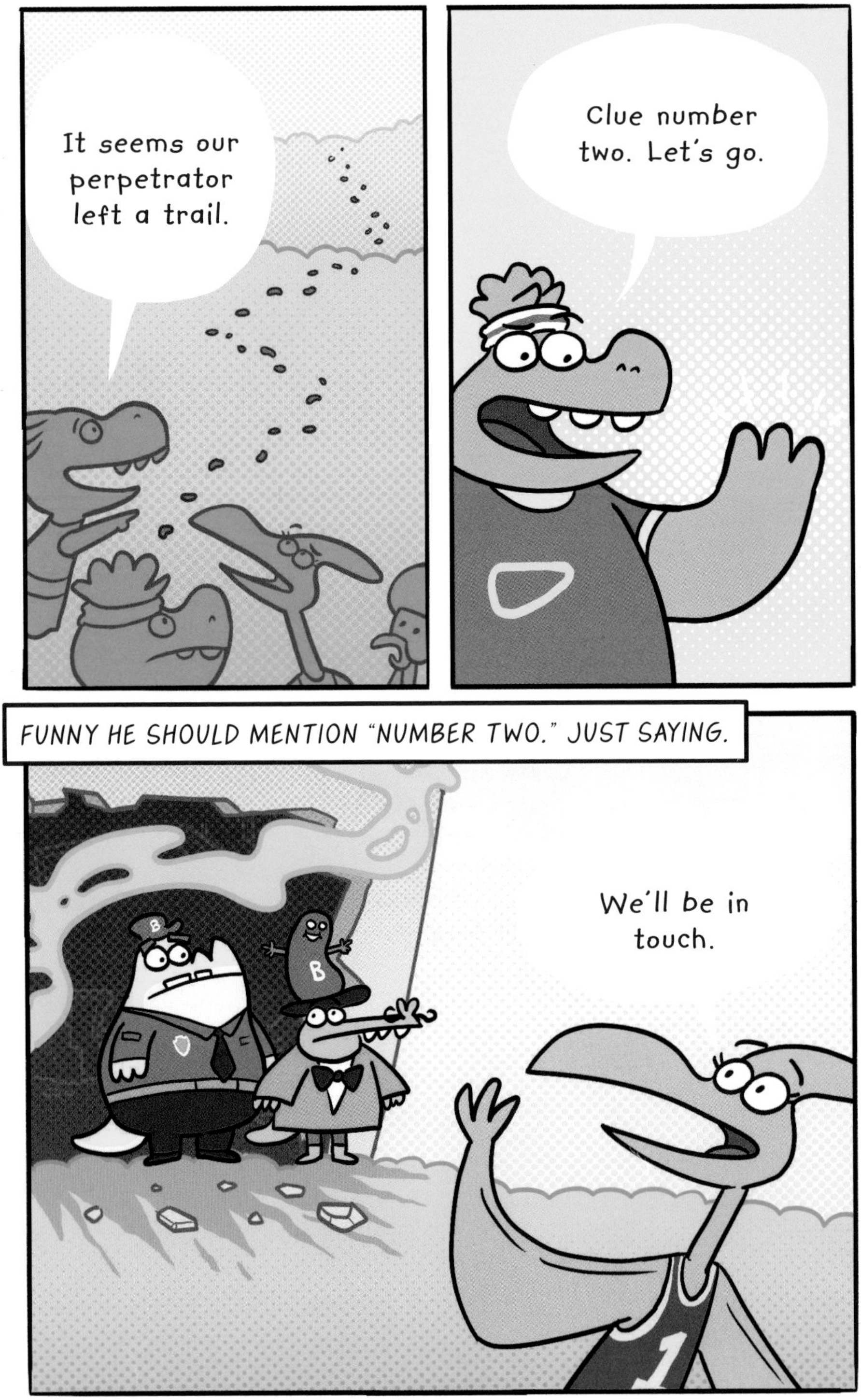
It seems our perpetrator left a trail.
Clue number two. Let's go.
FUNNY HE SHOULD MENTION "NUMBER TWO." JUST SAYING.
We'll be in touch.

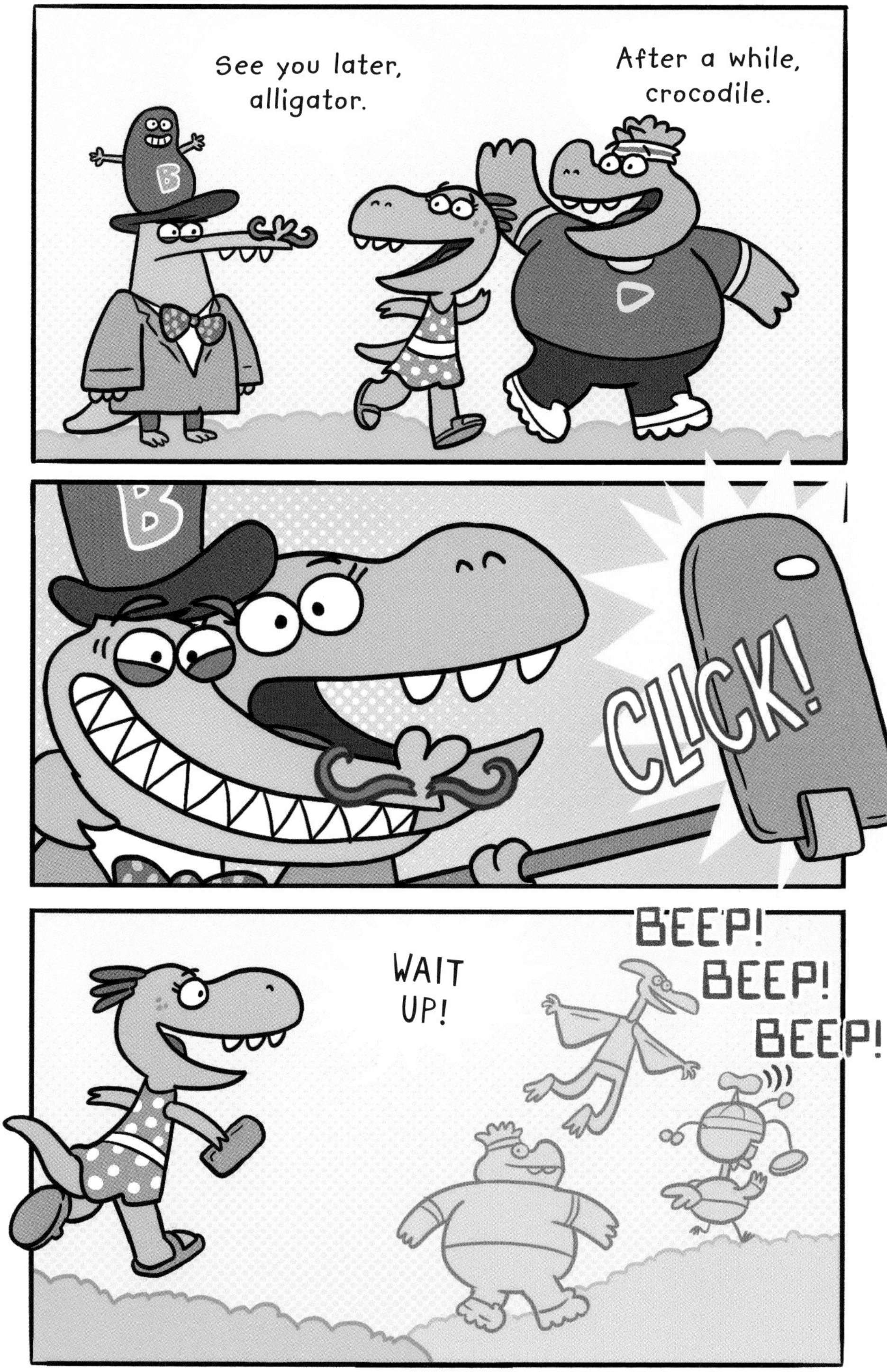
See you later, alligator.
After a while, crocodile.
CLICK!
WAIT UP!
BEEP!
BEEP!
BEEP!

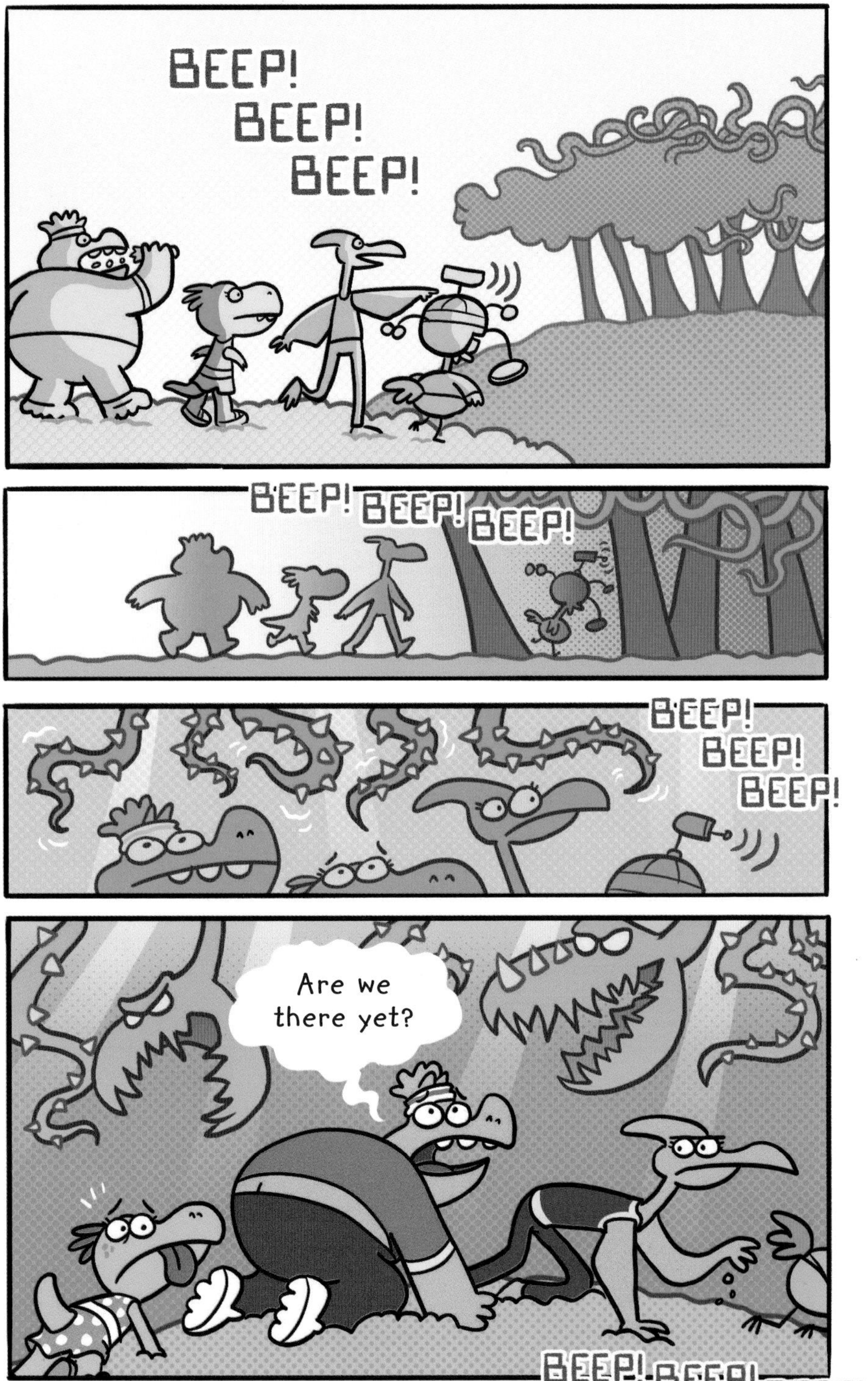
BEEP!
BEEP!
BEEP!
BEEP! BEEP! BEEP!
BEEP!
BEEP!
BEEP!
Are we there yet?
BEEP! BEEP! BEEP!

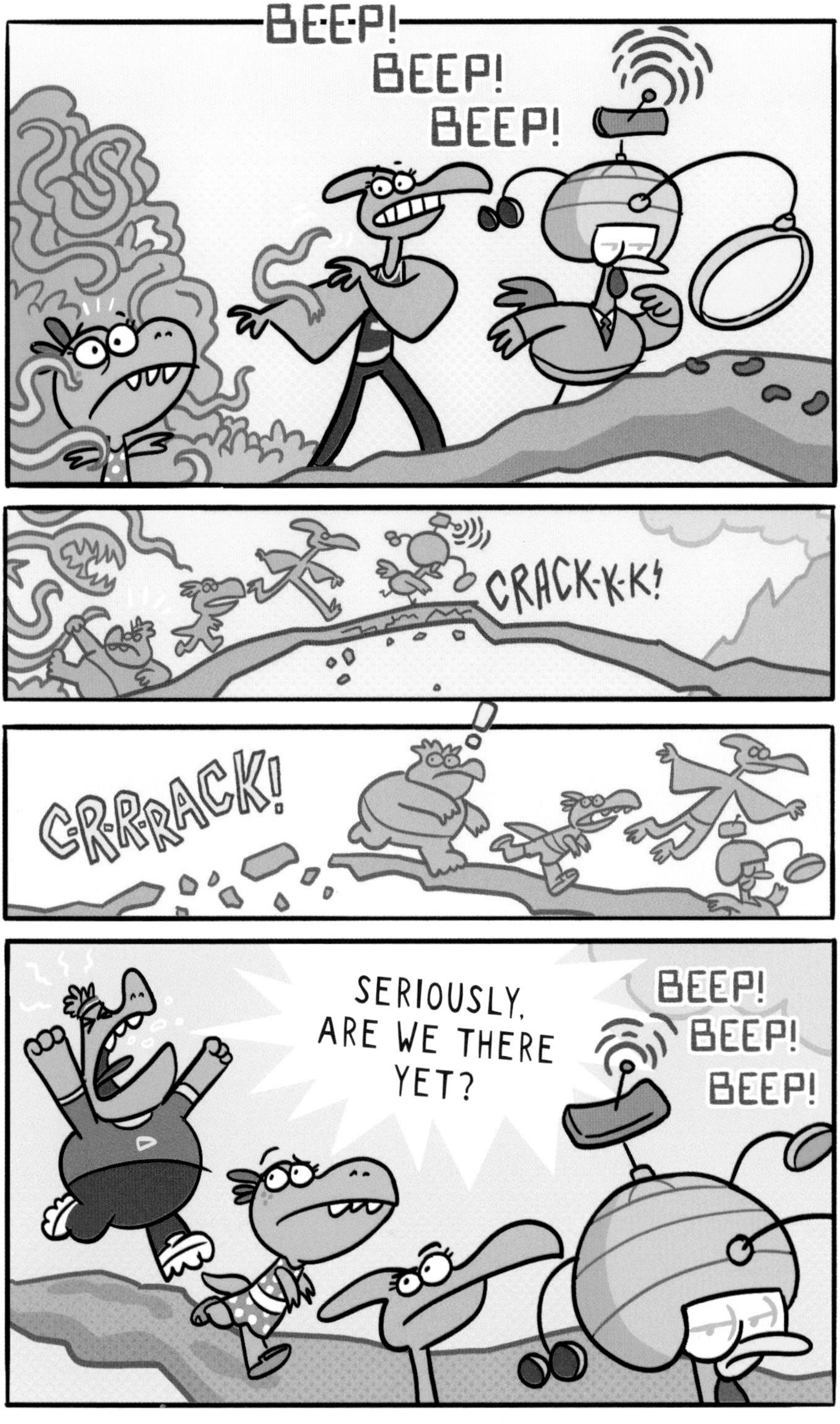

BE-E-P!
BEEP!
BEEP!
CRACK-K-K!
C-R-R-RACK!
SERIOUSLY, ARE WE THERE YET?
BEEP!
BEEP!
BEEP!

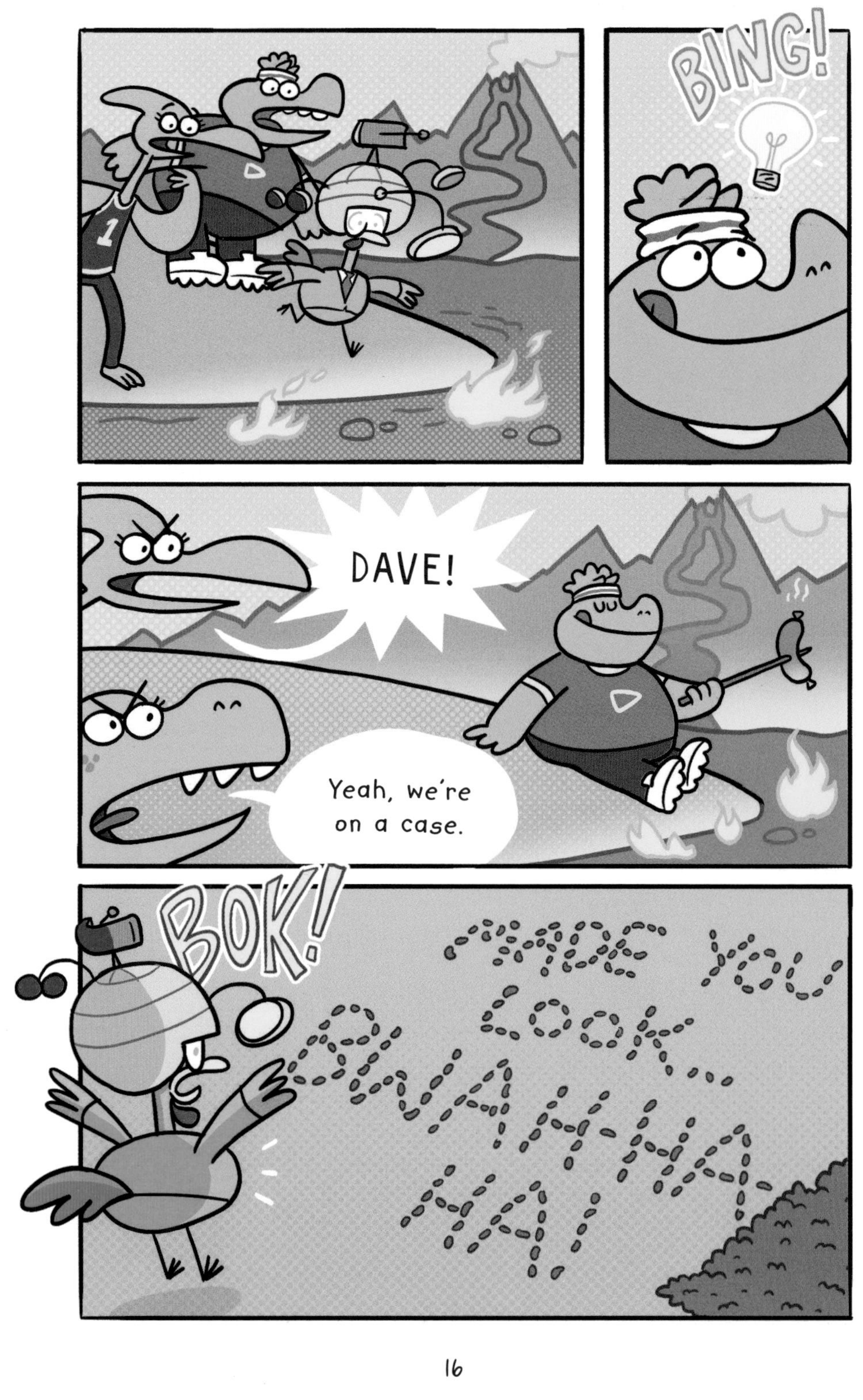
BING!
DAVE!
Yeah, we're on a case.
BOK!
MADE YOU LOOK...
BWAH-HA-HA
HA!

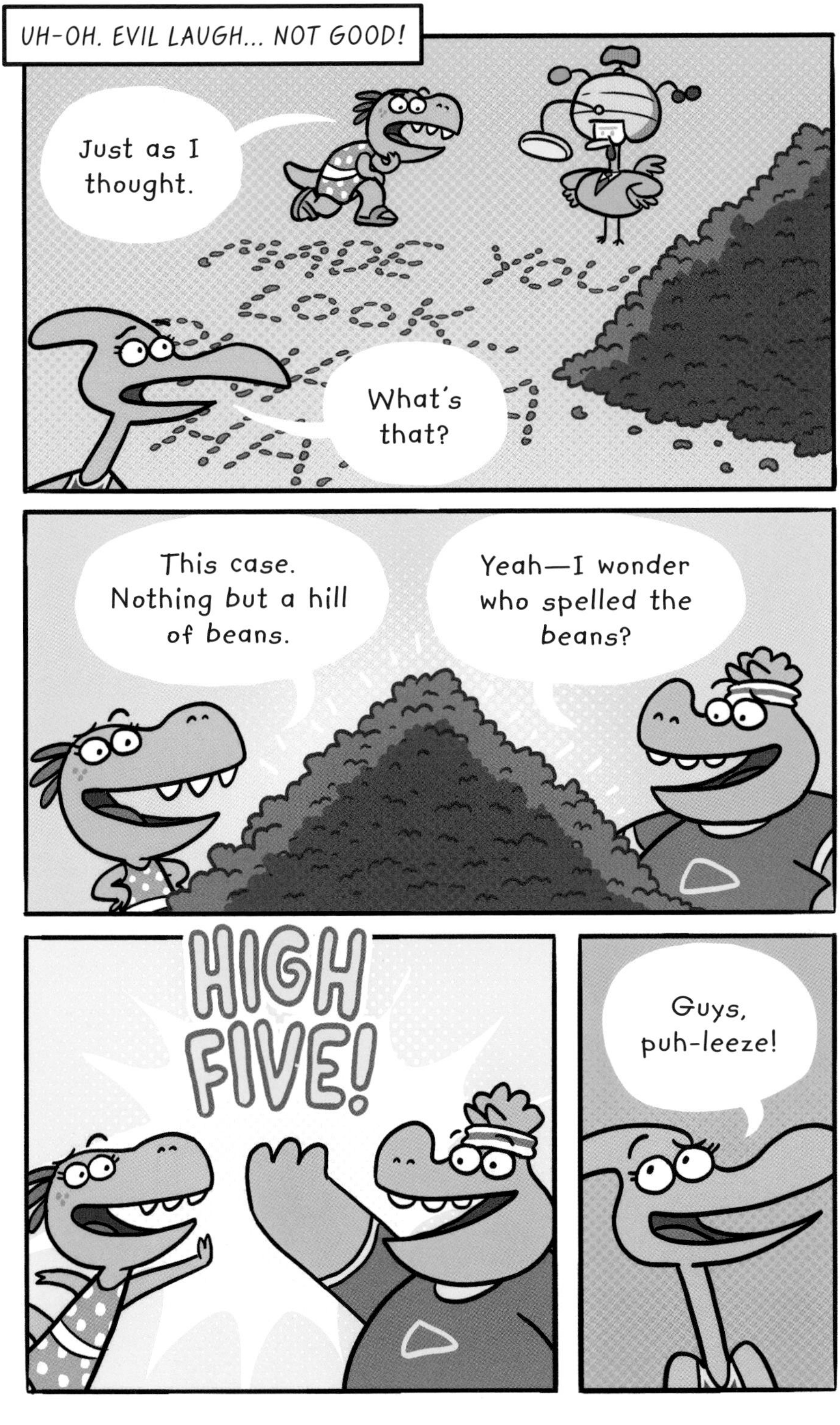
UH-OH. EVIL LAUGH... NOT GOOD!
Just as I thought.
What's that?
This case. Nothing but a hill of beans.
Yeah—I wonder who spelled the beans?
HIGH FIVE!
Guys, puh-leeze!

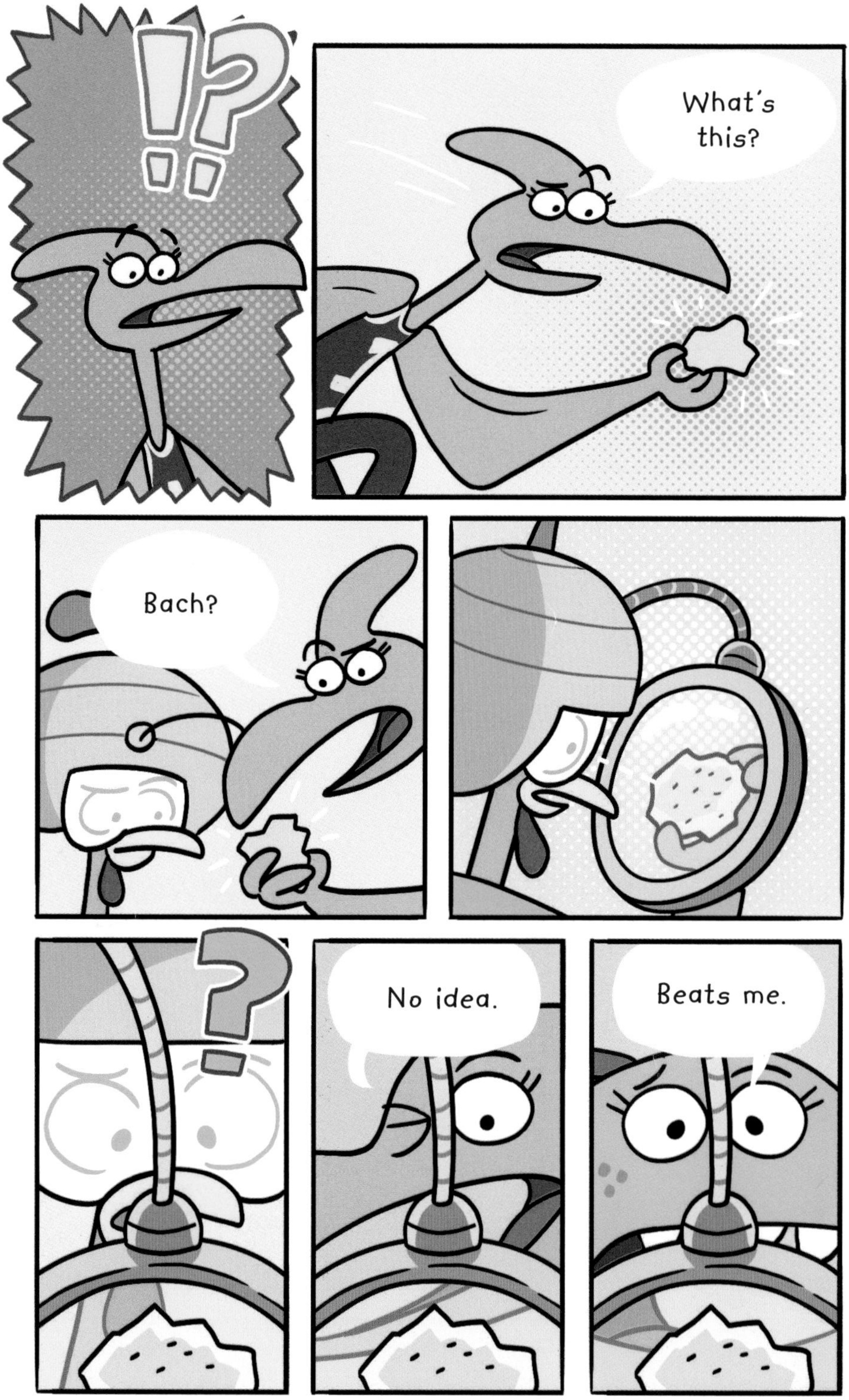
!?
!!
What's this?
Bach?
?
No idea.
Beats me.

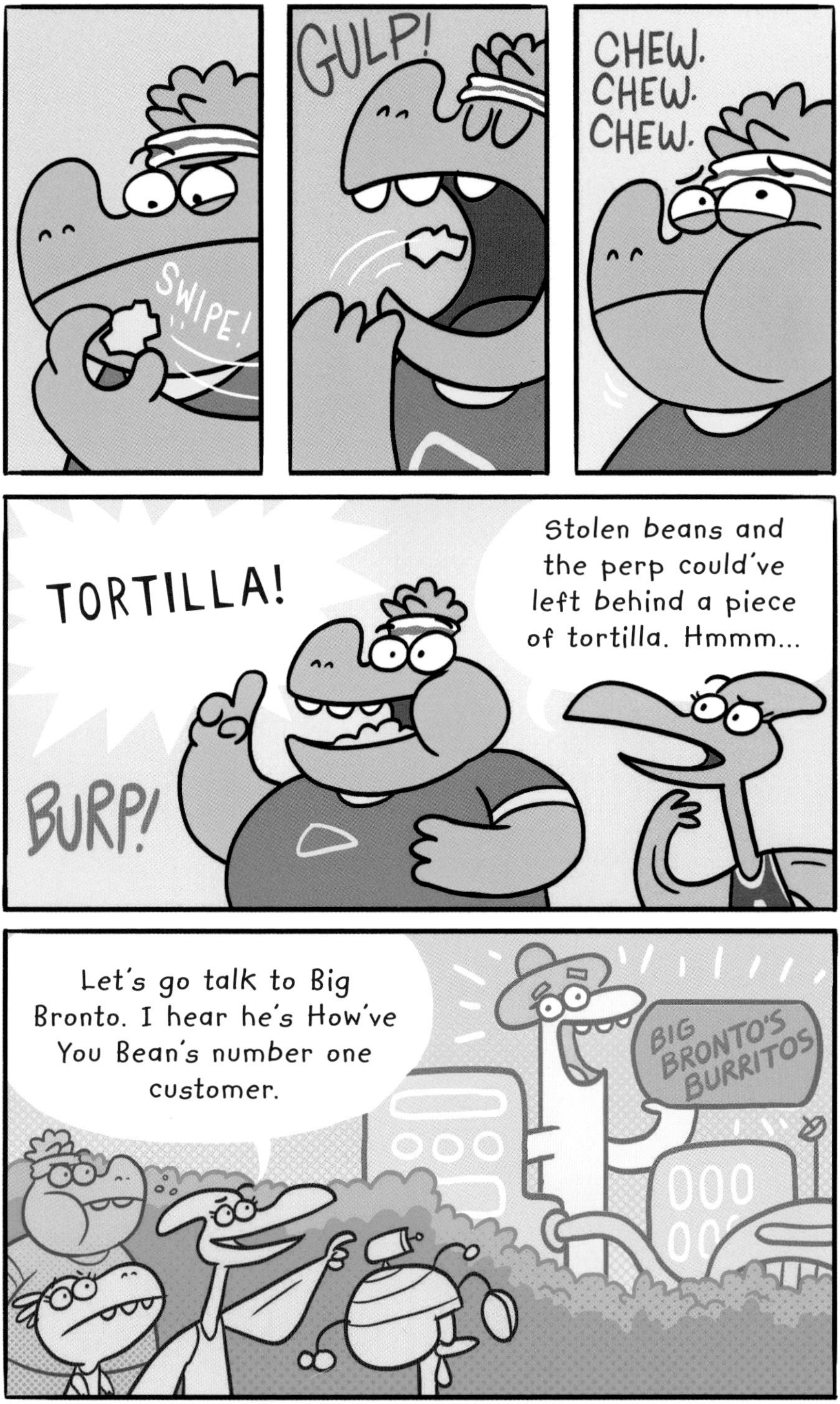
SWIPE!
GULP!
CHEW.
CHEW.
CHEW.
TORTILLA!
BURP!
Stolen beans and the perp could've left behind a piece of tortilla. Hmmm...
Let's go talk to Big Bronto. I hear he's How've You Bean's number one customer.
BIG BRONTO'S BURRITOS

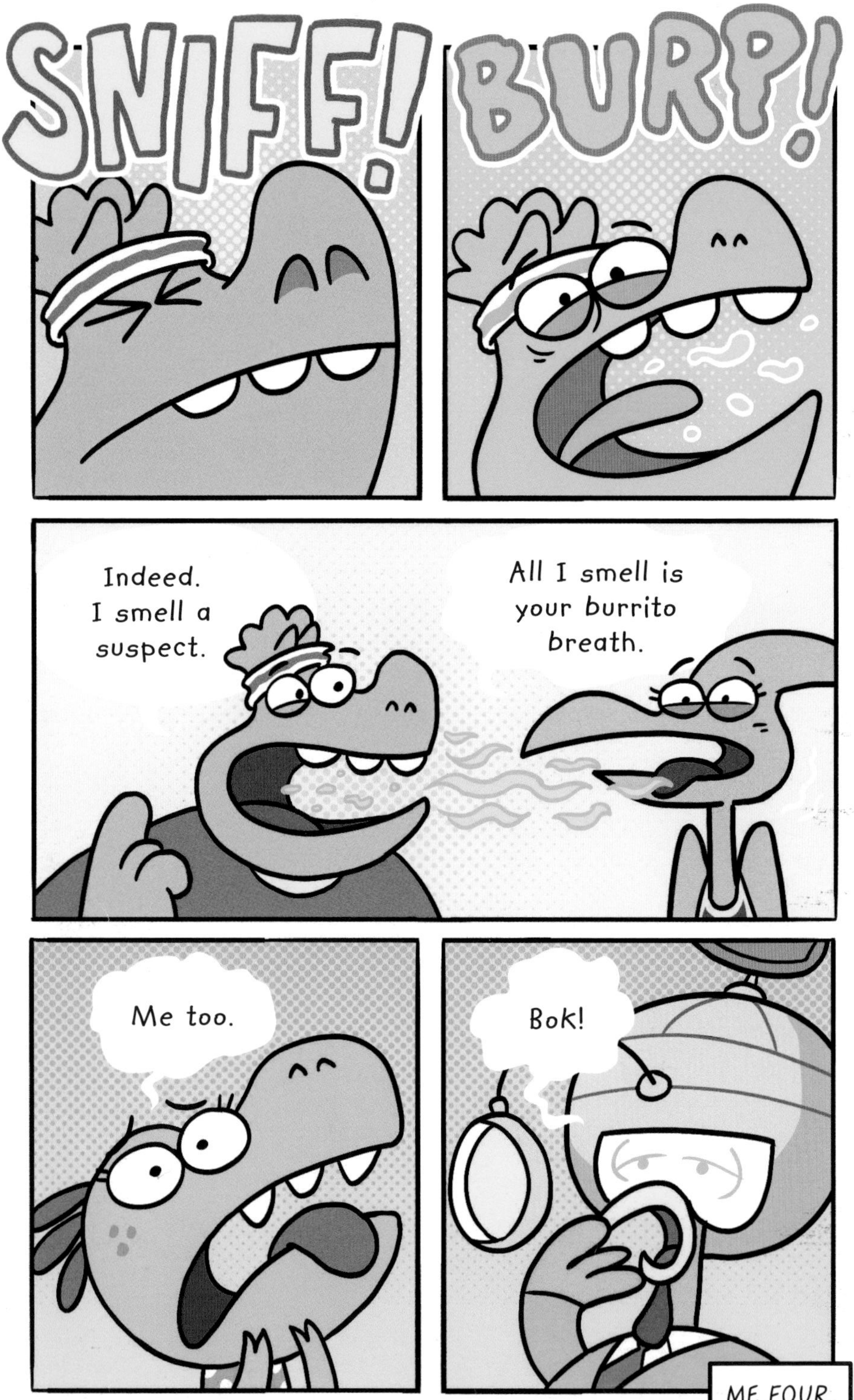
SNIFF!
BURP!
Indeed. I smell a suspect.
All I smell is your burrito breath.
Me too.
Bok!
ME FOUR.

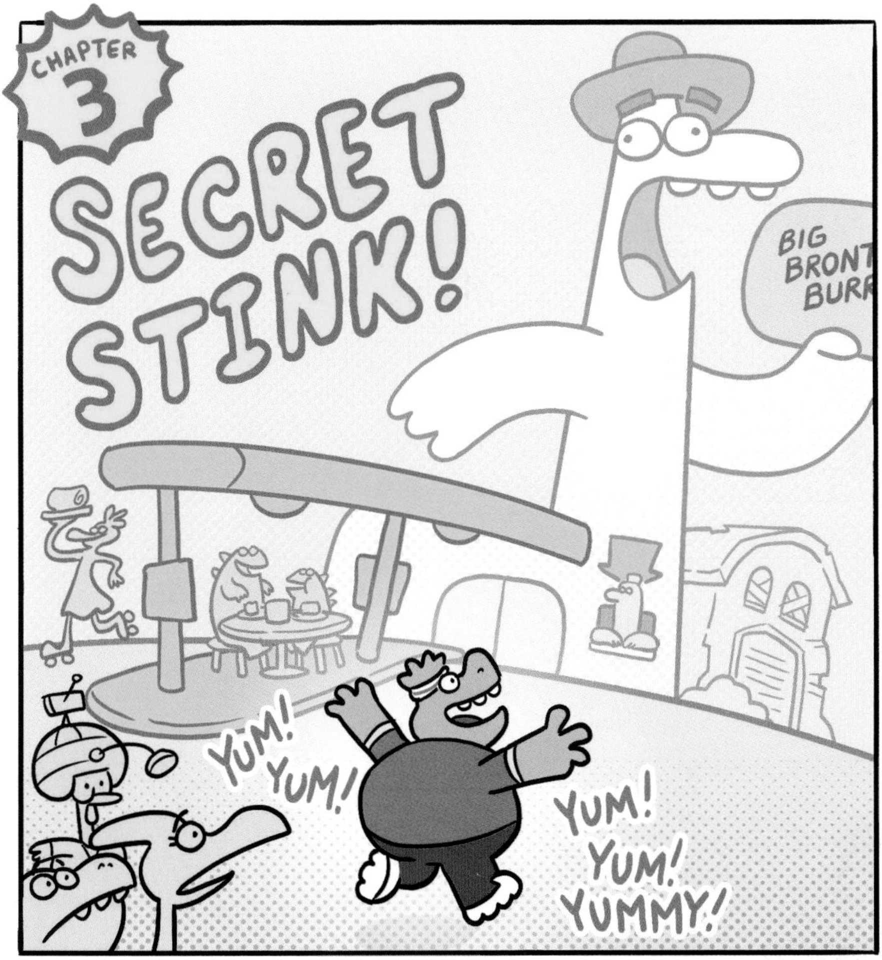
CHAPTER 3
SECRET STINK!
BIG BRONT BURR
YUM! YUM!
YUM! YUM! YUMMY!

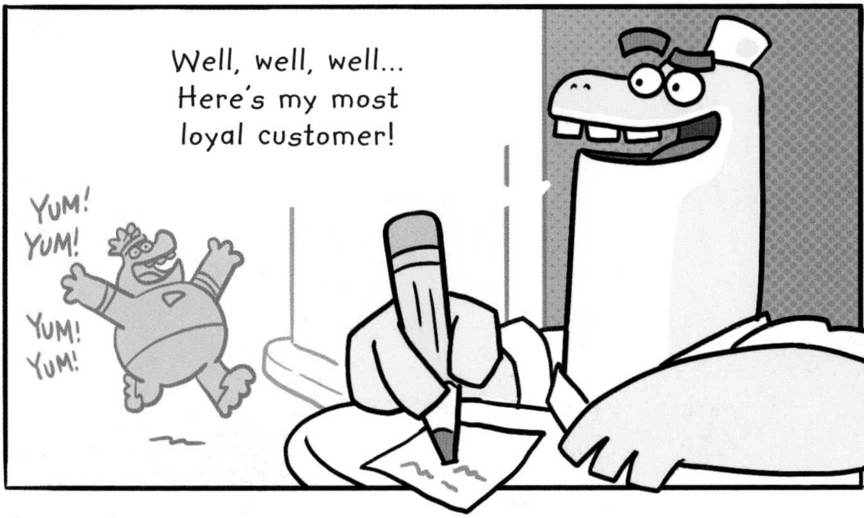
Well, well, well...
Here's my most loyal customer!
YUM! YUM!
YUM! YUM!

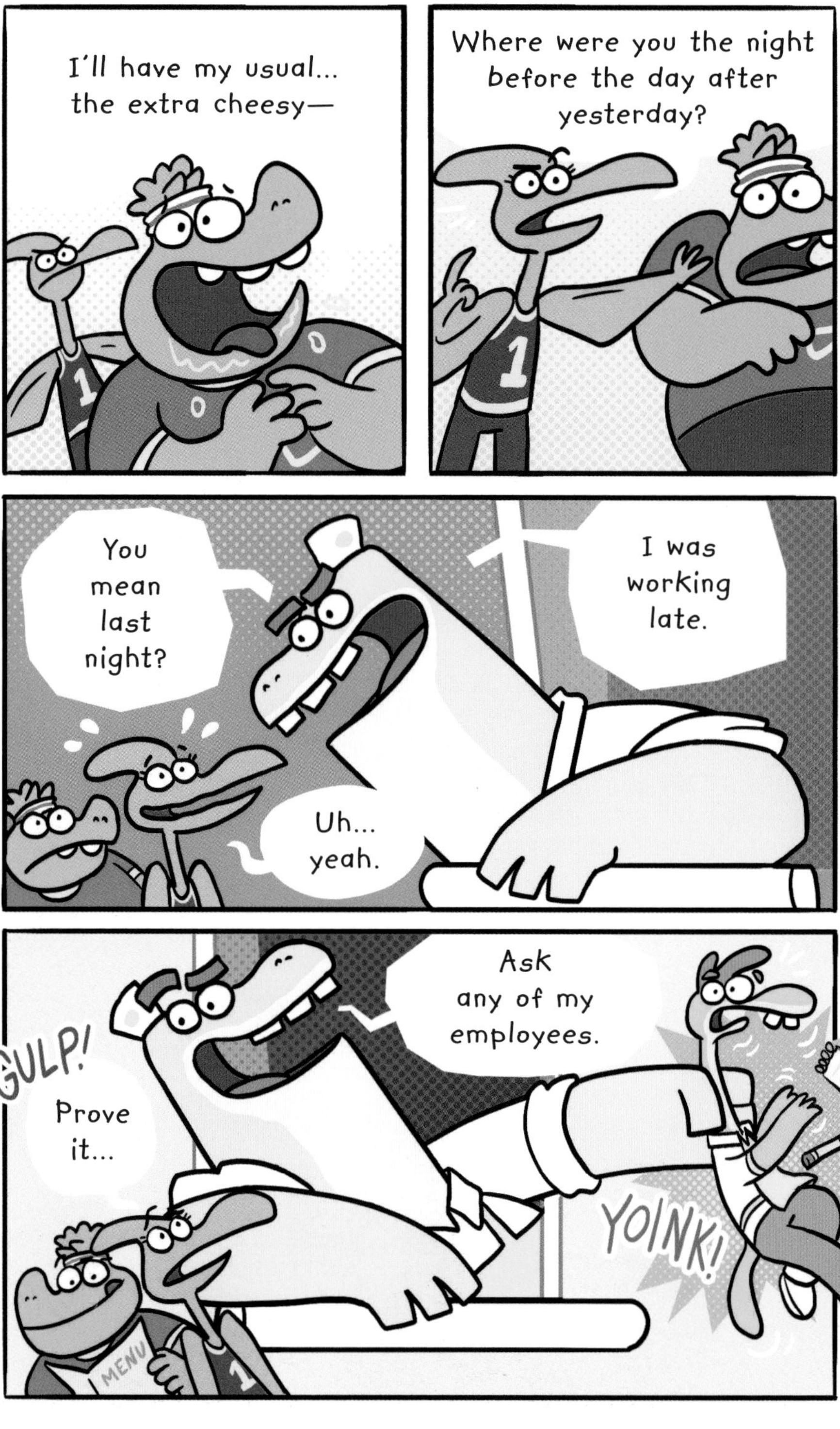
I'll have my usual... the extra cheesy—
Where were you the night before the day after yesterday?
You mean last night?
I was working late.
Uh... yeah.
Ask any of my employees.
GULP!
Prove it...
YOINK!
MENU

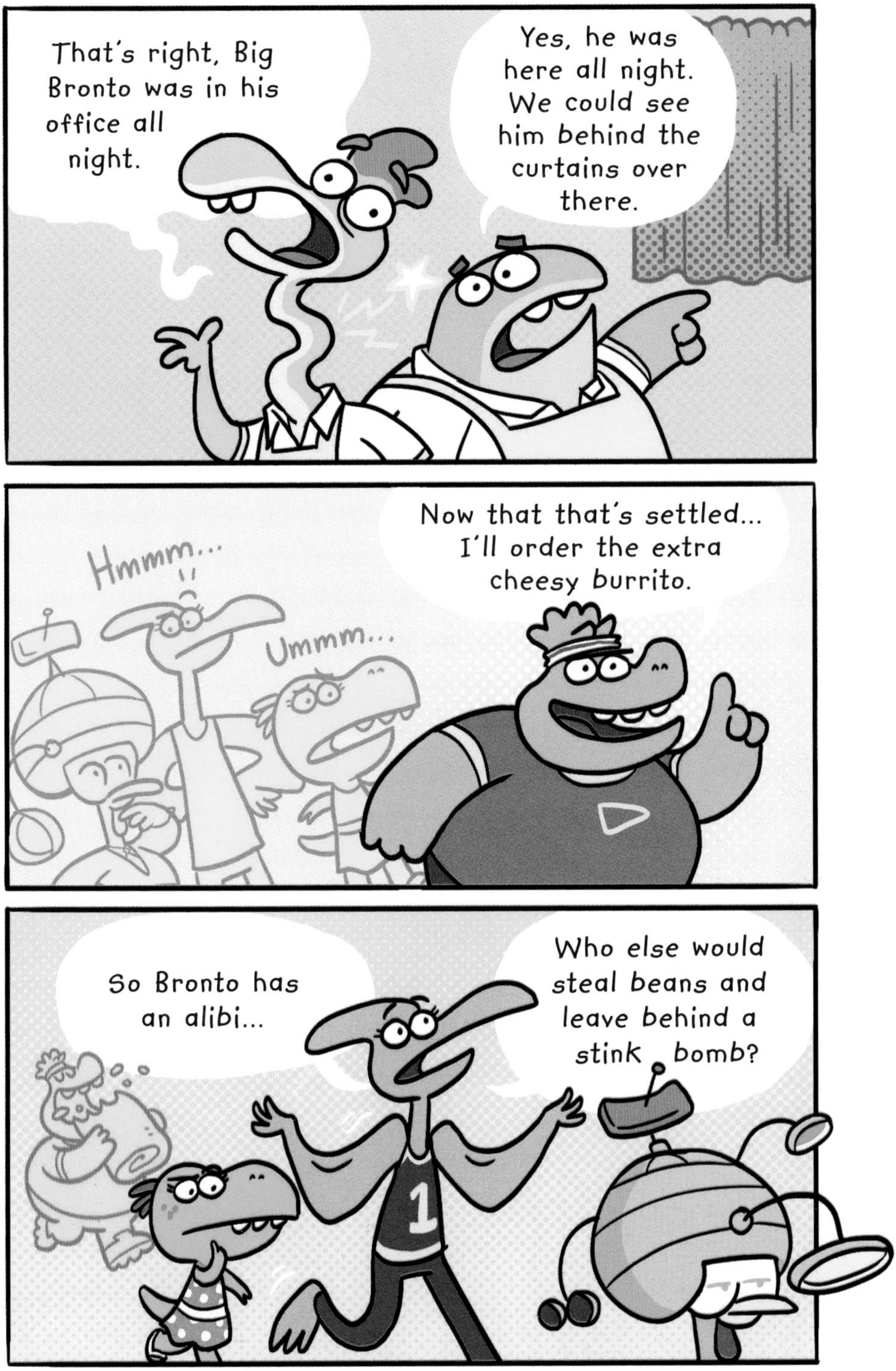
That's right, Big Bronto was in his office all night.
Yes, he was here all night. We could see him behind the curtains over there.
Hmmm...
Ummm...
Now that that's settled... I'll order the extra cheesy burrito.
So Bronto has an alibi...
Who else would steal beans and leave behind a stink bomb?

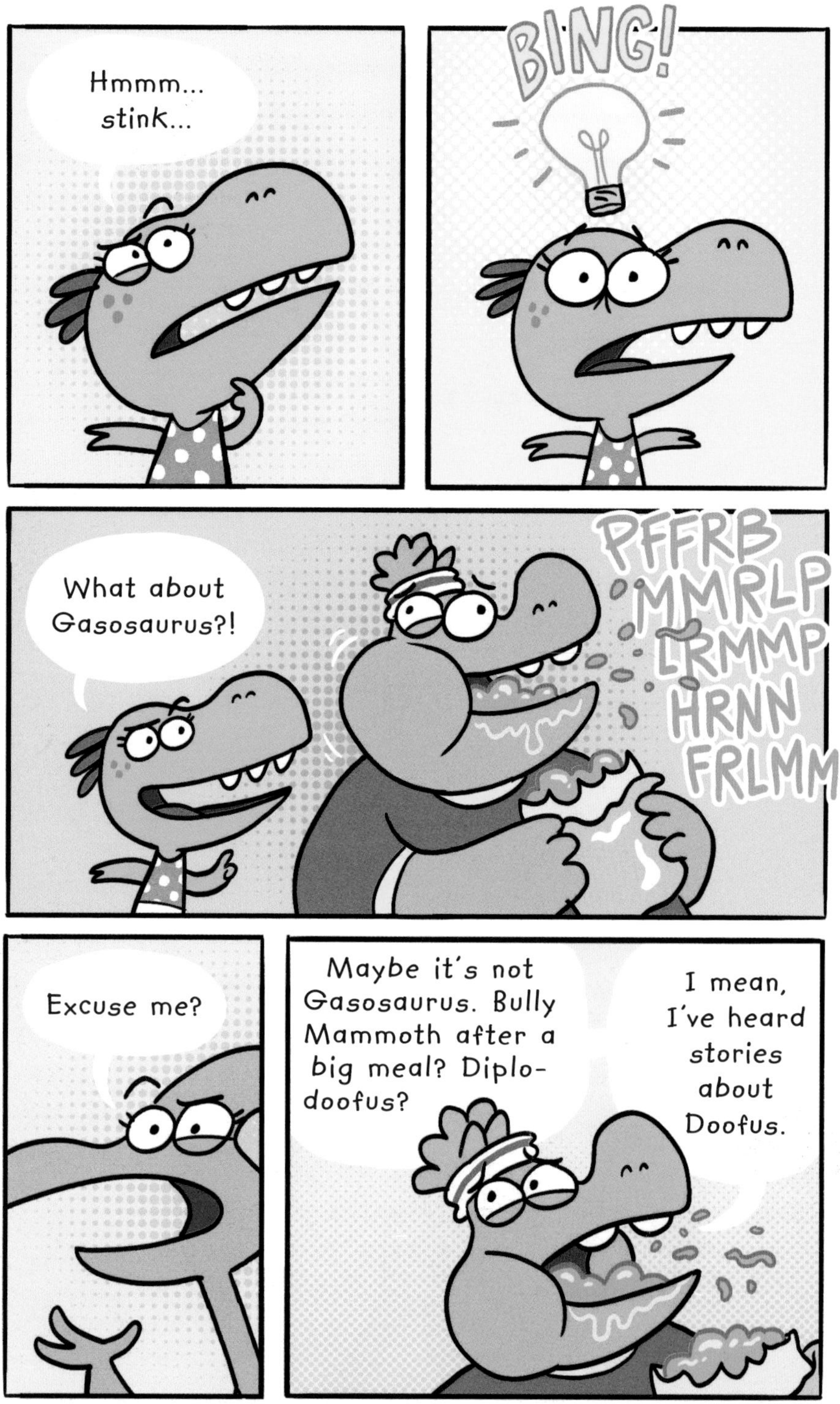
Hmmm... stink...
BING!
What about Gasosaurus?!
PFFRB MMRLP LRMMP HRNN FRLMM
Excuse me?
Maybe it's not Gasosaurus. Bully Mammoth after a big meal? Diplo-doofus?
I mean, I've heard stories about Doofus.

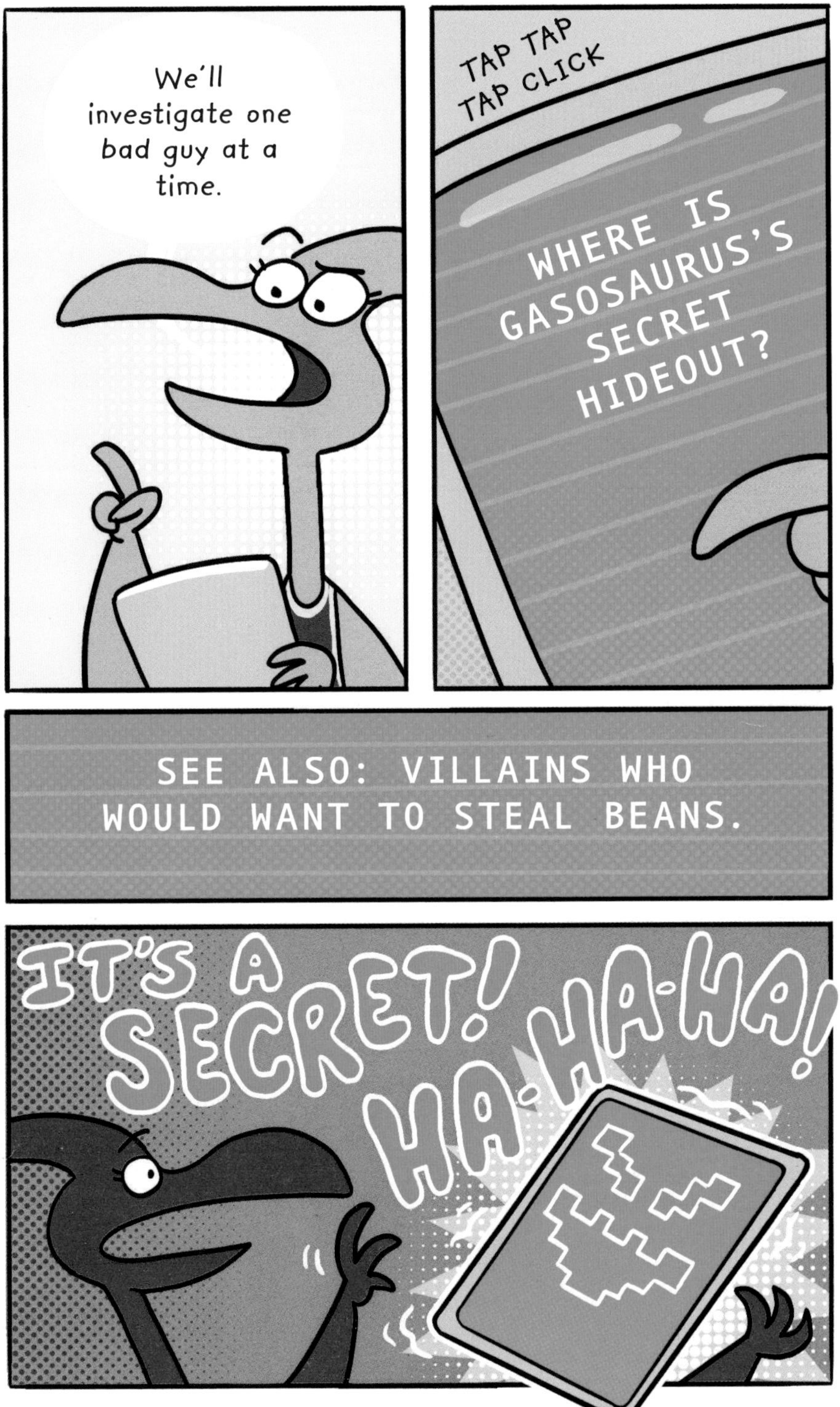
We'll investigate one bad guy at a time.
TAP TAP TAP CLICK
WHERE IS GASOSAURUS'S SECRET HIDEOUT?
SEE ALSO: VILLAINS WHO WOULD WANT TO STEAL BEANS.
IT'S A SECRET! HA-HA-HA-HA!

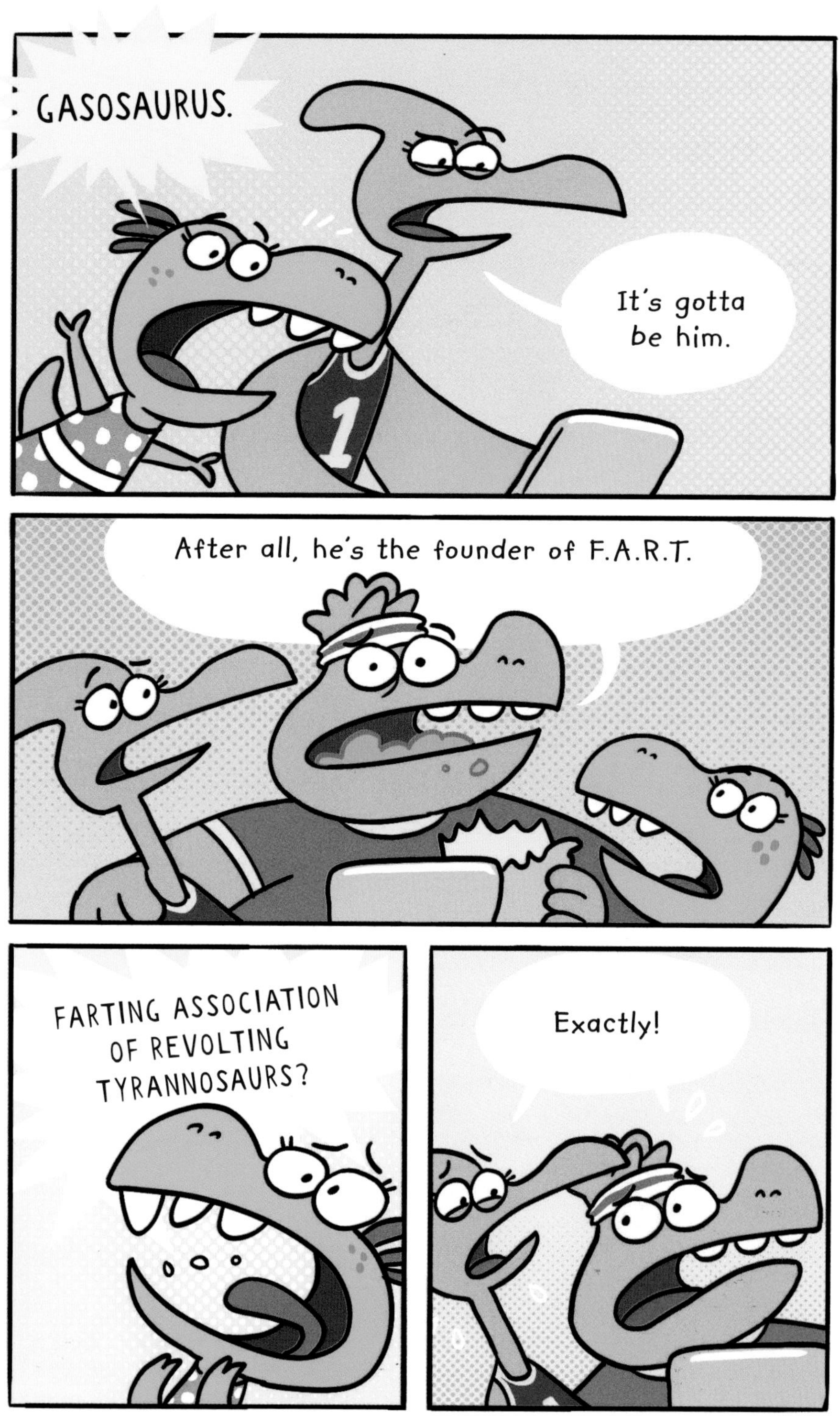
GASOSAURUS.
It's gotta be him.
After all, he's the founder of F.A.R.T.
FARTING ASSOCIATION OF REVOLTING TYRANNOSAURS?
Exactly!

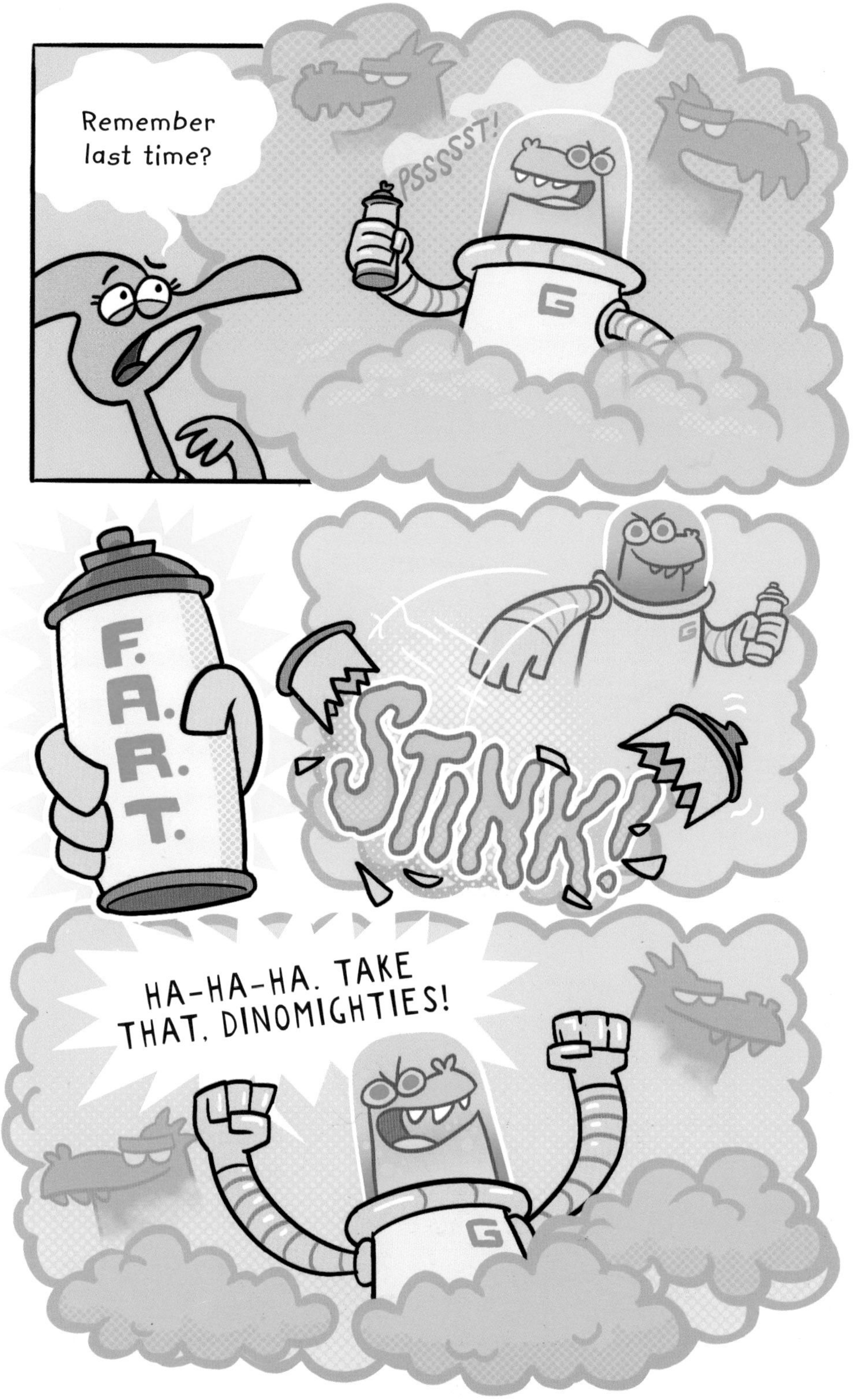
Remember last time?
PSSSSST!
F.A.R.T.
STINK!
HA-HA-HA. TAKE THAT, DINOMIGHTIES!

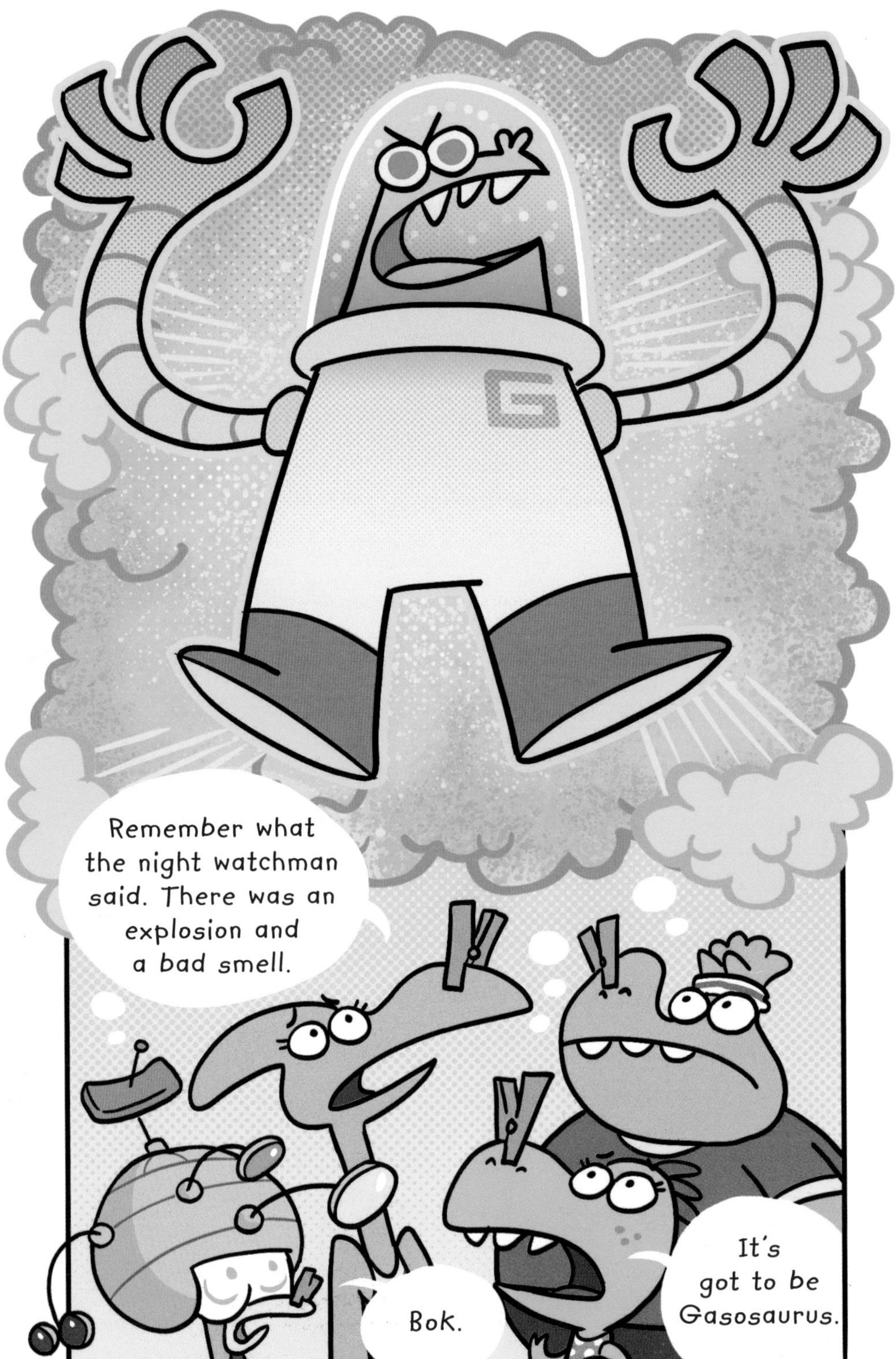
Remember what the night watchman said. There was an explosion and a bad smell.
Bok.
It's got to be Gasosaurus.

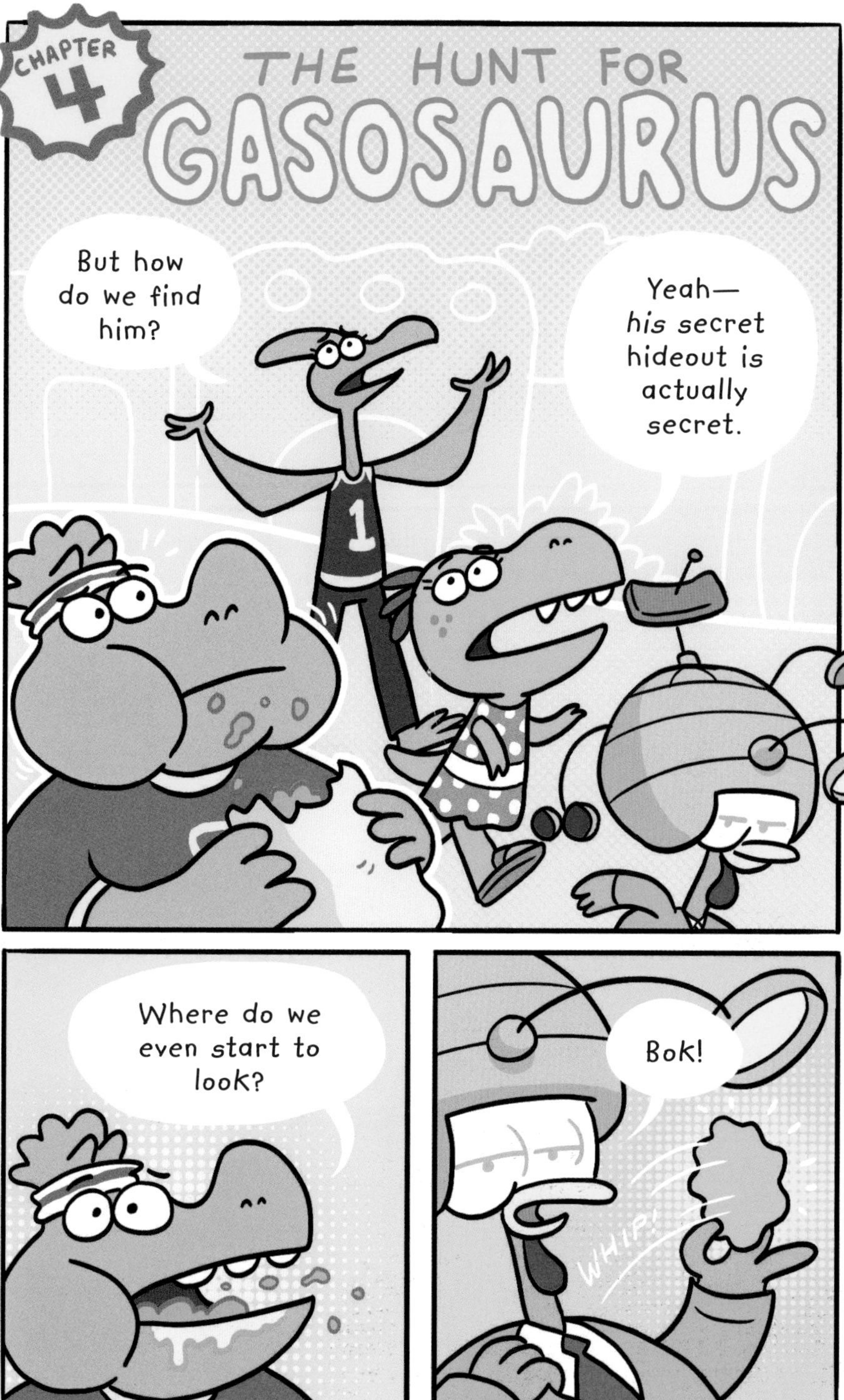
CHAPTER 4
THE HUNT FOR
GASOSAURUS
But how do we find him?
Yeah— *his* secret hideout is actually secret.
1
Where do we even start to look?
Bok!
WHIP!

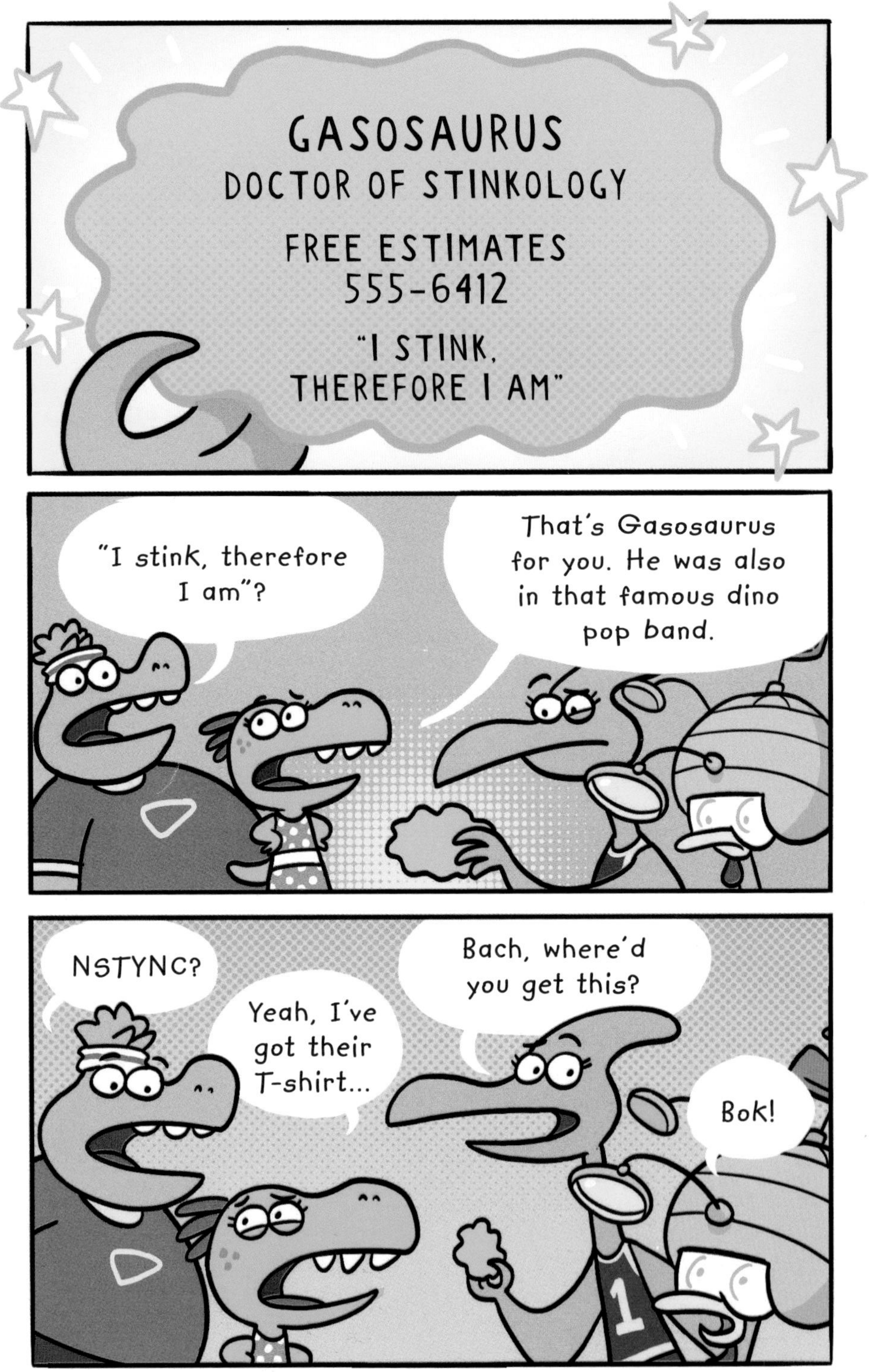
GASOSAURUS
DOCTOR OF STINKOLOGY
FREE ESTIMATES
555-6412
"I STINK, THEREFORE I AM"
"I stink, therefore I am"?
That's Gasosaurus for you. He was also in that famous dino pop band.
NSTYNC?
Yeah, I've got their T-shirt...
Bach, where'd you get this?
Bok!

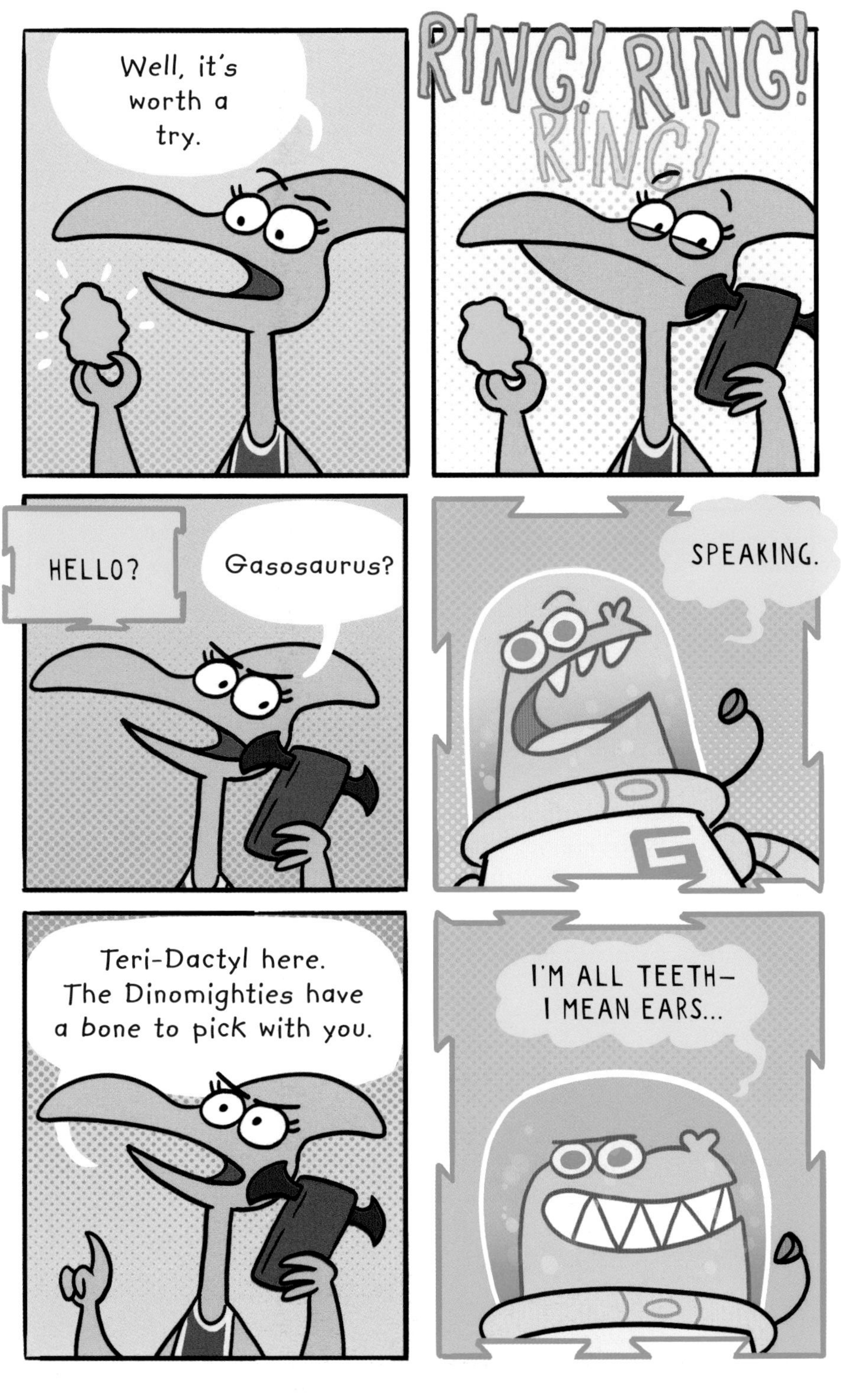
Well, it's worth a try.
RING! RING! RING!
HELLO?
Gasosaurus?
SPEAKING.
Teri-Dactyl here. The Dinomighties have a bone to pick with you.
I'M ALL TEETH—
I MEAN EARS...

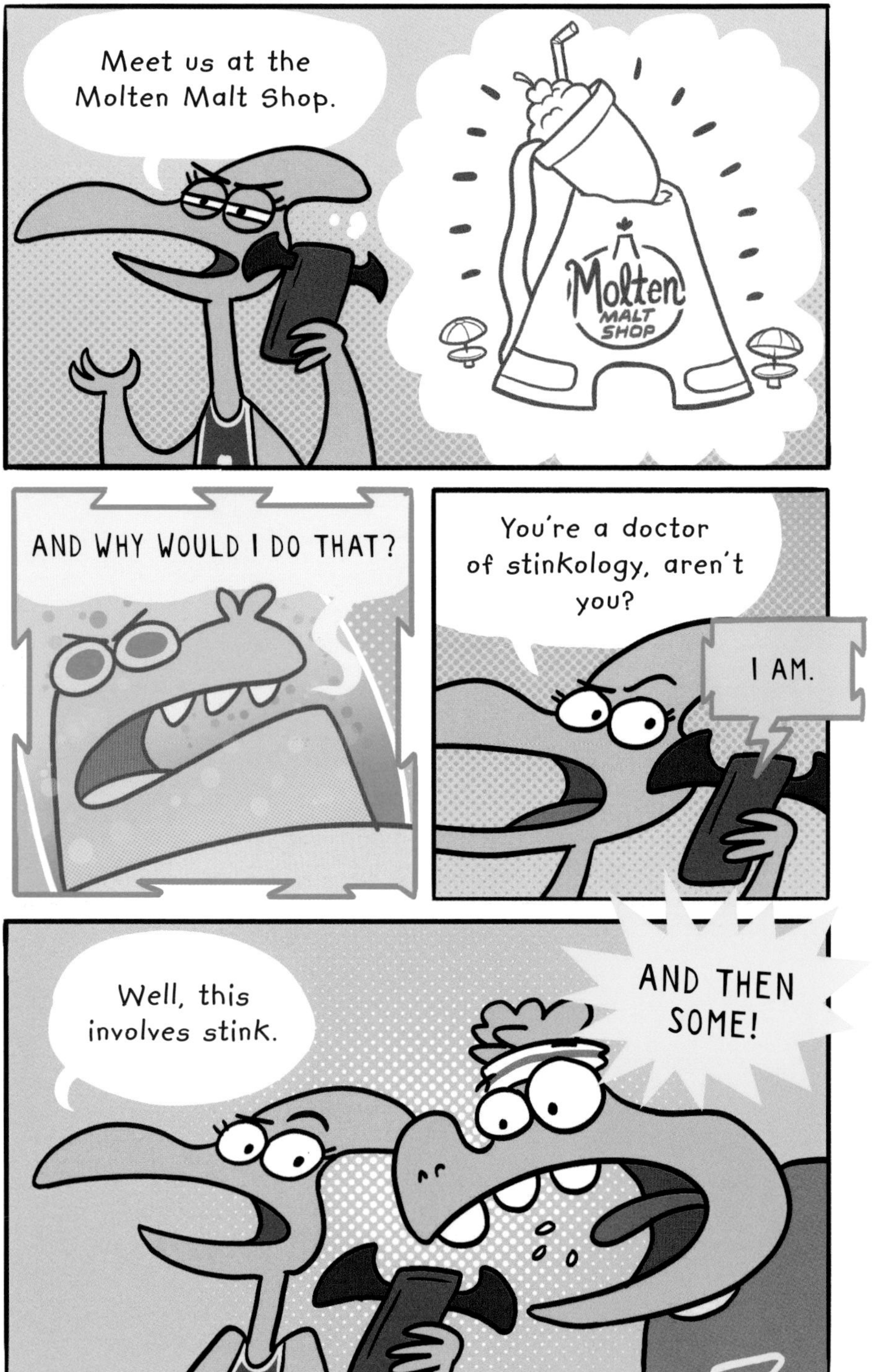
Meet us at the Molten Malt Shop.
Molten MALT SHOP
AND WHY WOULD I DO THAT?
You're a doctor of stinkology, aren't you?
I AM.
Well, this involves stink.
AND THEN SOME!

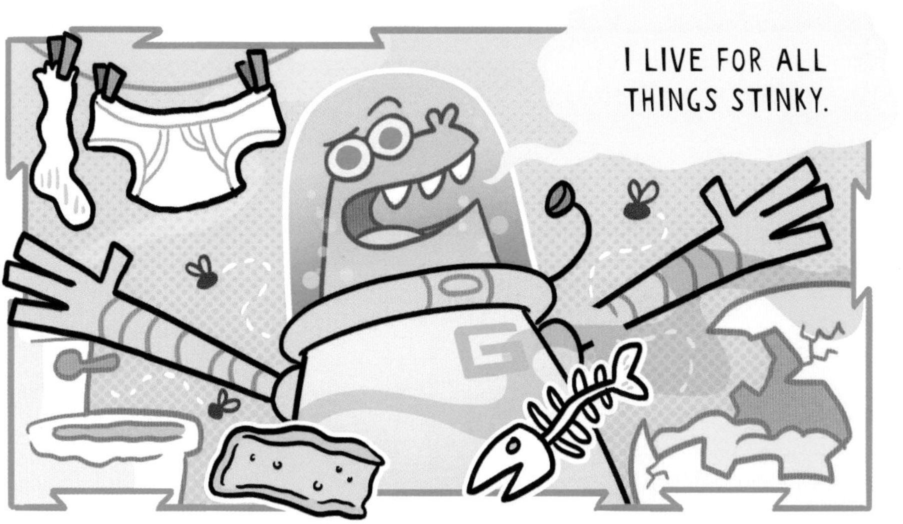
I LIVE FOR ALL THINGS STINKY.

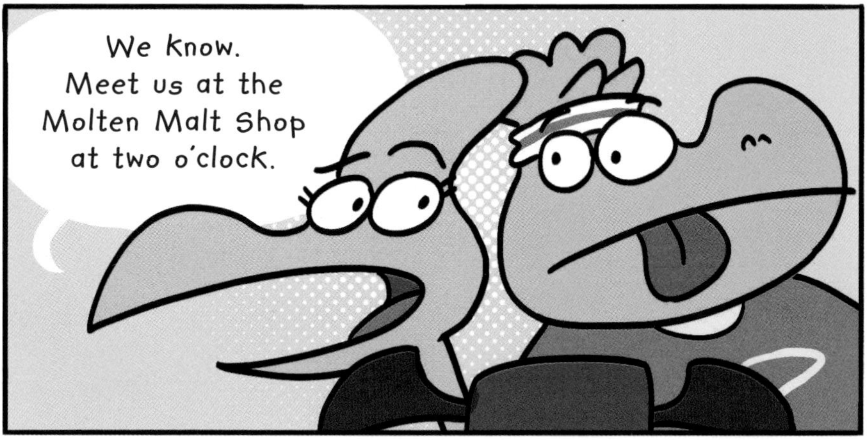
We know. Meet us at the Molten Malt Shop at two o'clock.

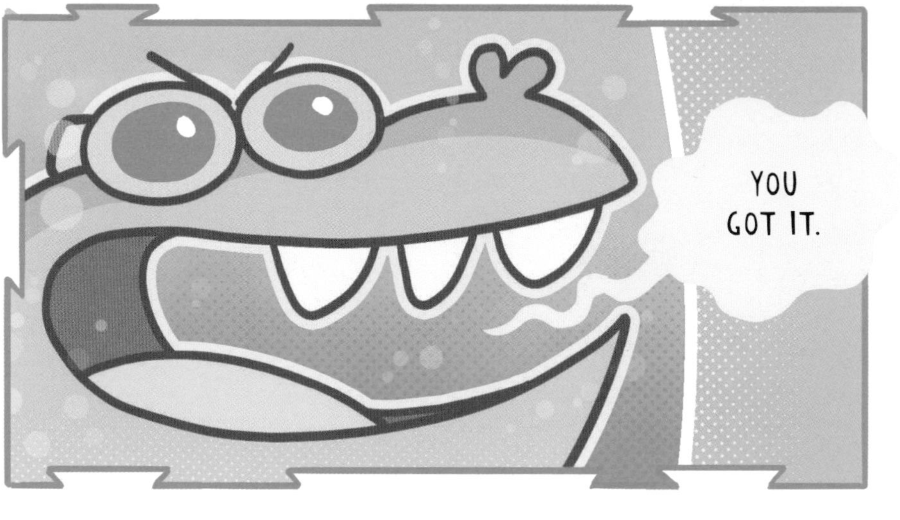
YOU GOT IT.

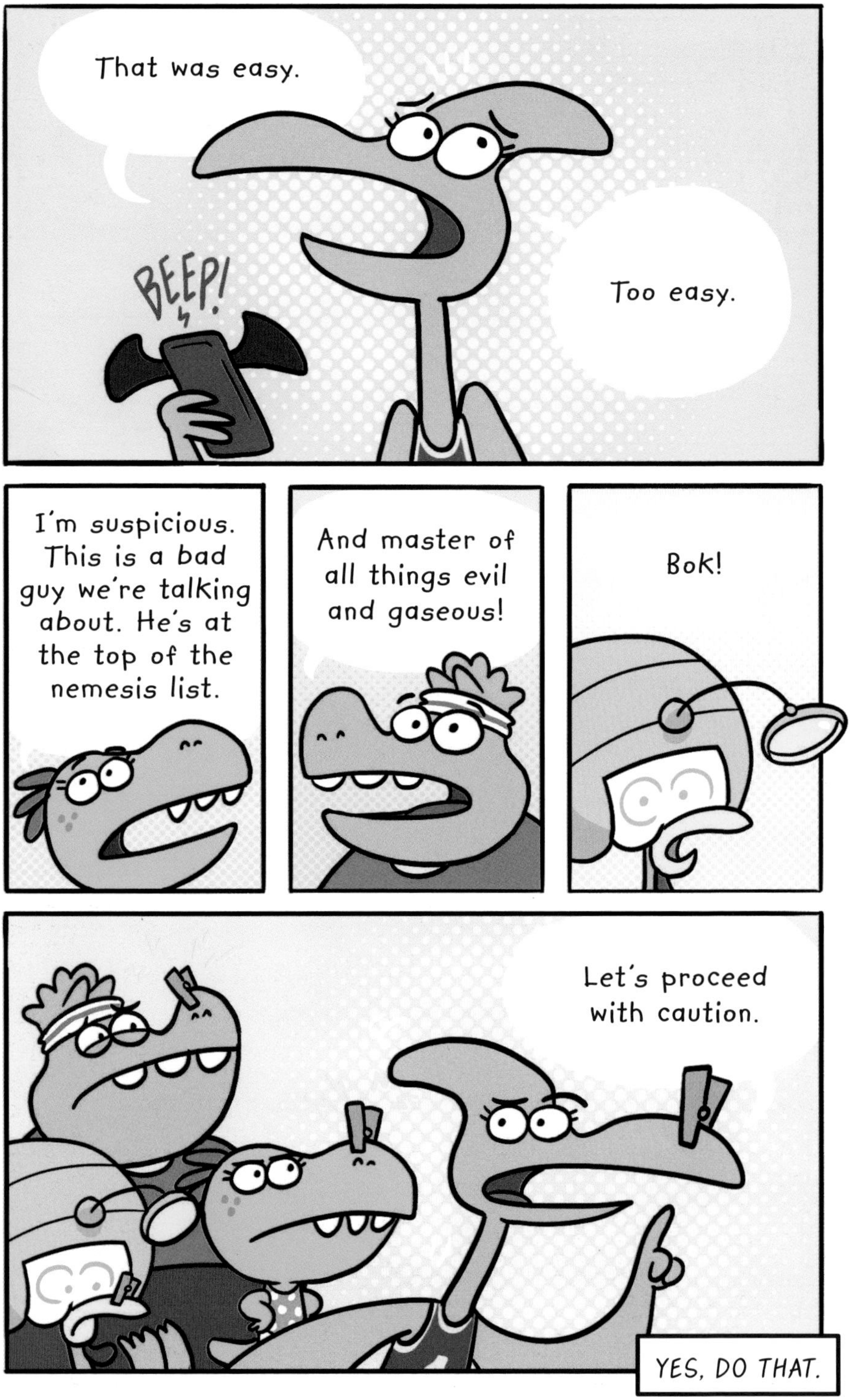
That was easy.
BEEP!
Too easy.
I'm suspicious. This is a bad guy we're talking about. He's at the top of the nemesis list.
And master of all things evil and gaseous!
Bok!
Let's proceed with caution.
YES, DO THAT.

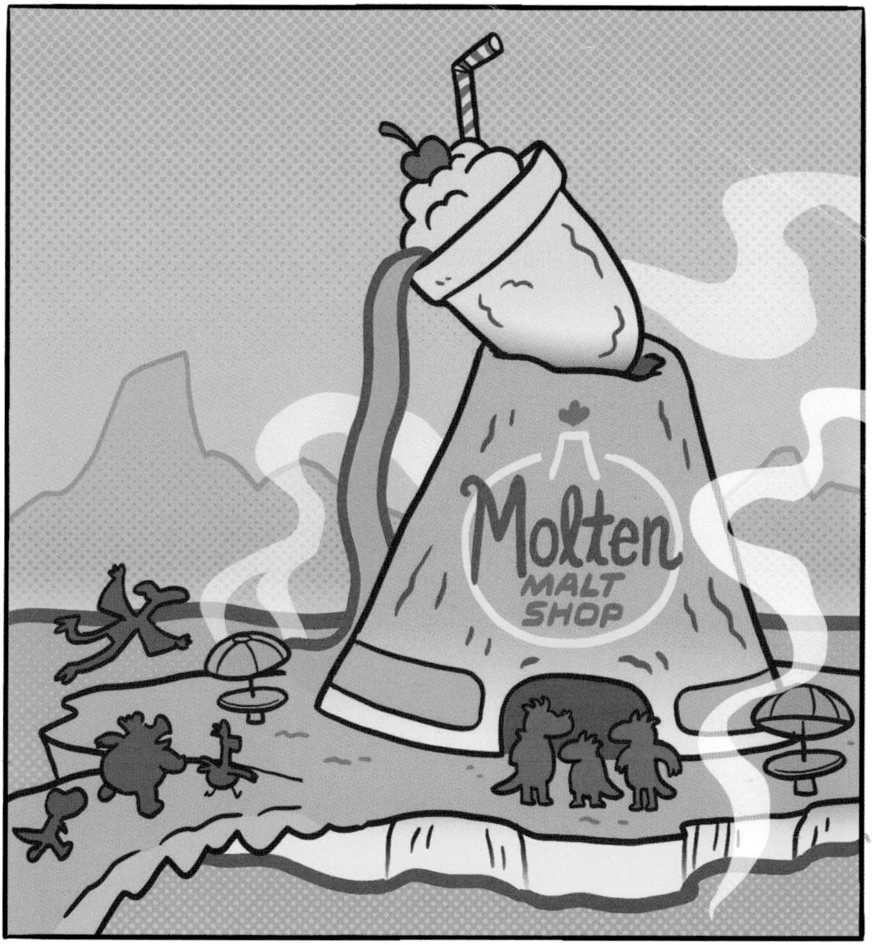
Molten
MALT
SHOP

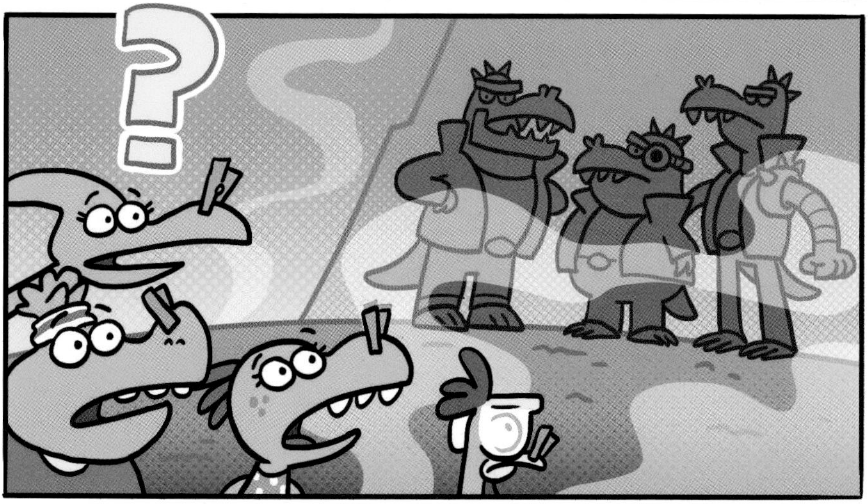
?

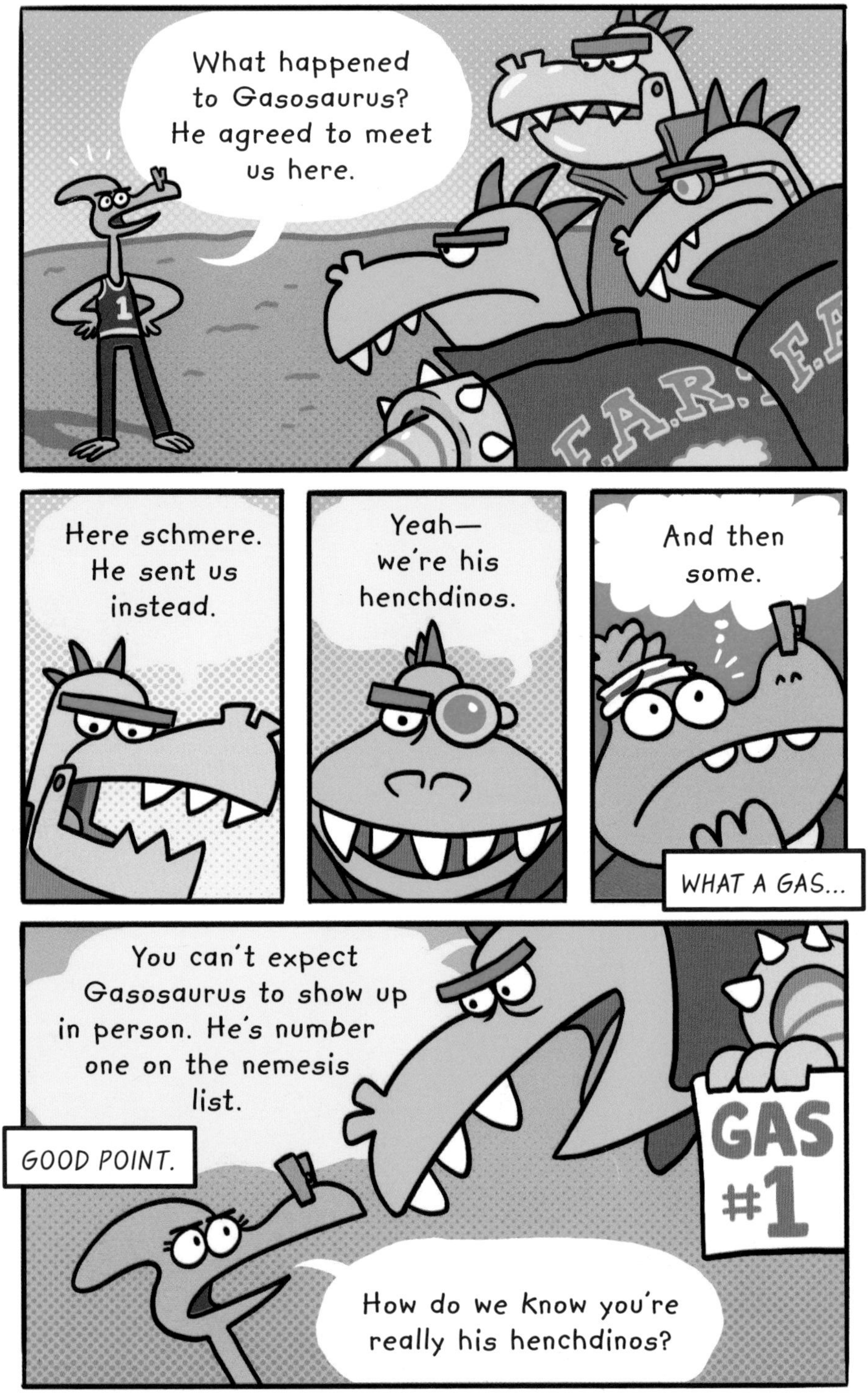

What happened to Gasosaurus? He agreed to meet us here.
F.A.R.T.
Here schmere. He sent us instead.
Yeah—we're his henchdinos.
And then some.
WHAT A GAS...
You can't expect Gasosaurus to show up in person. He's number one on the nemesis list.
GOOD POINT.
GAS #1
How do we know you're really his henchdinos?

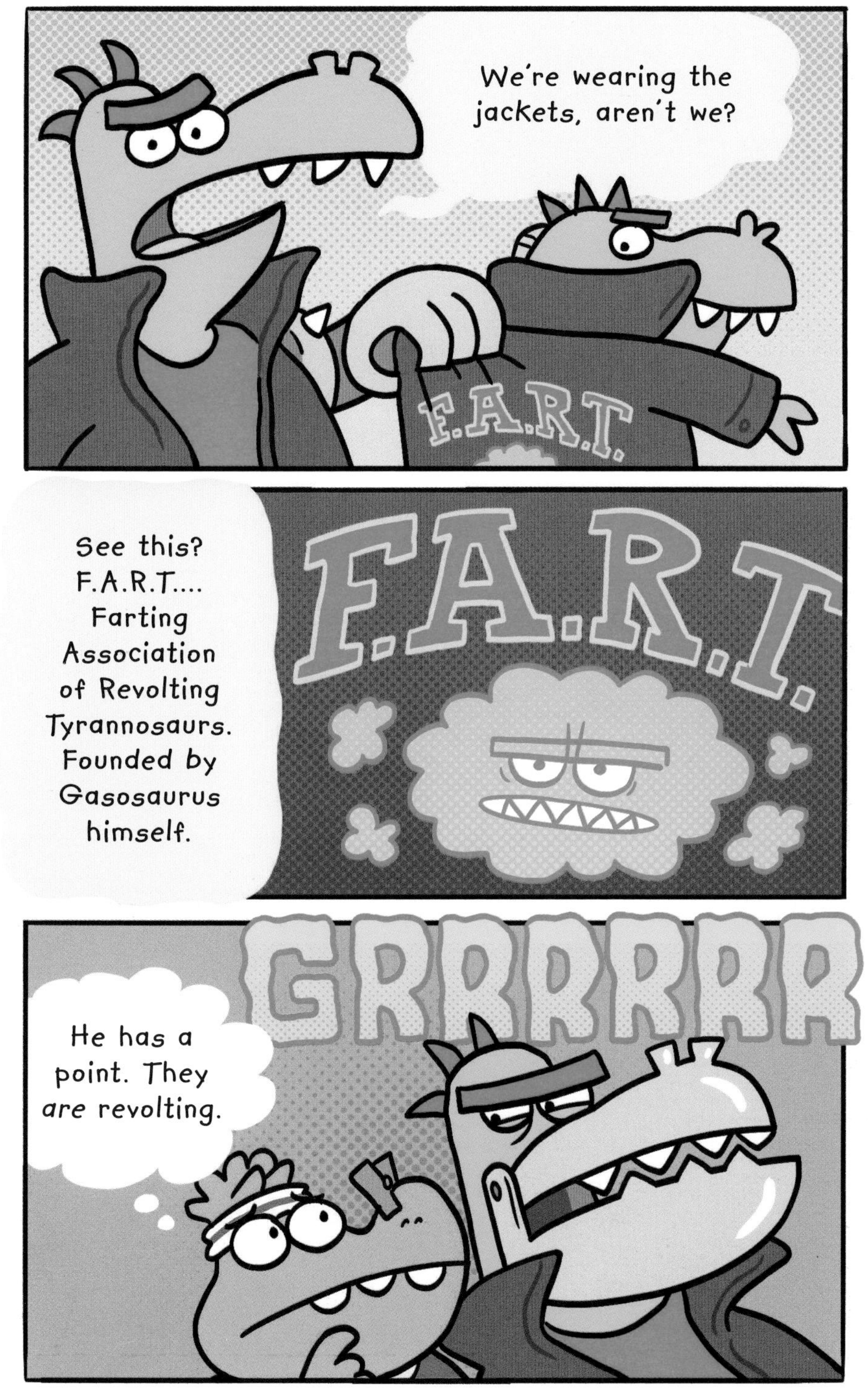

We're wearing the jackets, aren't we?
F.A.R.T.
See this? F.A.R.T.... Farting Association of Revolting Tyrannosaurs. Founded by Gasosaurus himself.
F.A.R.T.
GRRRRRR
He has a point. They *are* revolting.

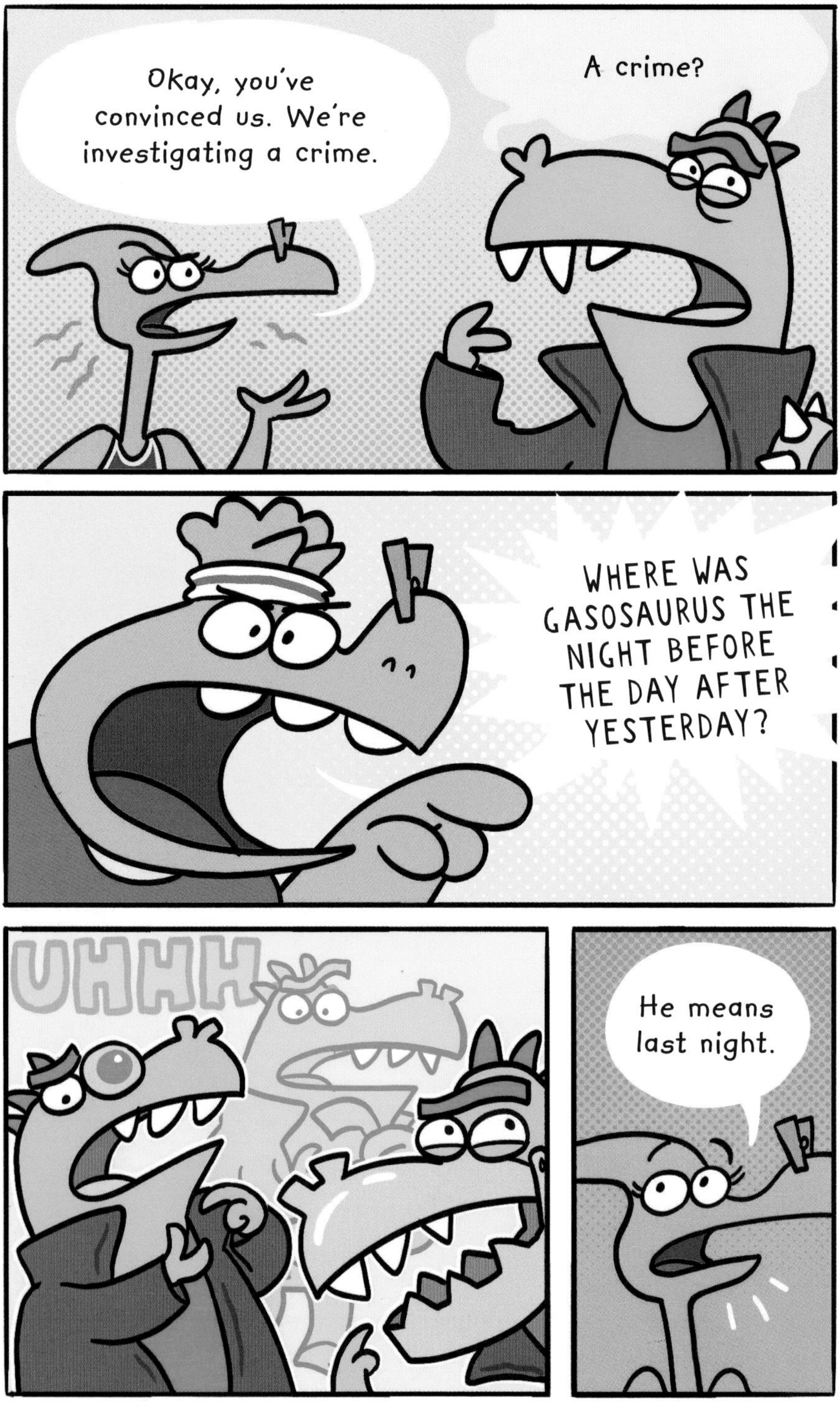
Okay, you've convinced us. We're investigating a crime.
A crime?
WHERE WAS GASOSAURUS THE NIGHT BEFORE THE DAY AFTER YESTERDAY?
UHHH
He means last night.

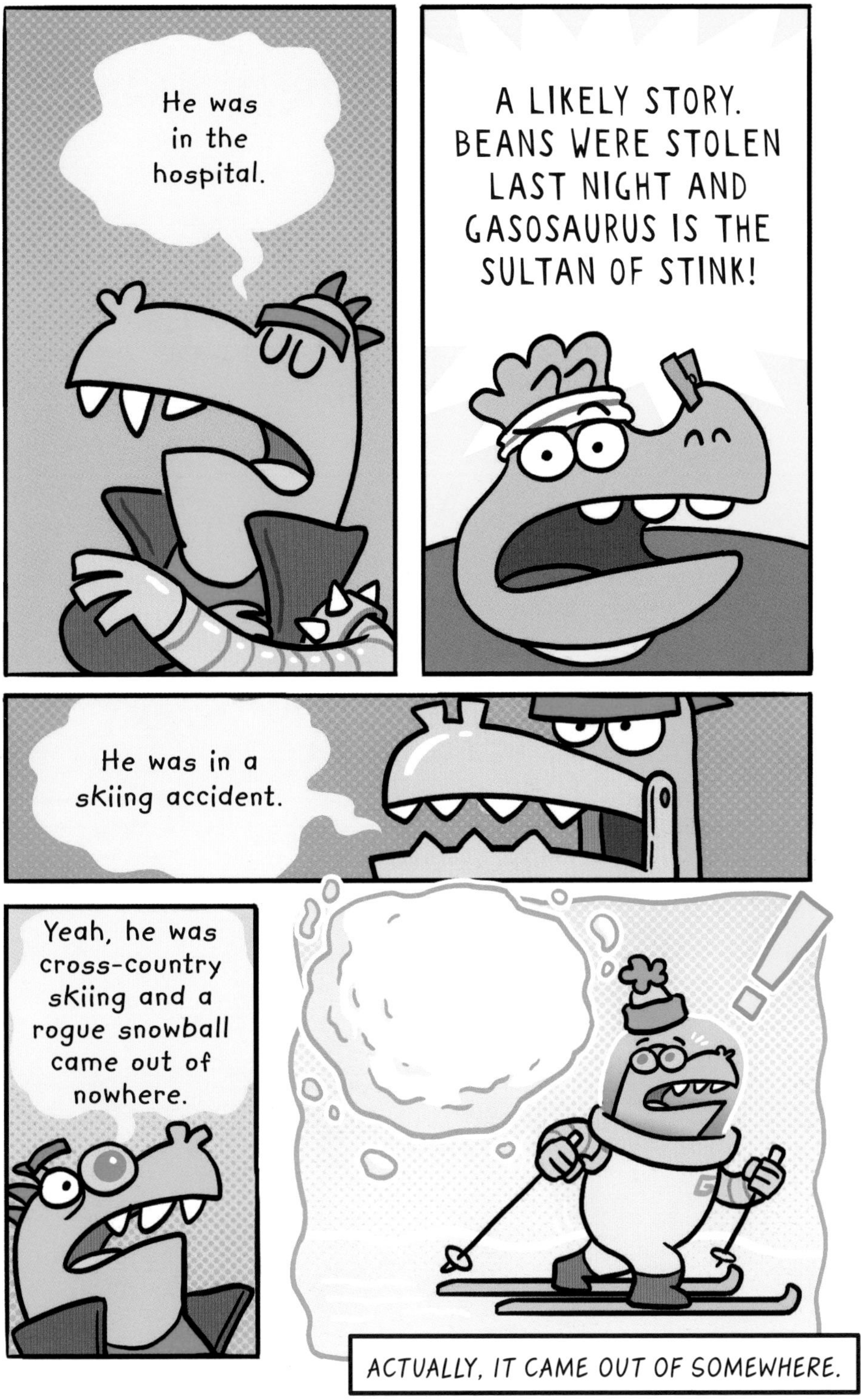
He was in the hospital.
A LIKELY STORY. BEANS WERE STOLEN LAST NIGHT AND GASOSAURUS IS THE SULTAN OF STINK!
He was in a skiing accident.
Yeah, he was cross-country skiing and a rogue snowball came out of nowhere.
ACTUALLY, IT CAME OUT OF SOMEWHERE.

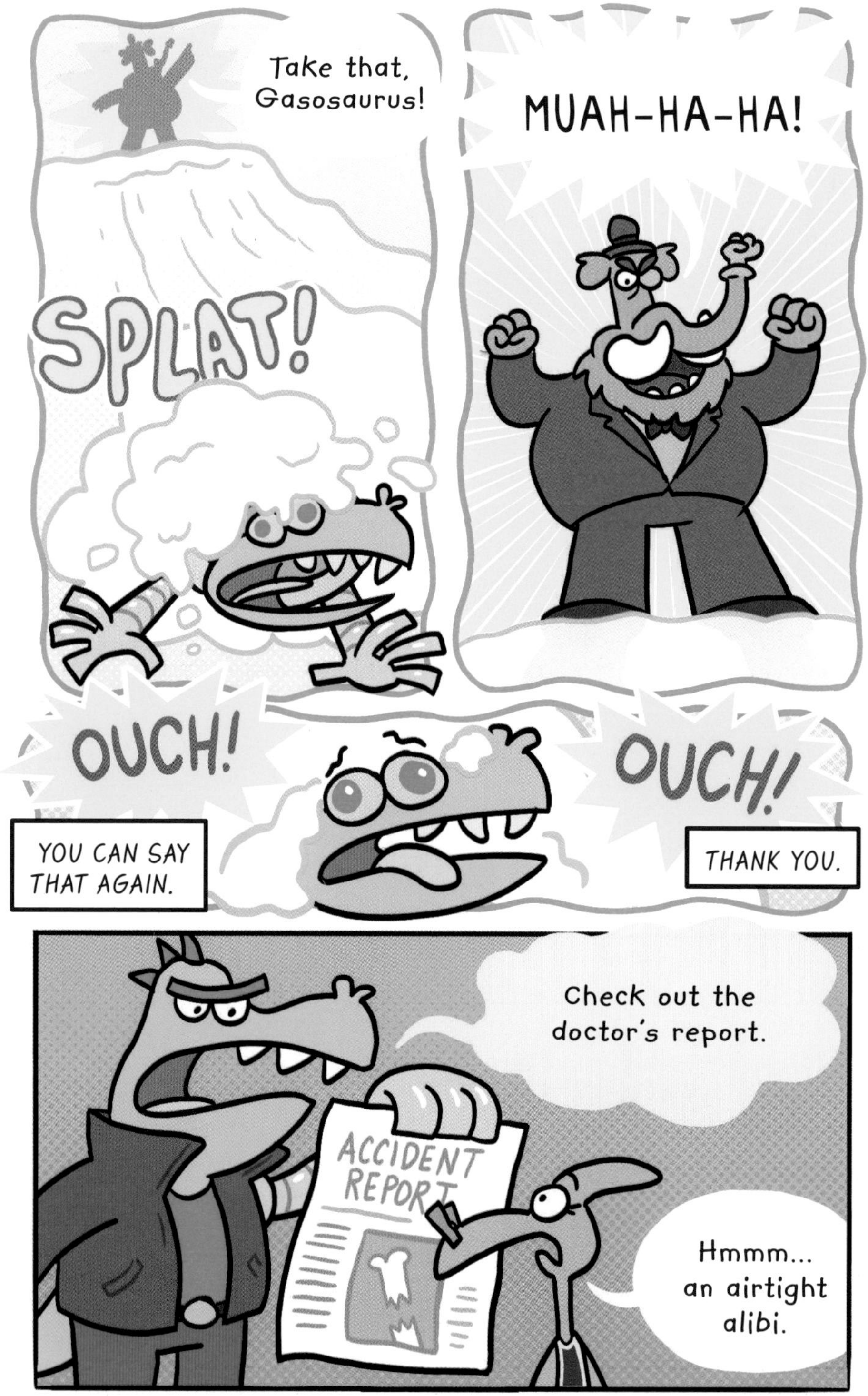

Take that, Gasosaurus!
SPLAT!
MUAH-HA-HA!
OUCH!
OUCH!
YOU CAN SAY THAT AGAIN.
THANK YOU.
Check out the doctor's report.
ACCIDENT REPORT
Hmmm... an airtight alibi.

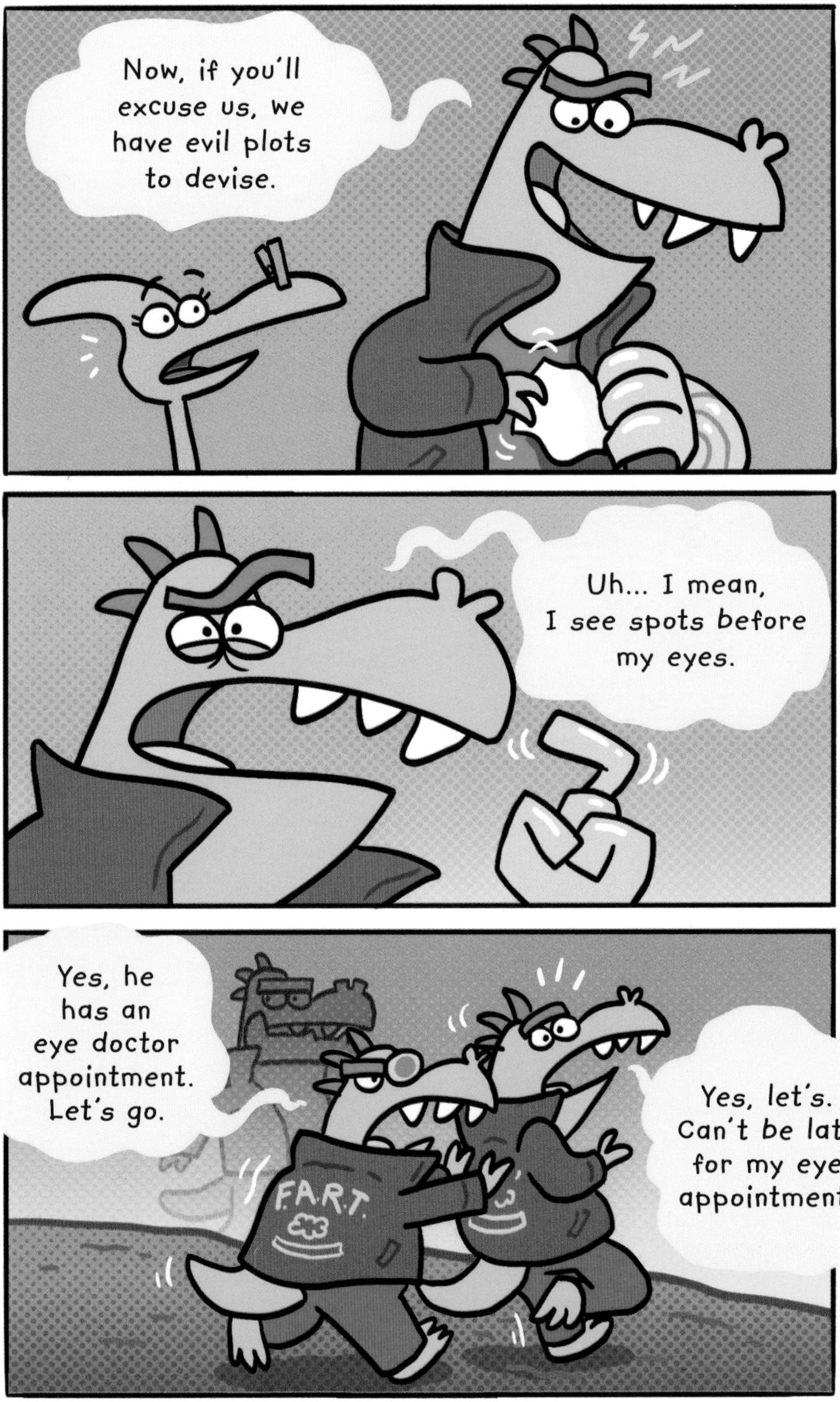
Now, if you'll excuse us, we have evil plots to devise.
Uh... I mean, I see spots before my eyes.
Yes, he has an eye doctor appointment. Let's go.
F.A.R.T.
Yes, let's. Can't be late for my eye appointment.

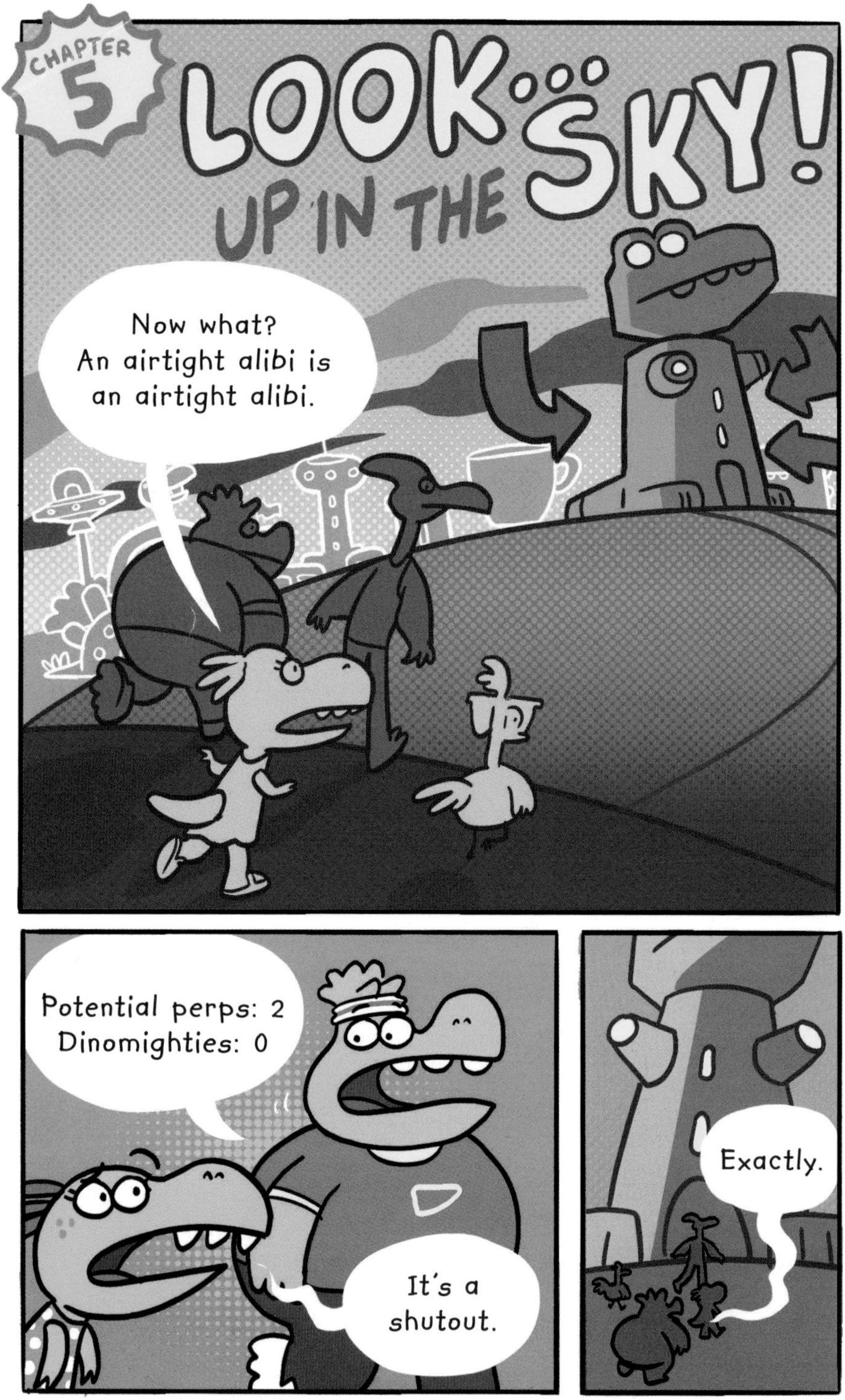
CHAPTER 5
LOOK... UP IN THE SKY!
Now what? An airtight alibi is an airtight alibi.
Potential perps: 2
Dinomighties: 0
It's a shutout.
Exactly.

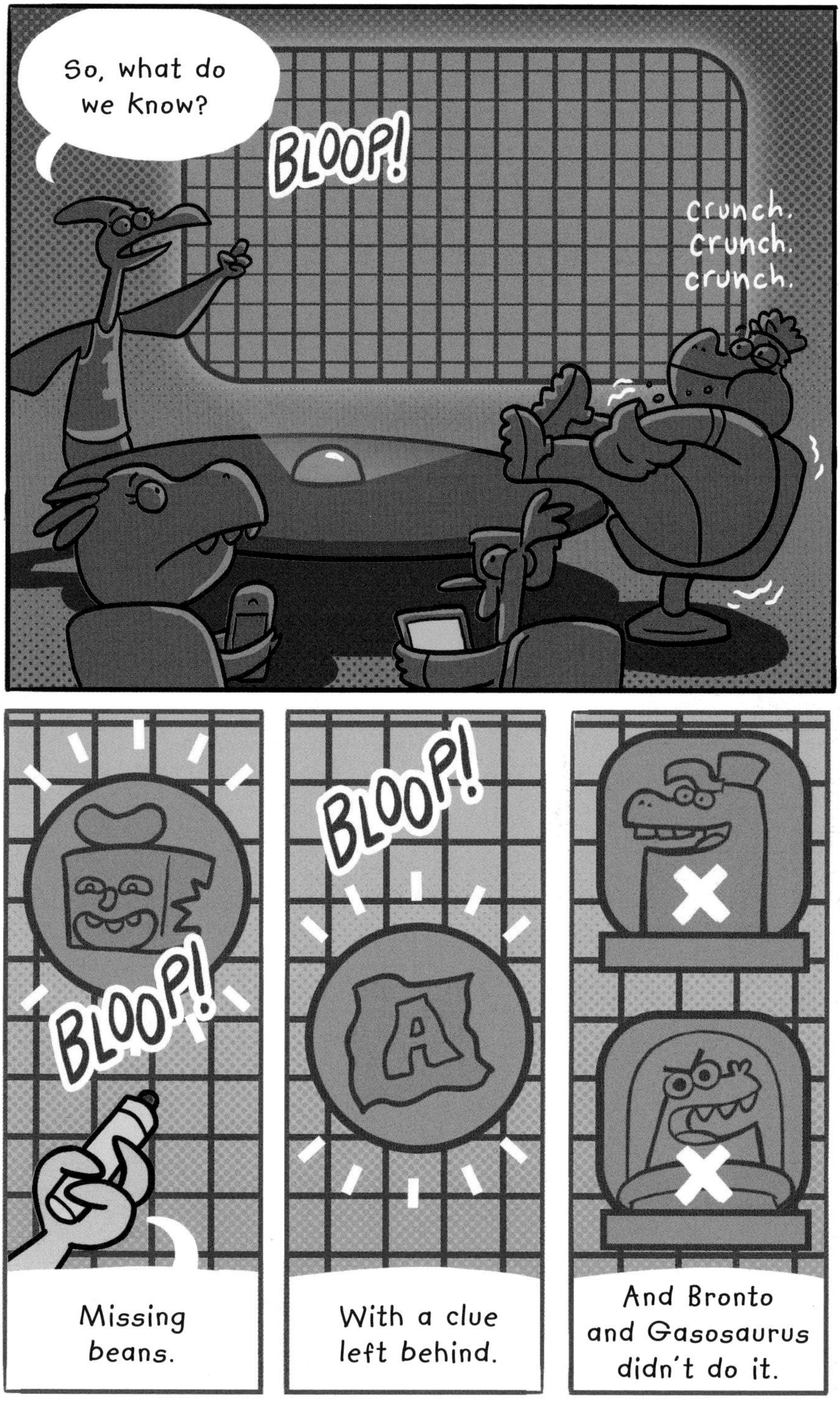
So, what do we know?
BLOOP!
crunch.
crunch.
crunch.
BLOOP!
Missing beans.
BLOOP!
With a clue left behind.
And Bronto and Gasosaurus didn't do it.

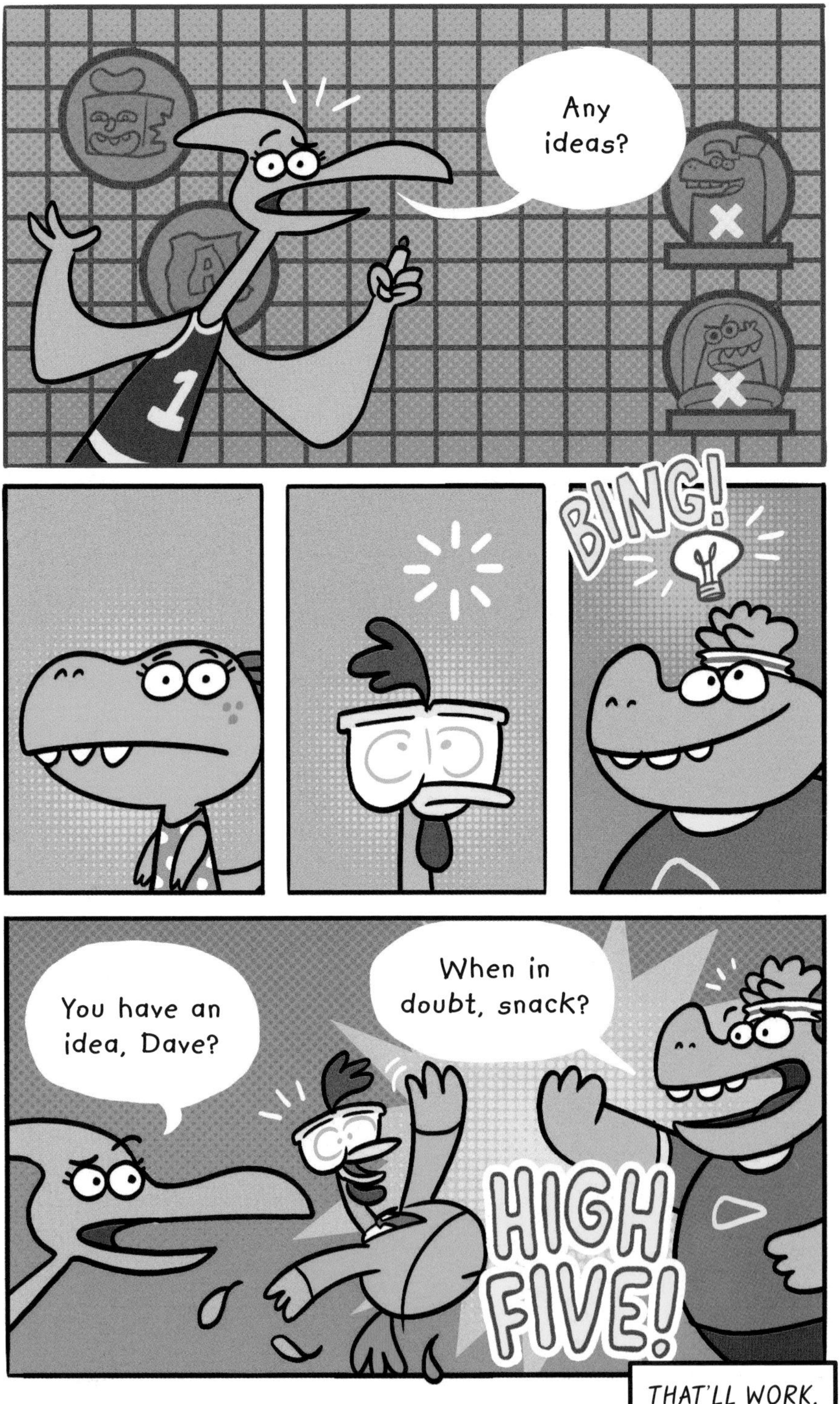
Any ideas?
BING!
You have an idea, Dave?
When in doubt, snack?
HIGH FIVE!
THAT'LL WORK.

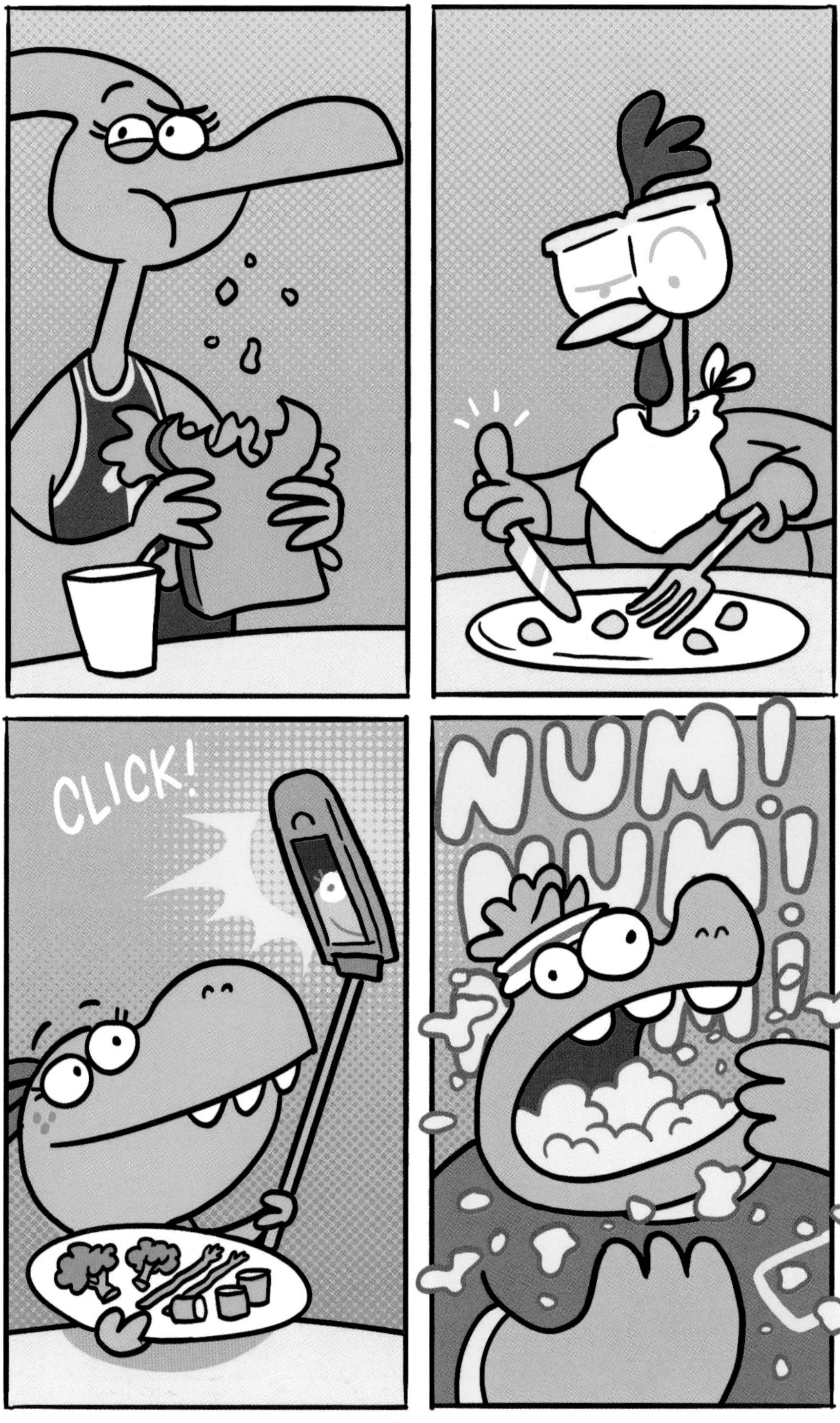
CLICK!
NUM! NUM! NUM!

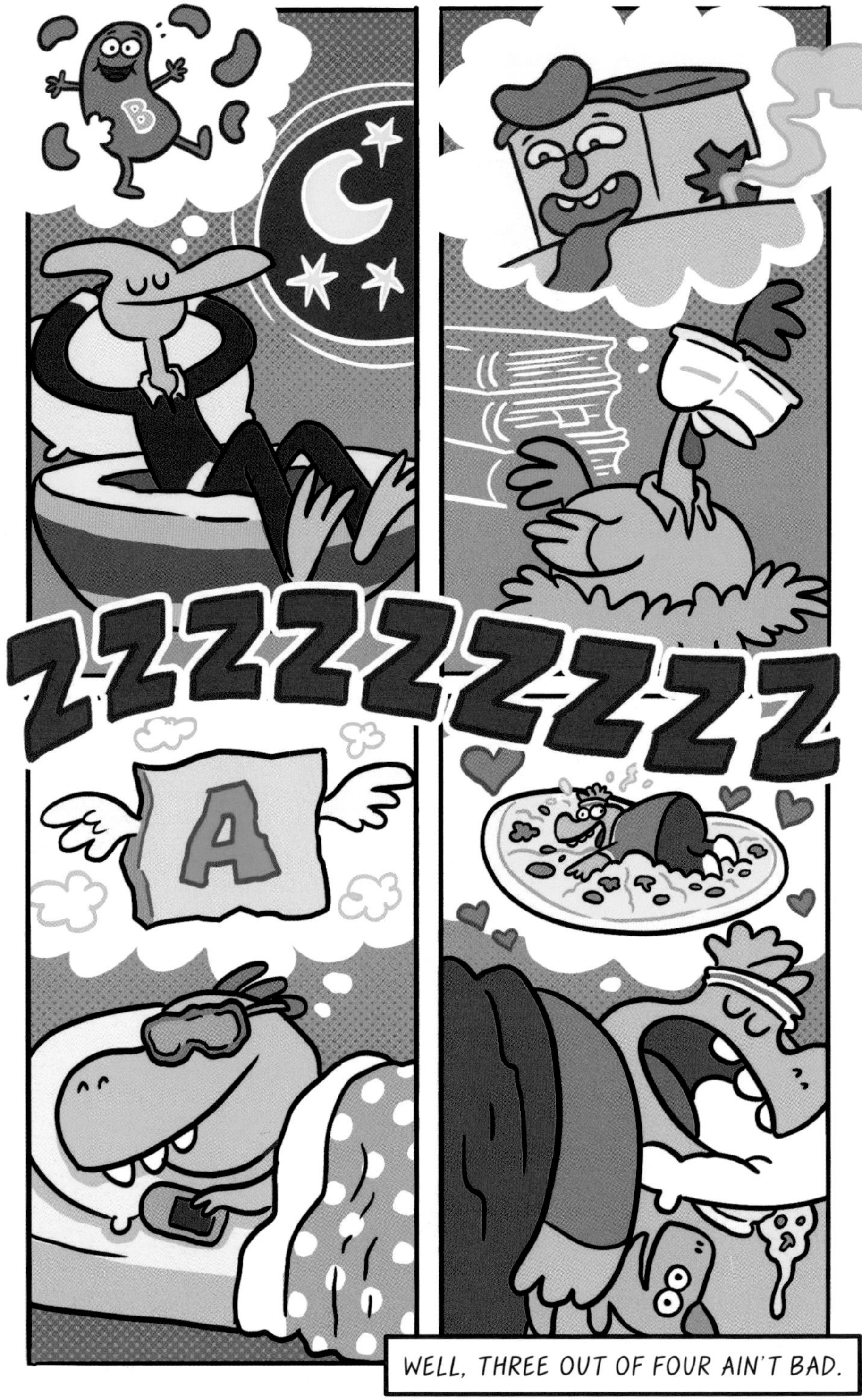
B
A
ZZZZZZZZZZZ
WELL, THREE OUT OF FOUR AIN'T BAD.

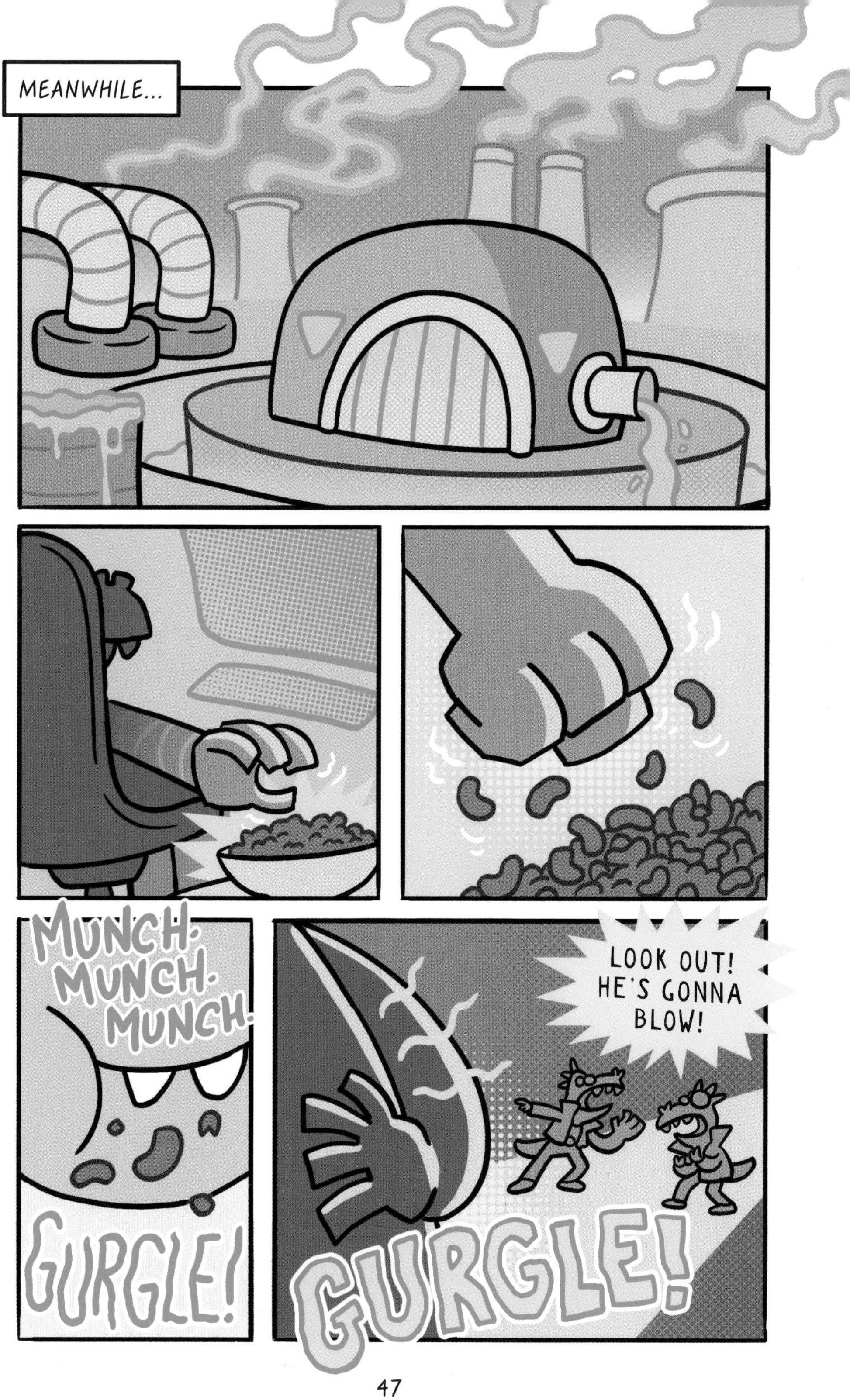
MEANWHILE...
MUNCH MUNCH MUNCH
GURGLE!
LOOK OUT! HE'S GONNA BLOW!
GURGLE!

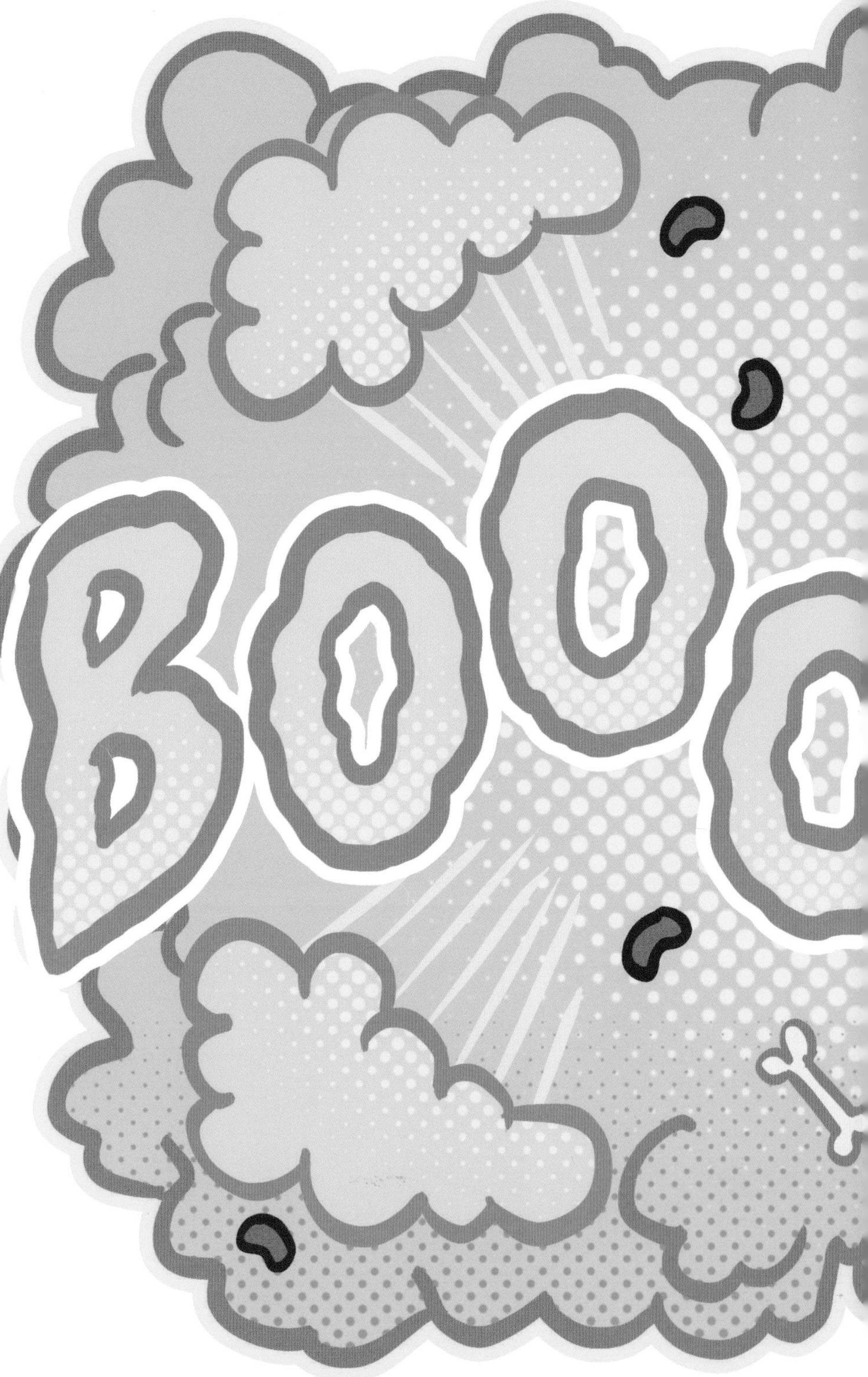
BOO

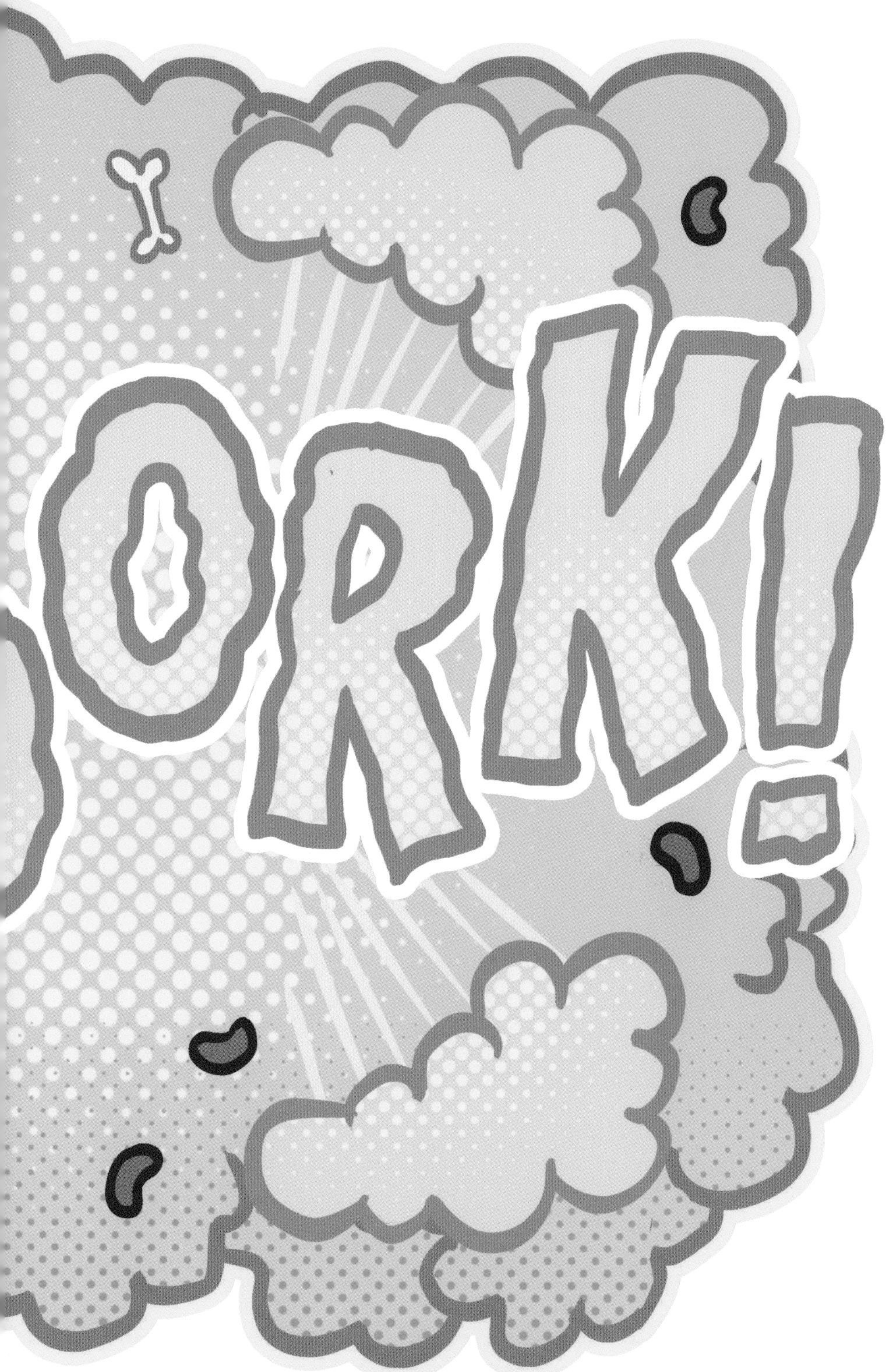
ORK!

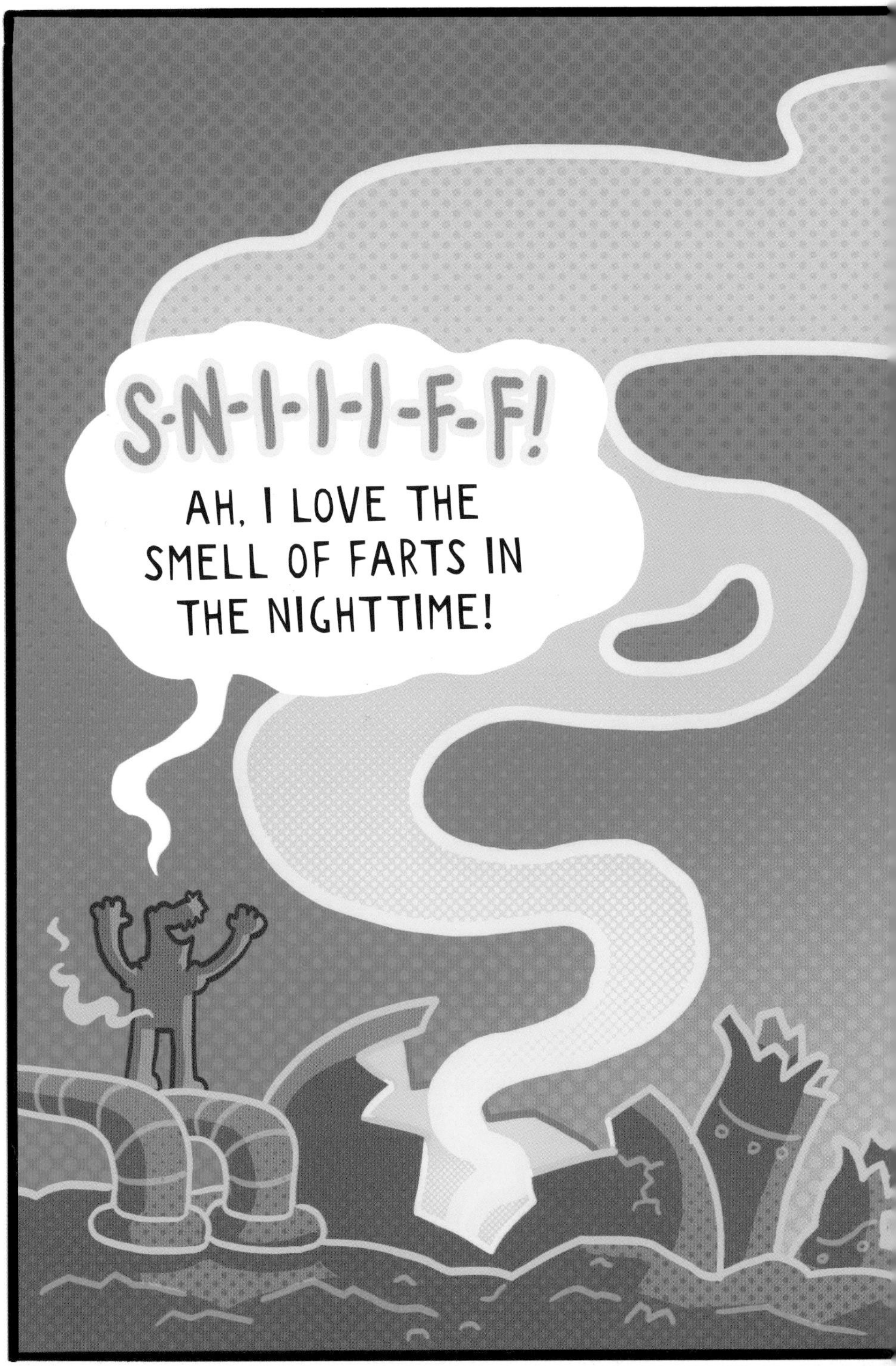
S-N-I-I-I-F-F!
AH, I LOVE THE SMELL OF FARTS IN THE NIGHTTIME!

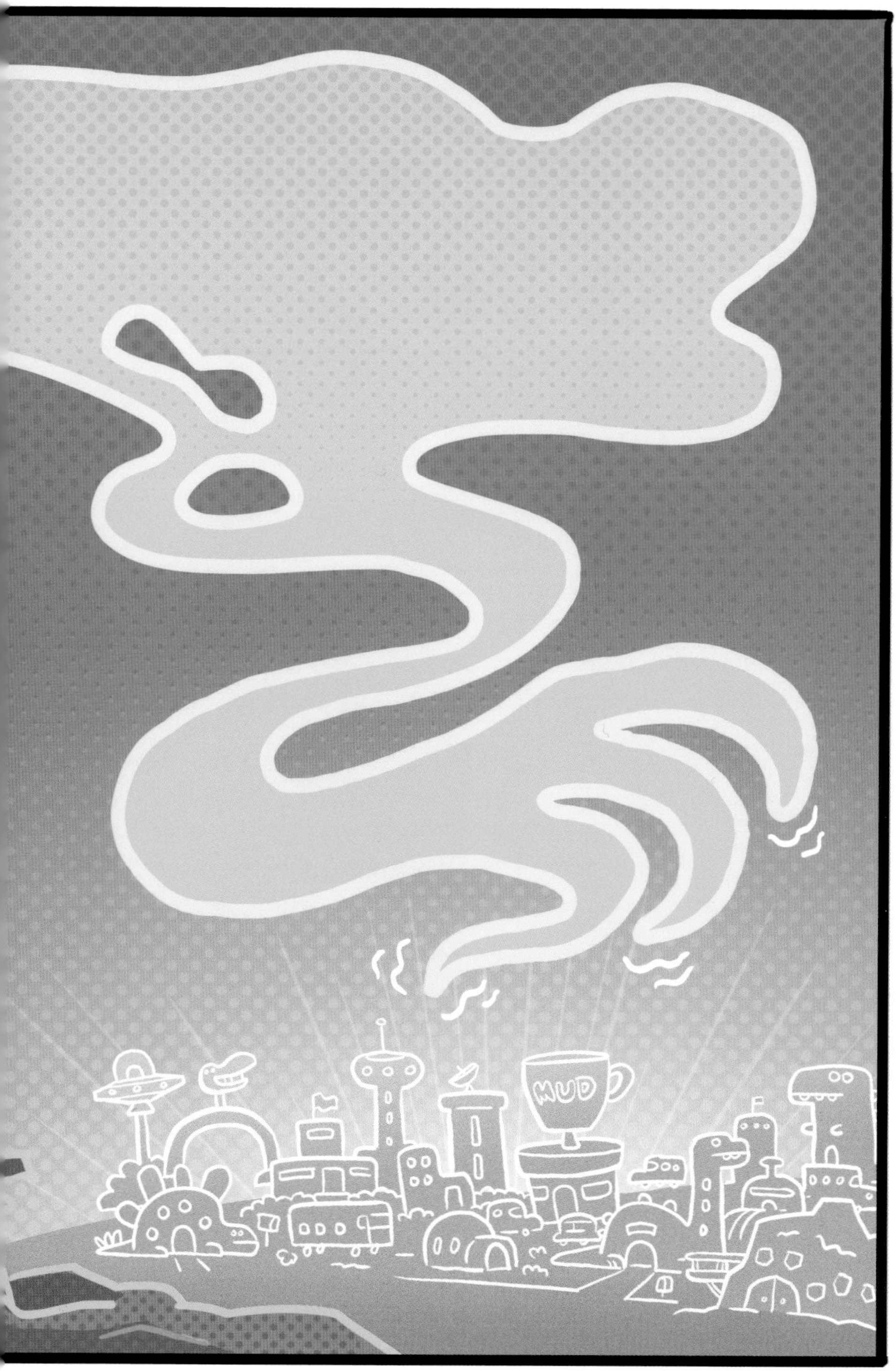
MUD

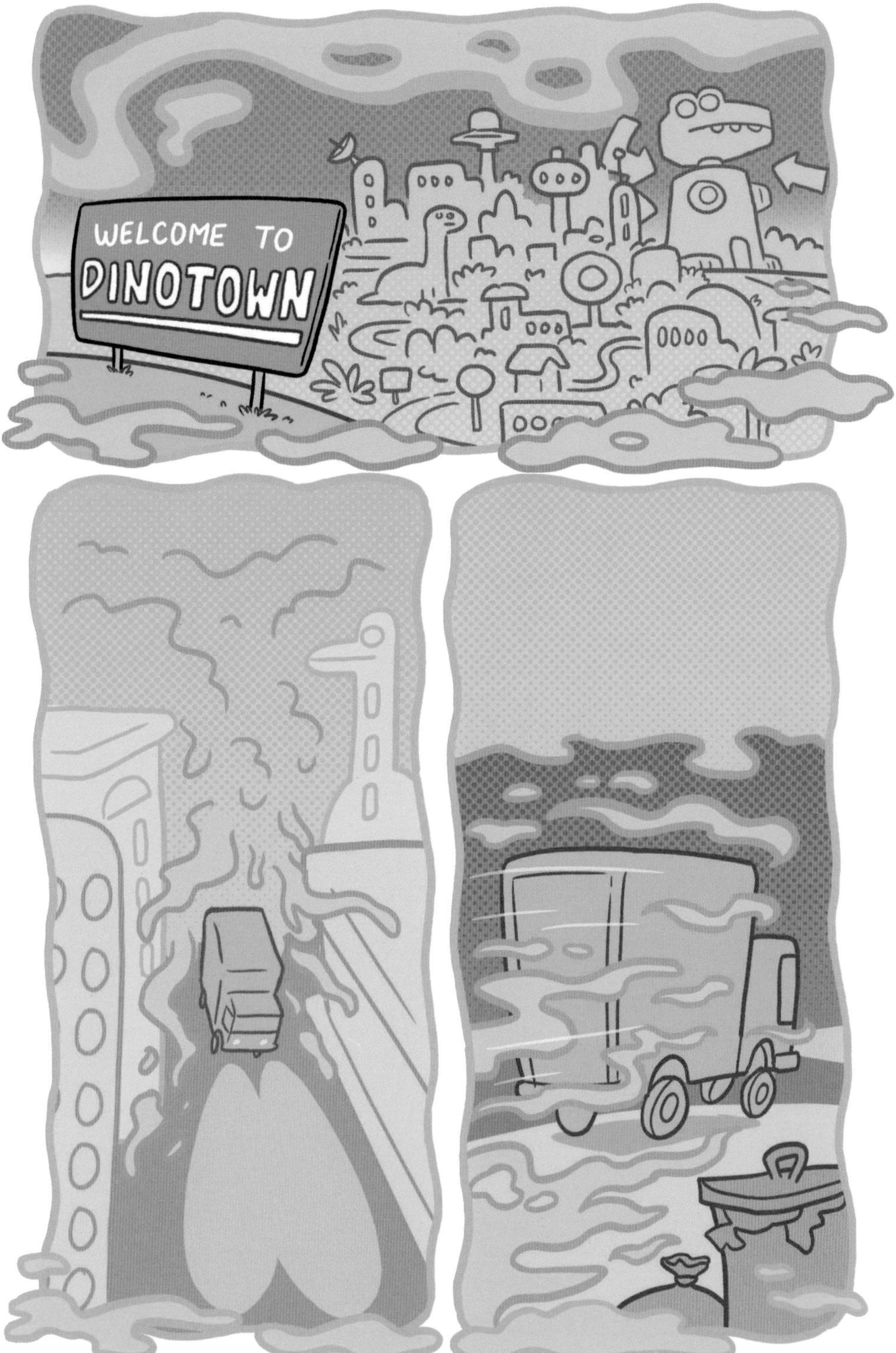
WELCOME TO
DINOTOWN

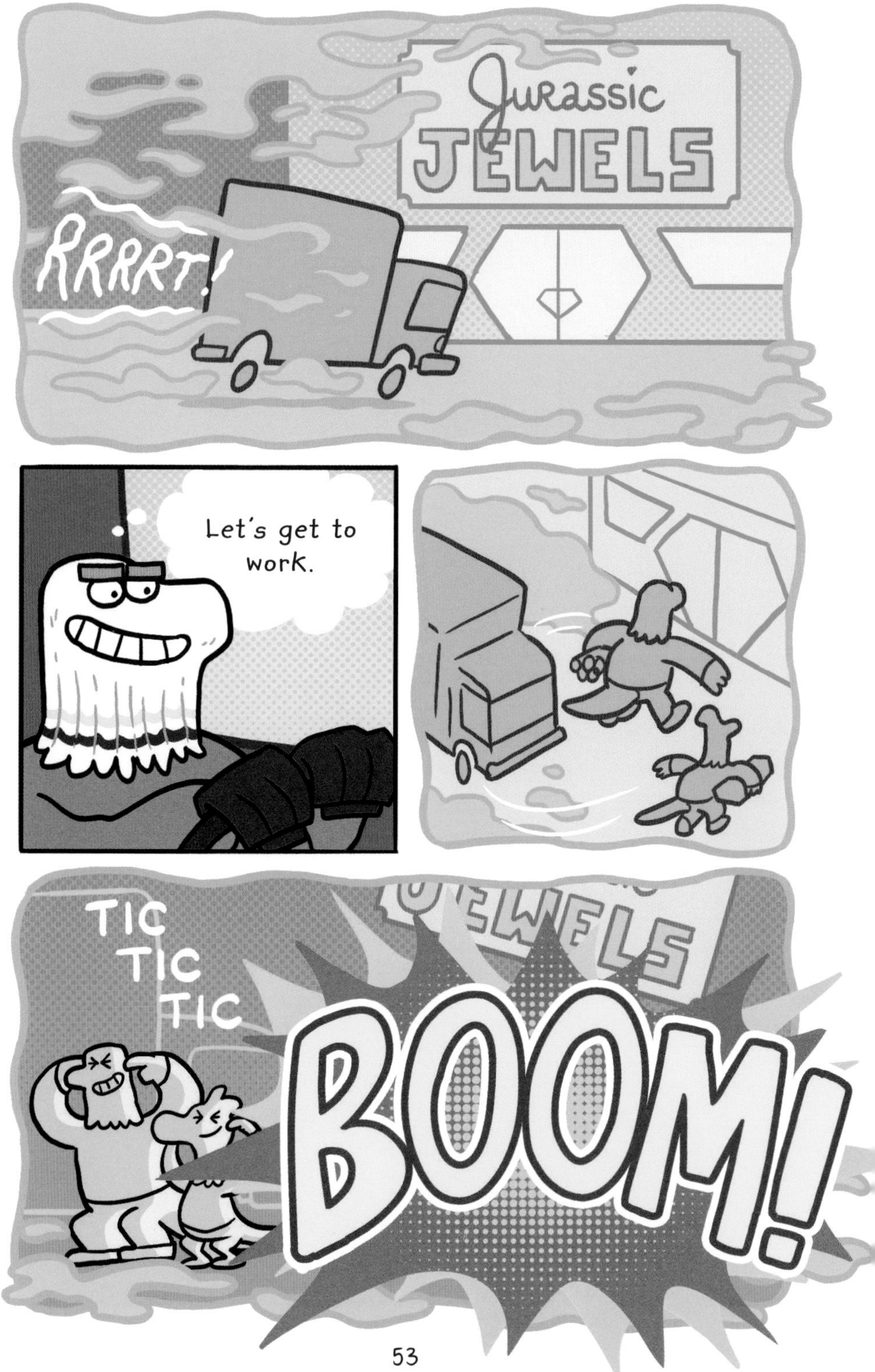
Jurassic
JEWELS
RRRRT!
Let's get to work.
JEWELS
TIC
TIC
TIC
BOOM!

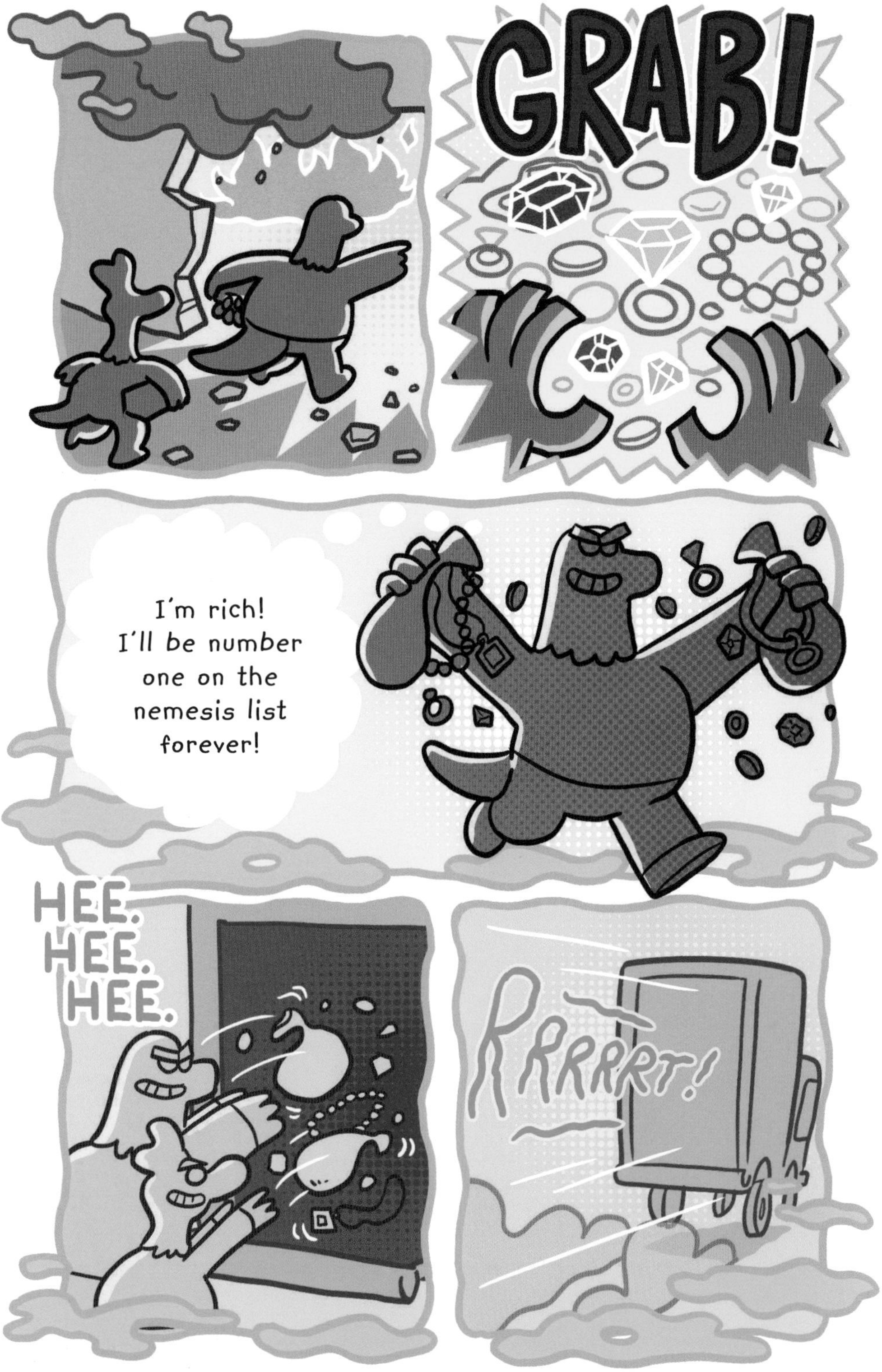
GRAB!
I'm rich! I'll be number one on the nemesis list forever!
HEE. HEE. HEE.
RRRRRT!

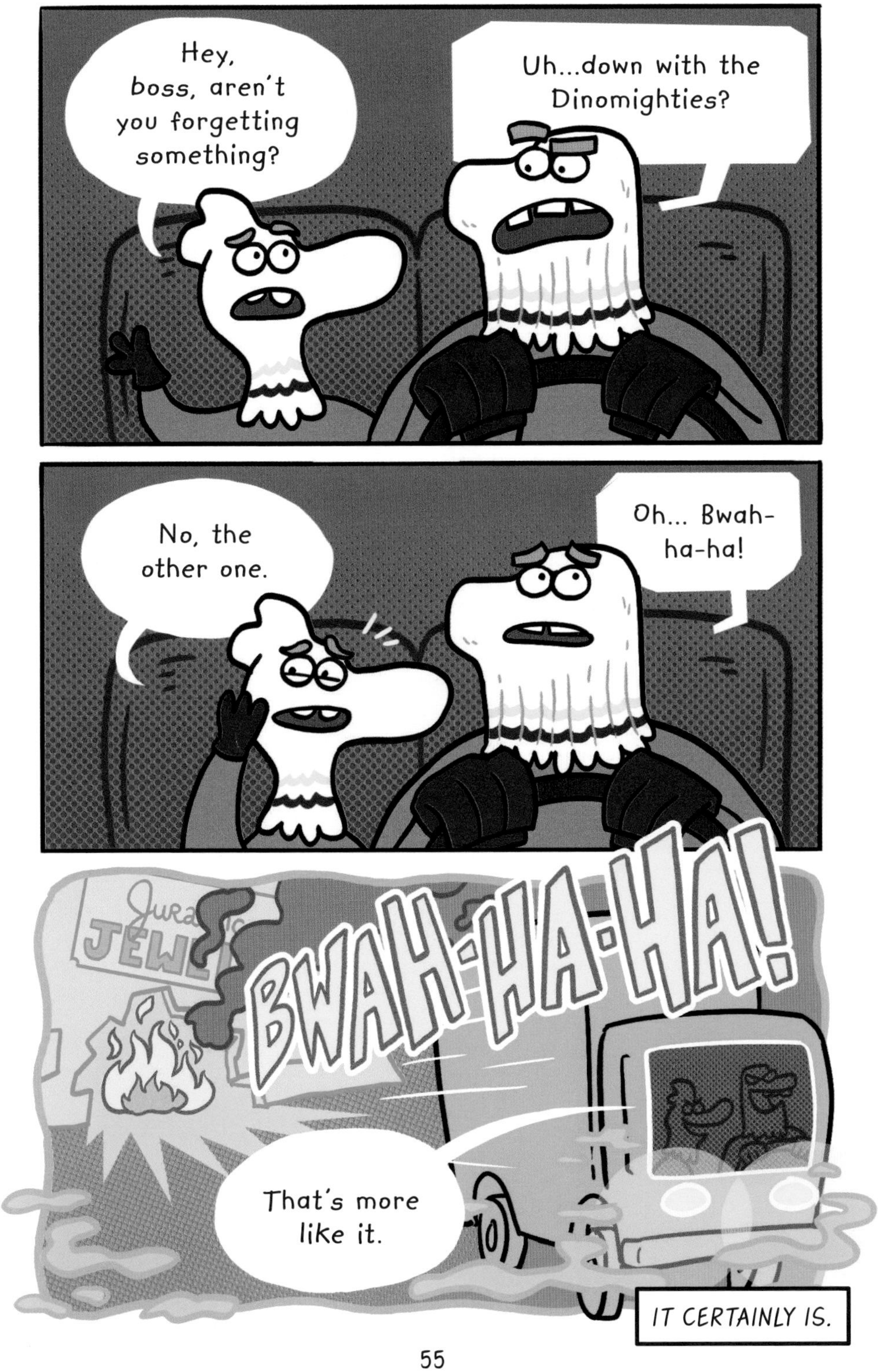
Hey, boss, aren't you forgetting something?
Uh...down with the Dinomighties?
No, the other one.
Oh... Bwah-ha-ha!
JEWEL
BWAH-HA-HA!
That's more like it.
IT CERTAINLY IS.

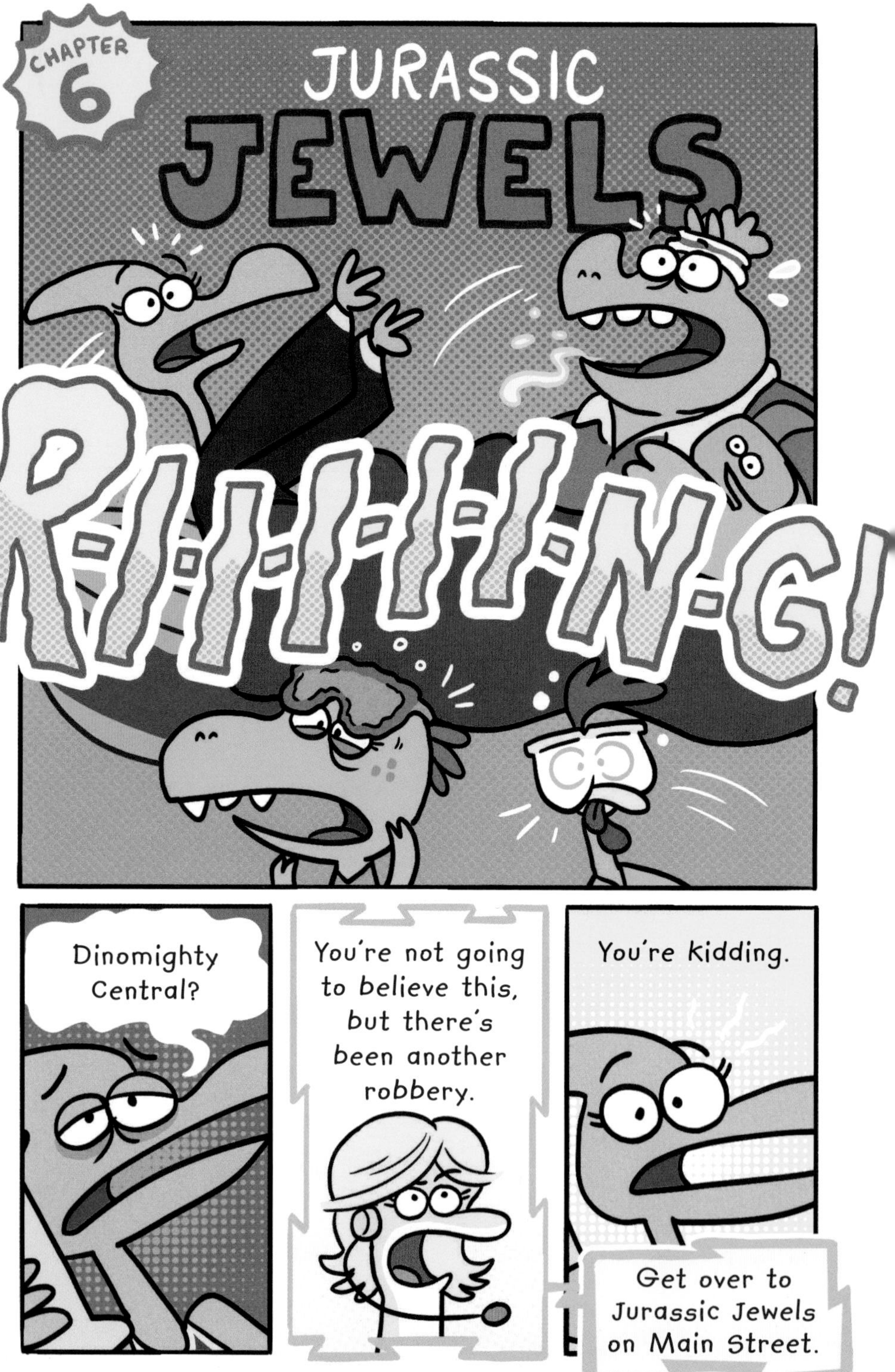
CHAPTER 6
JURASSIC JEWELS
R-I-I-I-I-N-G!
Dinomighty Central?
You're not going to believe this, but there's been another robbery.
You're kidding.
Get over to Jurassic Jewels on Main Street.

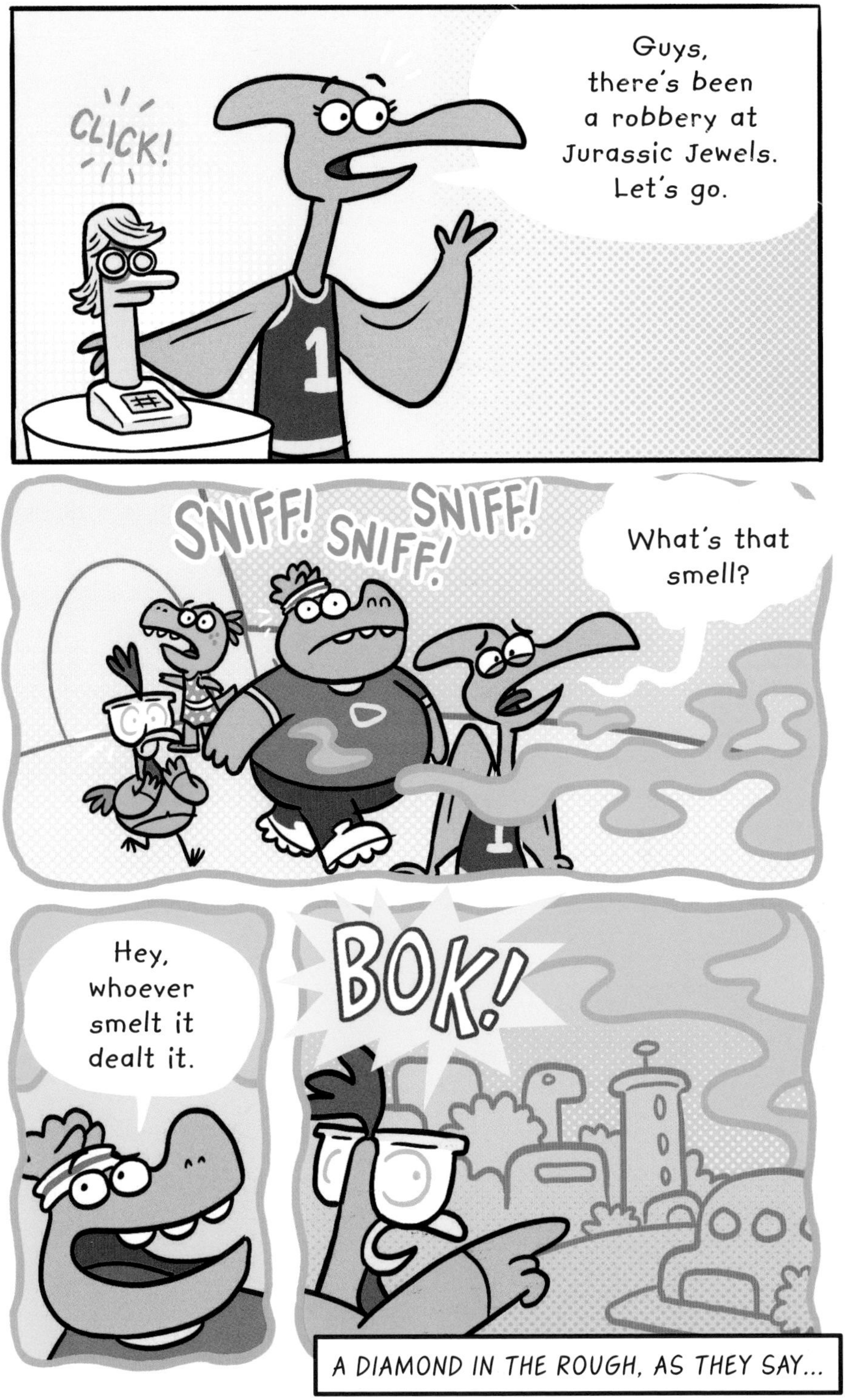
CLICK!
Guys, there's been a robbery at Jurassic Jewels. Let's go.
SNIFF! SNIFF! SNIFF!
What's that smell?
Hey, whoever smelt it dealt it.
BOK!
A DIAMOND IN THE ROUGH, AS THEY SAY...

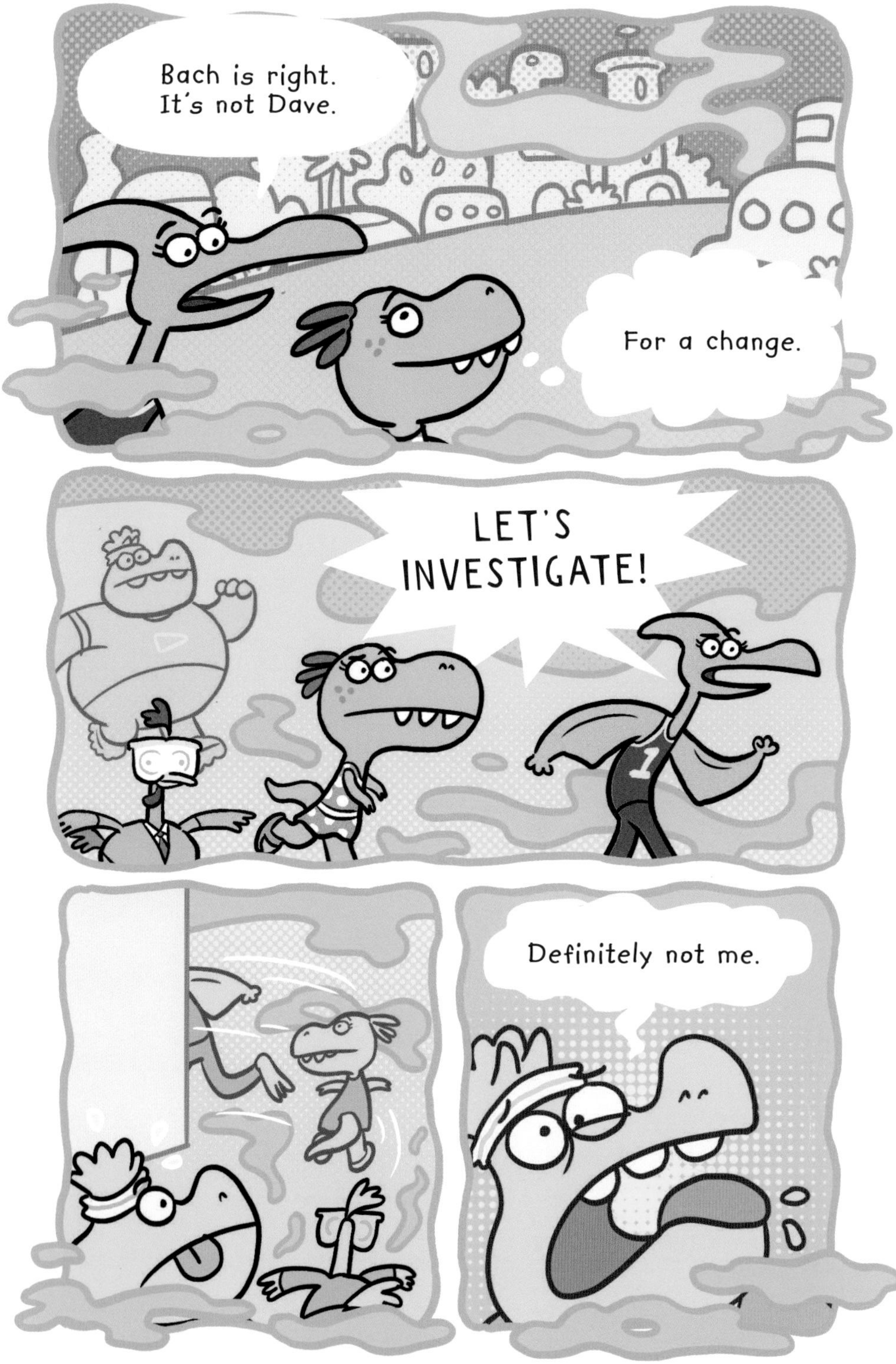

Bach is right.
It's not Dave.
For a change.
LET'S INVESTIGATE!
Definitely not me.

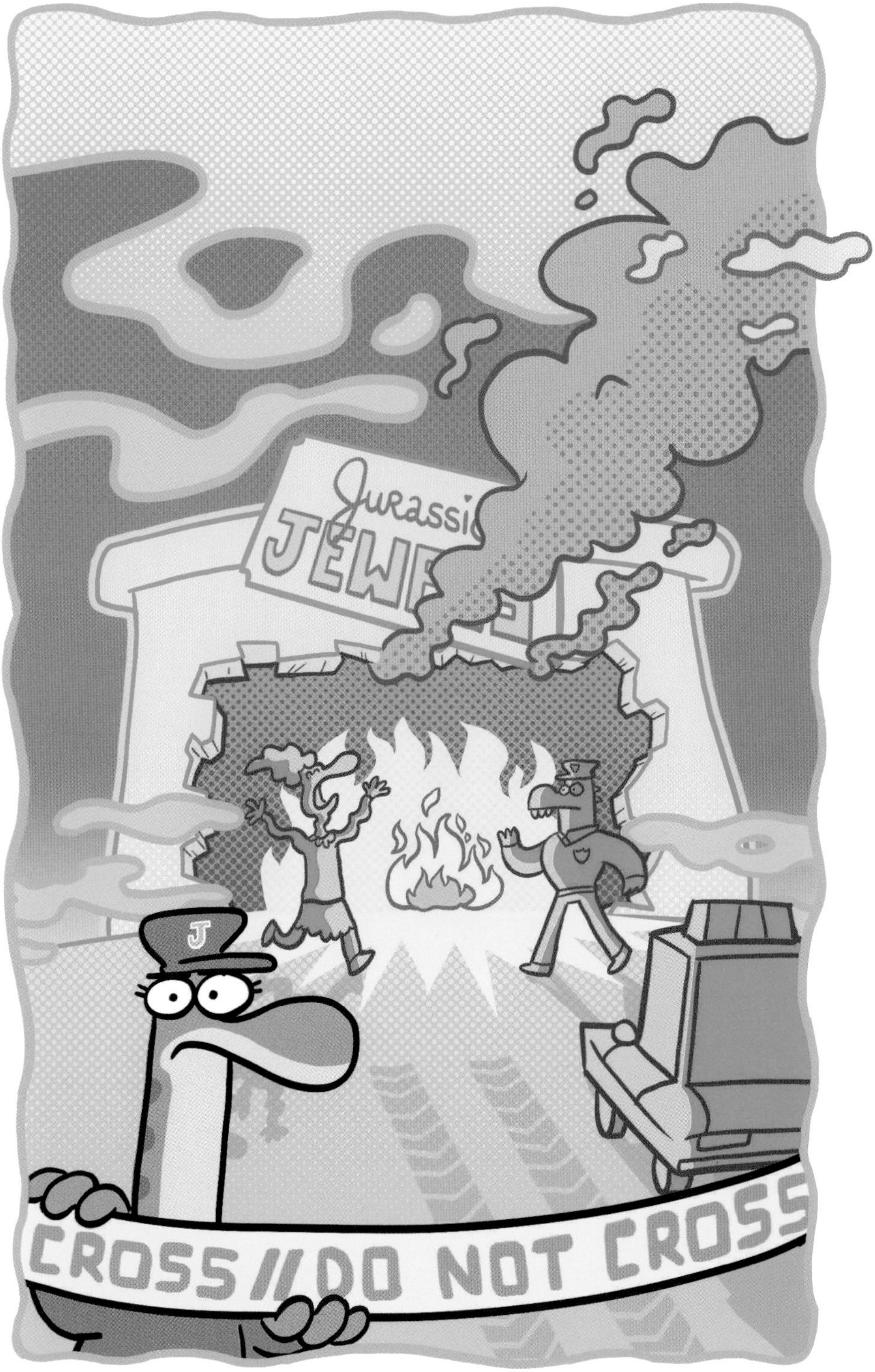
Jurassi
JEW
J
CROSS // DO NOT CROSS

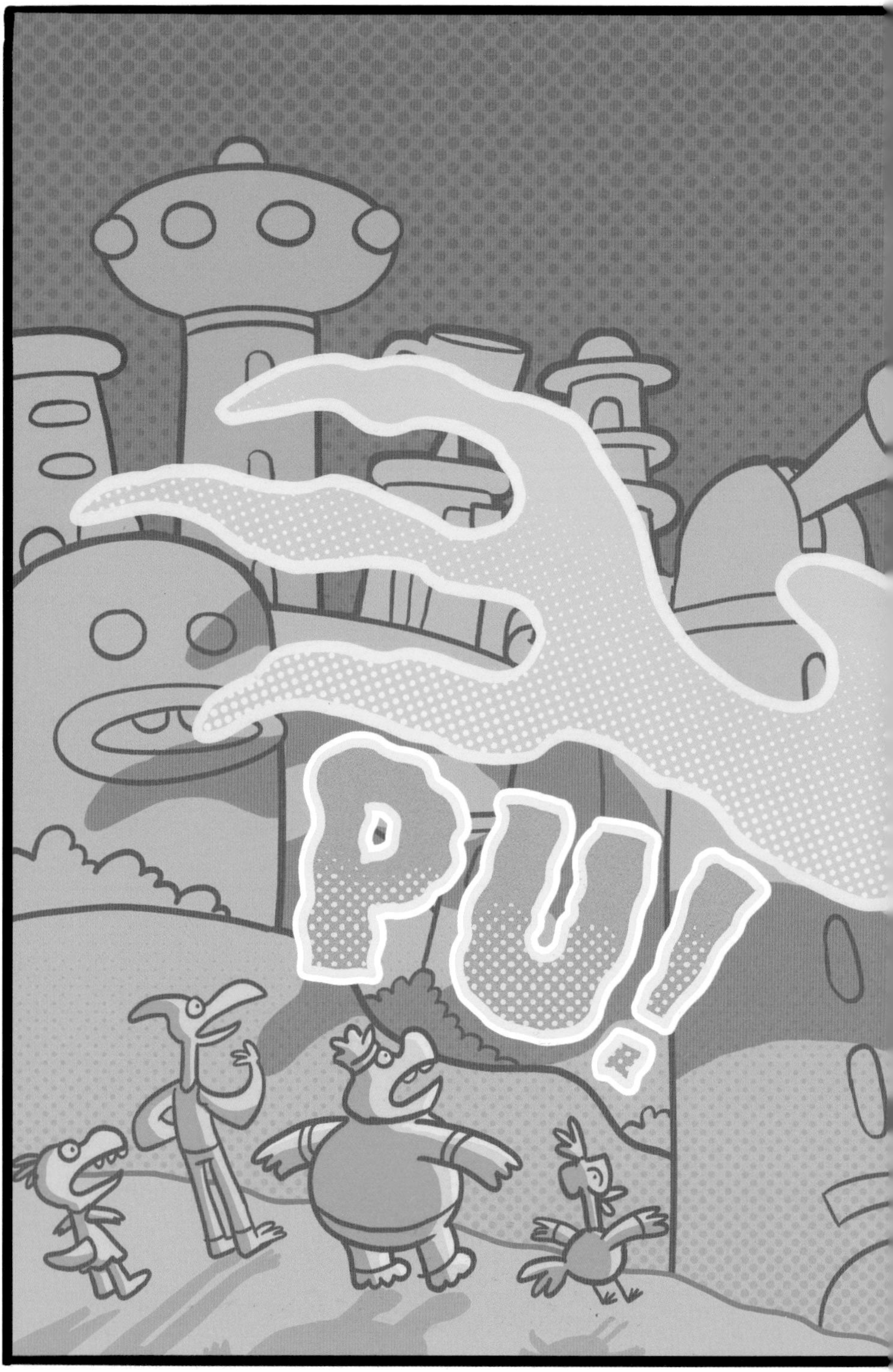
PU!!

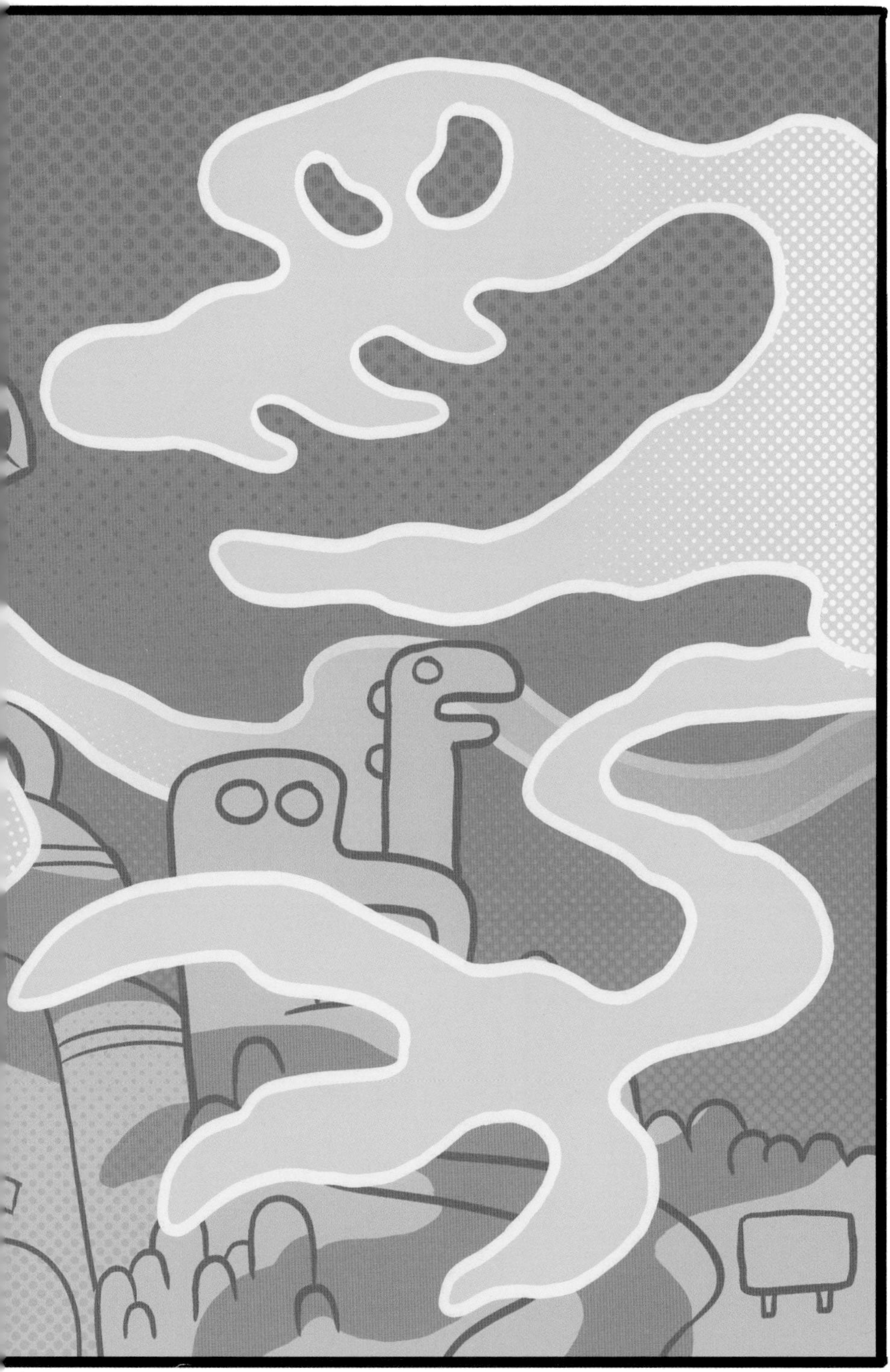

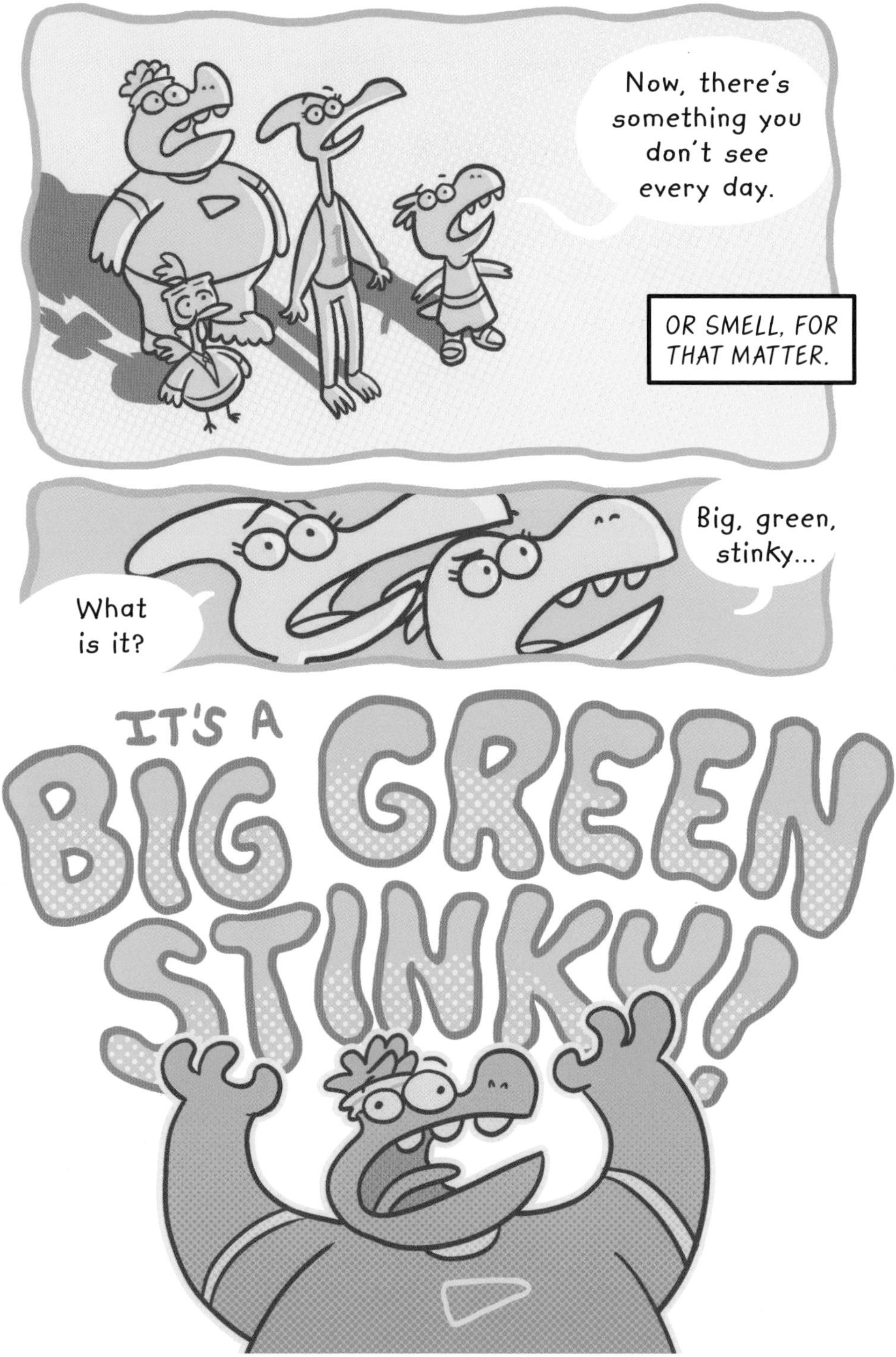
Now, there's something you don't see every day.
OR SMELL, FOR THAT MATTER.
What is it?
Big, green, stinky...
IT'S A BIG GREEN STINKY!

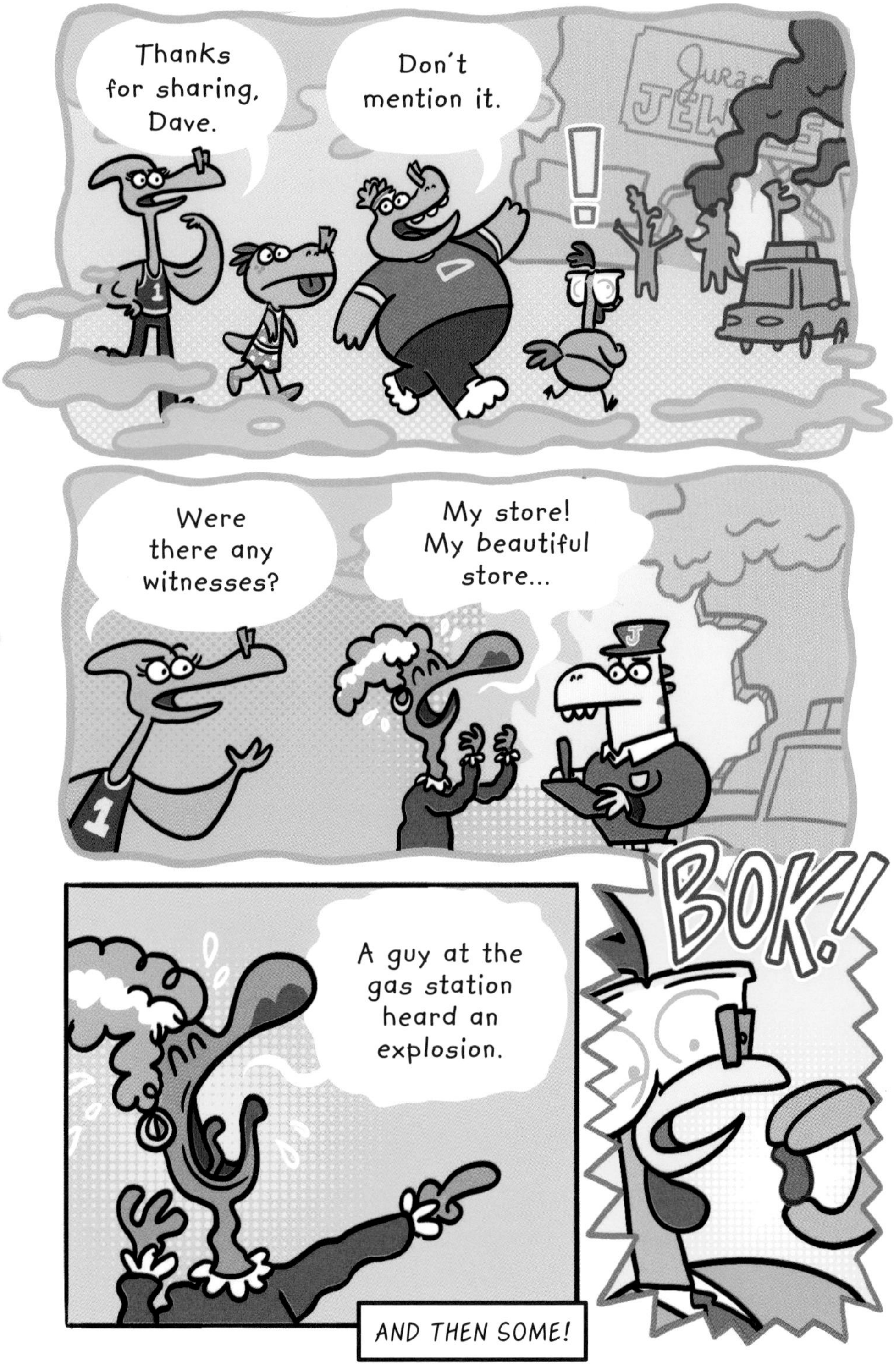

Thanks for sharing, Dave.
Don't mention it.
!
Were there any witnesses?
My store! My beautiful store...
A guy at the gas station heard an explosion.
AND THEN SOME!
BOK!

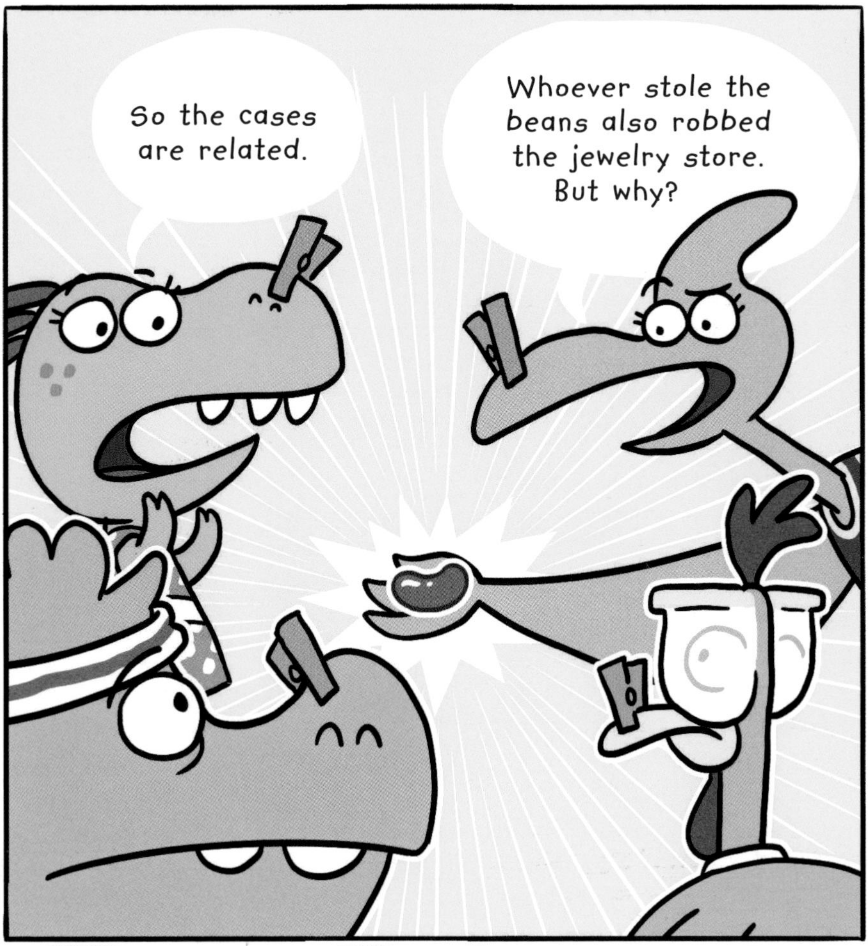
So the cases are related.
Whoever stole the beans also robbed the jewelry store. But why?

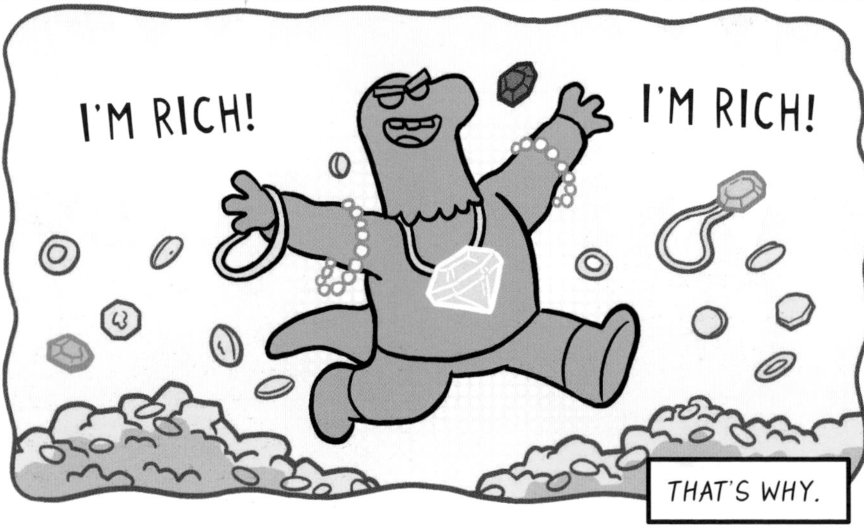
I'M RICH!
I'M RICH!
THAT'S WHY.

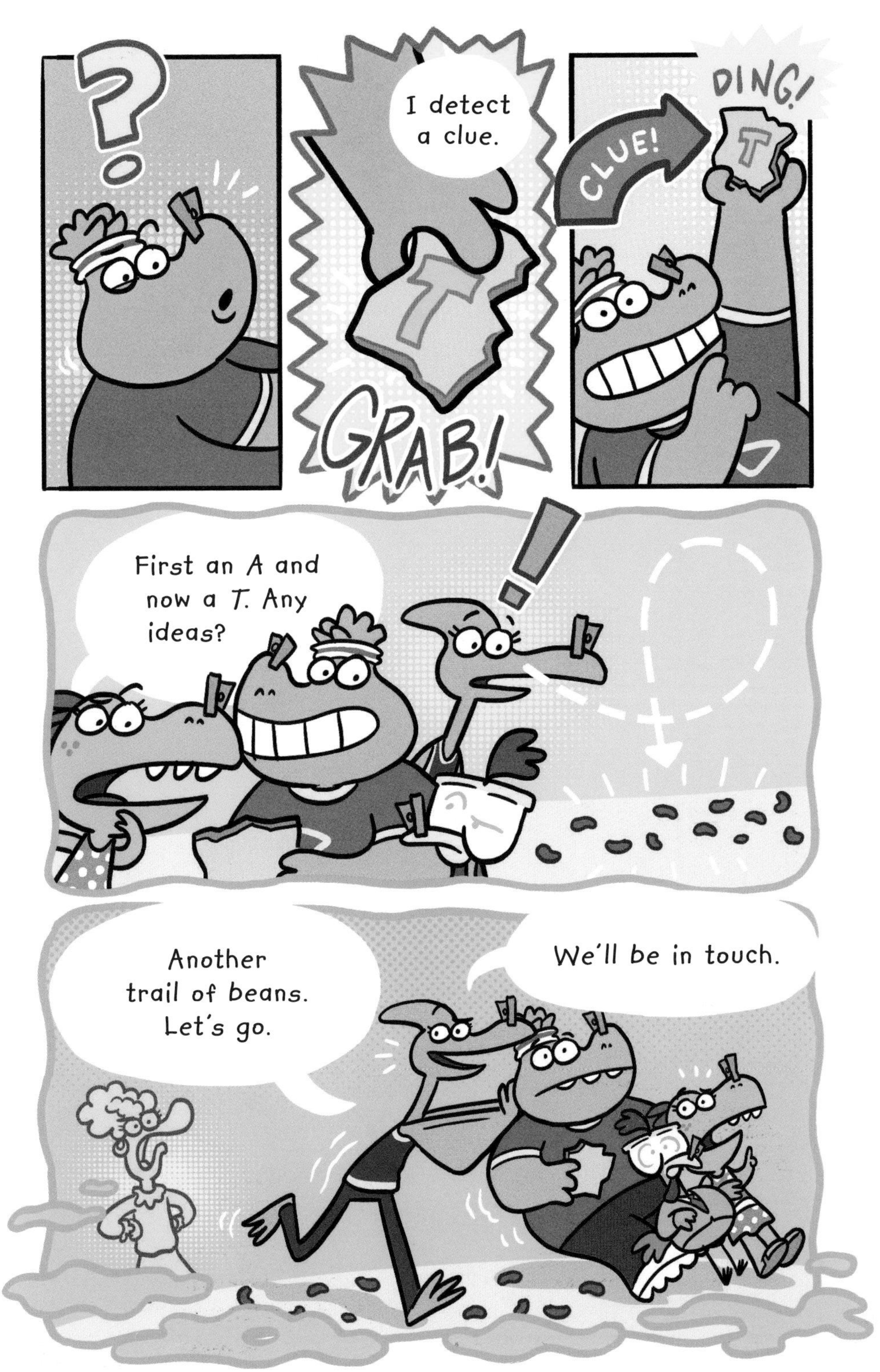
?
I detect a clue.
GRAB!
CLUE!
DING!
T
!
First an A and now a T. Any ideas?
Another trail of beans. Let's go.
We'll be in touch.

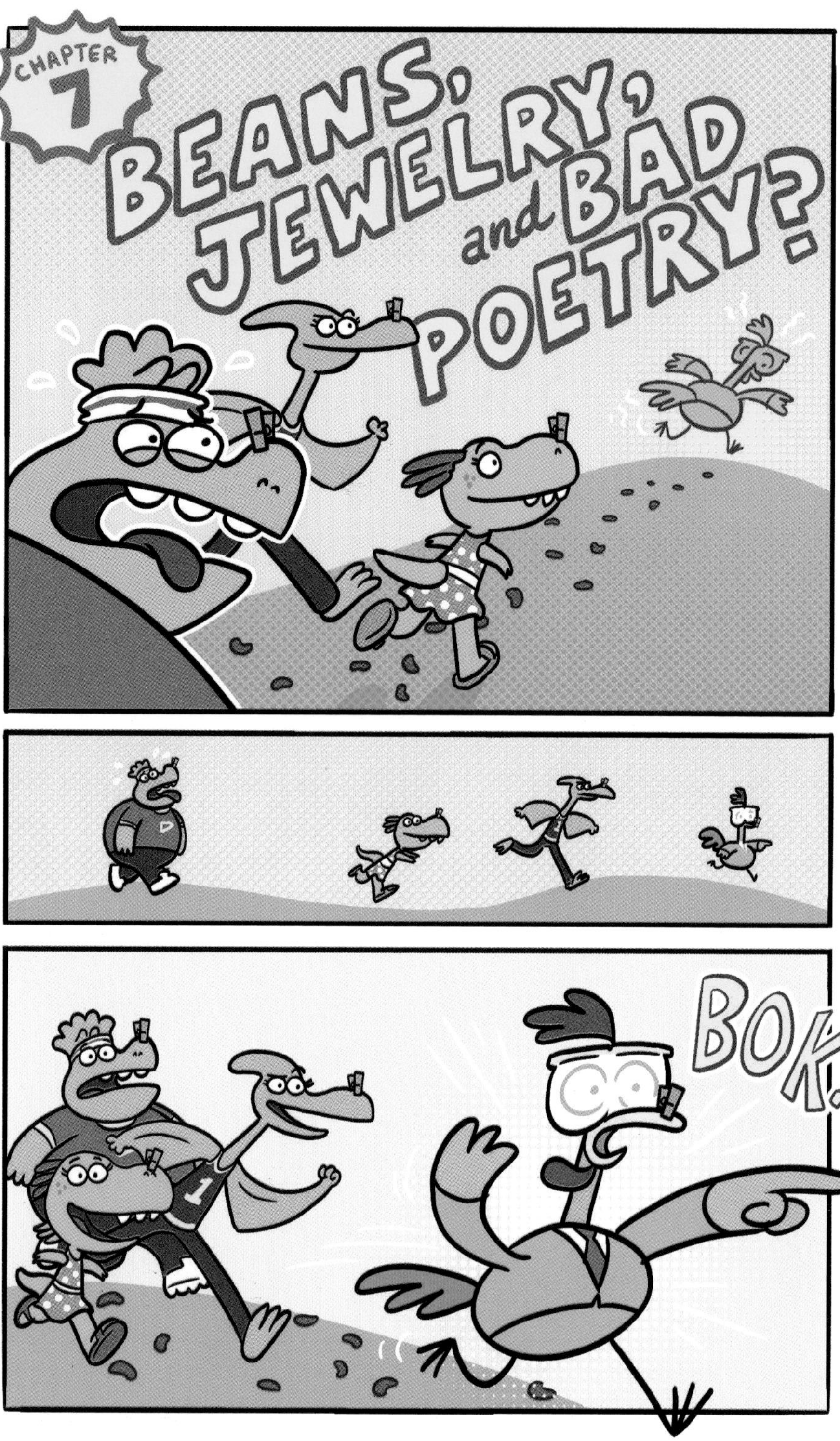
CHAPTER 7
BEANS, JEWELRY, and BAD POETRY?
BOK!

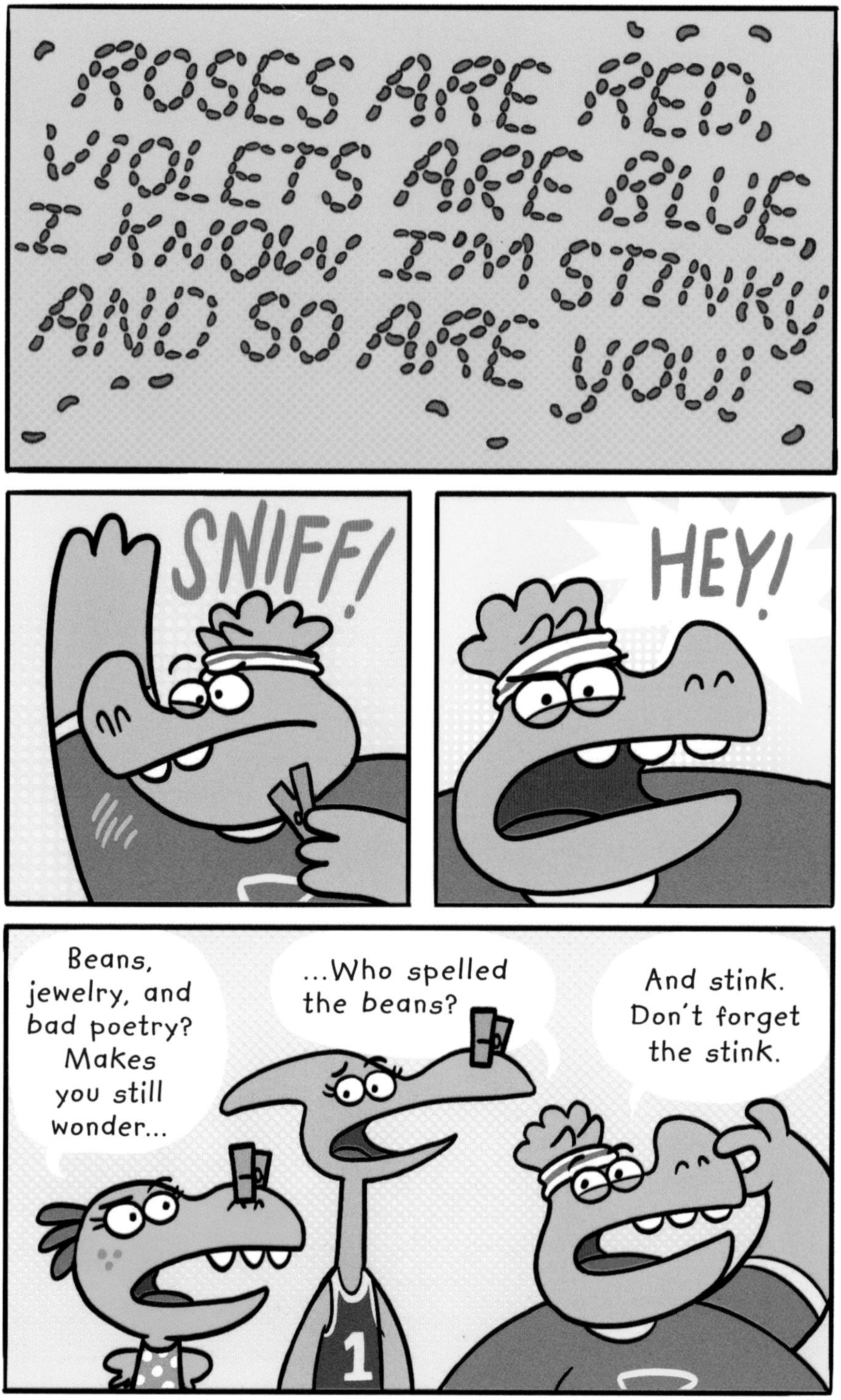

ROSES ARE RED, VIOLETS ARE BLUE, I KNOW I'M STINKY AND SO ARE YOU!
SNIFF!
HEY!
Beans, jewelry, and bad poetry? Makes you still wonder...
...Who spelled the beans?
And stink. Don't forget the stink.
1

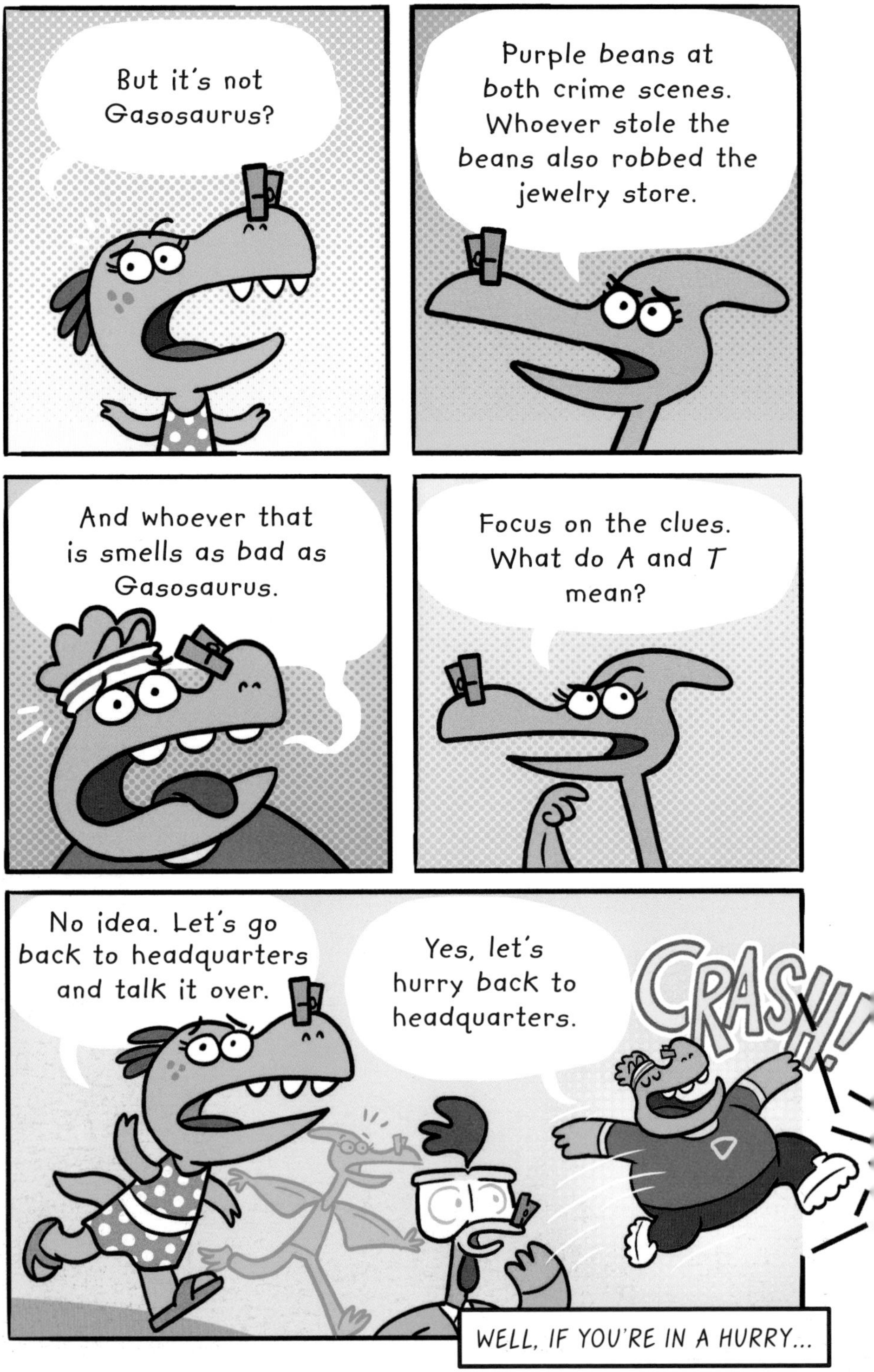
But it's not Gasosaurus?
Purple beans at both crime scenes. Whoever stole the beans also robbed the jewelry store.
And whoever that is smells as bad as Gasosaurus.
Focus on the clues. What do A and T mean?
No idea. Let's go back to headquarters and talk it over.
Yes, let's hurry back to headquarters.
CRASH!!
WELL, IF YOU'RE IN A HURRY...

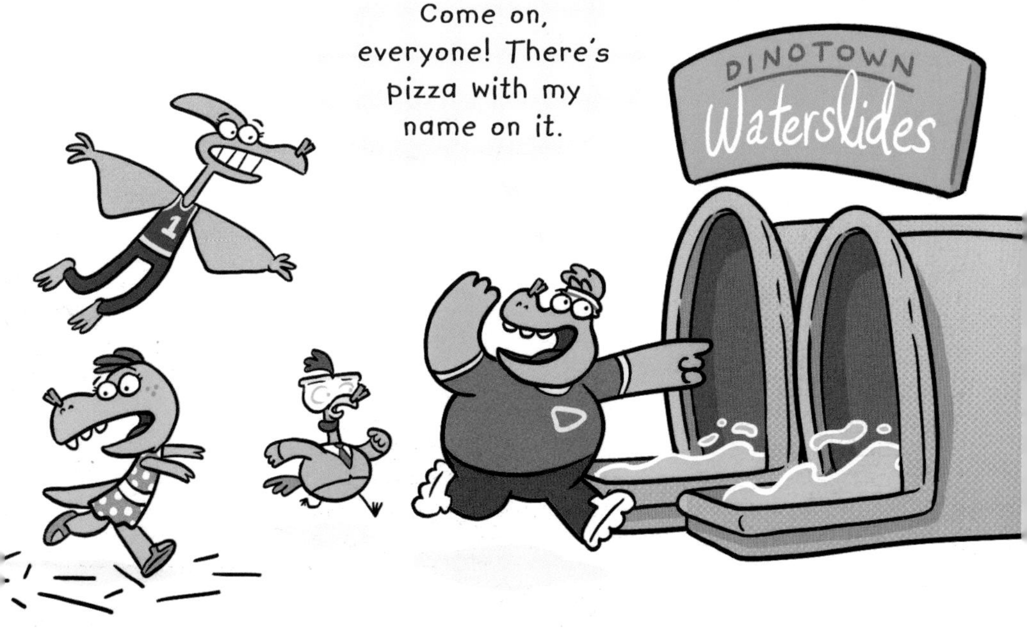
Come on, everyone! There's pizza with my name on it.
DINOTOWN
Waterslides

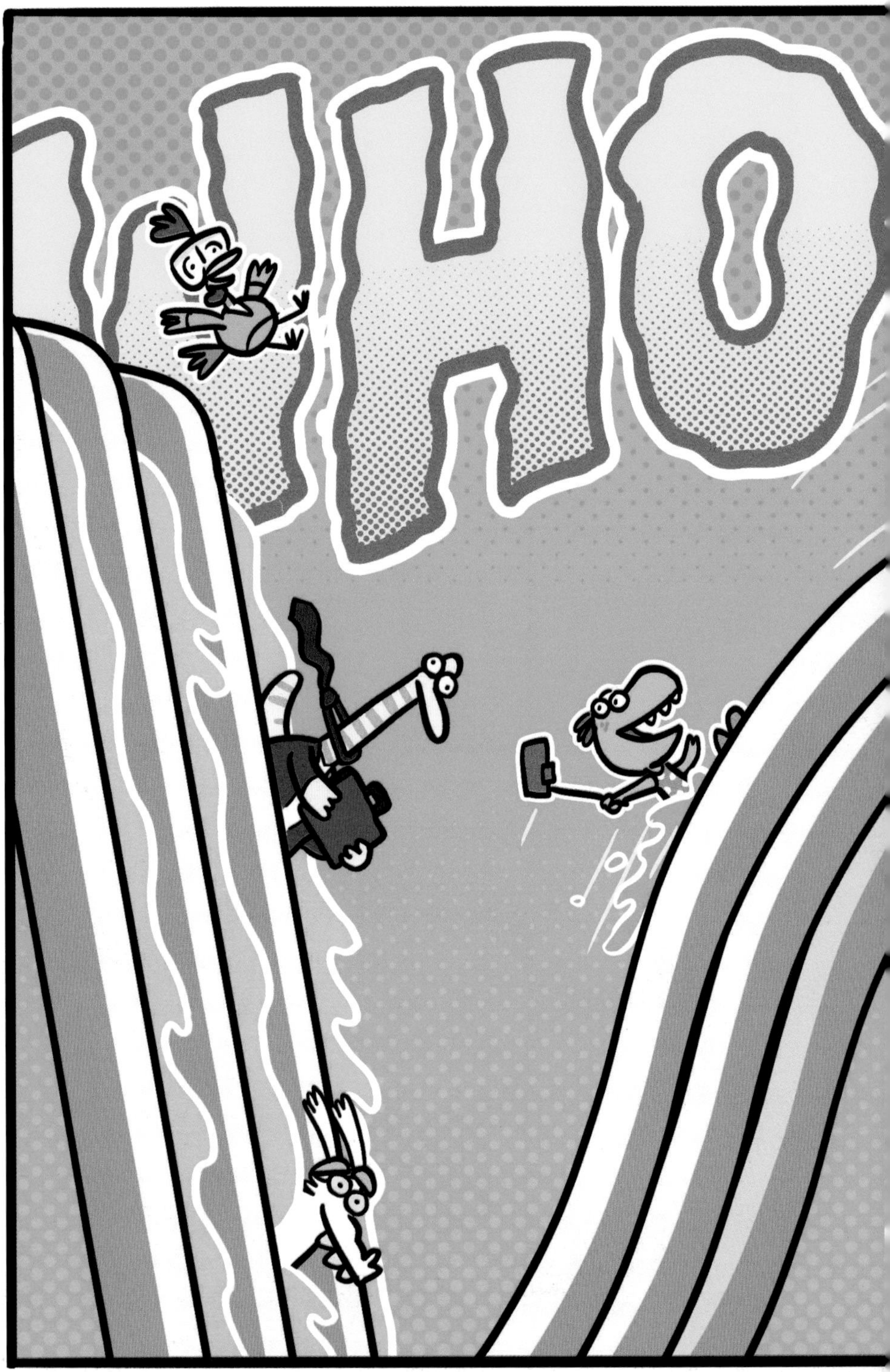

WHO

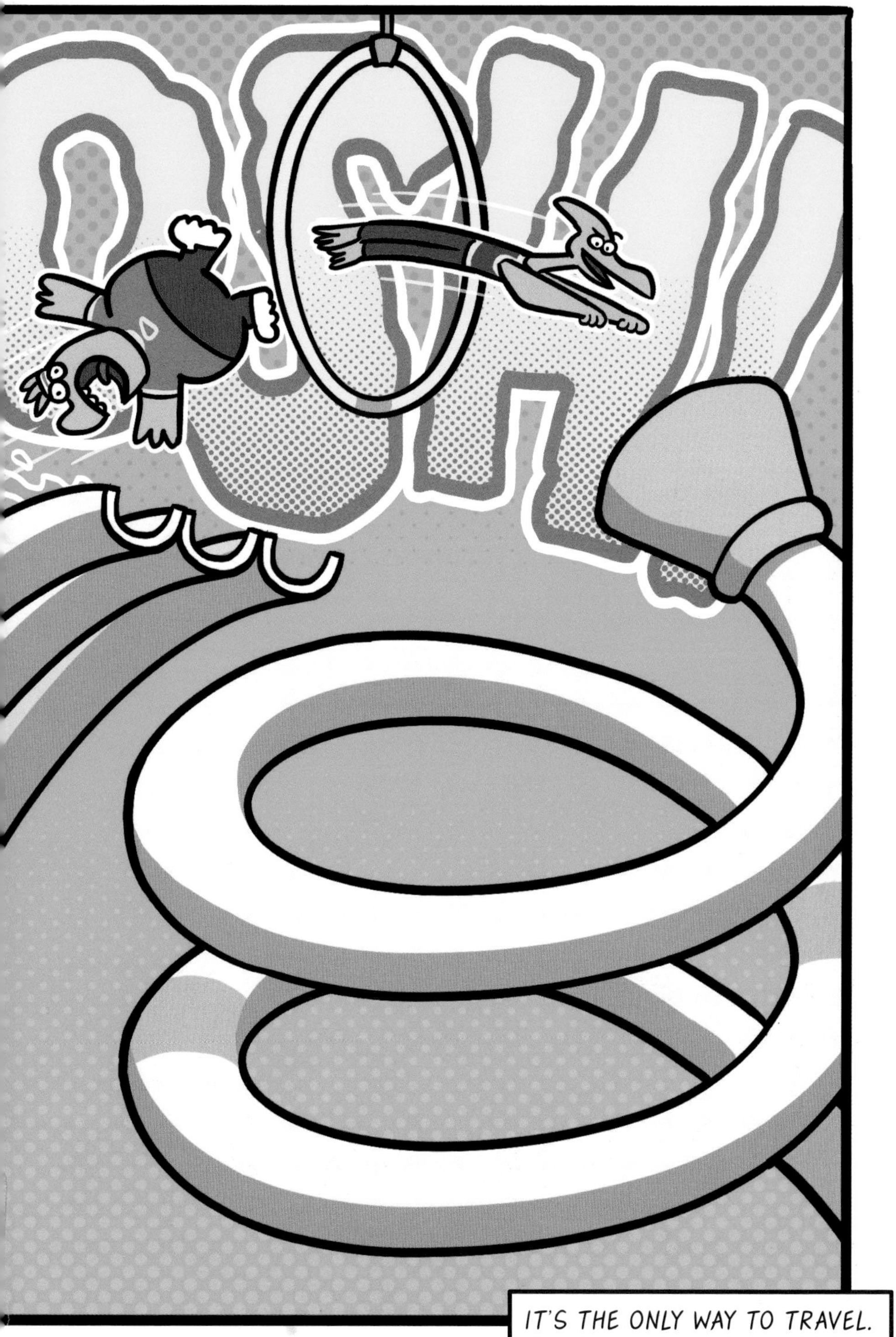
IT'S THE ONLY WAY TO TRAVEL.

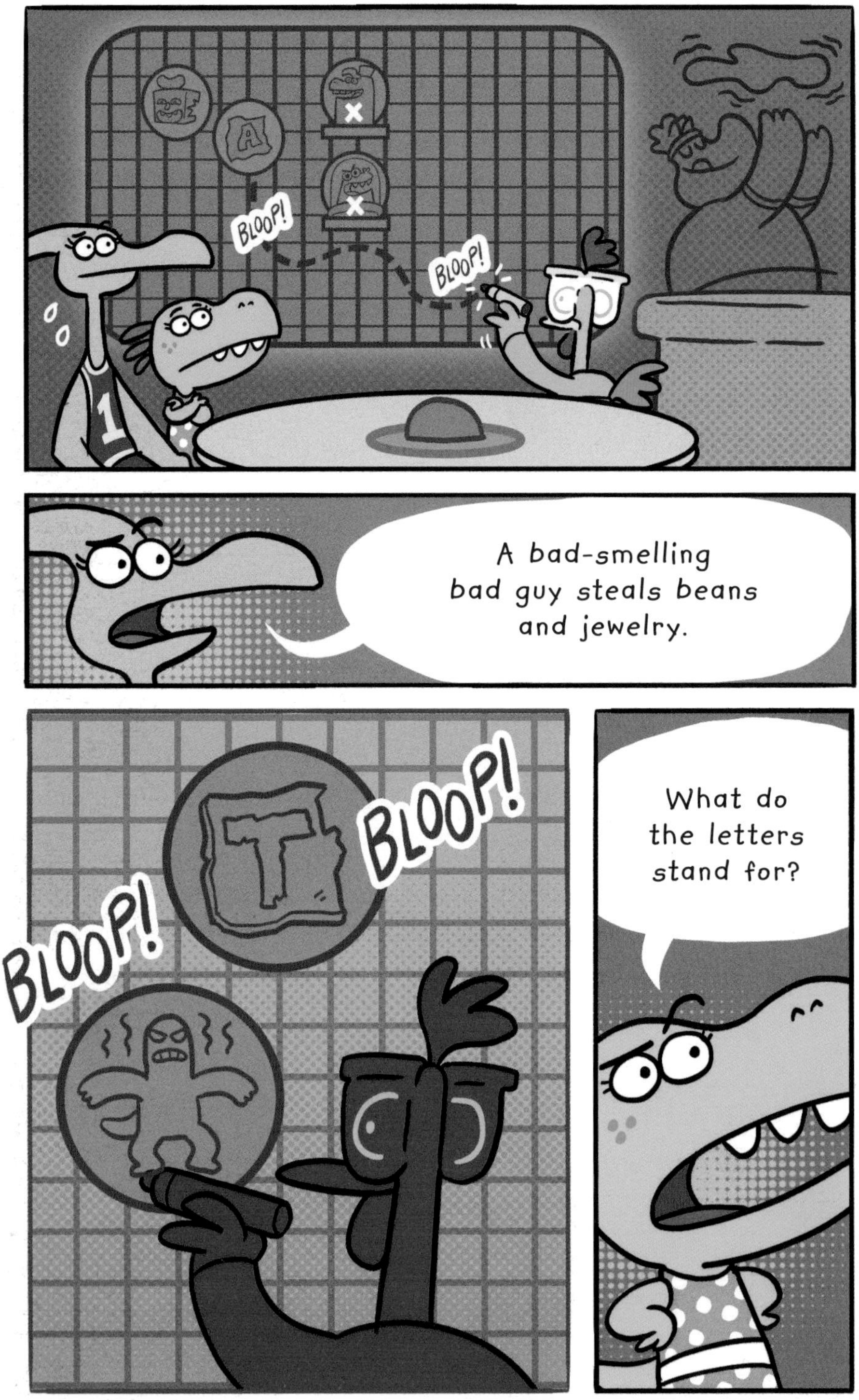
BLOOP!
BLOOP!
A bad-smelling
bad guy steals beans
and jewelry.
BLOOP!
BLOOP!
What do
the letters
stand for?

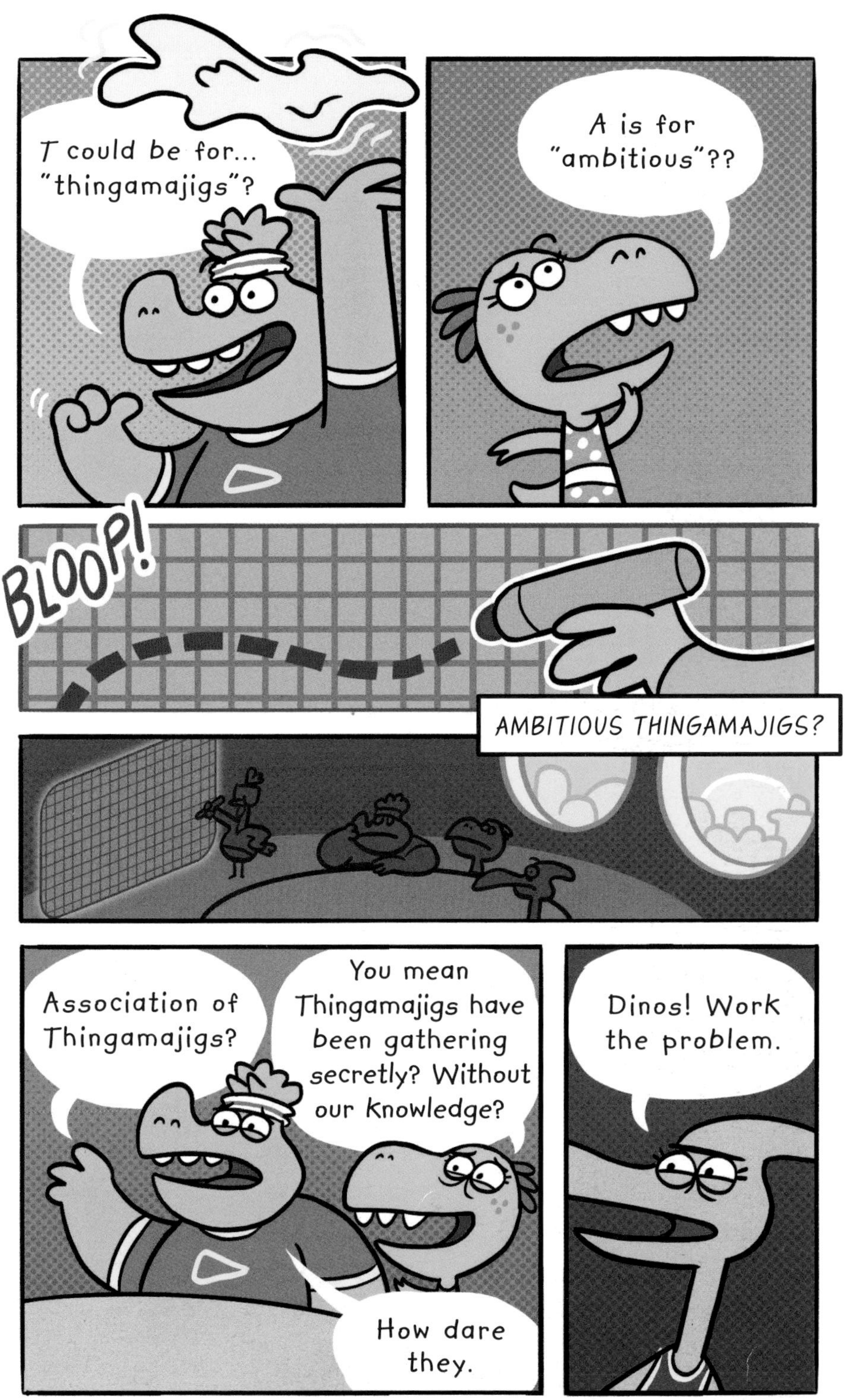
T could be for... "thingamajigs"?
A is for "ambitious"??
BLOOP!
AMBITIOUS THINGAMAJIGS?
Association of Thingamajigs?
You mean Thingamajigs have been gathering secretly? Without our knowledge?
How dare they.
Dinos! Work the problem.

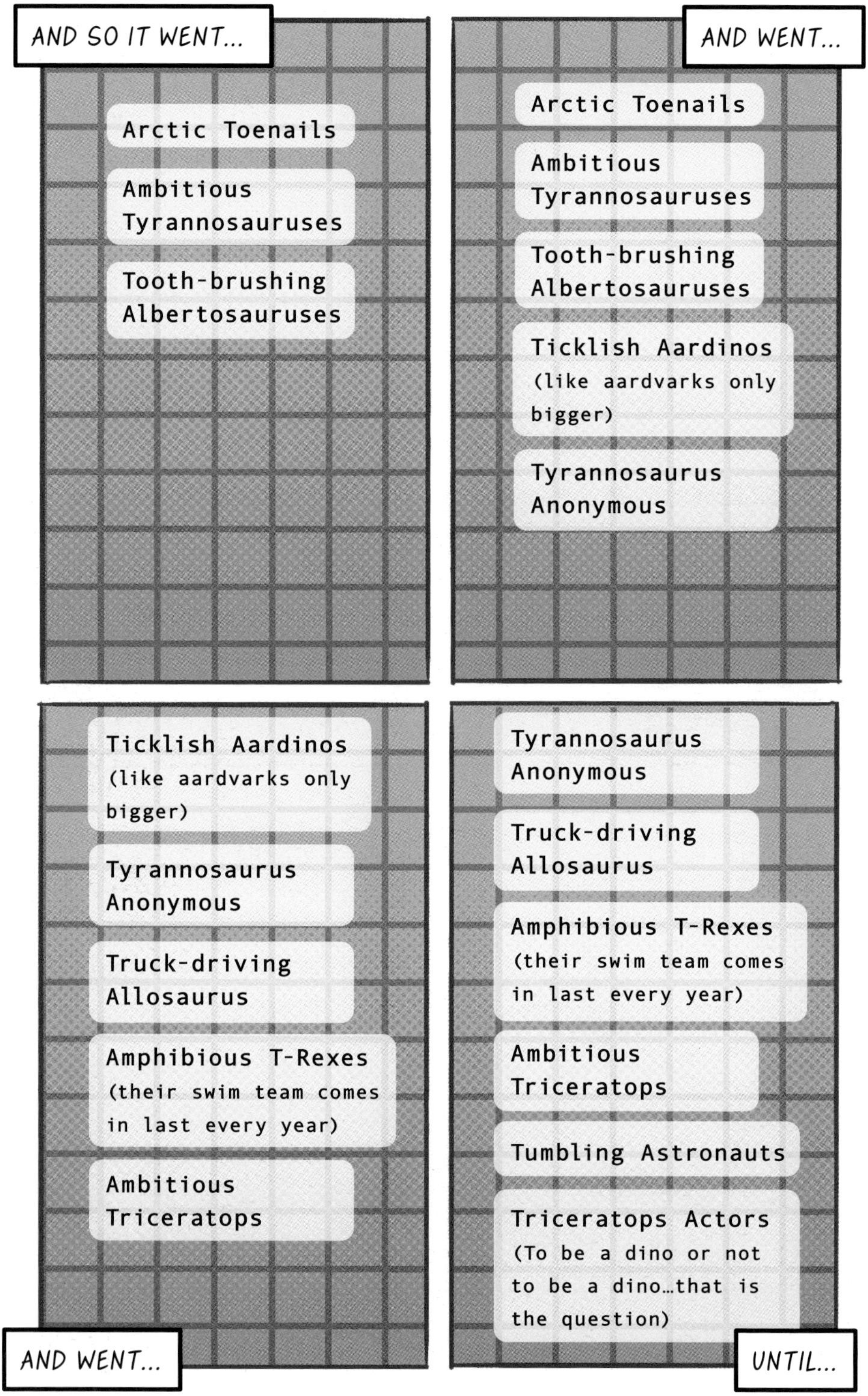
AND SO IT WENT...
Arctic Toenails
Ambitious Tyrannosauruses
Tooth-brushing Albertosauruses
AND WENT...
Arctic Toenails
Ambitious Tyrannosauruses
Tooth-brushing Albertosauruses
Ticklish Aardinos (like aardvarks only bigger)
Tyrannosaurus Anonymous
Ticklish Aardinos (like aardvarks only bigger)
Tyrannosaurus Anonymous
Truck-driving Allosaurus
Amphibious T-Rexes (their swim team comes in last every year)
Ambitious Triceratops
AND WENT...
Tyrannosaurus Anonymous
Truck-driving Allosaurus
Amphibious T-Rexes (their swim team comes in last every year)
Ambitious Triceratops
Tumbling Astronauts
Triceratops Actors (To be a dino or not to be a dino…that is the question)
UNTIL...

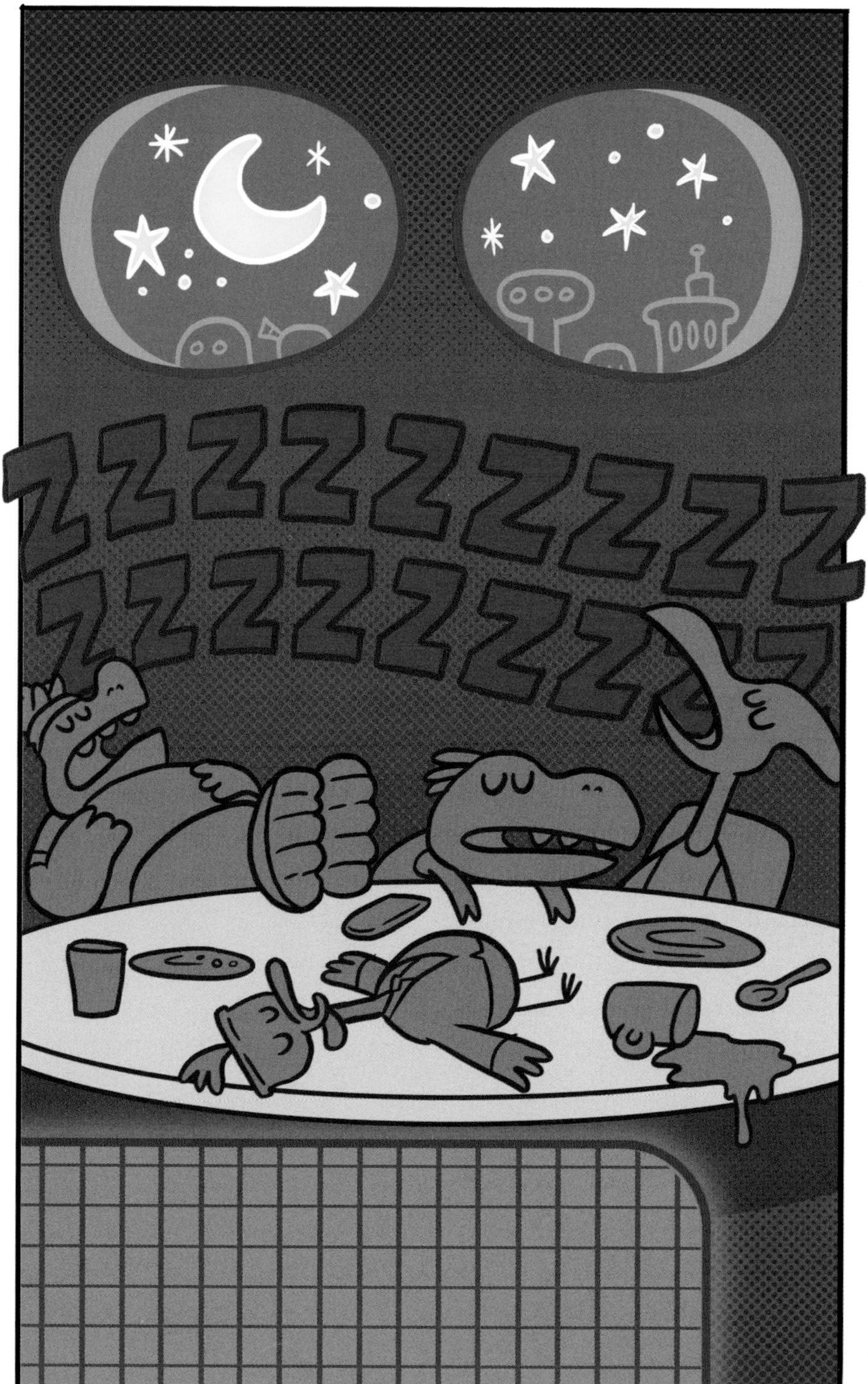
ZZZZZZZZZ
ZZZZZZZZZ

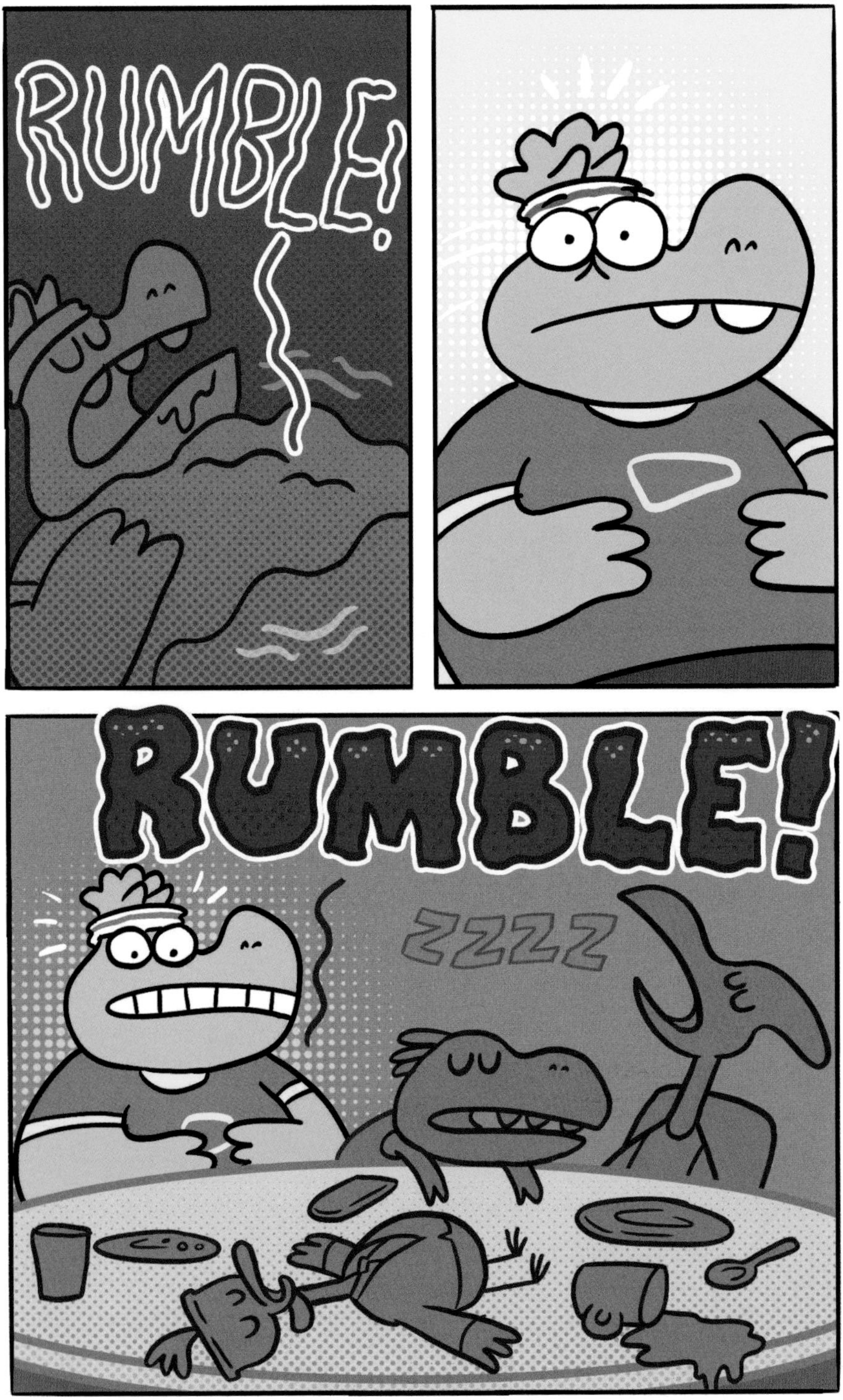
RUMBLE!
RUMBLE!
ZZZZ

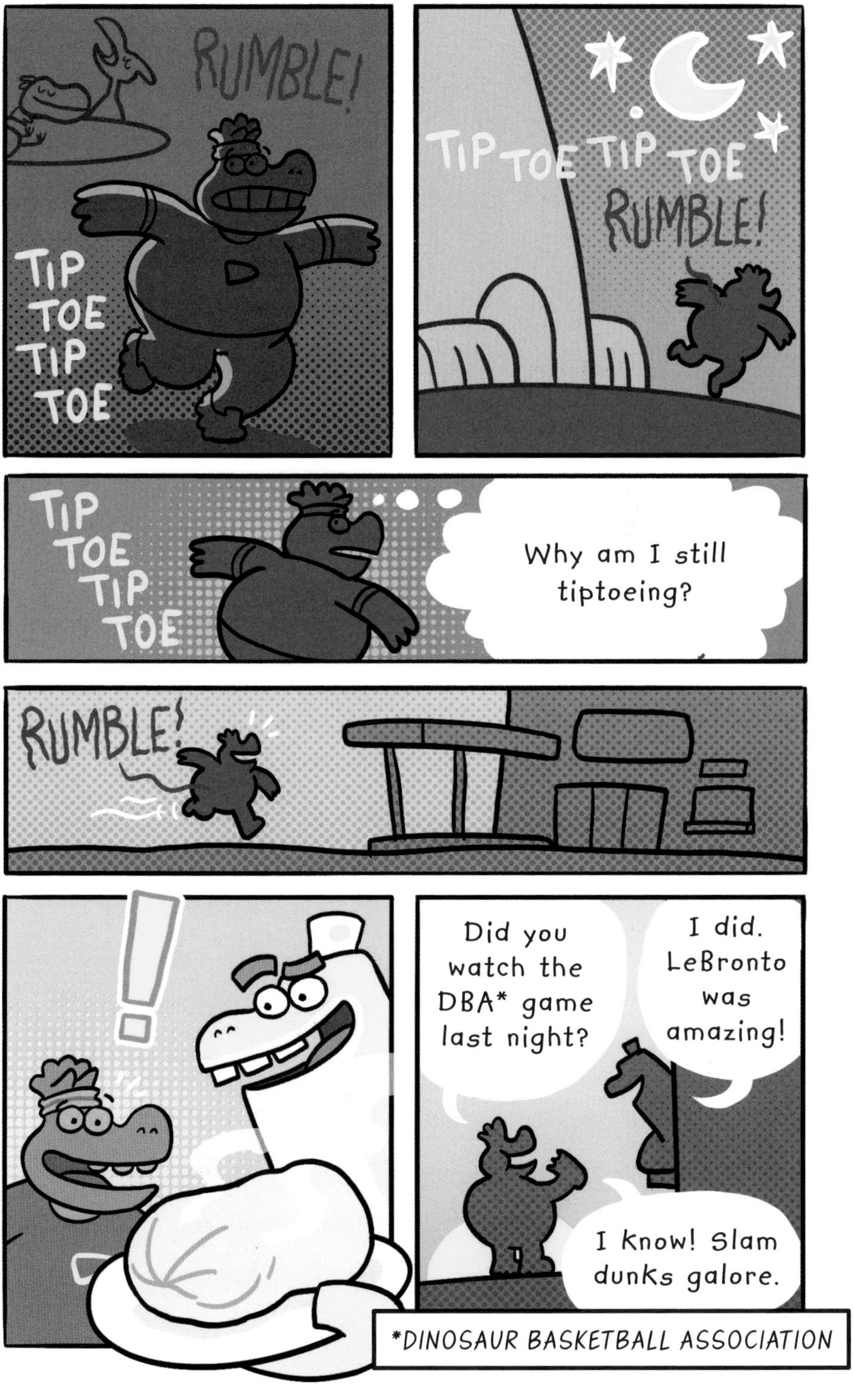

RUMBLE!
TIP TOE TIP TOE
TIP TOE TIP TOE
RUMBLE!
TIP TOE TIP TOE
Why am I still tiptoeing?
RUMBLE!
!
Did you watch the DBA* game last night?
I did. LeBronto was amazing!
I know! Slam dunks galore.
*DINOSAUR BASKETBALL ASSOCIATION

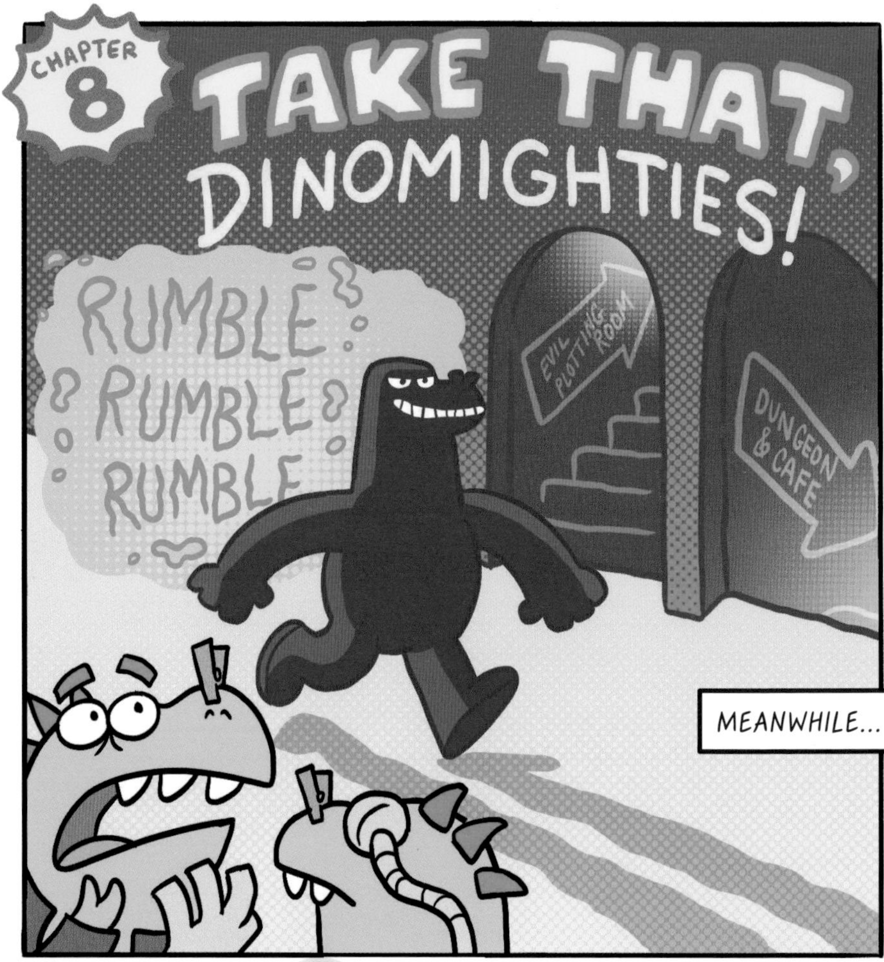
CHAPTER 8
TAKE THAT, DINOMIGHTIES!
RUMBLE RUMBLE RUMBLE
EVIL PLOTTING ROOM
DUNGEON & CAFE
MEANWHILE...

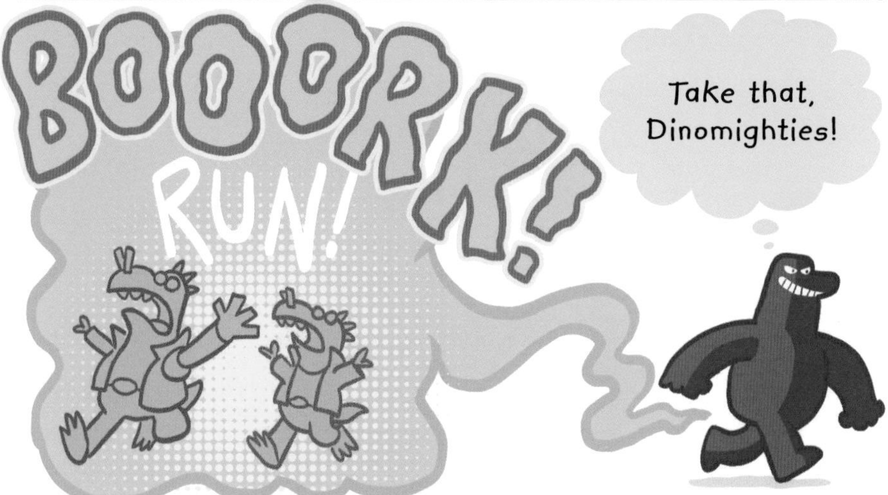
BOOORK!
RUN!
Take that, Dinomighties!

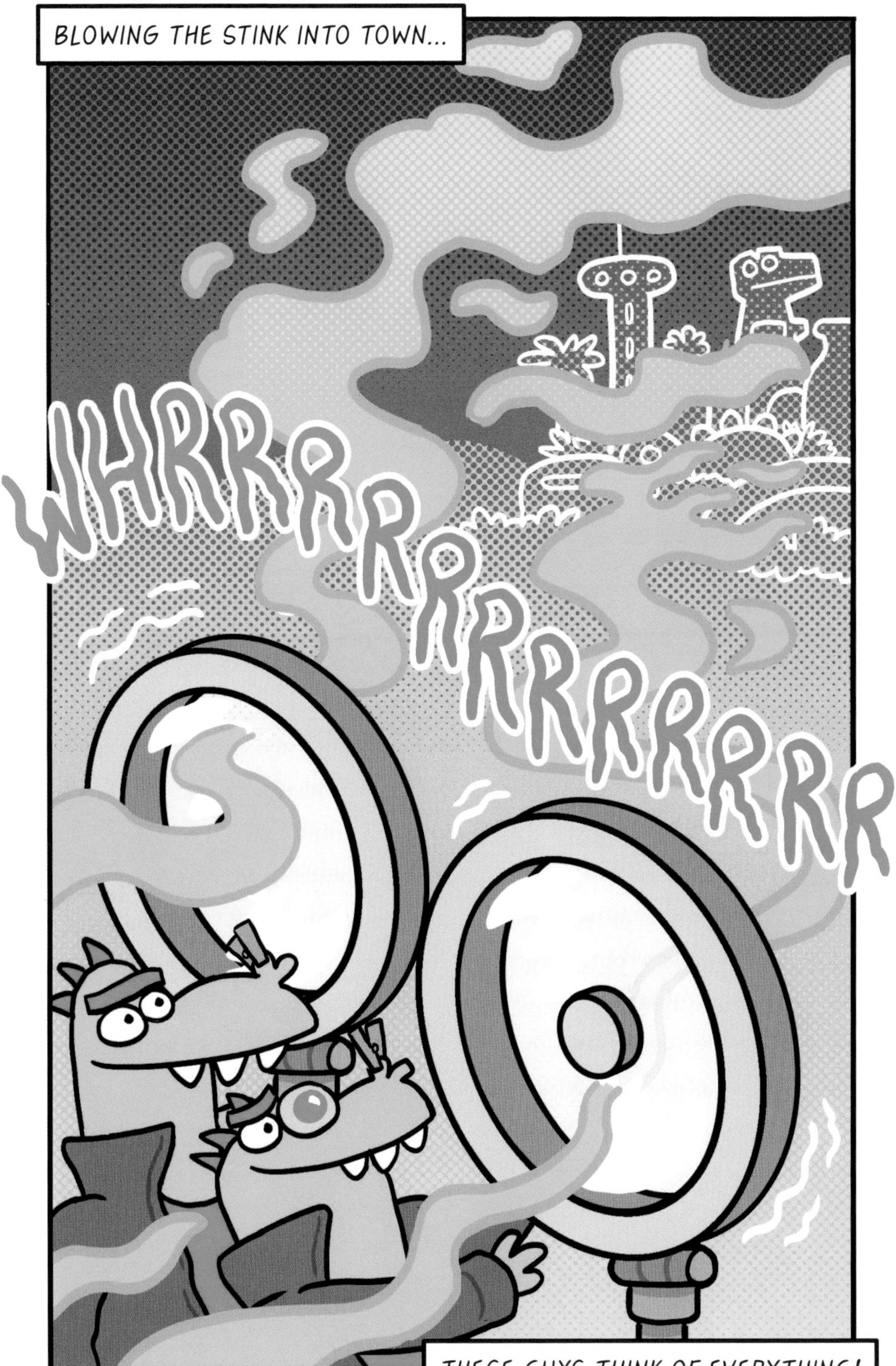
BLOWING THE STINK INTO TOWN...
WHRRRRRRRRRRRRRRR
THESE GUYS THINK OF EVERYTHING!

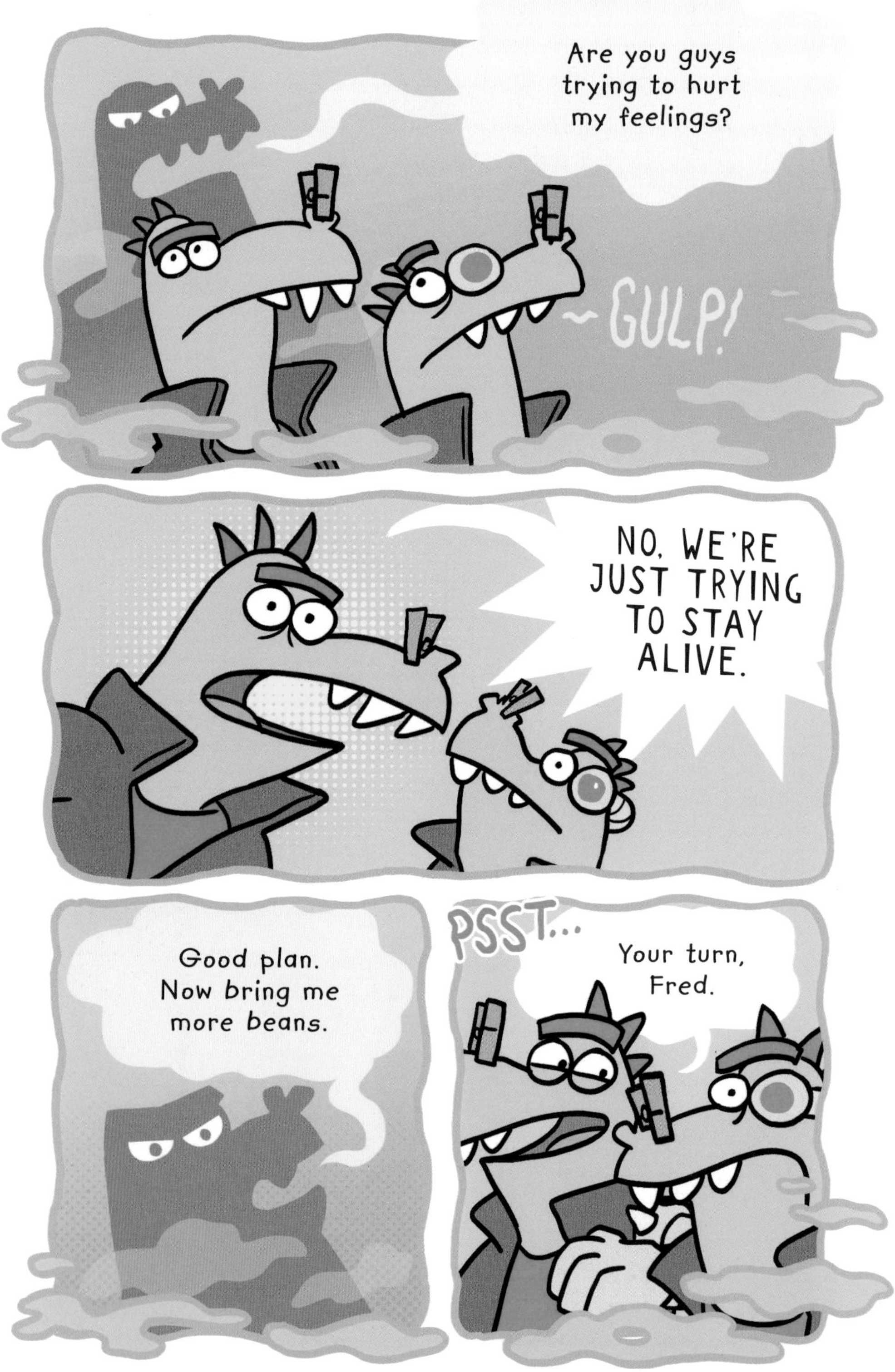
Are you guys trying to hurt my feelings?
GULP!
NO, WE'RE JUST TRYING TO STAY ALIVE.
Good plan. Now bring me more beans.
PSST...
Your turn, Fred.

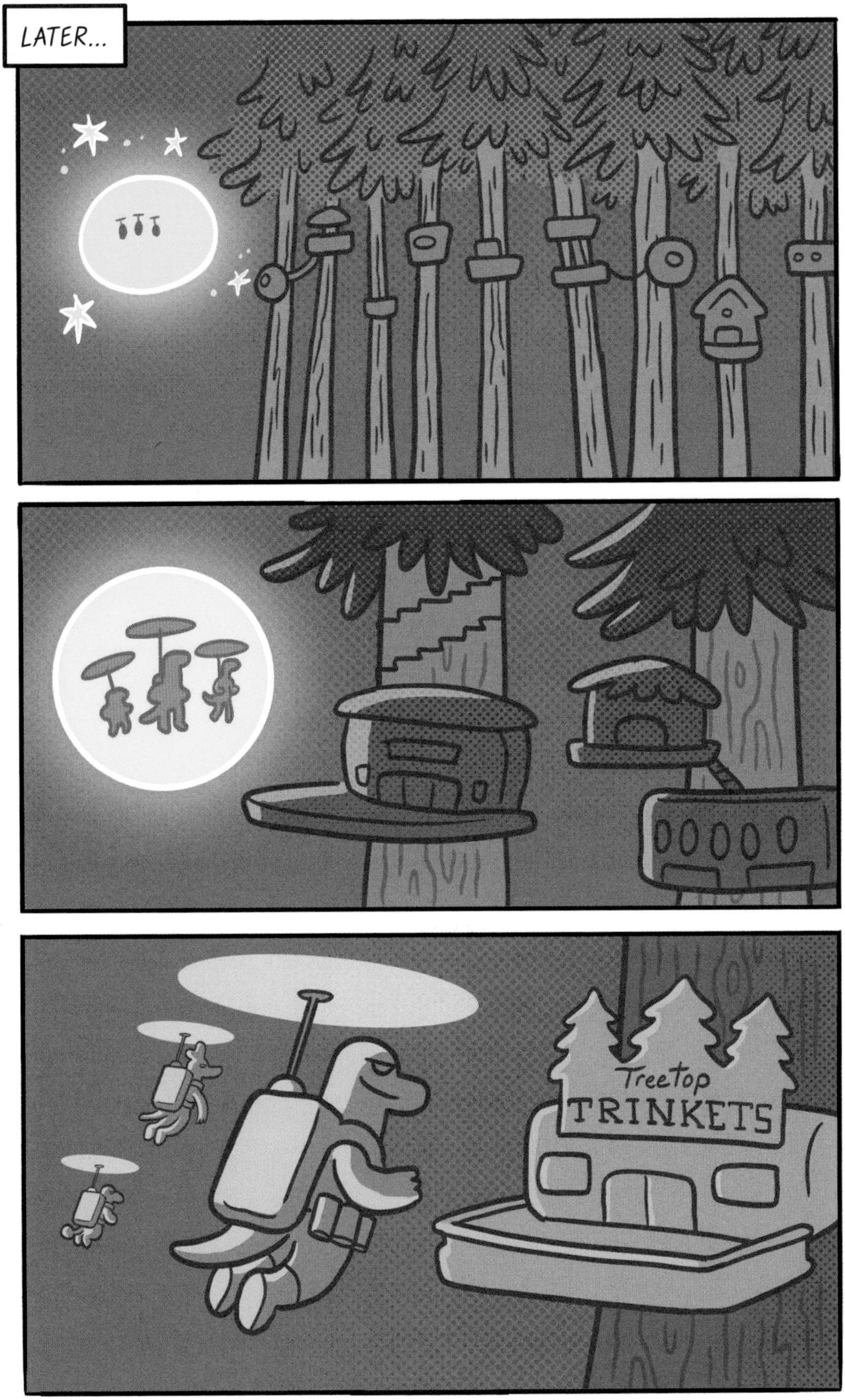
LATER...
Treetop
TRINKETS

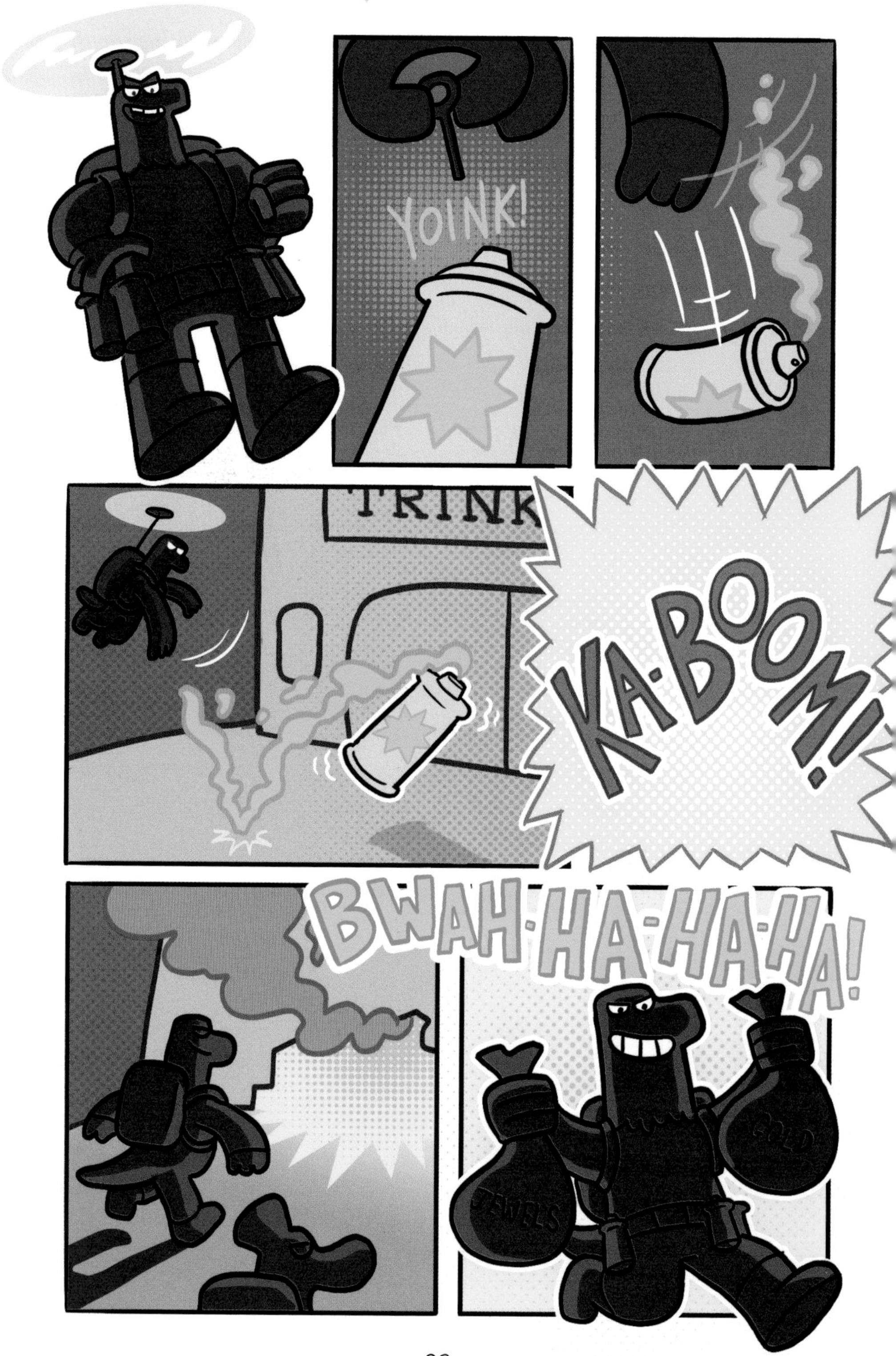
YOINK!
TRINK
KA-BOOM!!
BWAH-HA-HA-HA!
GOLD
JEWELS

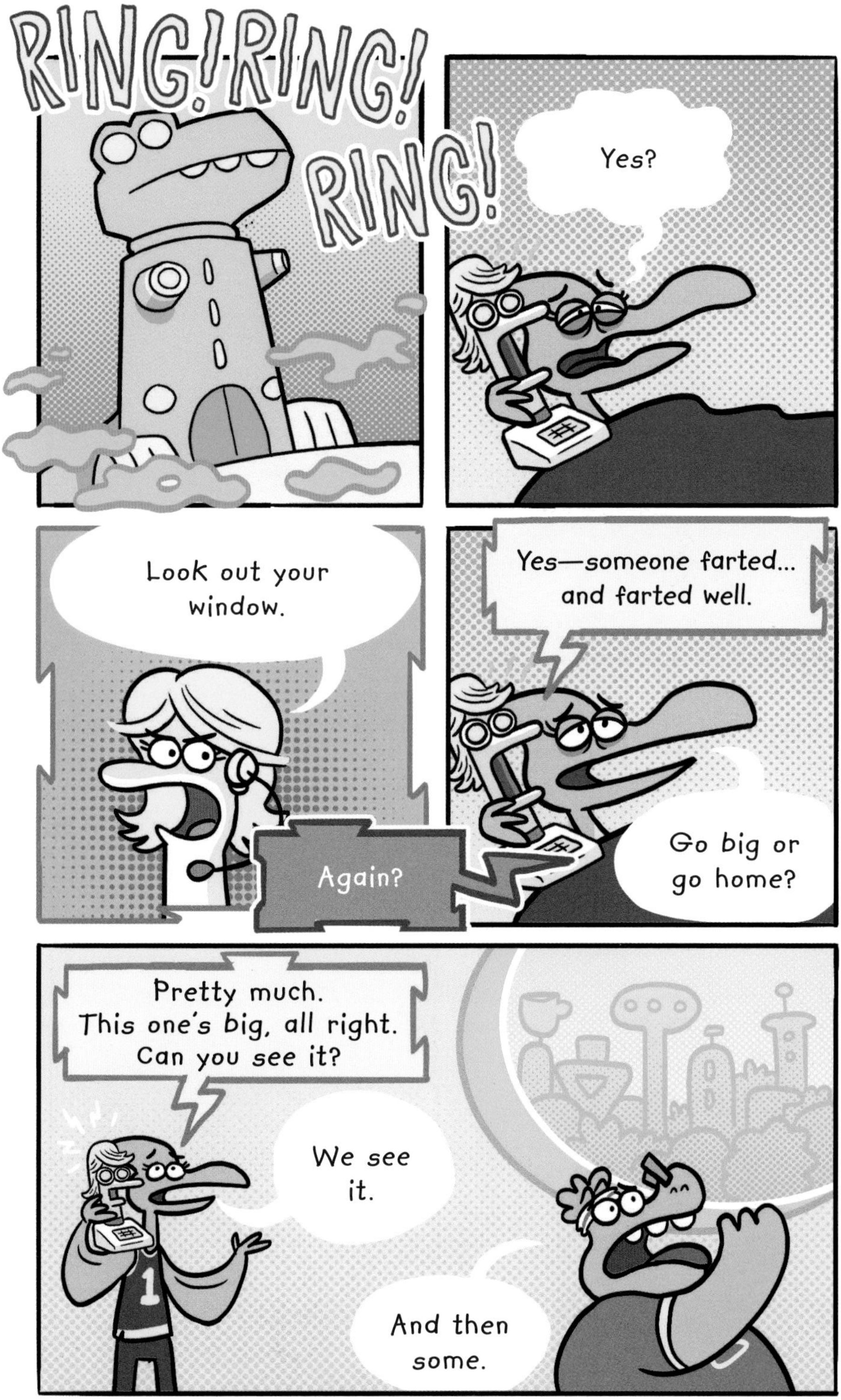
RING! RING! RING!
Yes?
Look out your window.
Yes—someone farted... and farted well.
Again?
Go big or go home?
Pretty much. This one's big, all right. Can you see it?
We see it.
And then some.

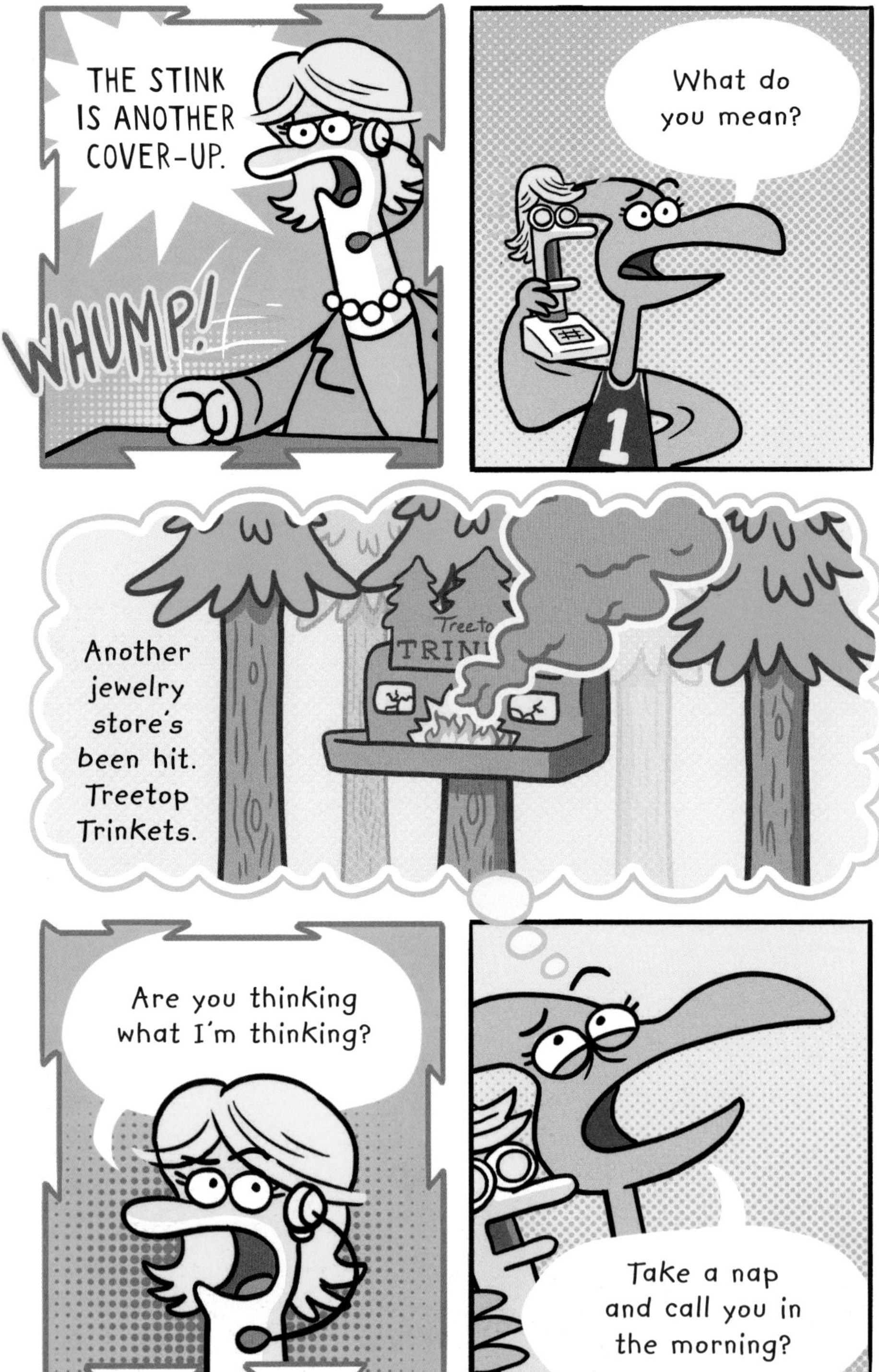
THE STINK IS ANOTHER COVER-UP.
WHUMP!
What do you mean?
Another jewelry store's been hit. Treetop Trinkets.
Treeto
TRIN
Are you thinking what I'm thinking?
Take a nap and call you in the morning?

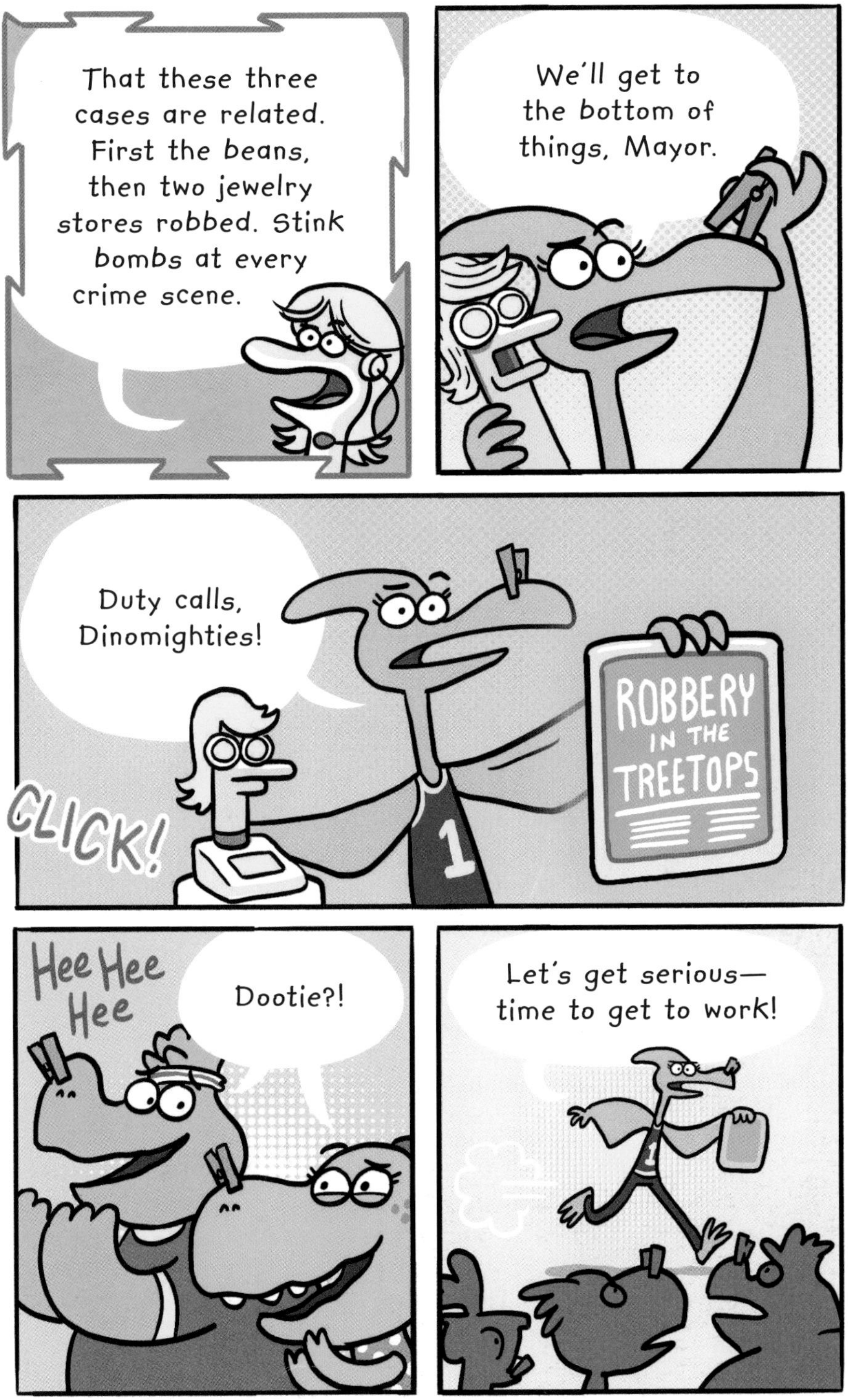
That these three cases are related. First the beans, then two jewelry stores robbed. Stink bombs at every crime scene.
We'll get to the bottom of things, Mayor.
Duty calls, Dinomighties!
CLICK!
ROBBERY IN THE TREETOPS
Hee Hee Hee
Dootie?!
Let's get serious—time to get to work!

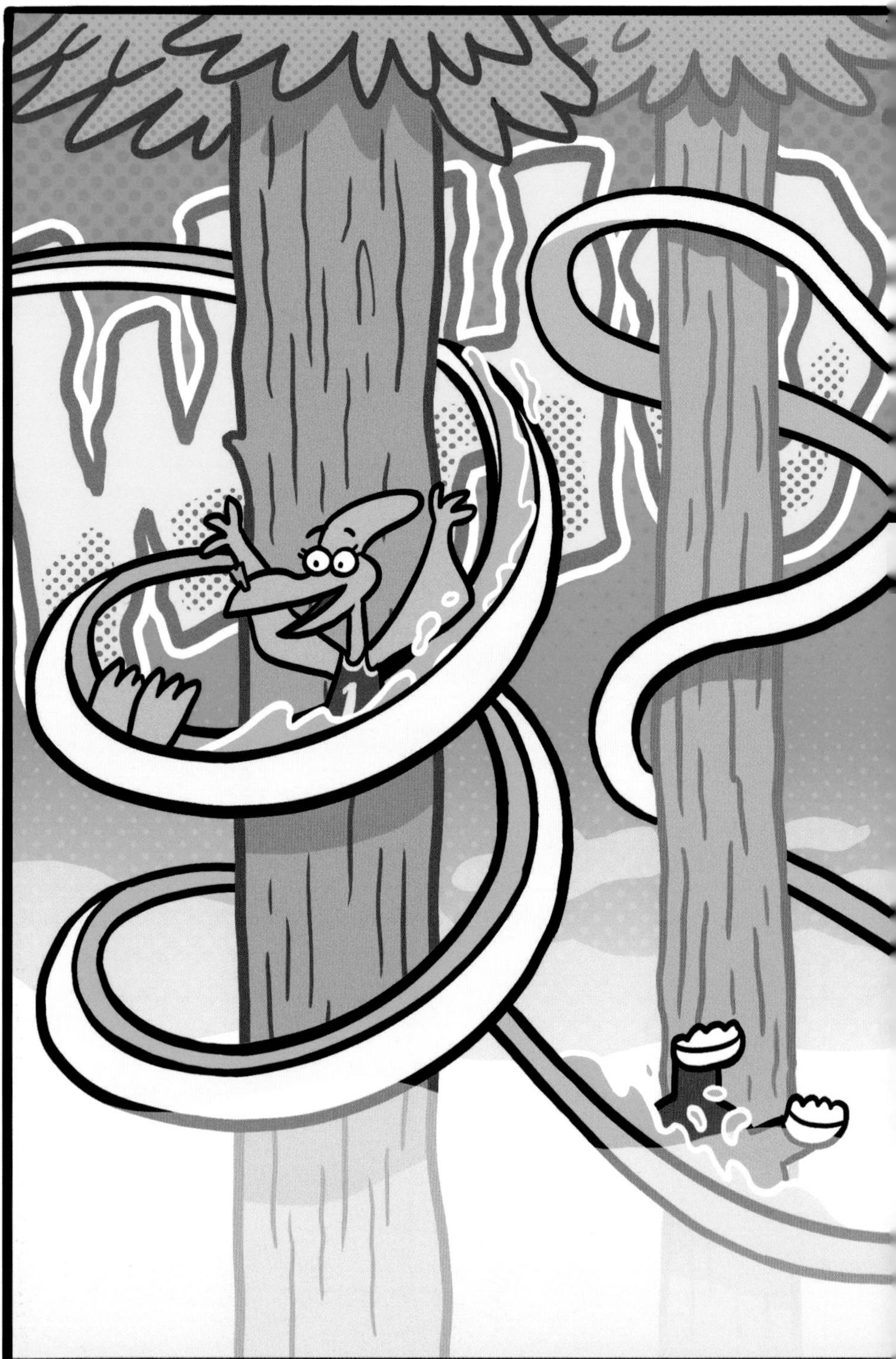

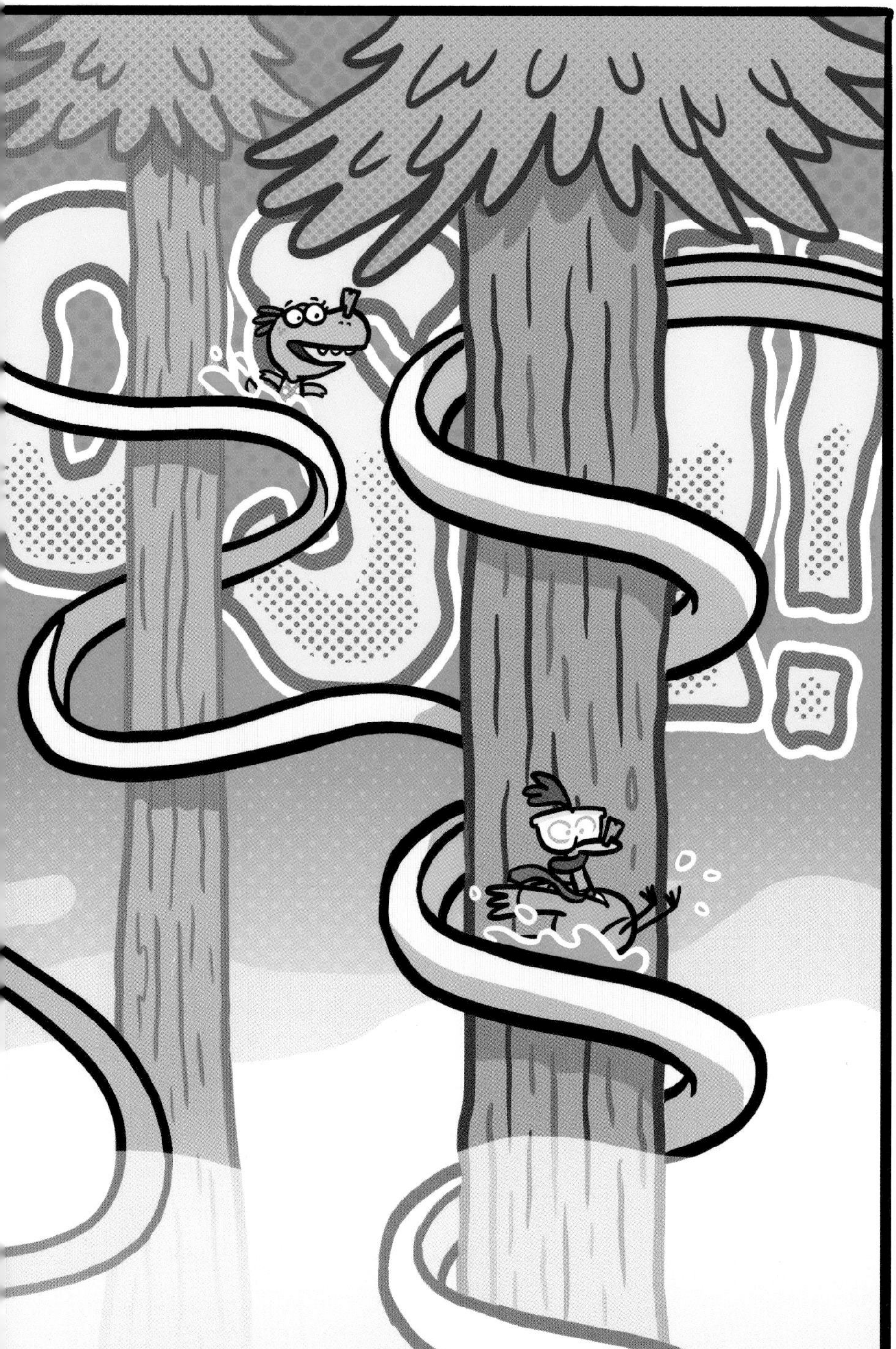

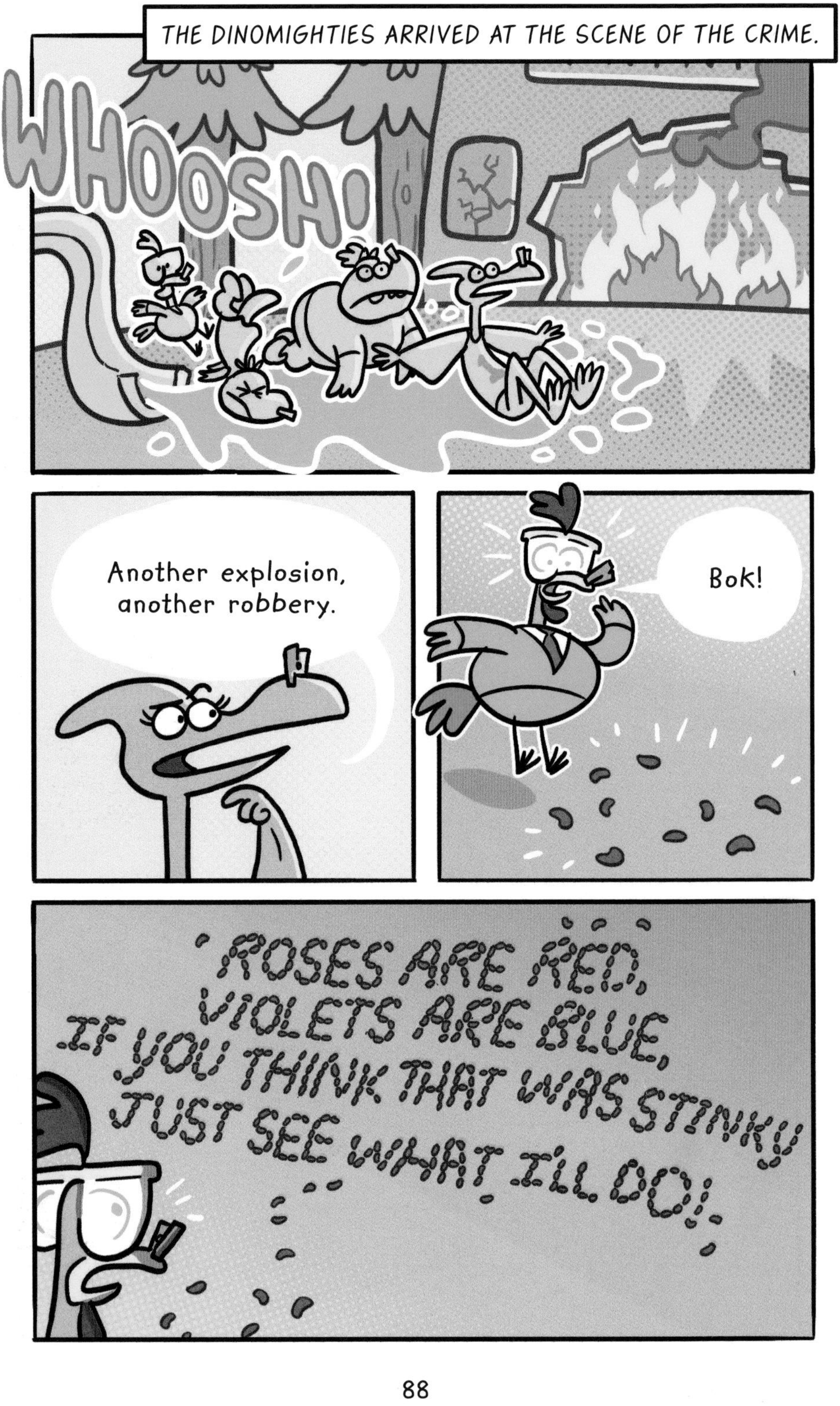
THE DINOMIGHTIES ARRIVED AT THE SCENE OF THE CRIME.
WHOOSH!
Another explosion, another robbery.
Bok!
ROSES ARE RED,
VIOLETS ARE BLUE,
IF YOU THINK THAT WAS STINKY
JUST SEE WHAT I'LL DO!

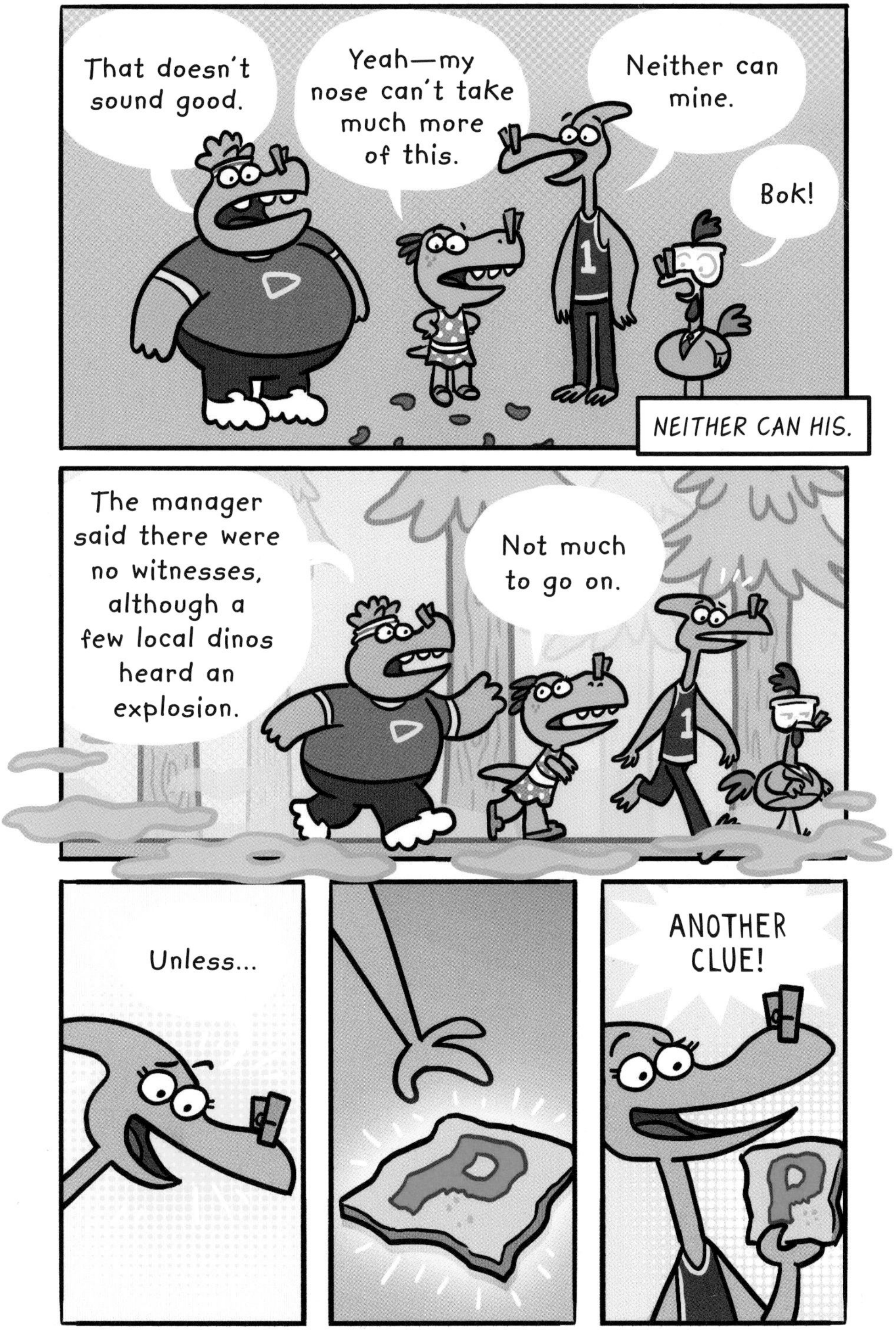
That doesn't sound good.
Yeah—my nose can't take much more of this.
Neither can mine.
Bok!
NEITHER CAN HIS.
The manager said there were no witnesses, although a few local dinos heard an explosion.
Not much to go on.
Unless...
ANOTHER CLUE!

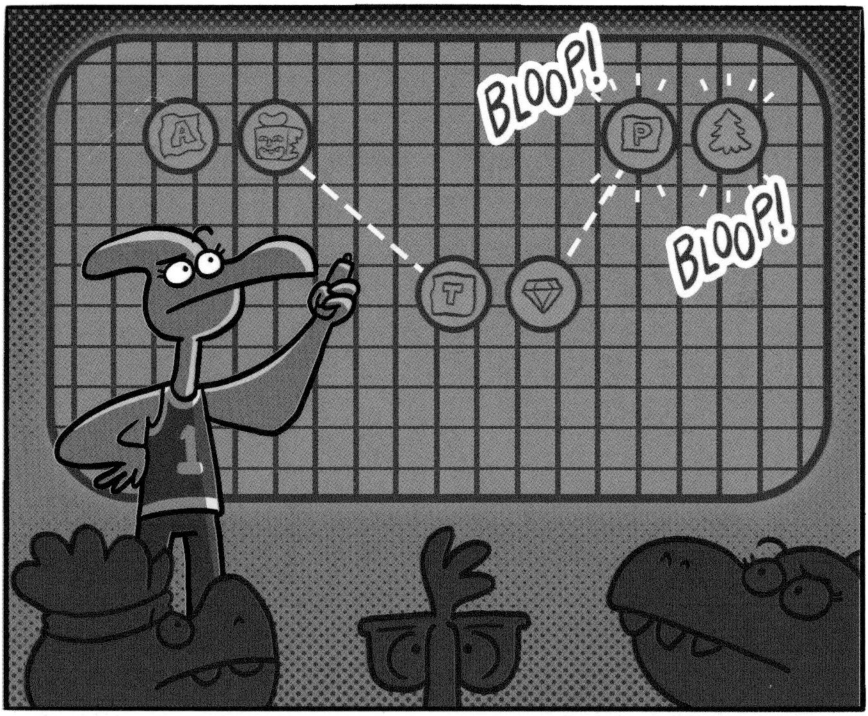
BLOOP!
BLOOP!

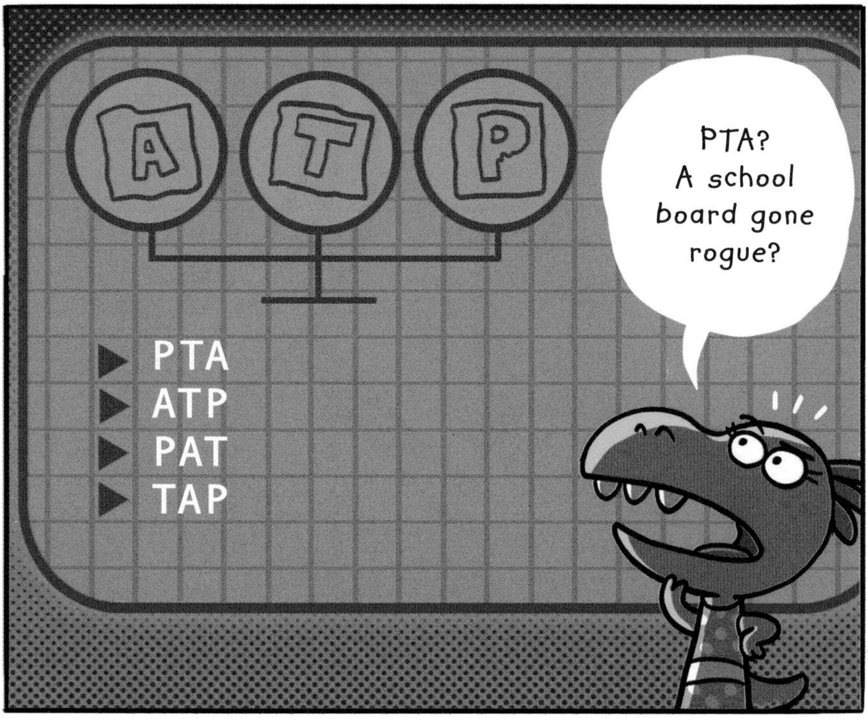
A
T
P
PTA
ATP
PAT
TAP
PTA? A school board gone rogue?

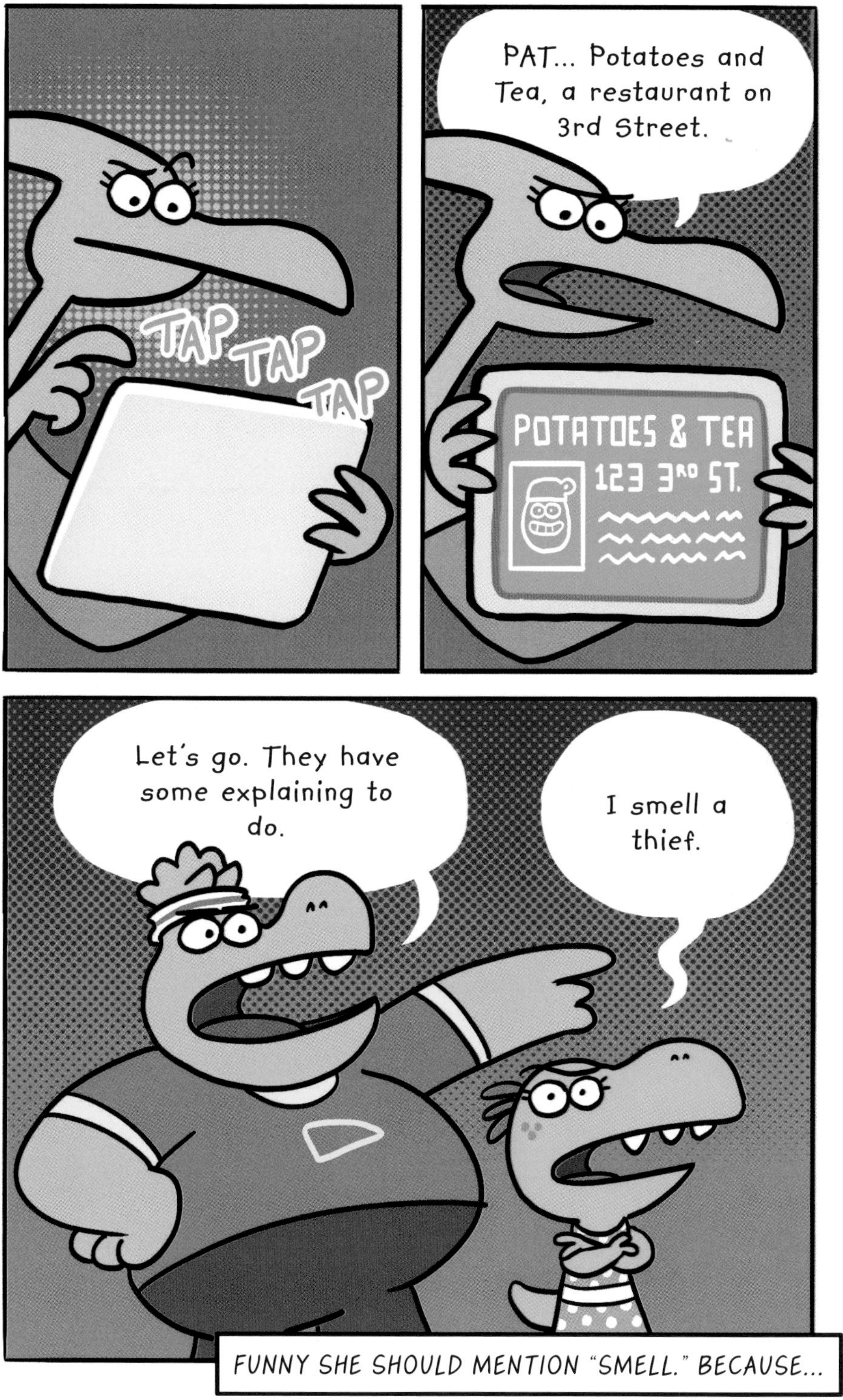
TAP TAP TAP
PAT... Potatoes and Tea, a restaurant on 3rd Street.
POTATOES & TEA
123 3RD ST.
Let's go. They have some explaining to do.
I smell a thief.
FUNNY SHE SHOULD MENTION "SMELL." BECAUSE...

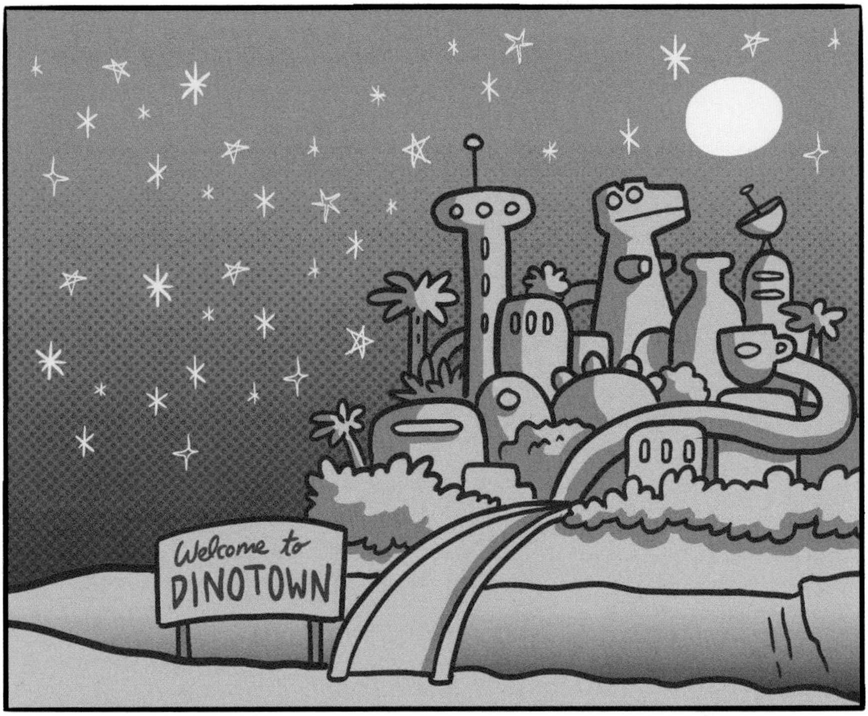
Welcome to
DINOTOWN

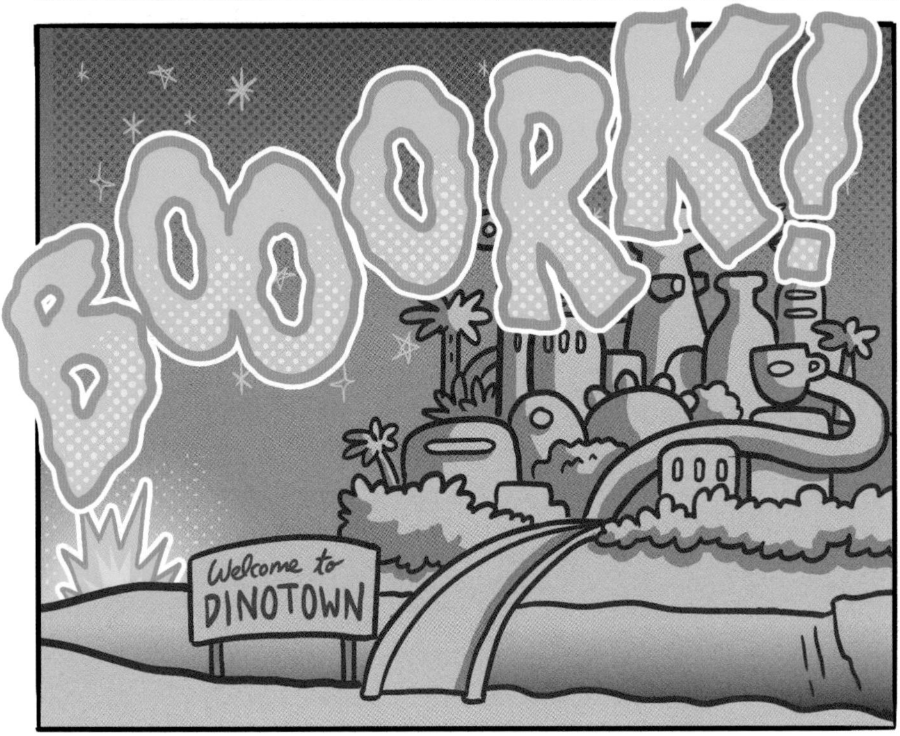
BOOORK!
Welcome to
DINOTOWN

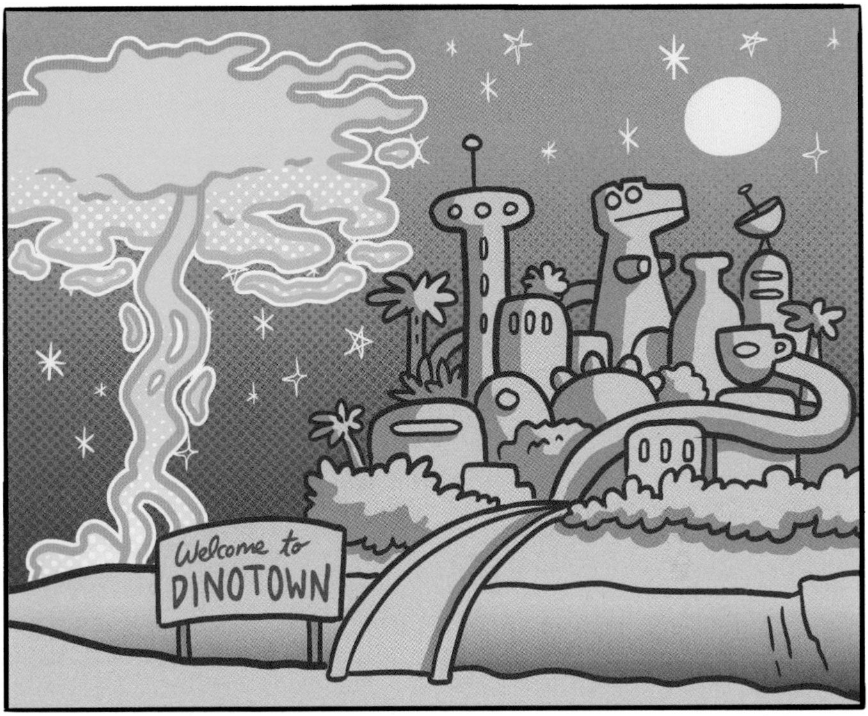
Welcome to
DINOTOWN

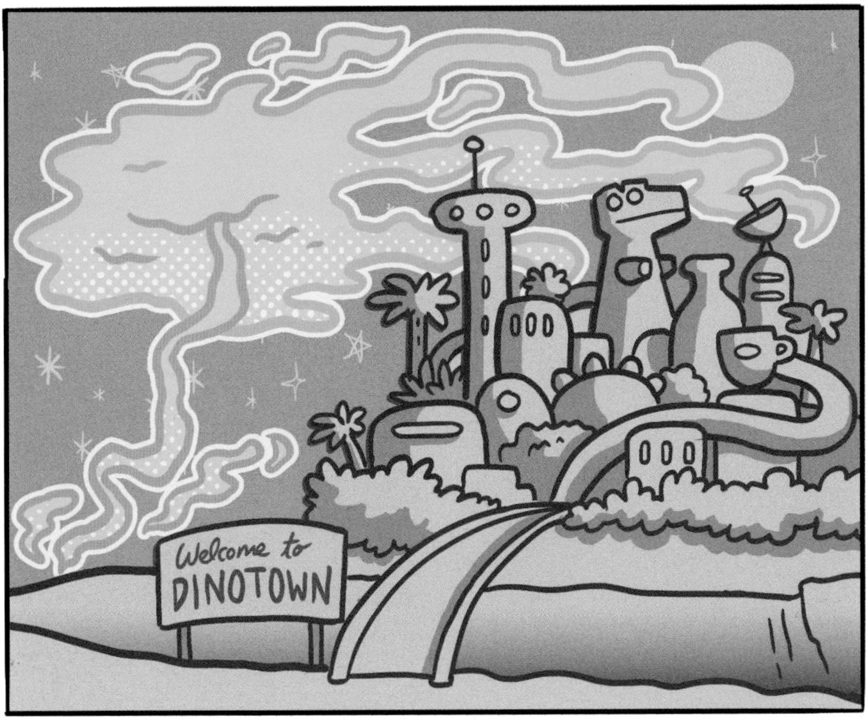
Welcome to
DINOTOWN

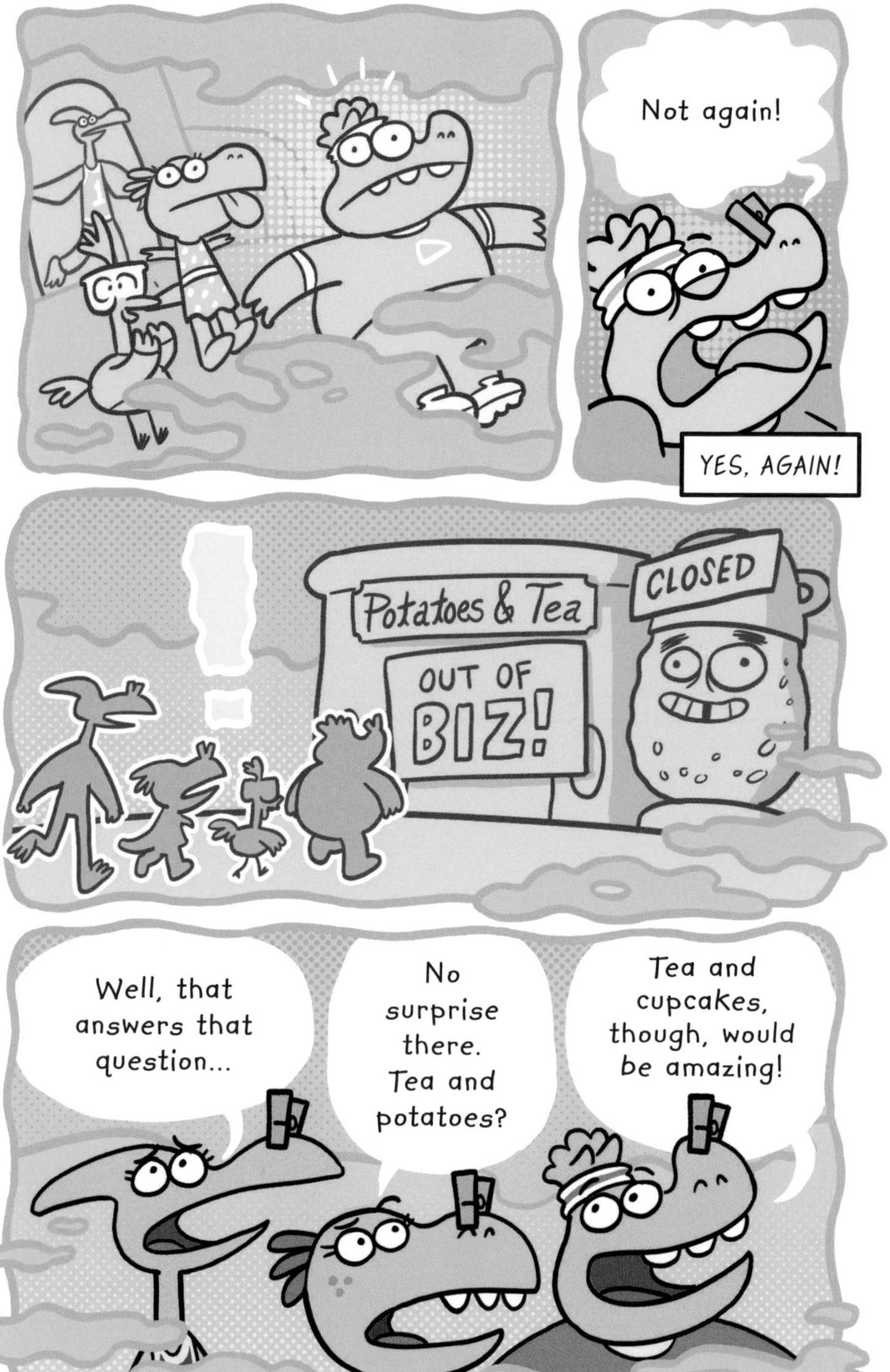
Not again!
YES, AGAIN!
Potatoes & Tea
CLOSED
OUT OF BIZ!
Well, that answers that question...
No surprise there. Tea and potatoes?
Tea and cupcakes, though, would be amazing!

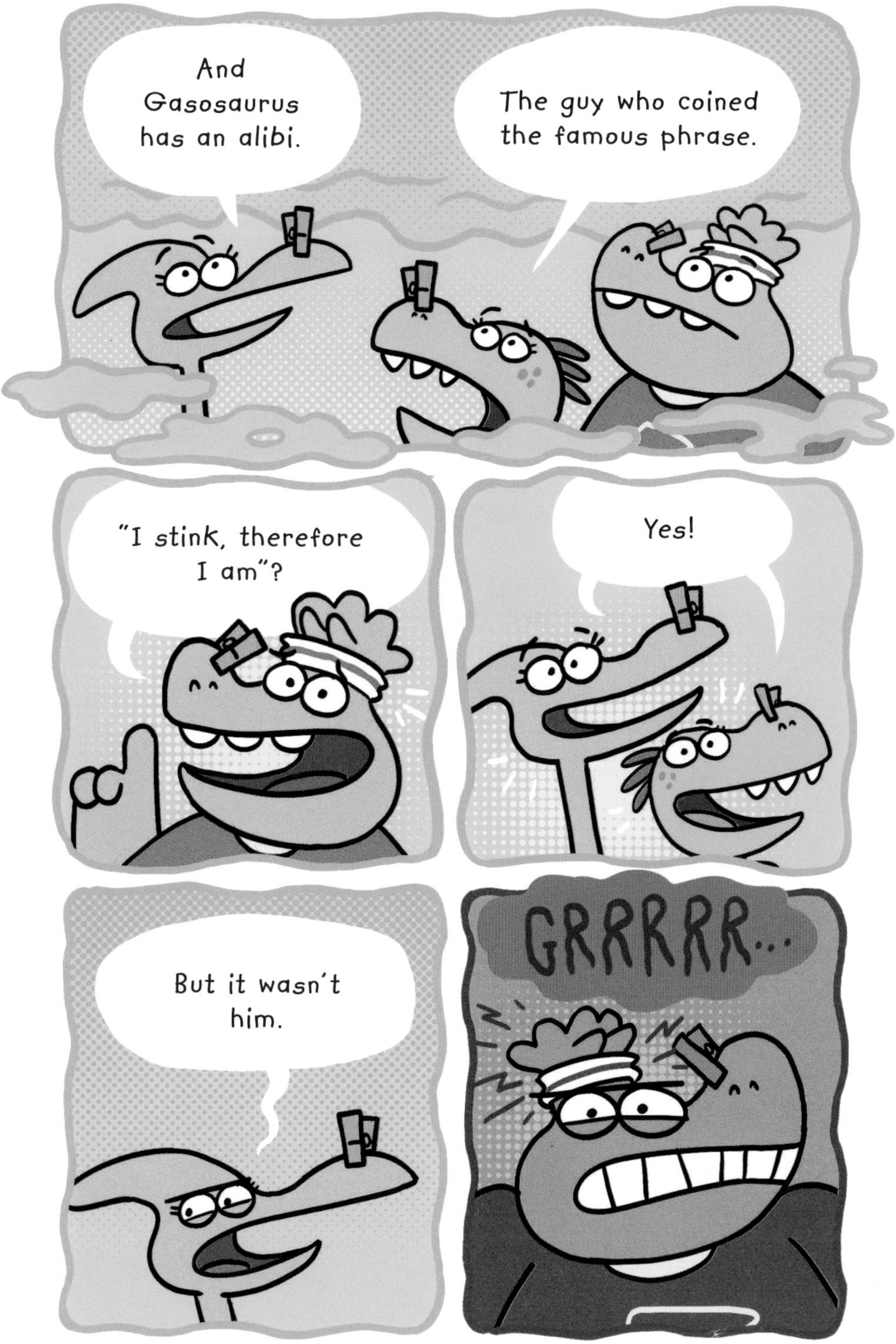
And Gasosaurus has an alibi.
The guy who coined the famous phrase.
"I stink, therefore I am"?
Yes!
But it wasn't him.
GRRRRR...

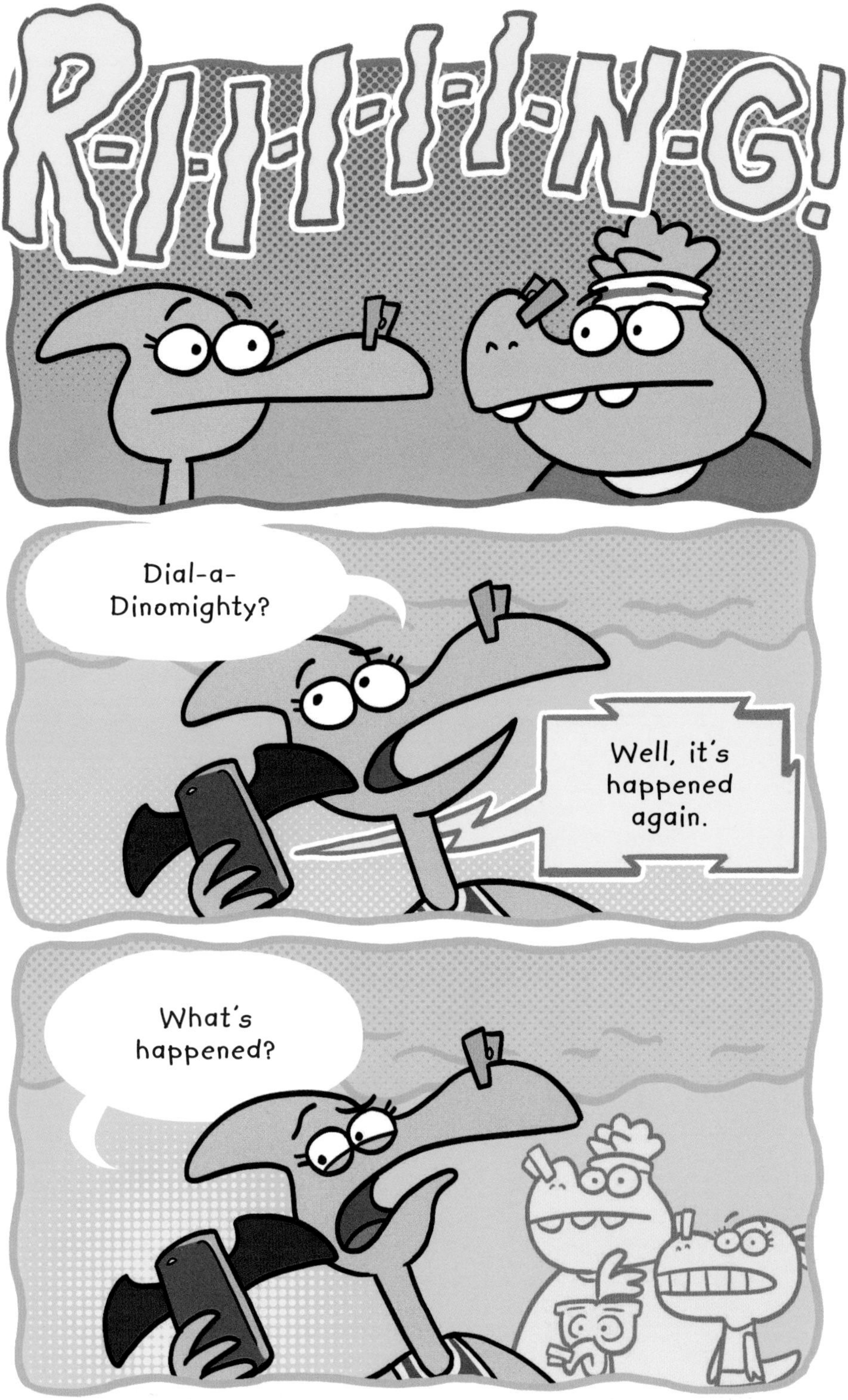
R-I-I-I-I-I-N-G!
Dial-a-Dinomighty?
Well, it's happened again.
What's happened?

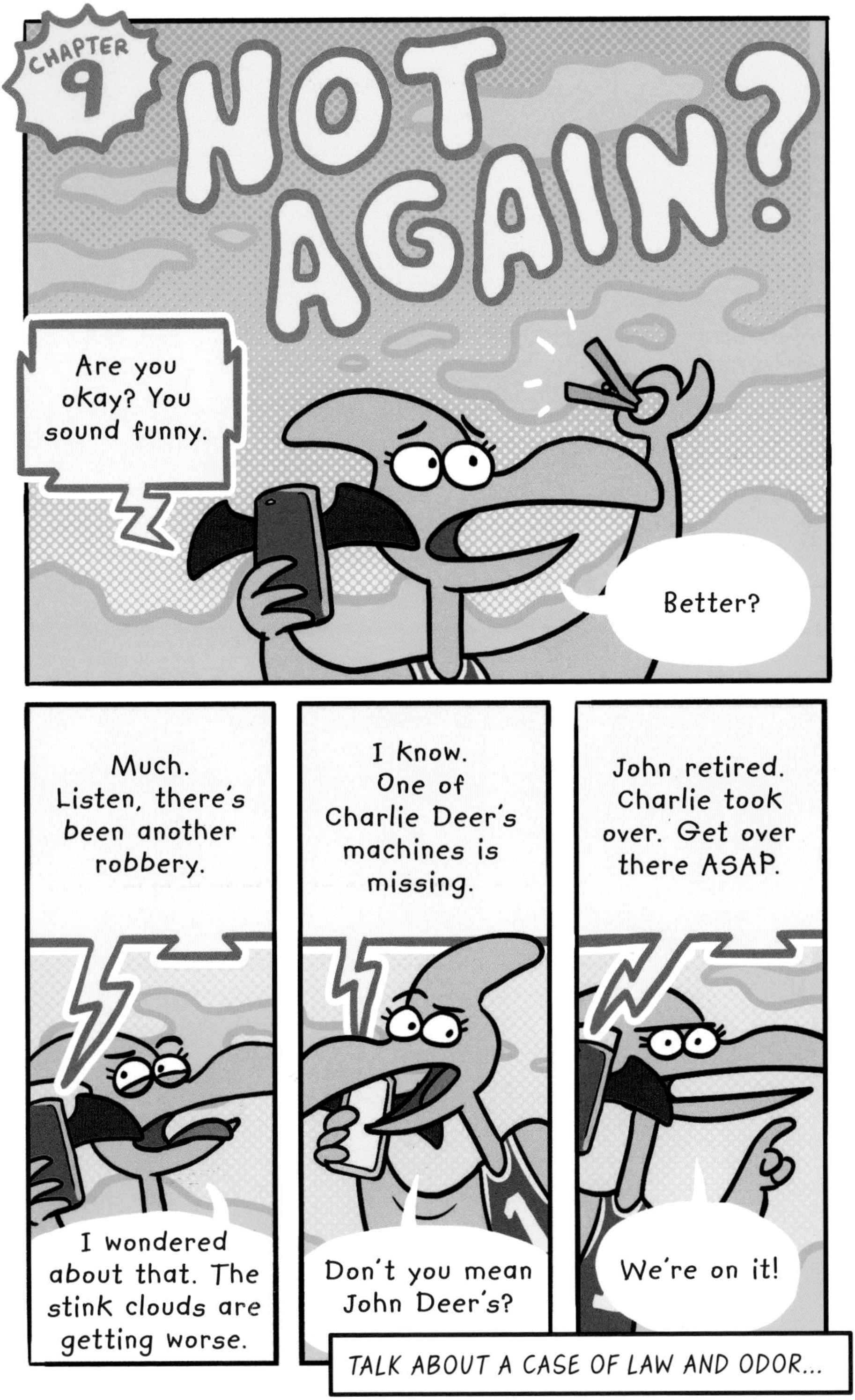
CHAPTER 9
NOT AGAIN?
Are you okay? You sound funny.
Better?
Much. Listen, there's been another robbery.
I wondered about that. The stink clouds are getting worse.
I know. One of Charlie Deer's machines is missing.
Don't you mean John Deer's?
John retired. Charlie took over. Get over there ASAP.
We're on it!
TALK ABOUT A CASE OF LAW AND ODOR...

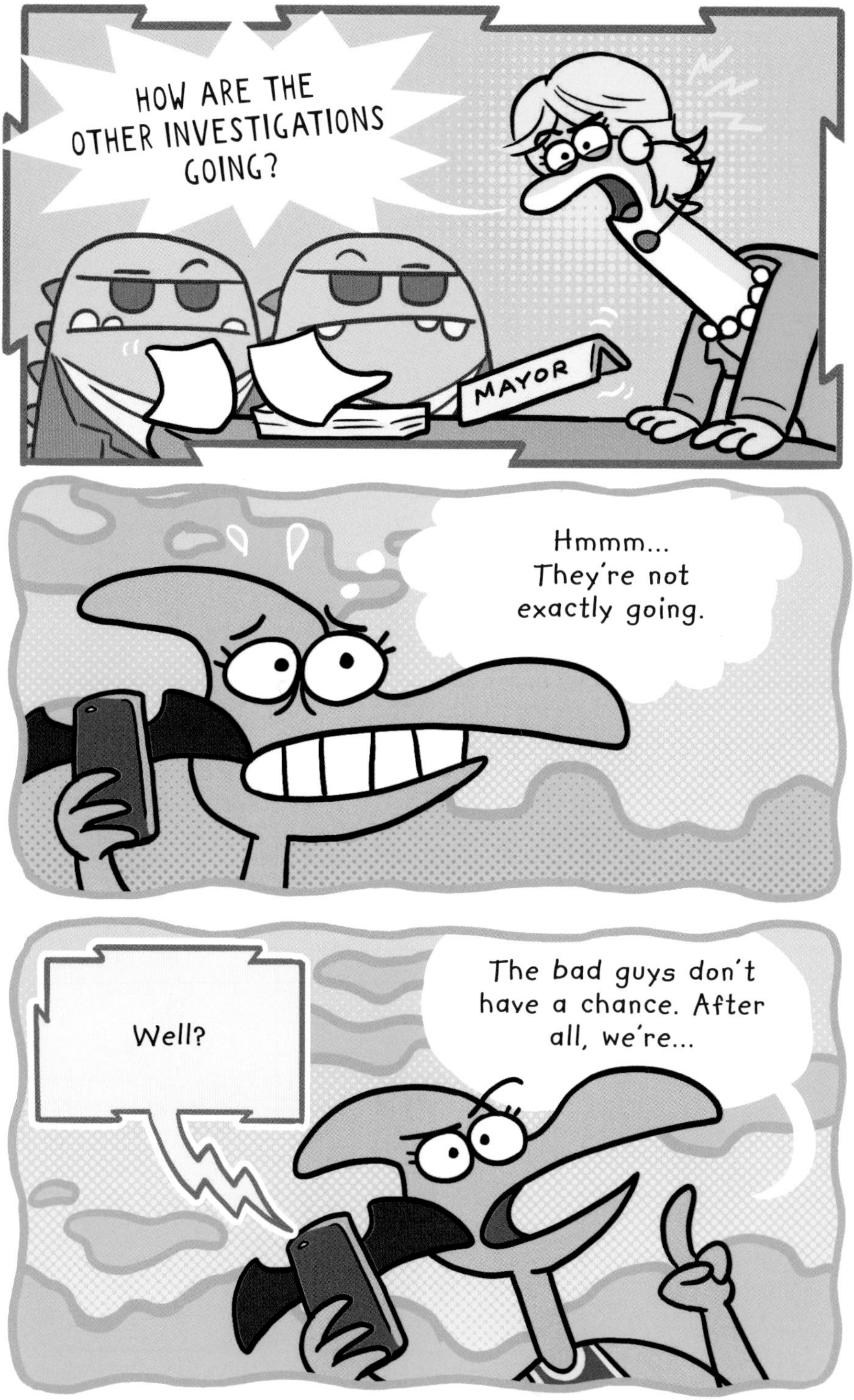
HOW ARE THE OTHER INVESTIGATIONS GOING?
MAYOR
Hmmm... They're not exactly going.
Well?
The bad guys don't have a chance. After all, we're...

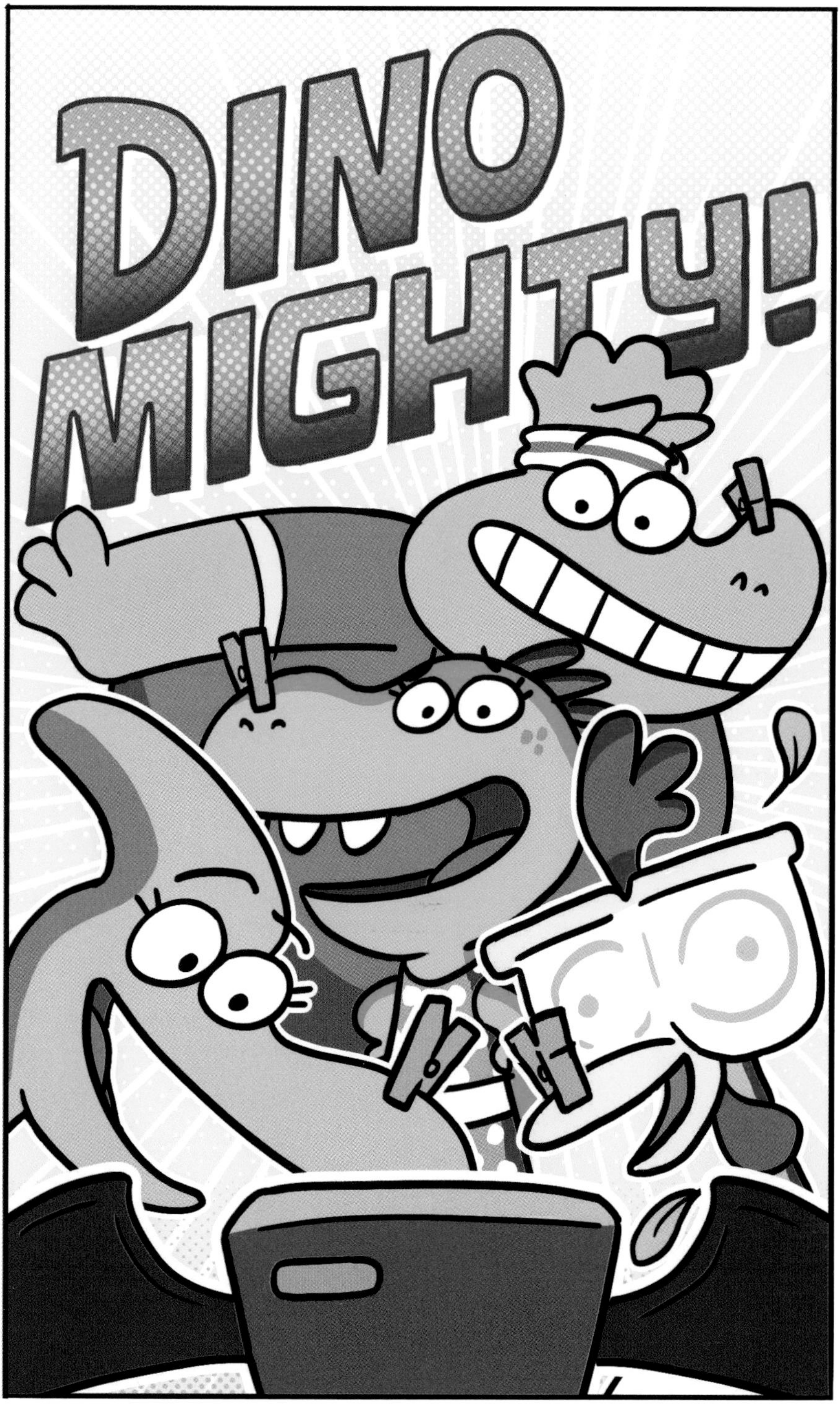
DINO MIGHTY!

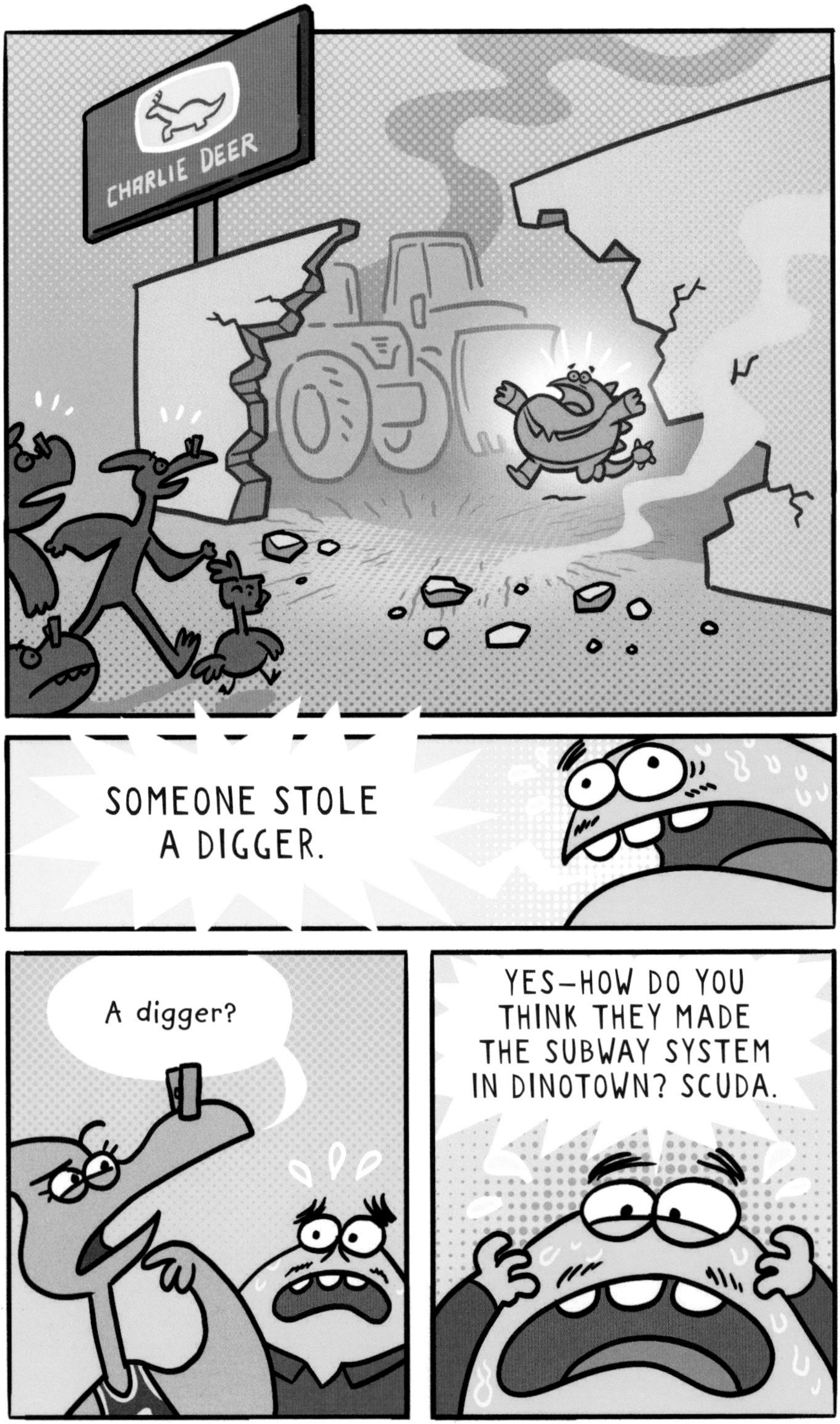
CHARLIE DEER
SOMEONE STOLE A DIGGER.
A digger?
YES—HOW DO YOU THINK THEY MADE THE SUBWAY SYSTEM IN DINOTOWN? SCUDA.

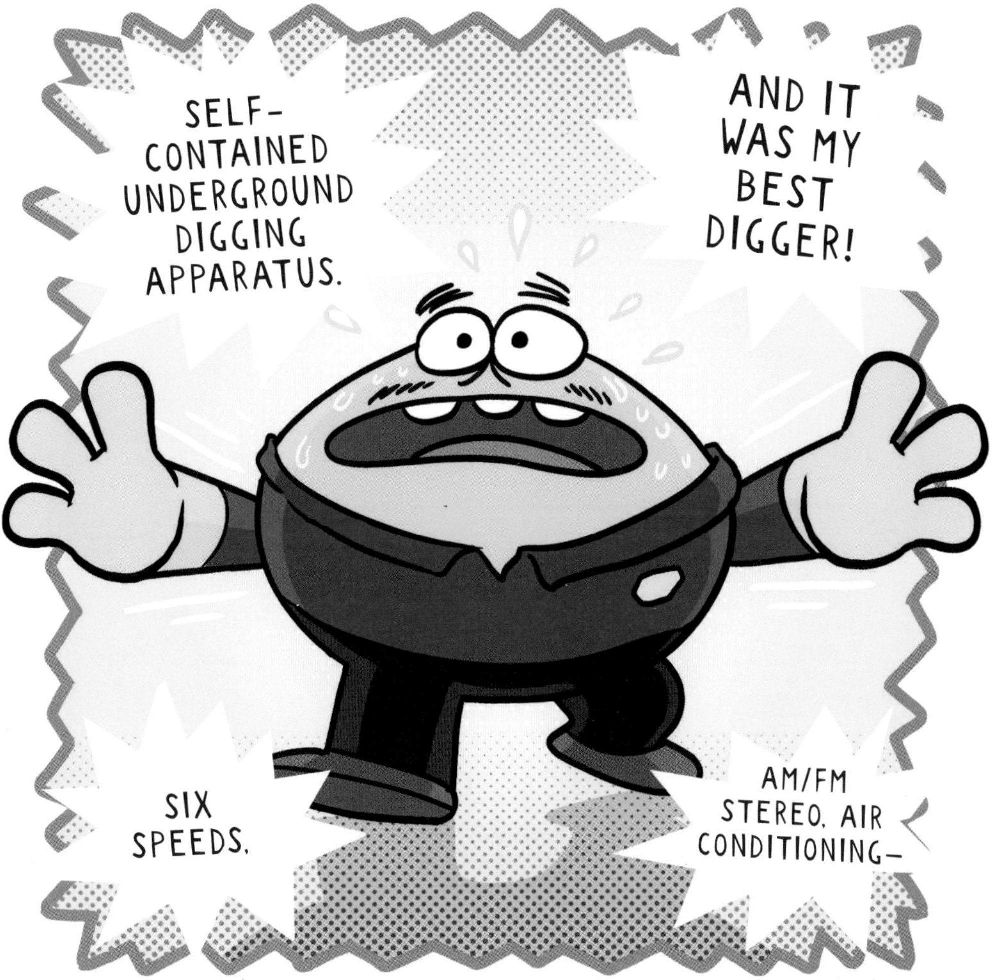
SELF-CONTAINED UNDERGROUND DIGGING APPARATUS.
AND IT WAS MY BEST DIGGER!
SIX SPEEDS.
AM/FM STEREO. AIR CONDITIONING—

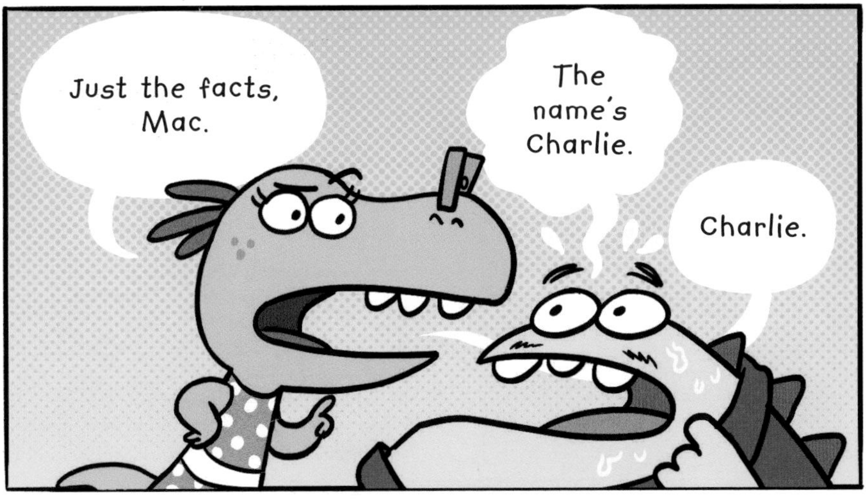
Just the facts, Mac.
The name's Charlie.
Charlie.

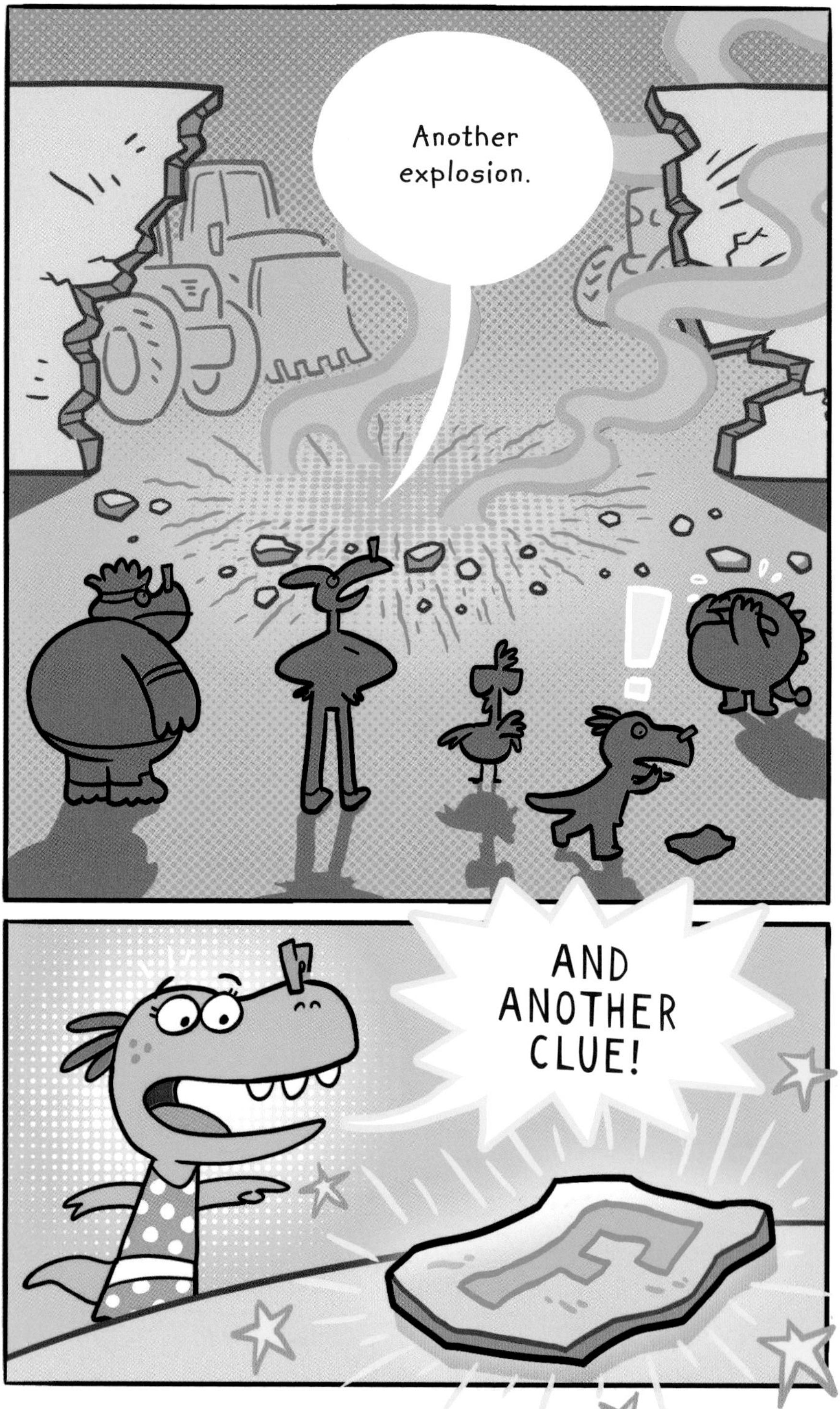
Another explosion.
AND ANOTHER CLUE!

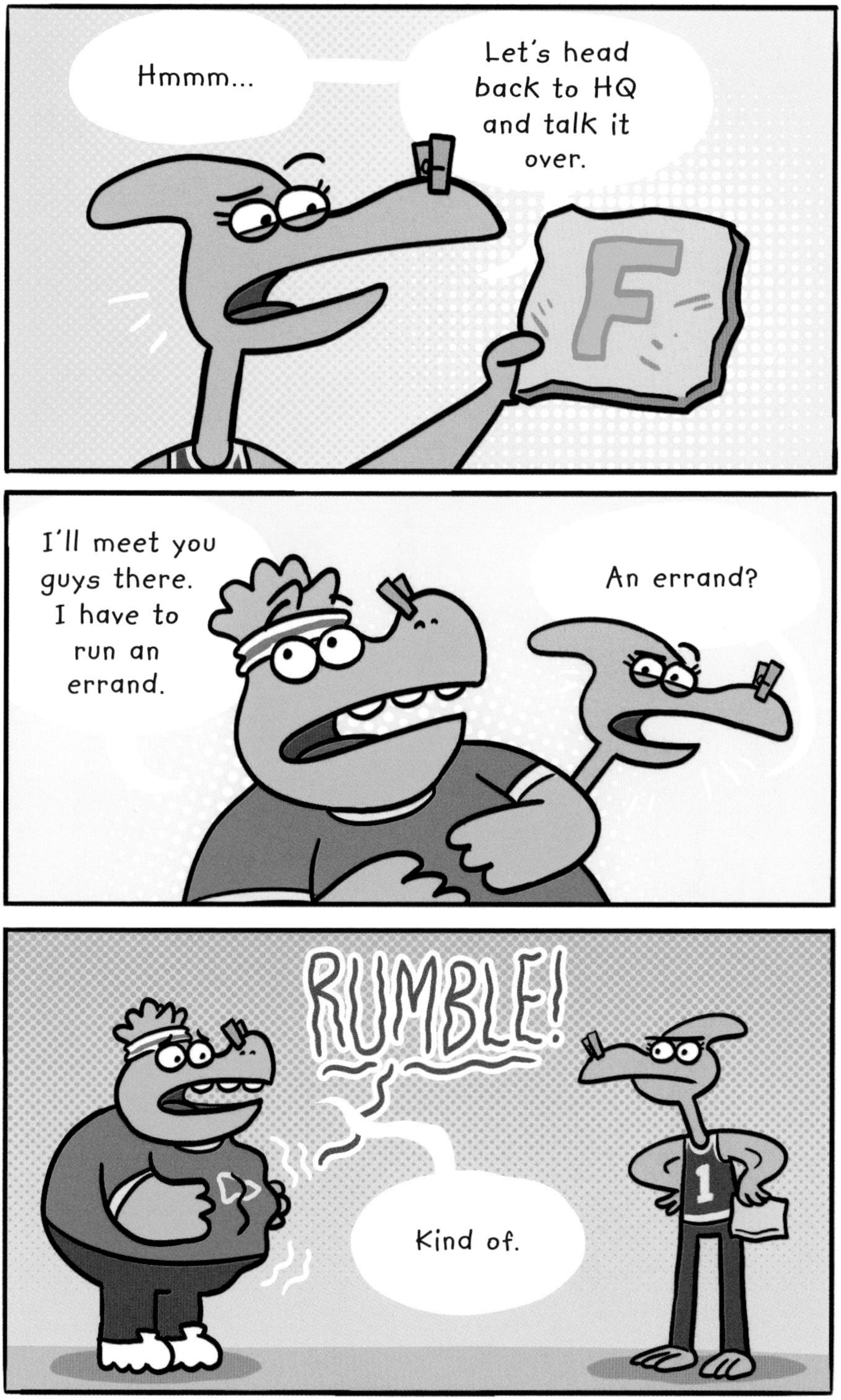
Hmmm...
Let's head back to HQ and talk it over.
F
I'll meet you guys there. I have to run an errand.
An errand?
RUMBLE!
Kind of.
1

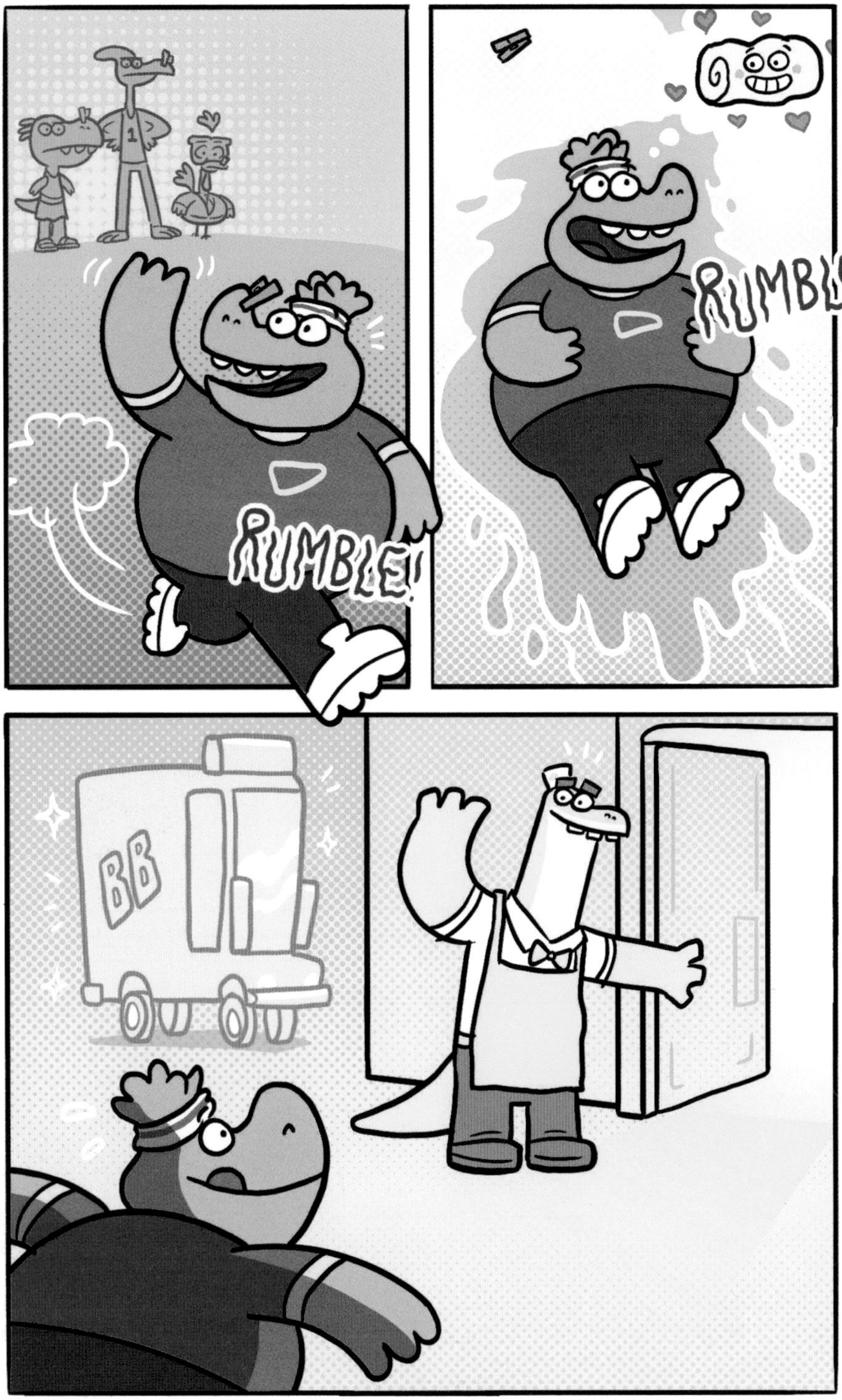
RUMBLE!
RUMBLE!
BB

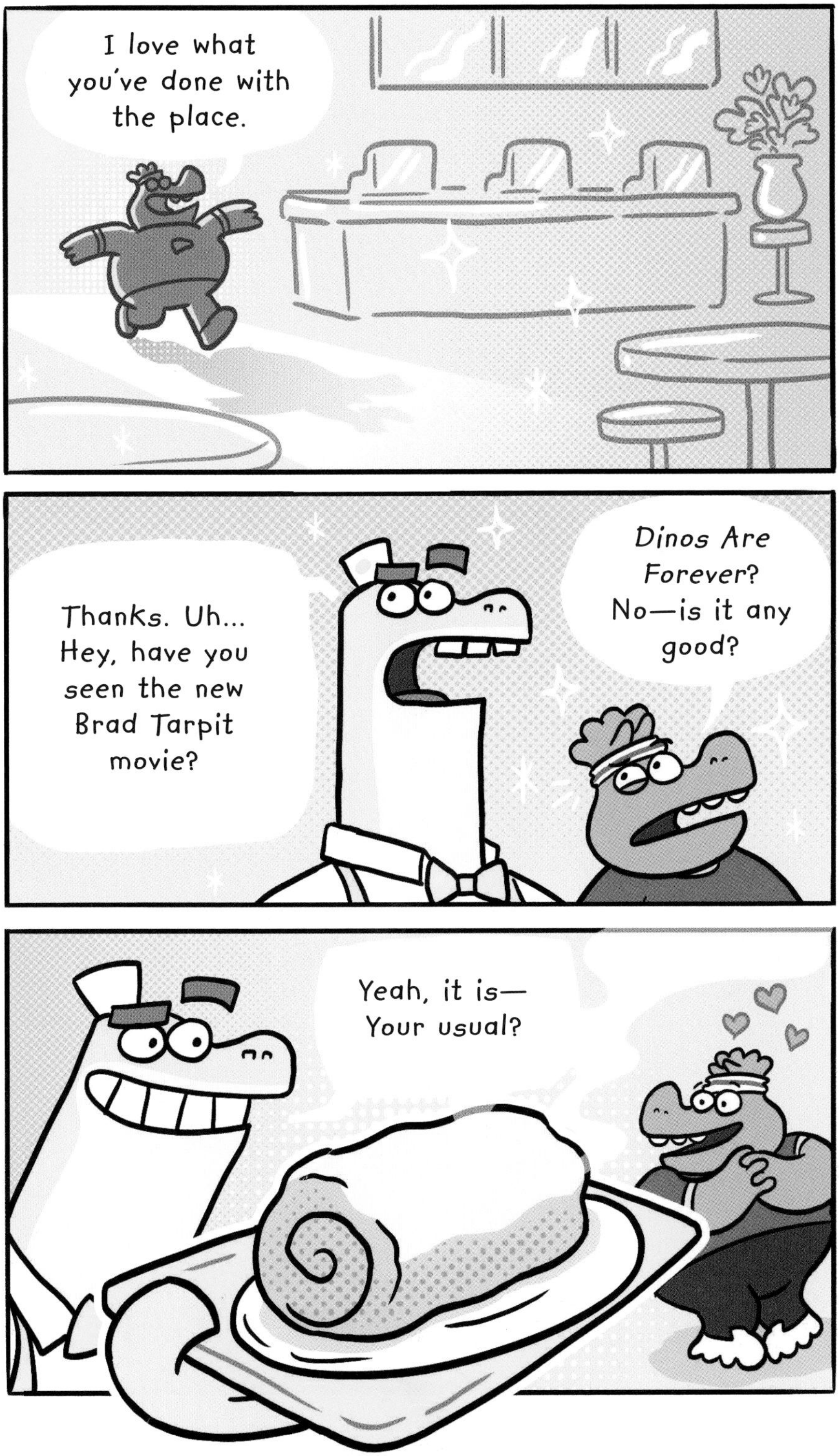
I love what you've done with the place.
Thanks. Uh... Hey, have you seen the new Brad Tarpit movie?
Dinos Are Forever? No—is it any good?
Yeah, it is— Your usual?

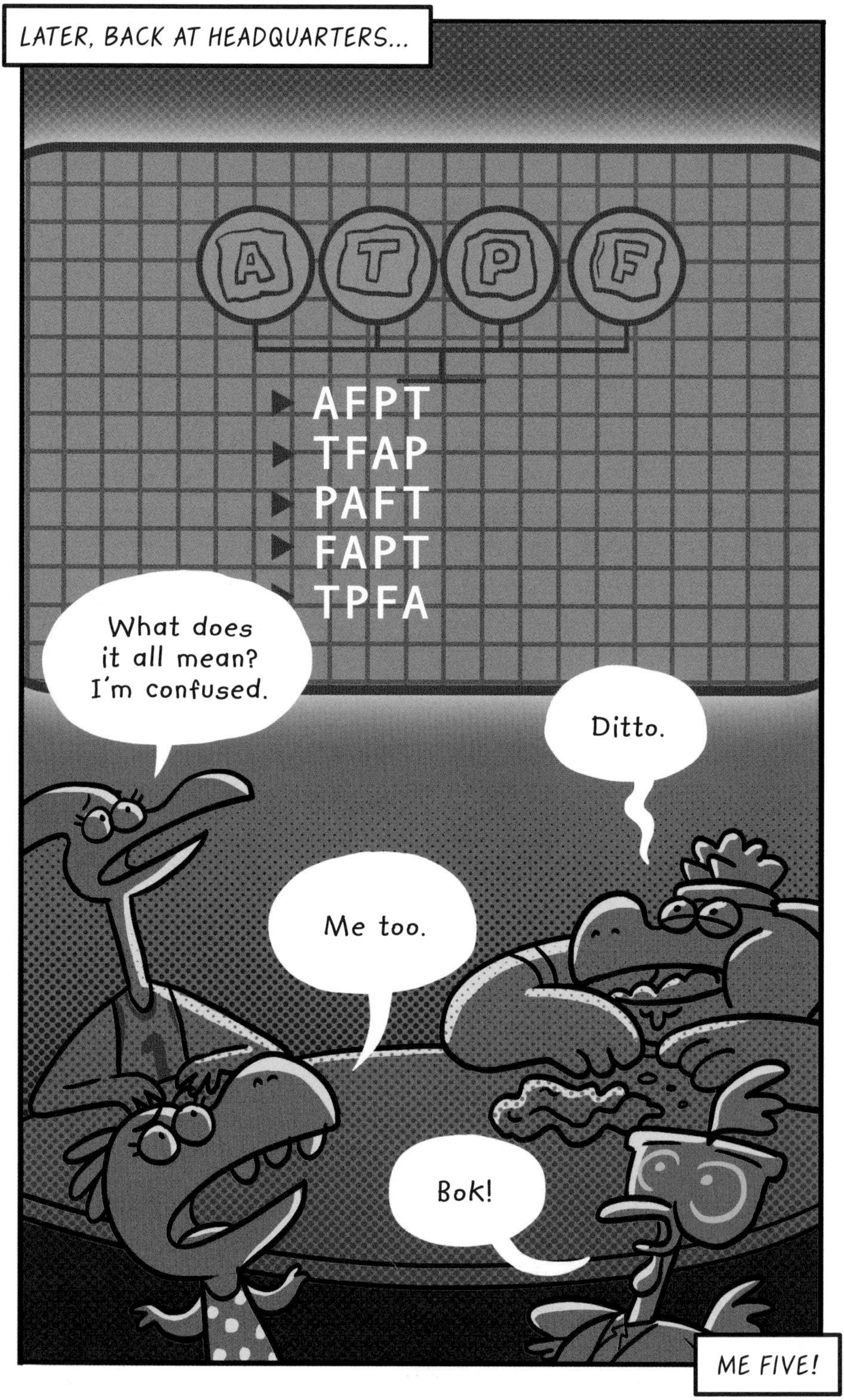
LATER, BACK AT HEADQUARTERS...
A T P F
AFPT
TFAP
PAFT
FAPT
TPFA
What does it all mean? I'm confused.
Ditto.
Me too.
Bok!
ME FIVE!

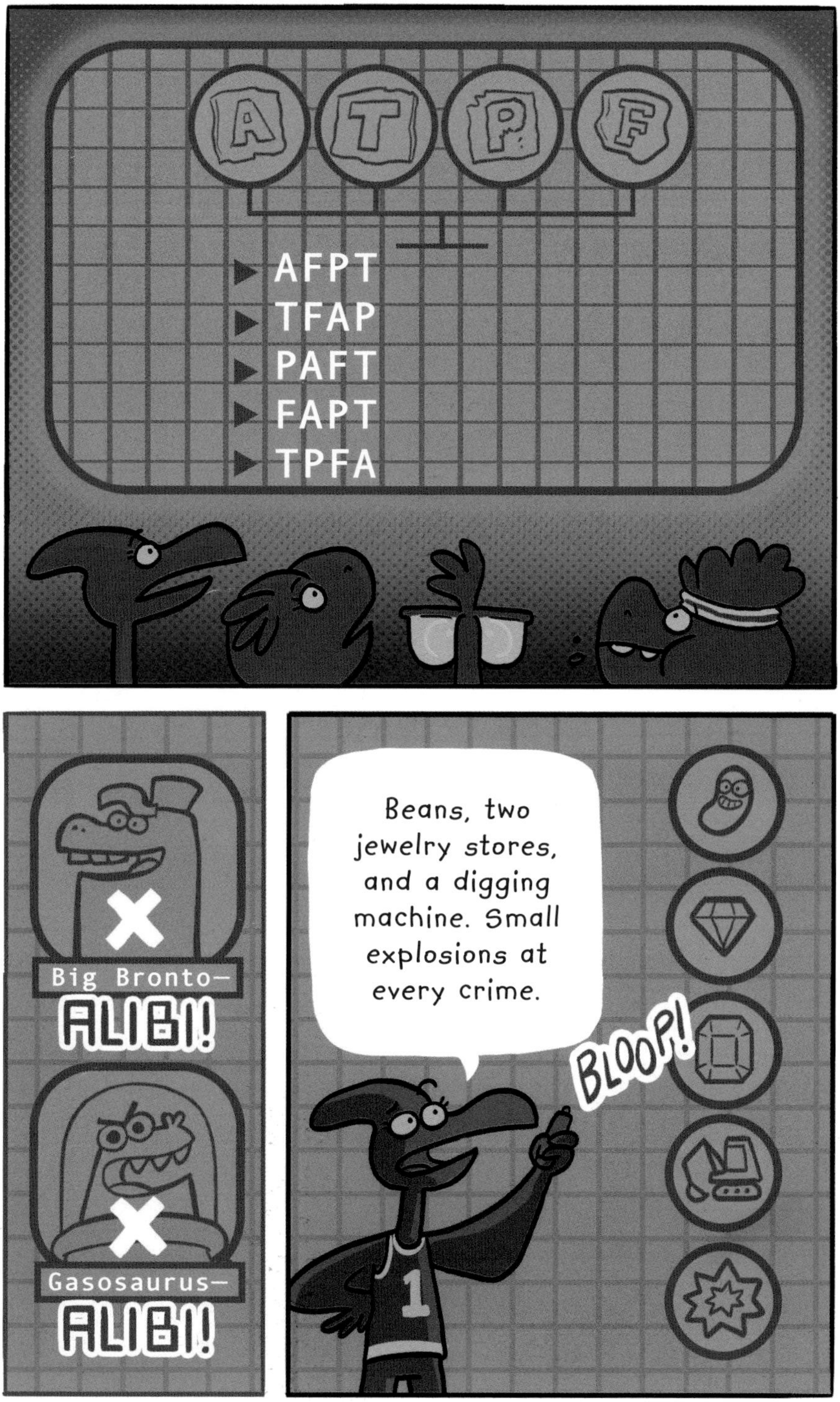
A
T
P
F
AFPT
TFAP
PAFT
FAPT
TPFA
Big Bronto—
ALIBI!
Gasosaurus—
ALIBI!
Beans, two jewelry stores, and a digging machine. Small explosions at every crime.
BLOOP!
1

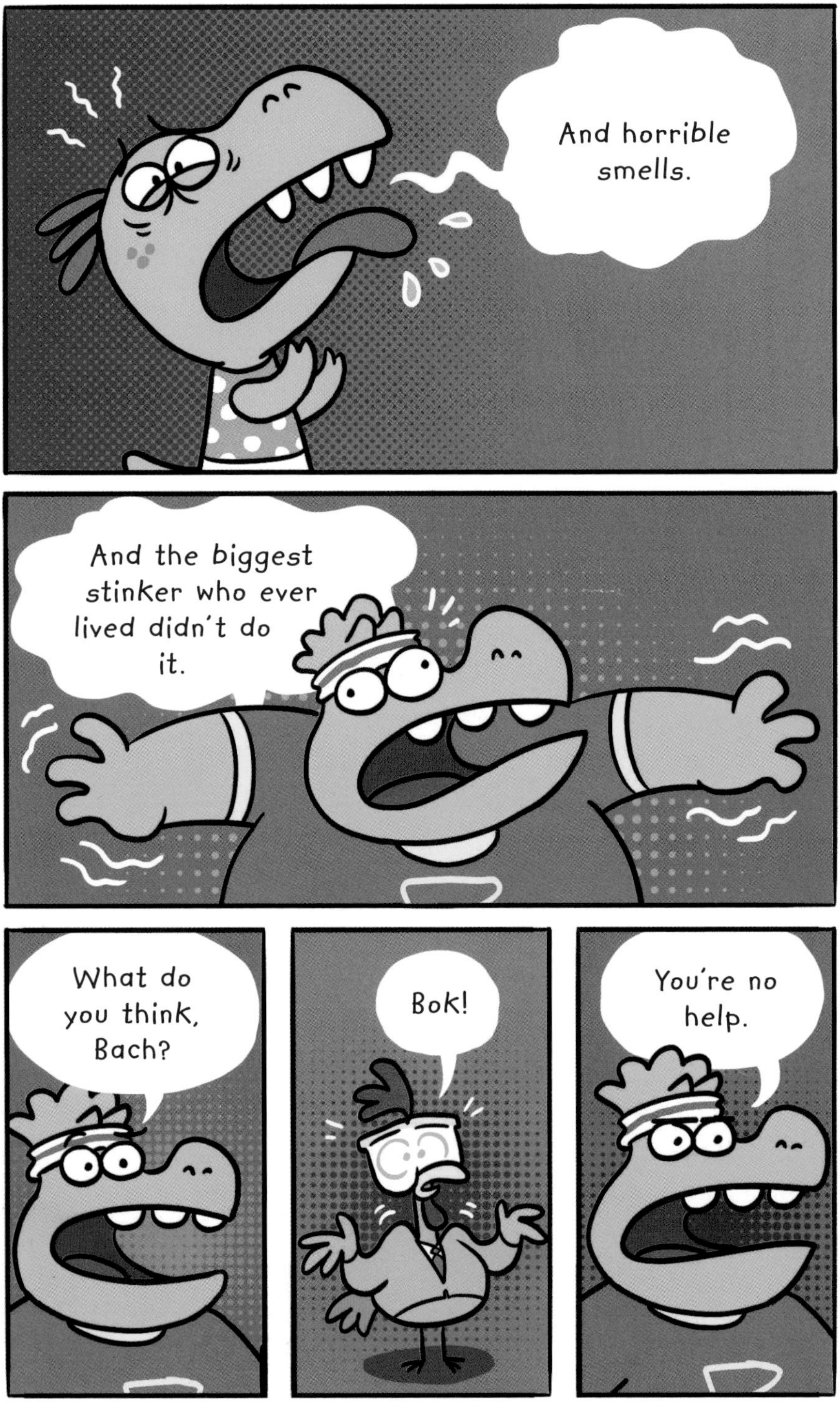
And horrible smells.
And the biggest stinker who ever lived didn't do it.
What do you think, Bach?
Bok!
You're no help.

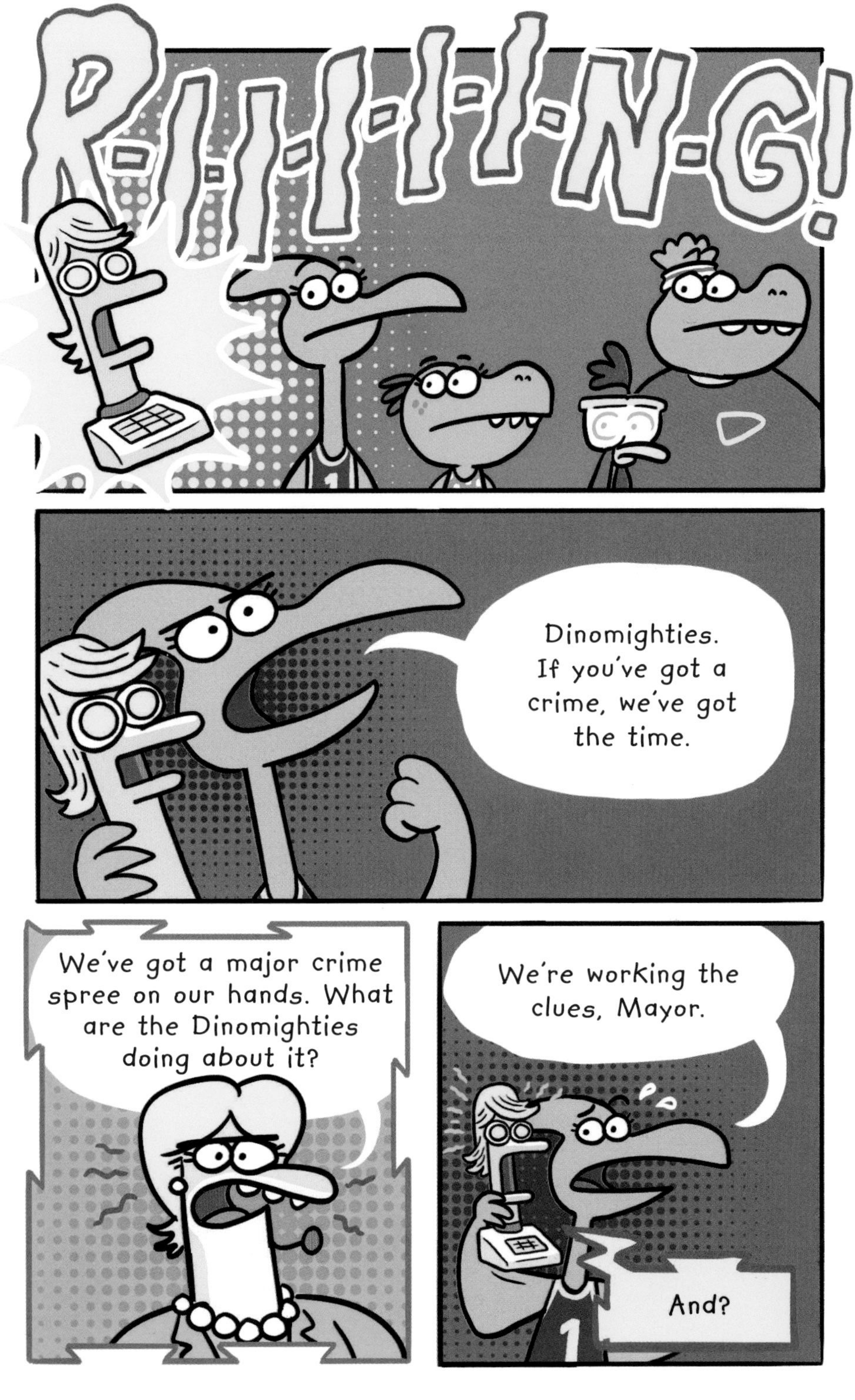
R-I-I-I-I-I-N-G!
Dinomighties. If you've got a crime, we've got the time.
We've got a major crime spree on our hands. What are the Dinomighties doing about it?
We're working the clues, Mayor.
And?

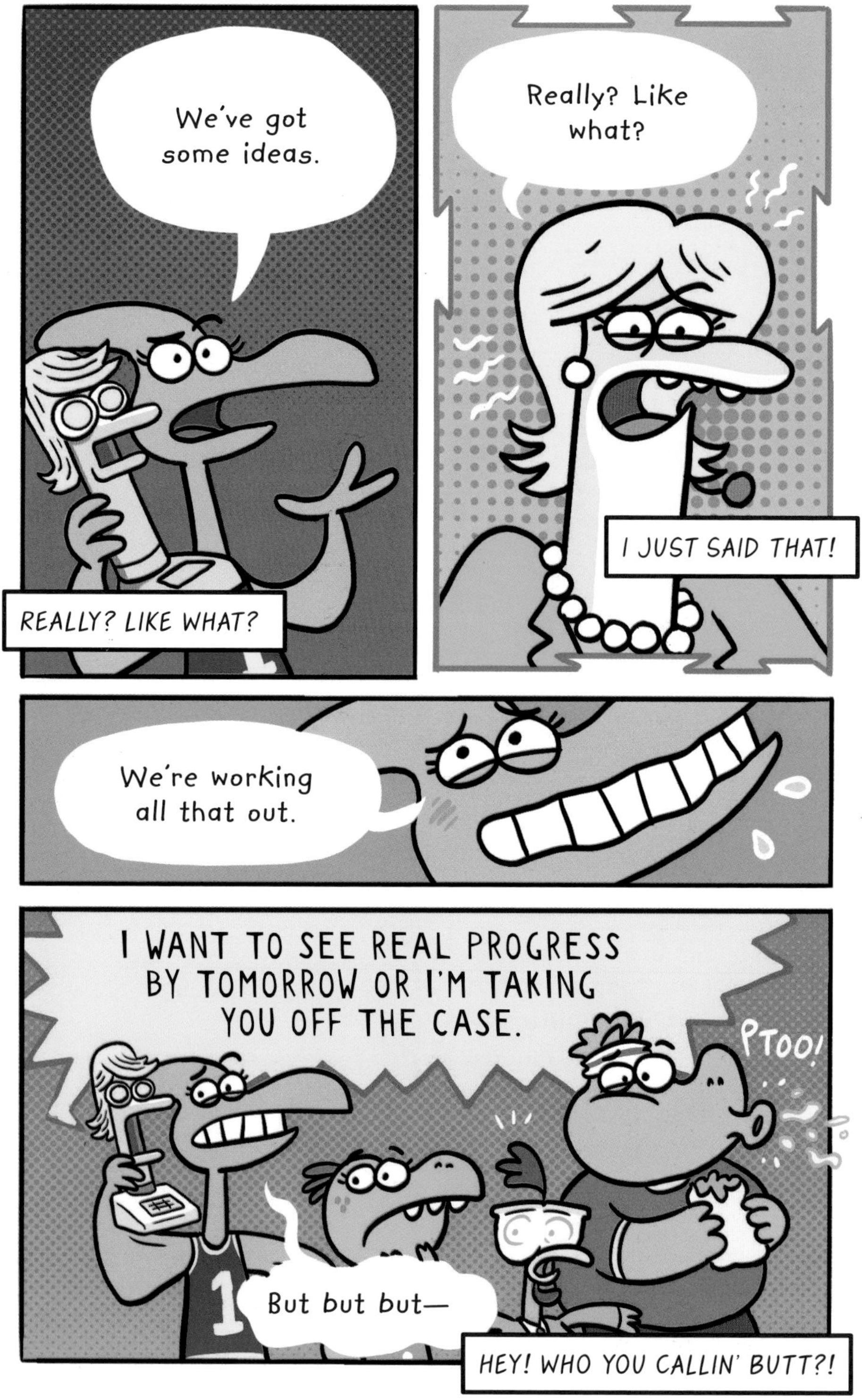
We've got some ideas.
REALLY? LIKE WHAT?
Really? Like what?
I JUST SAID THAT!
We're working all that out.
I WANT TO SEE REAL PROGRESS BY TOMORROW OR I'M TAKING YOU OFF THE CASE.
PTOO!
But but but—
HEY! WHO YOU CALLIN' BUTT?!

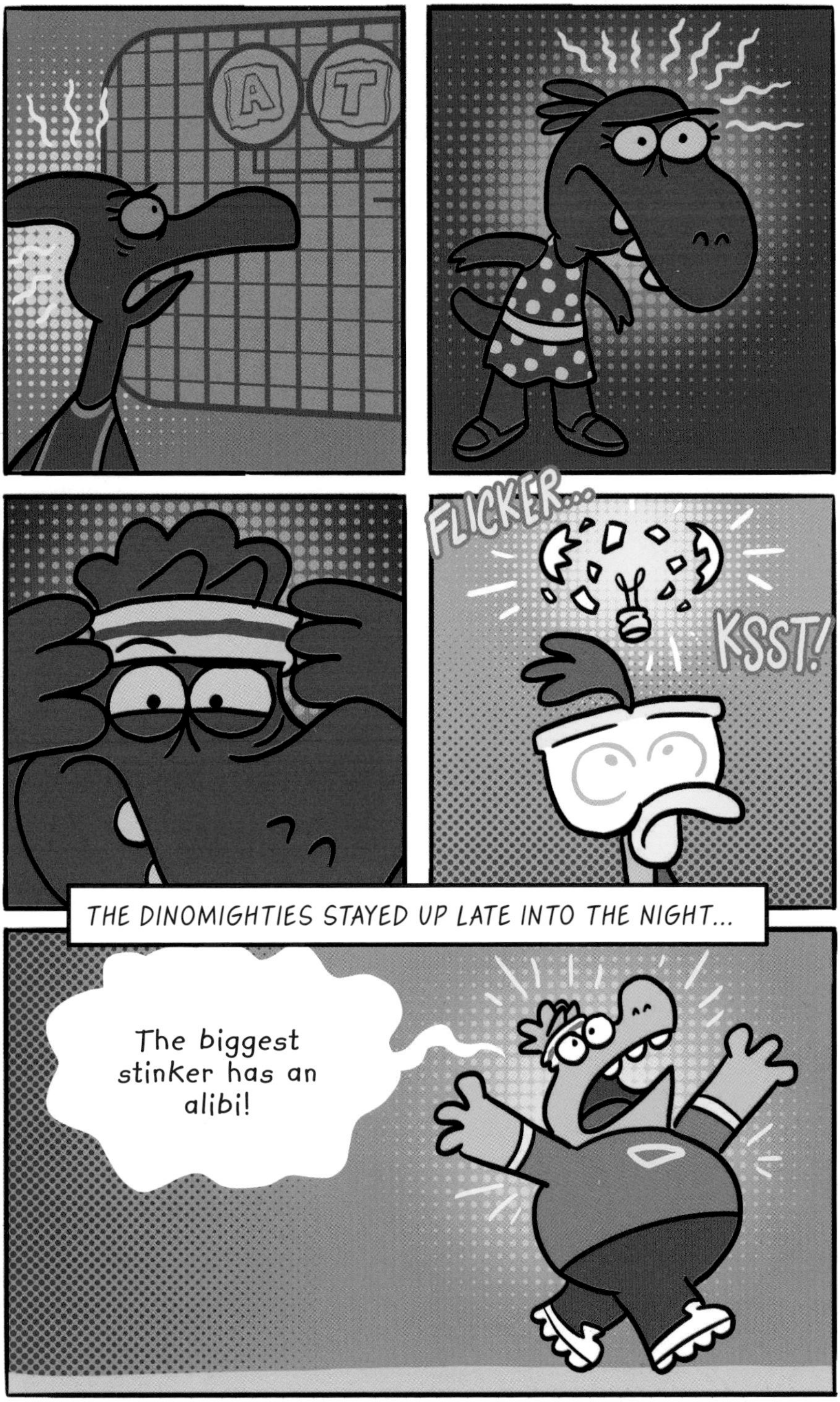
FLICKER...
KSST!
THE DINOMIGHTIES STAYED UP LATE INTO THE NIGHT...
The biggest stinker has an alibi!

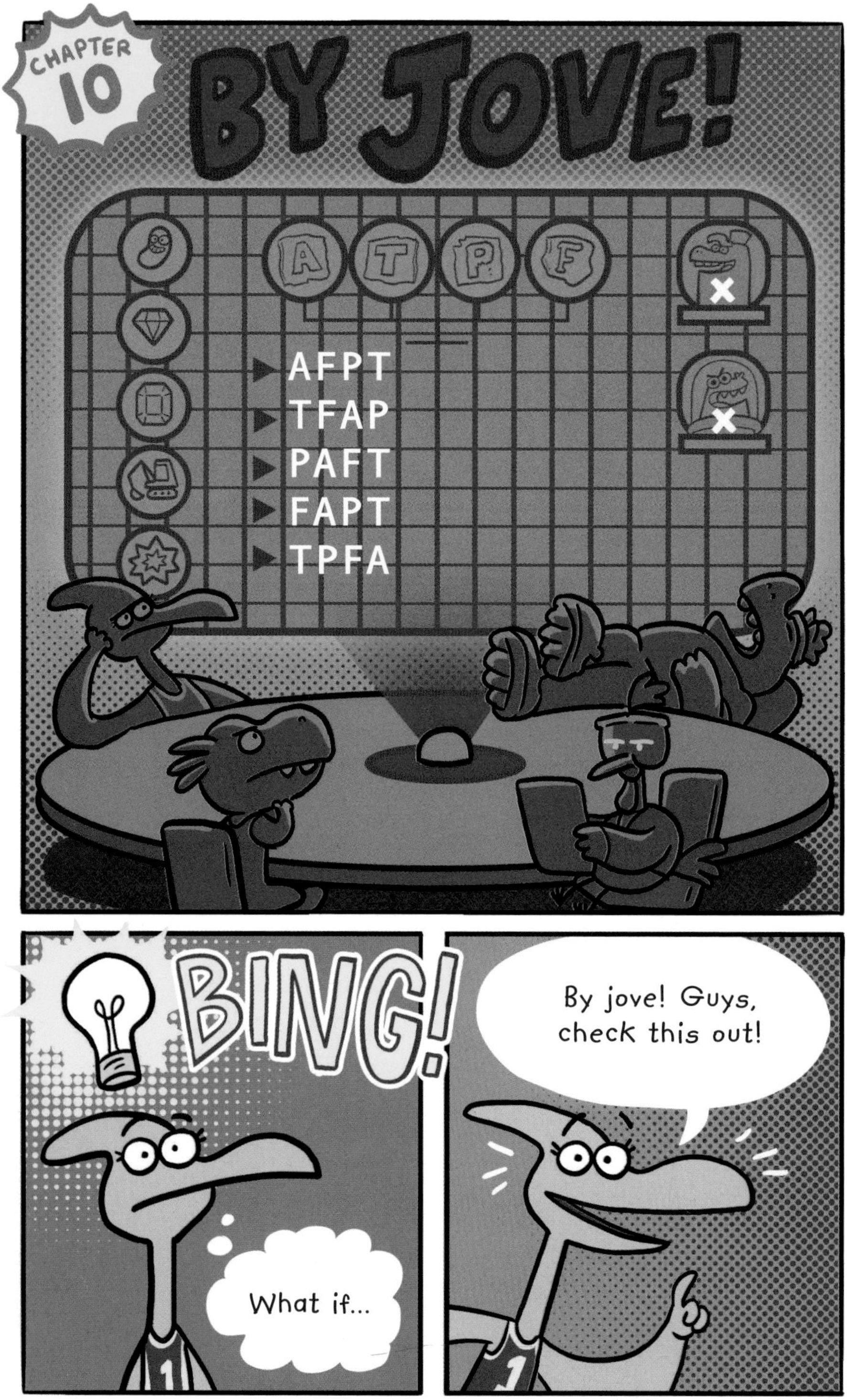
CHAPTER 10
BY JOVE!
A
T
P
F
AFPT
TFAP
PAFT
FAPT
TPFA
BING!
What if...
By jove! Guys, check this out!

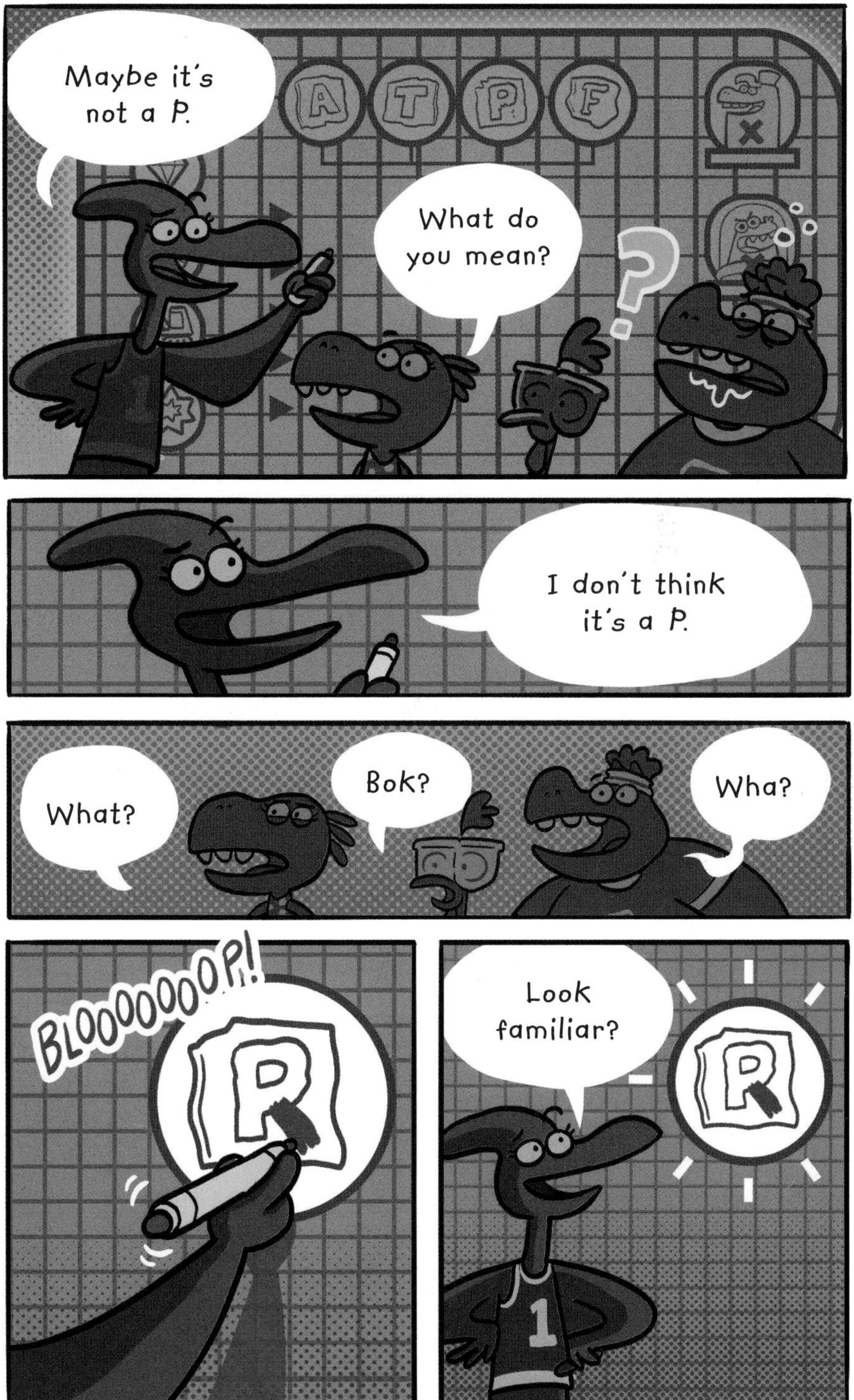
Maybe it's not a P.
What do you mean?
I don't think it's a P.
What?
Bok?
Wha?
BLOOOOOOOP!
Look familiar?

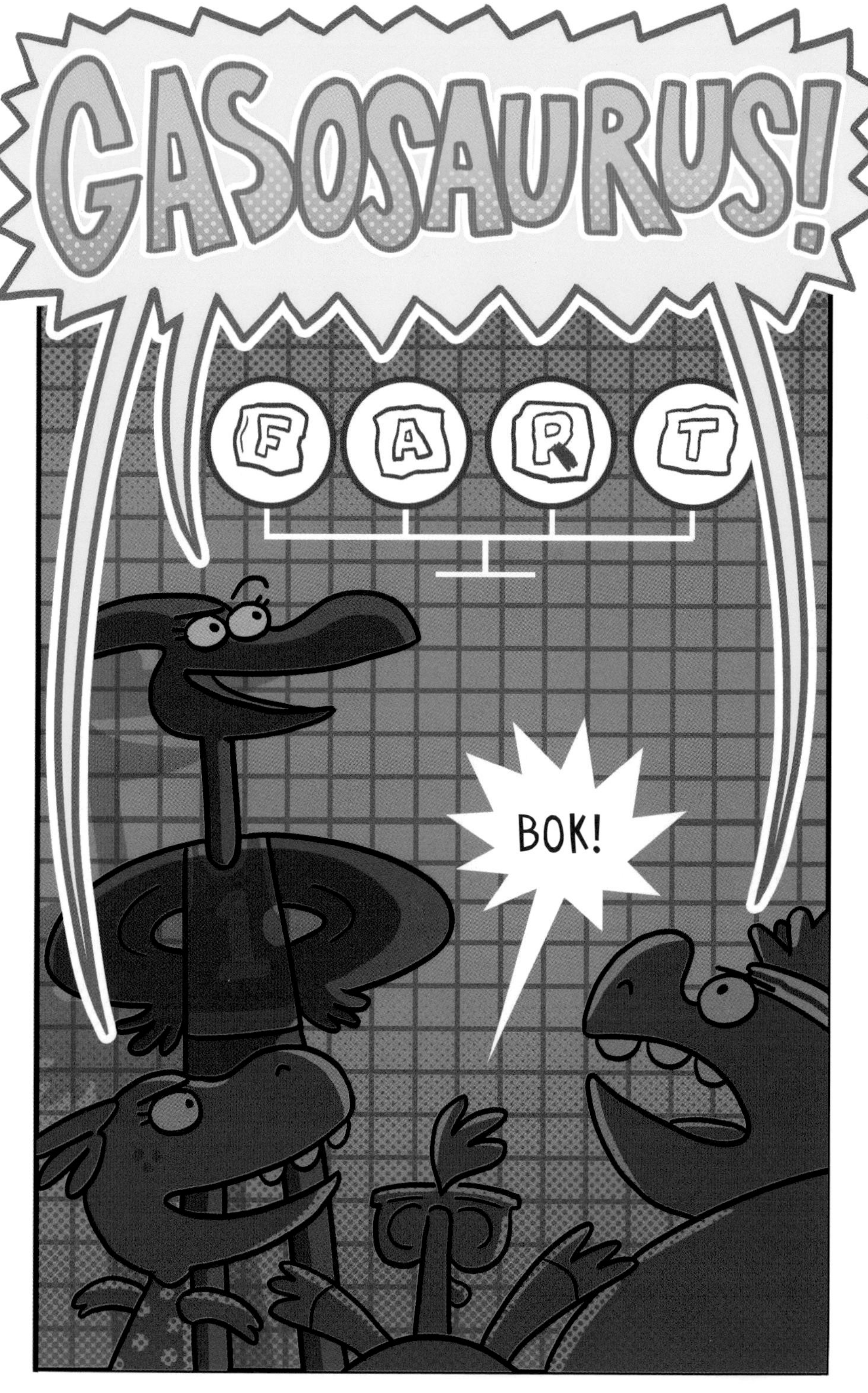
GASOSAURUS!
F A R T
BOK!

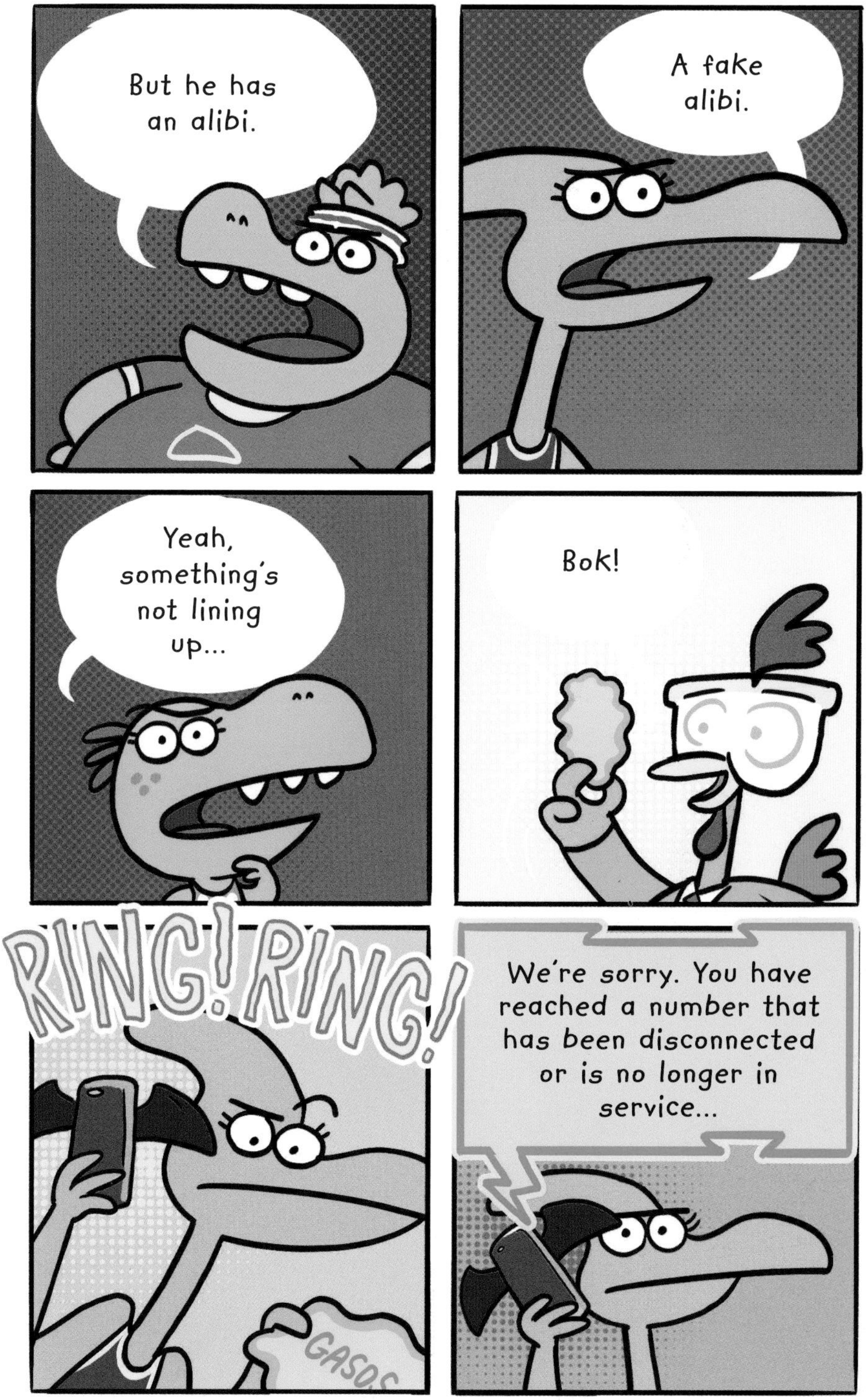
But he has an alibi.
A fake alibi.
Yeah, something's not lining up...
Bok!
RING! RING!
We're sorry. You have reached a number that has been disconnected or is no longer in service...

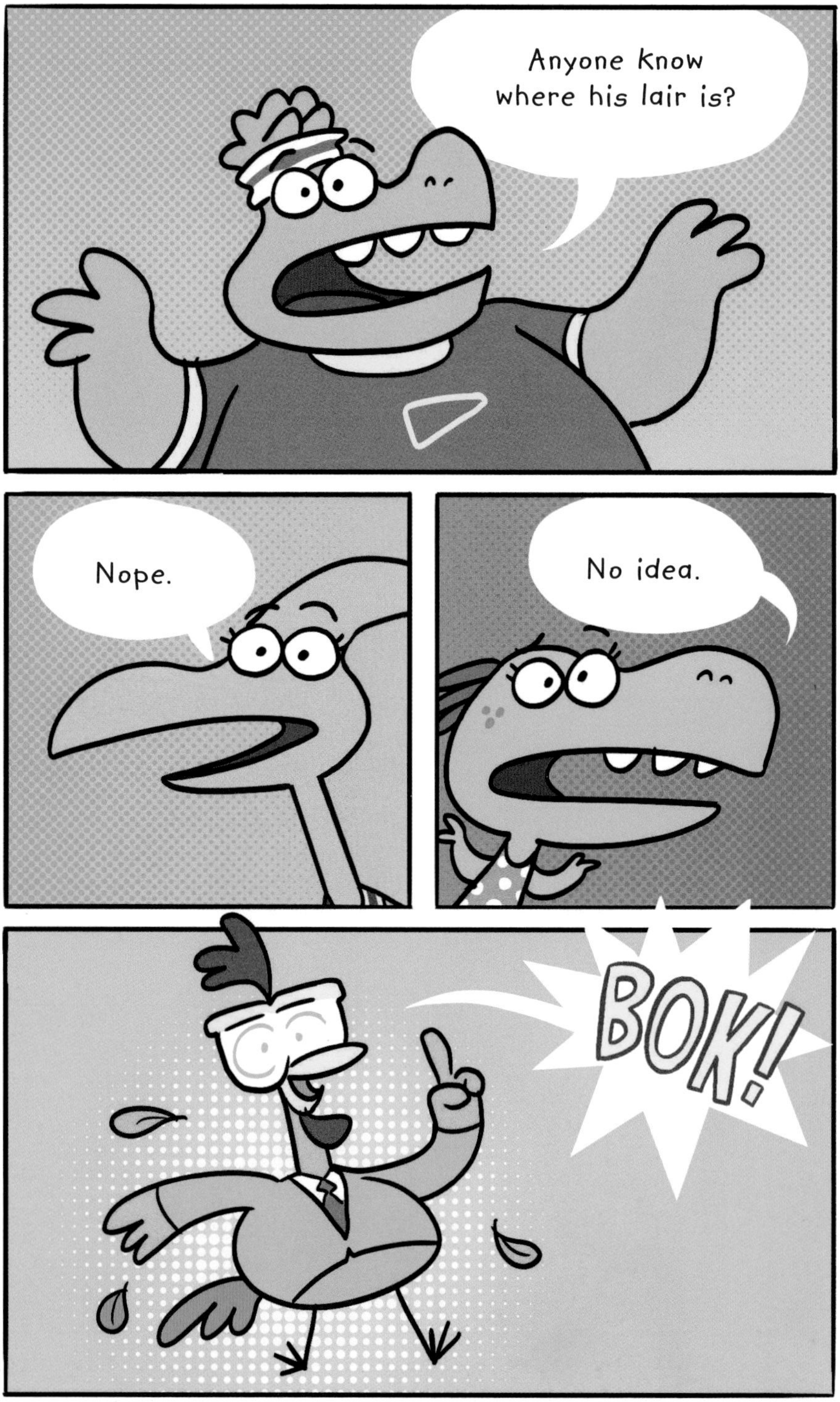
Anyone know where his lair is?
Nope.
No idea.
BOK!

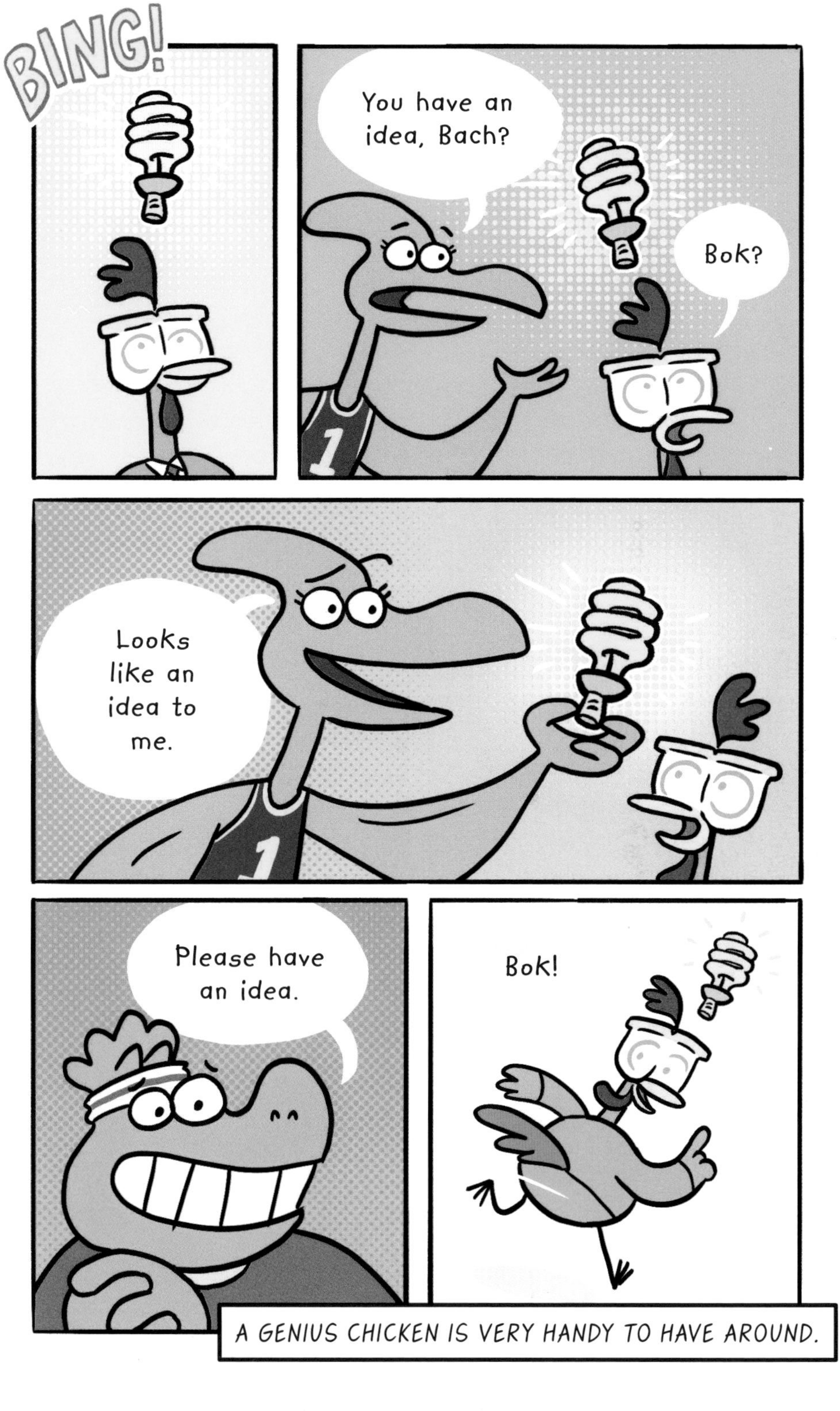
BING!
You have an idea, Bach?
Bok?
Looks like an idea to me.
Please have an idea.
Bok!
A GENIUS CHICKEN IS VERY HANDY TO HAVE AROUND.

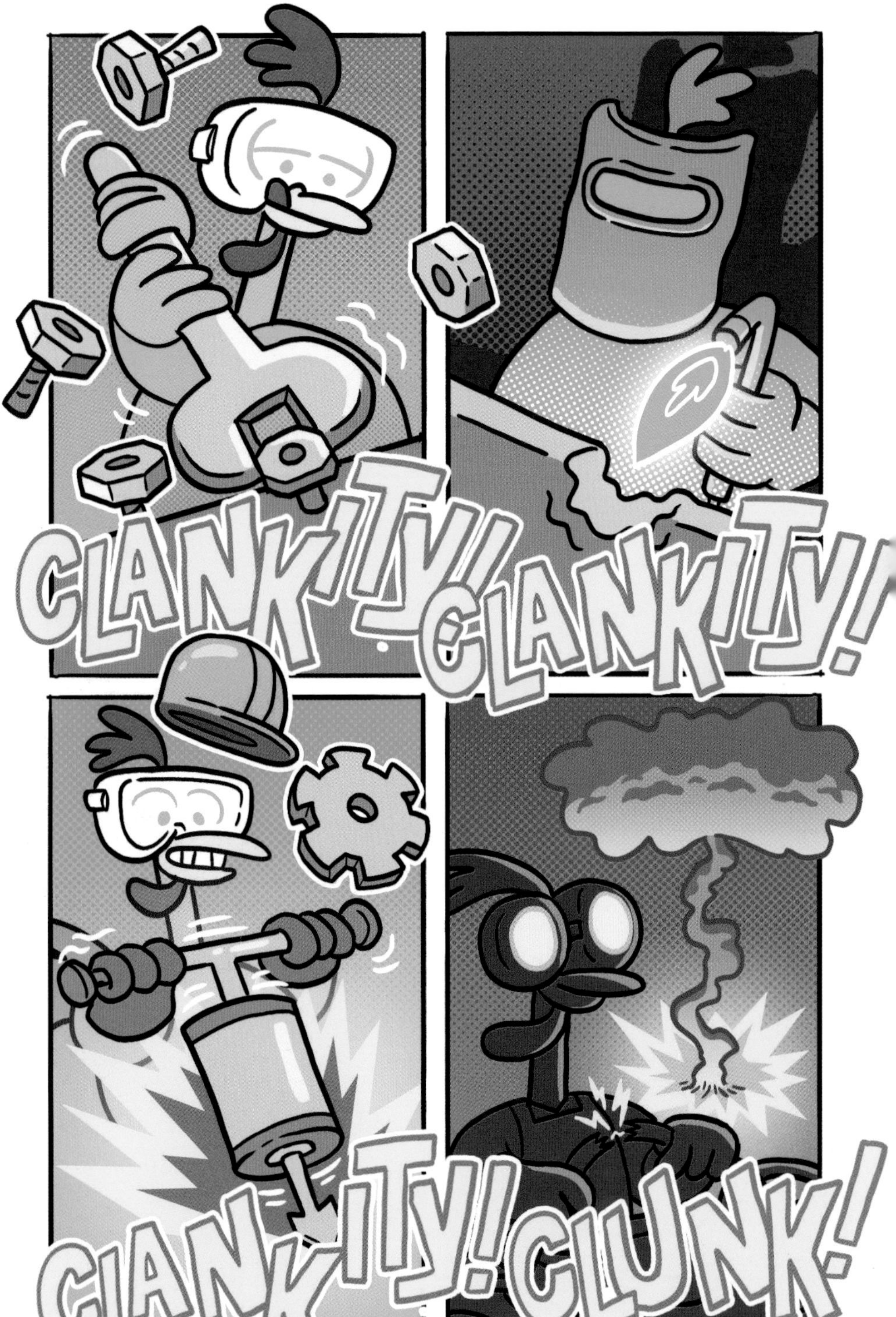
CLANKITY!
CLANKITY!
CLANKITY!
CLUNK!

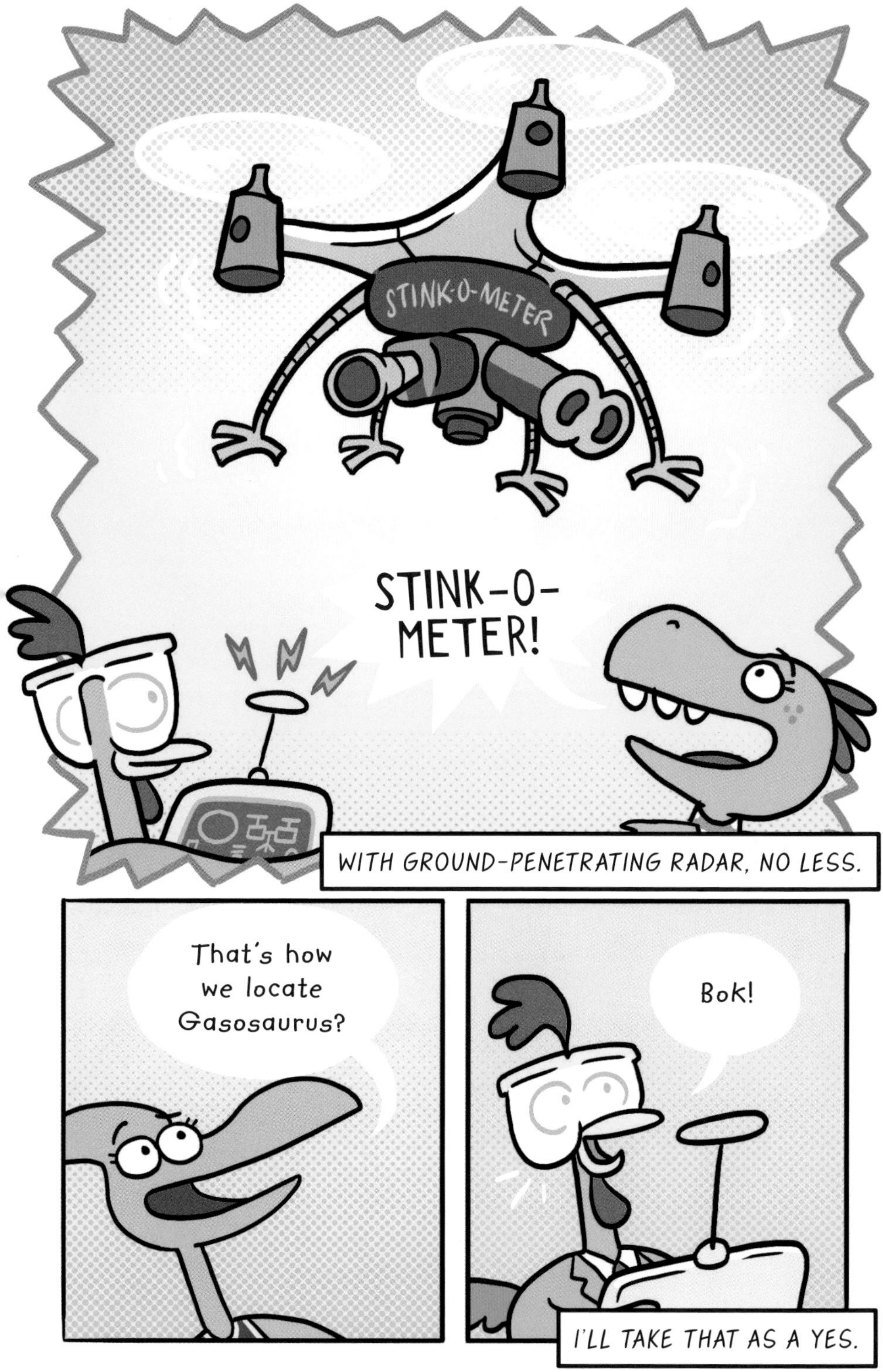

STINK-O-METER
STINK-O-METER!
WITH GROUND-PENETRATING RADAR, NO LESS.
That's how we locate Gasosaurus?
Bok!
I'LL TAKE THAT AS A YES.

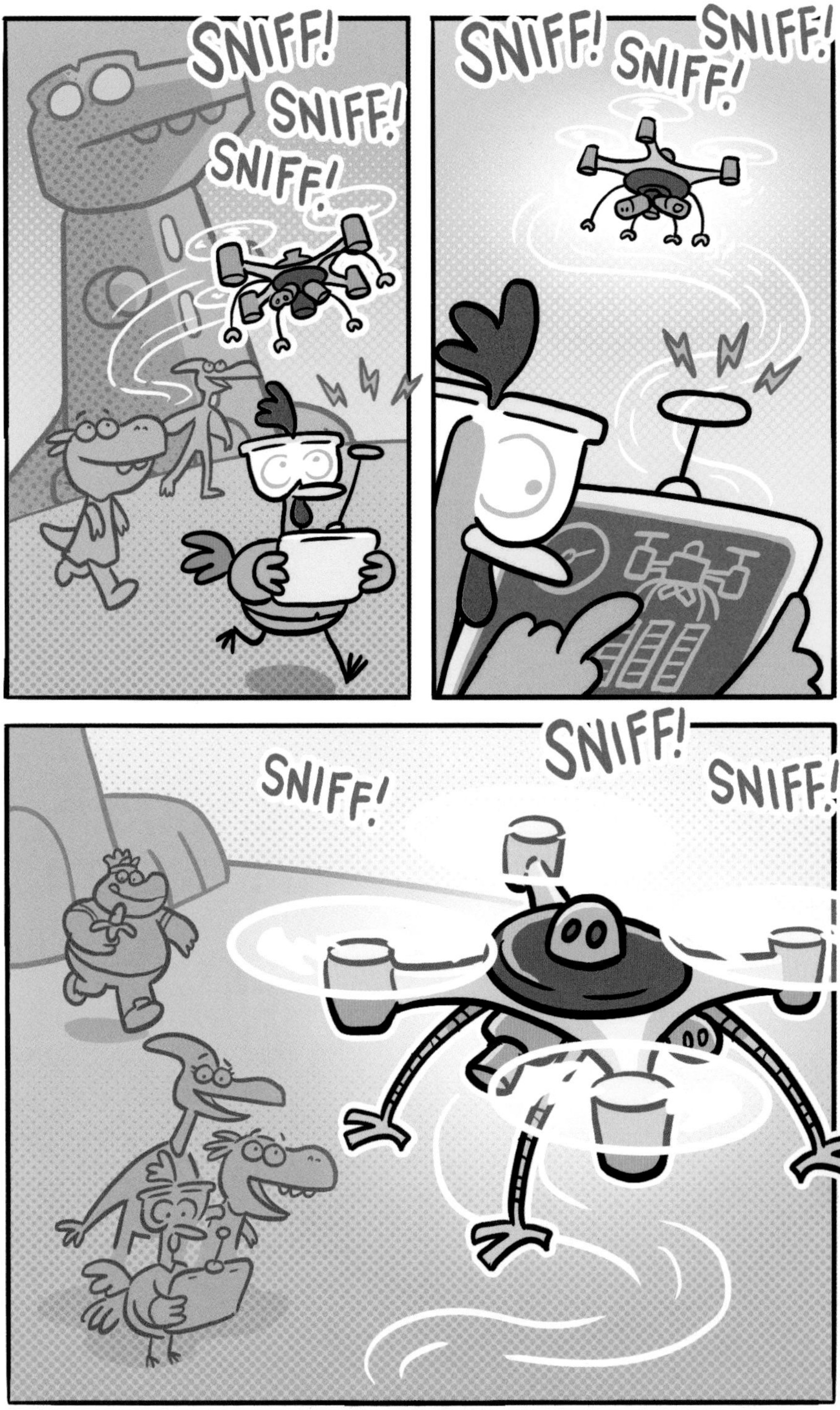
SNIFF!
SNIFF!
SNIFF!
SNIFF!
SNIFF!
SNIFF!
SNIFF!
SNIFF!
SNIFF!

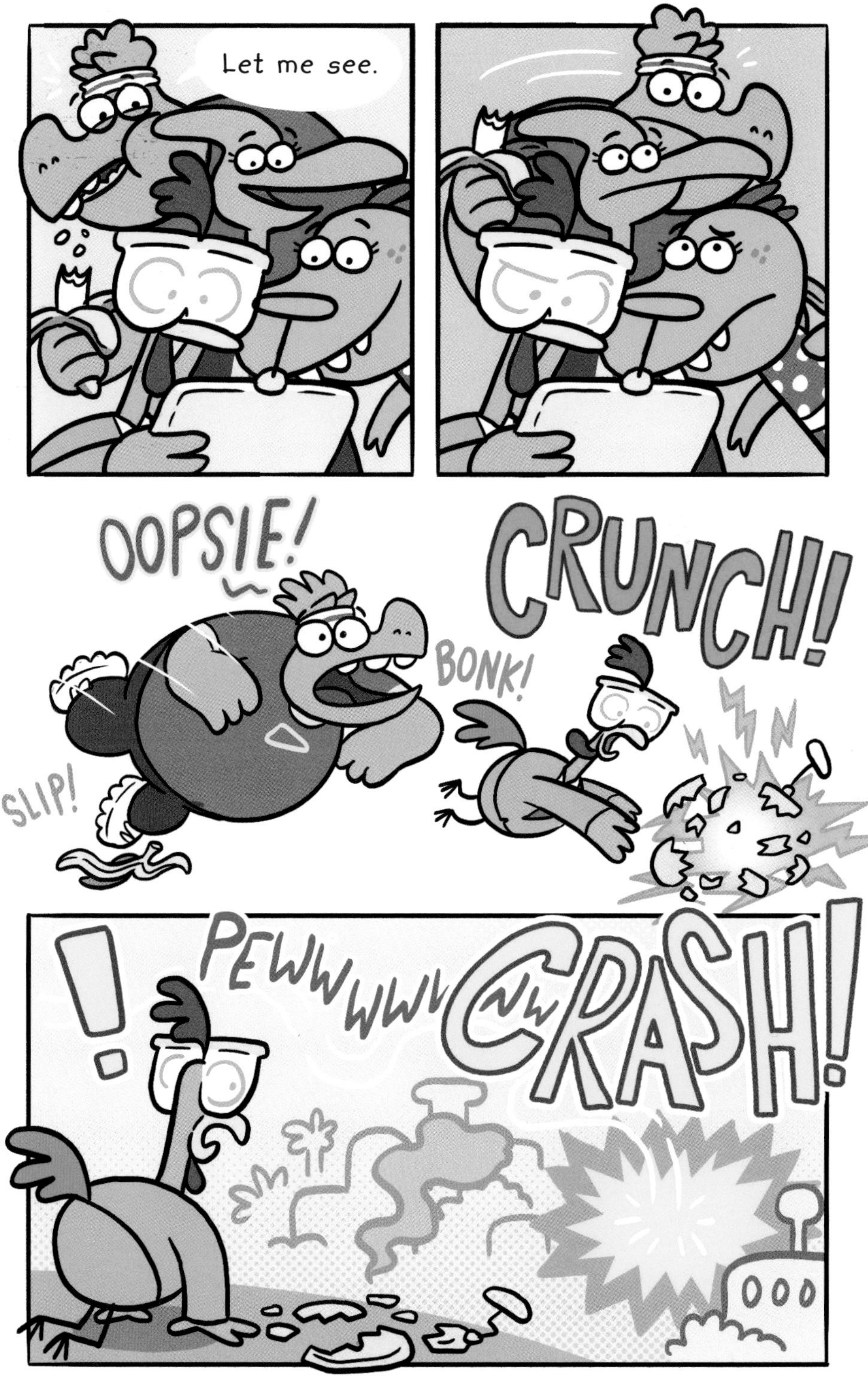
Let me see.
OOPSIE!
SLIP!
BONK!
CRUNCH!
!
PEWWWWWWWWW
CRASH!

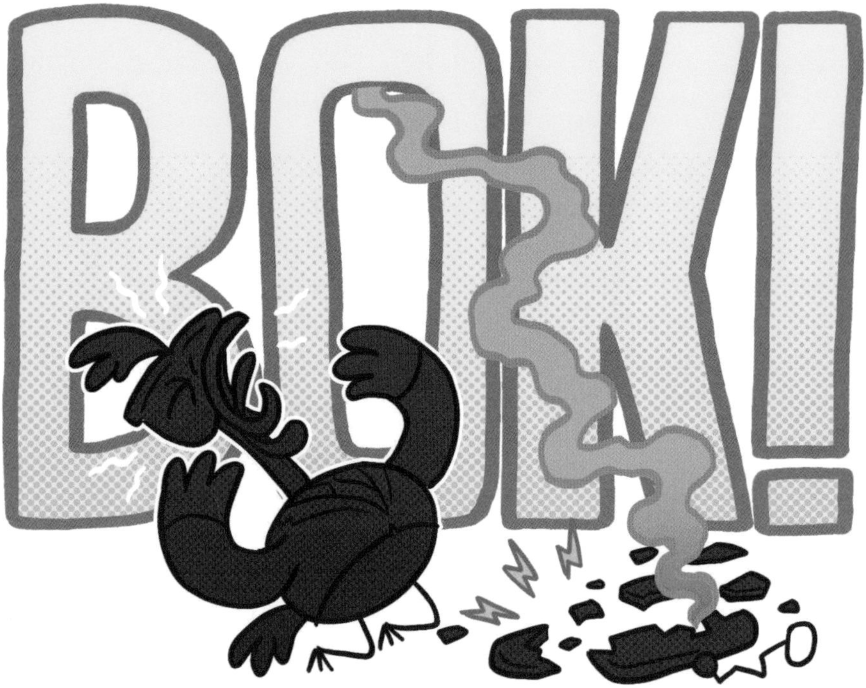
BOK!

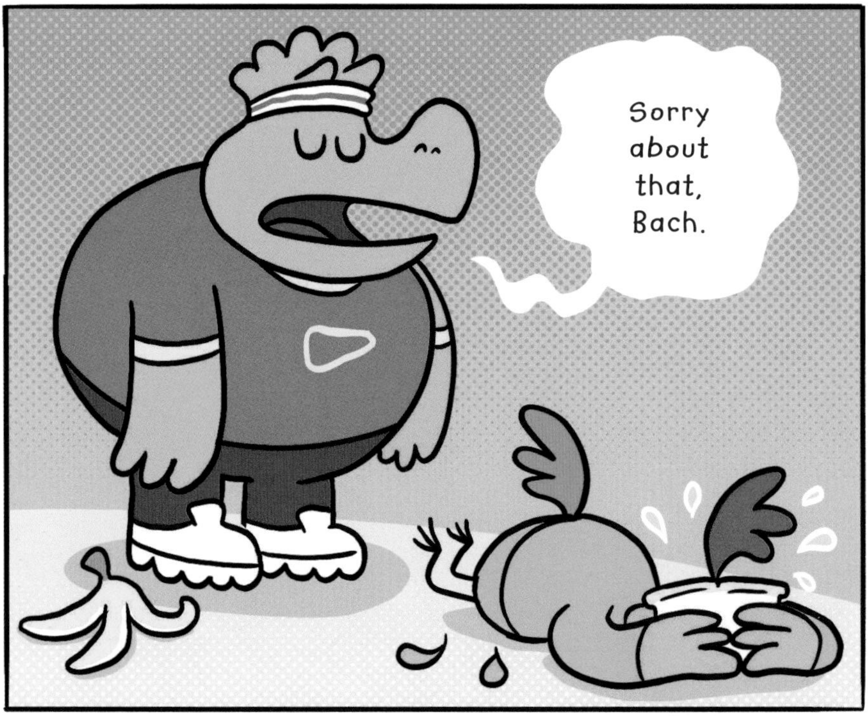
Sorry about that, Bach.

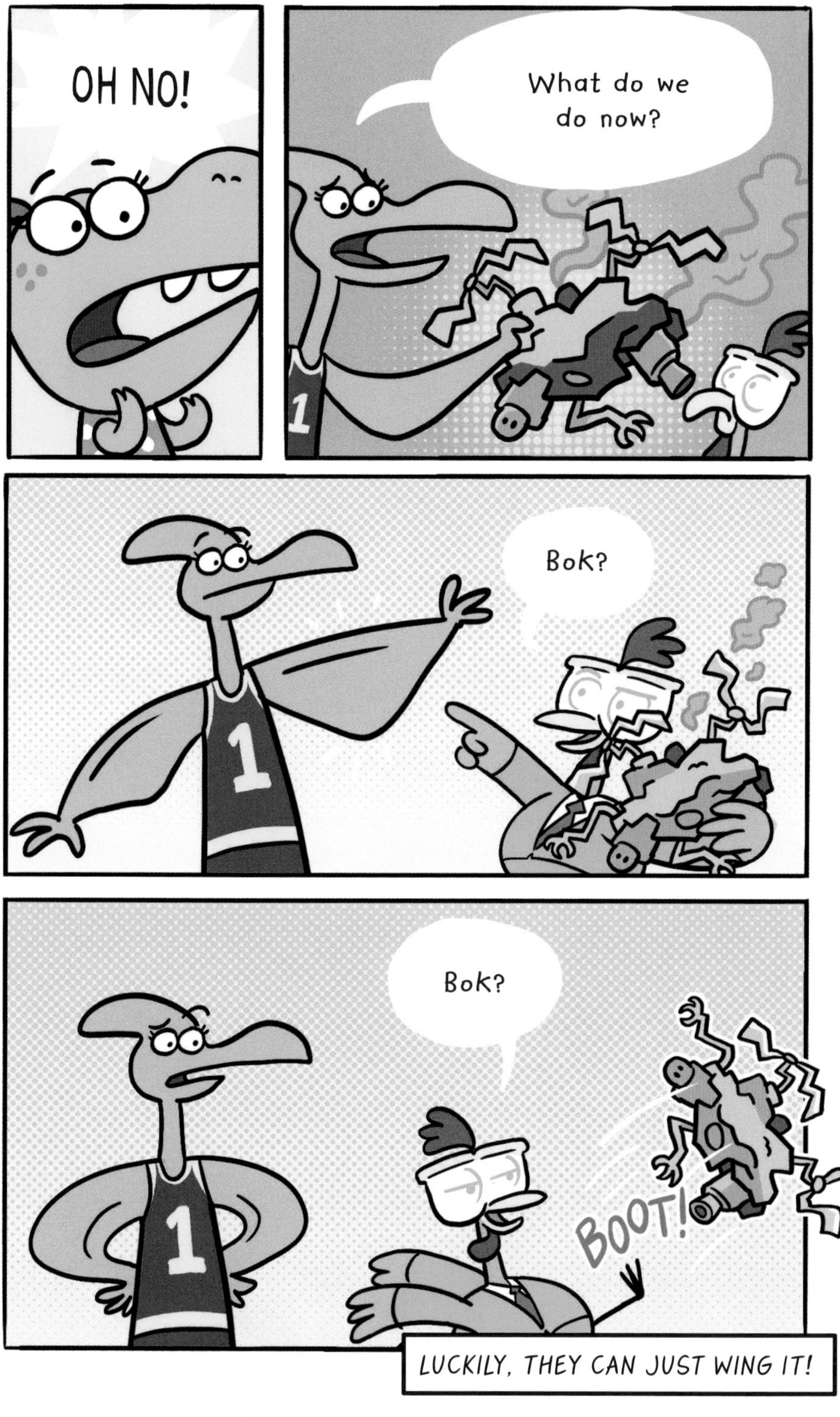
OH NO!
What do we do now?
Bok?
Bok?
BOOT!
LUCKILY, THEY CAN JUST WING IT!

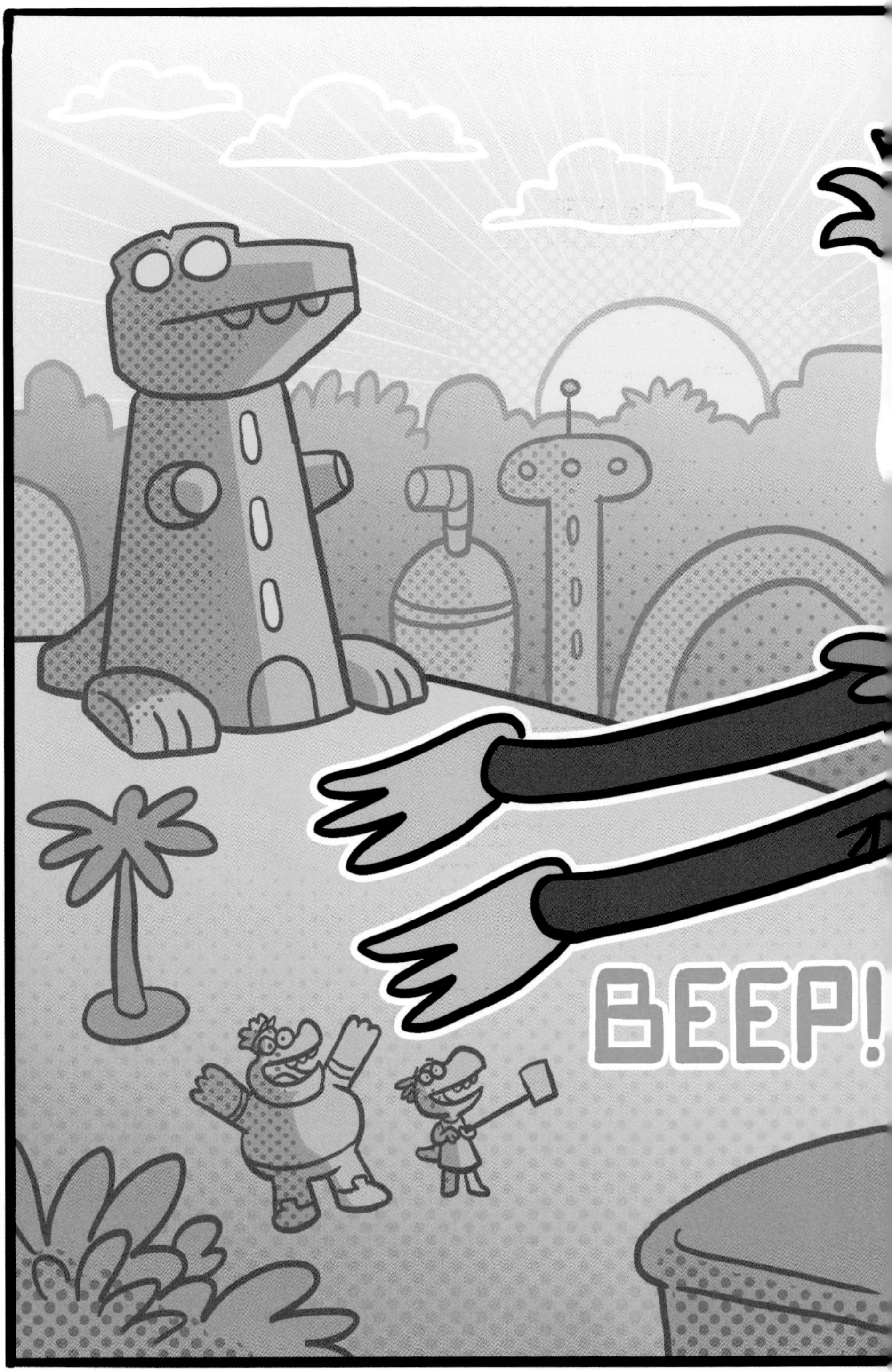
BEEP!

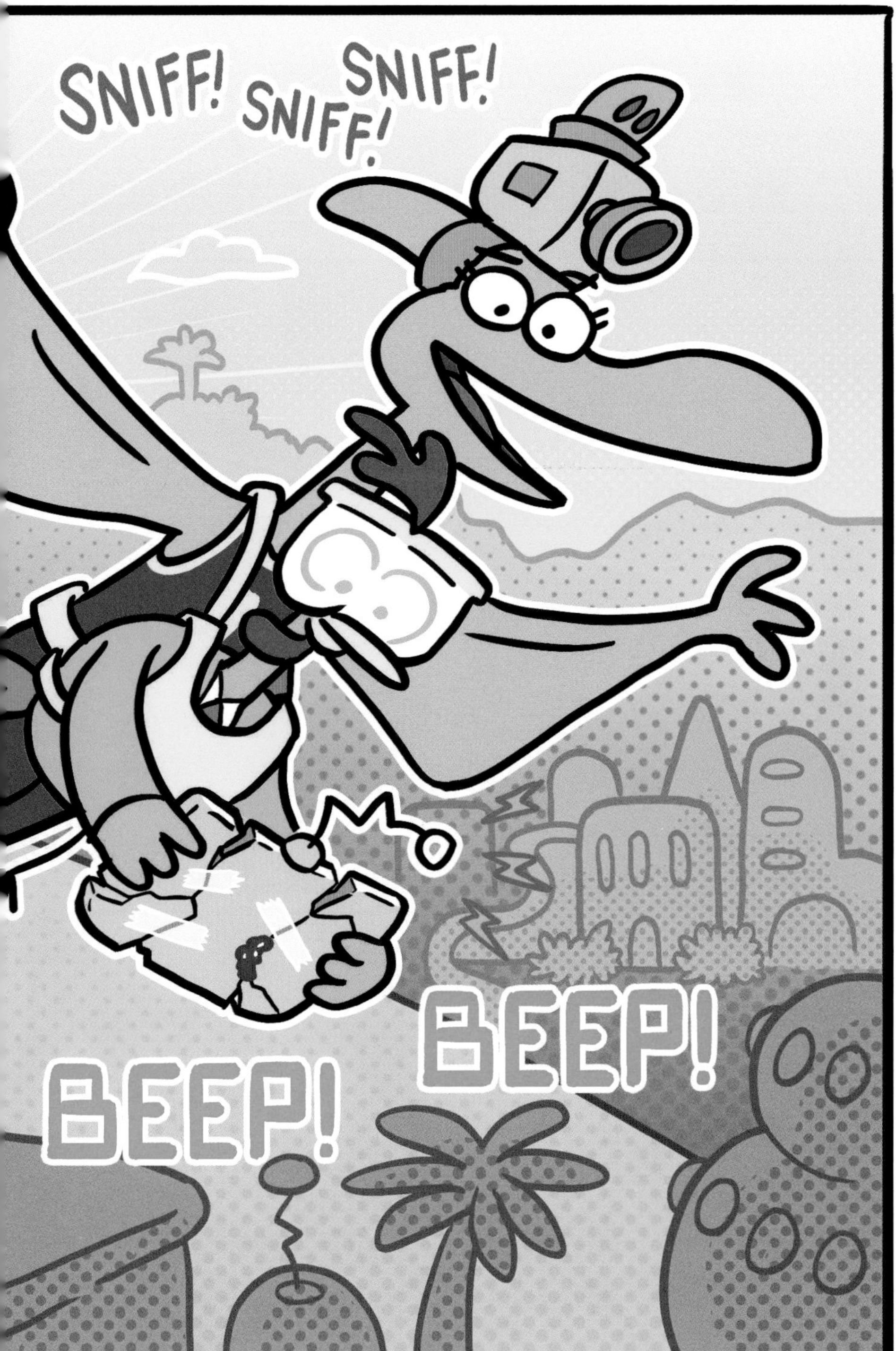
SNIFF! SNIFF! SNIFF!
BEEP! BEEP!

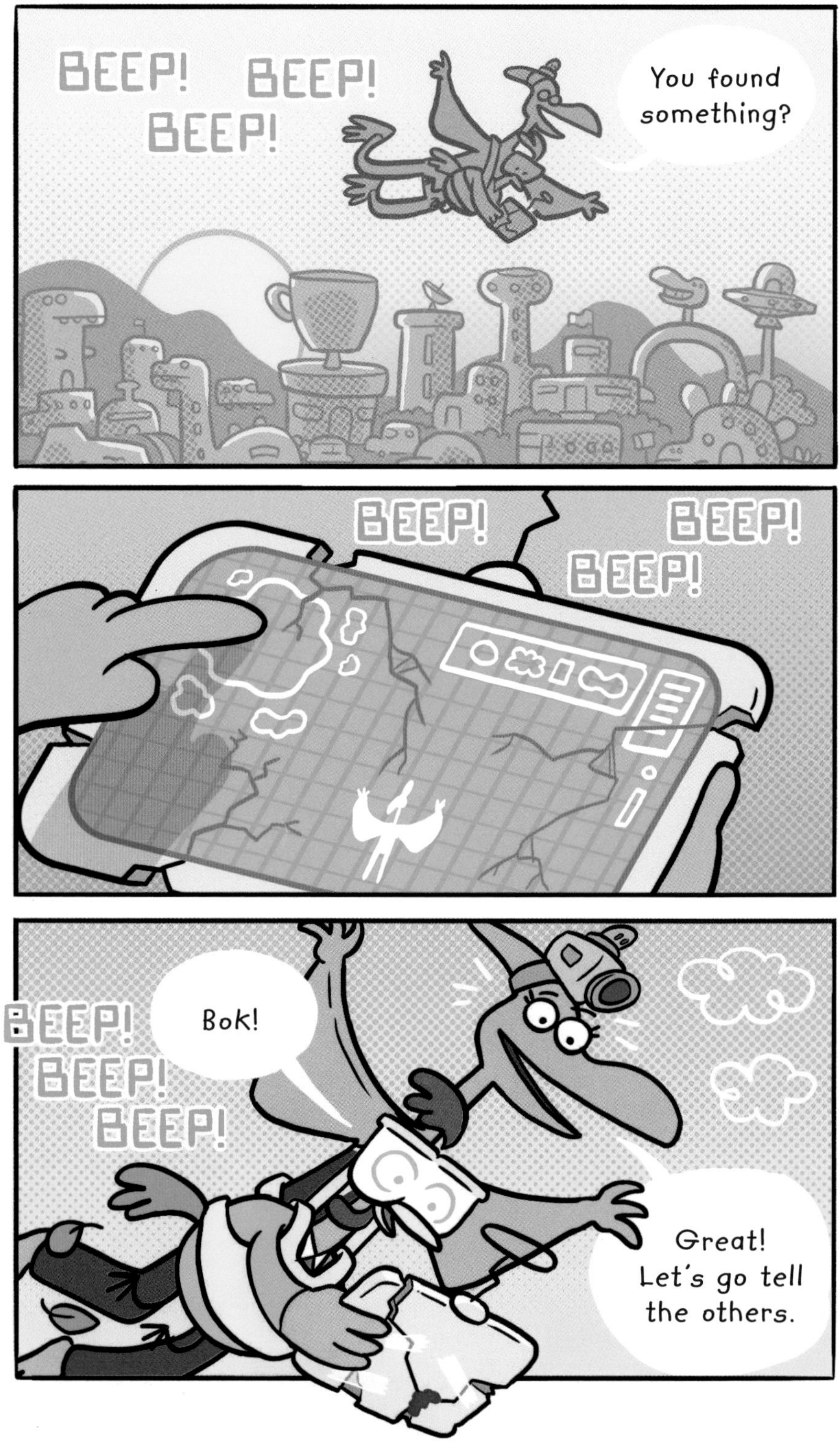
BEEP! BEEP! BEEP!
You found something?
BEEP! BEEP! BEEP!
BEEP! BEEP! BEEP!
Bok!
Great! Let's go tell the others.

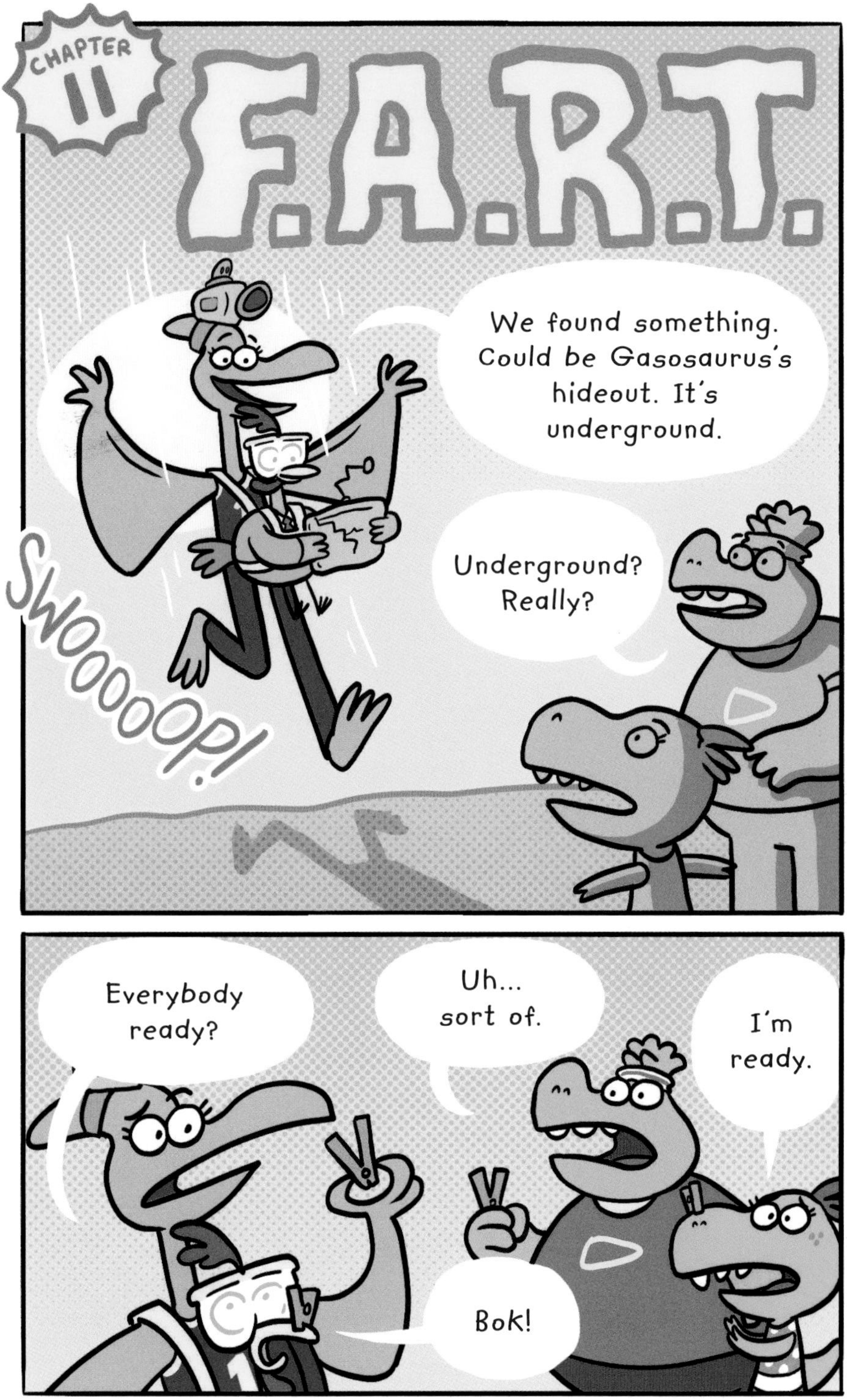
CHAPTER 11
F.A.R.T.
We found something. Could be Gasosaurus's hideout. It's underground.
SWOOOOOOP!
Underground? Really?
Everybody ready?
Uh... sort of.
I'm ready.
Bok!

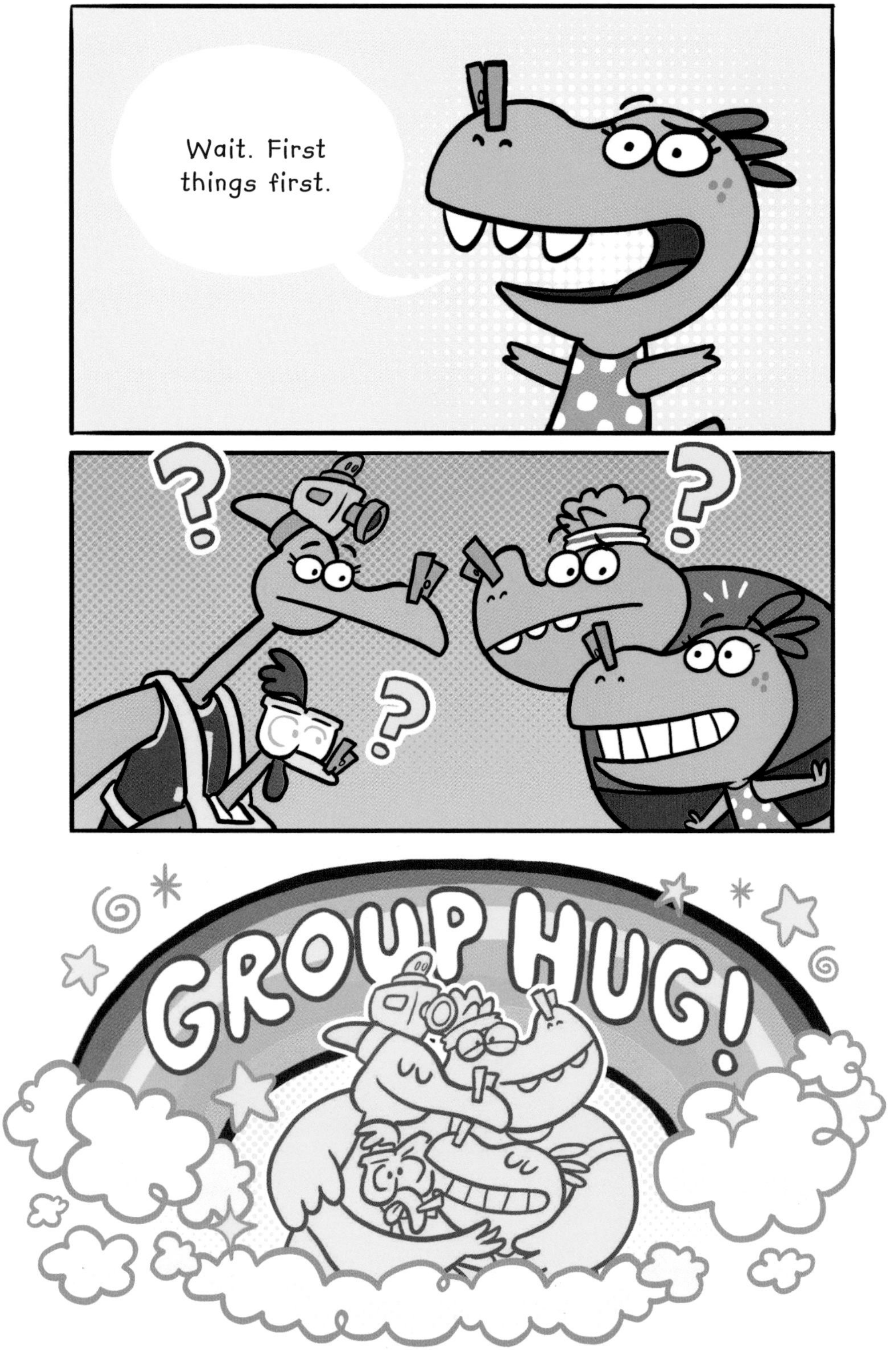
Wait. First things first.
?
?
?
GROUP HUG!

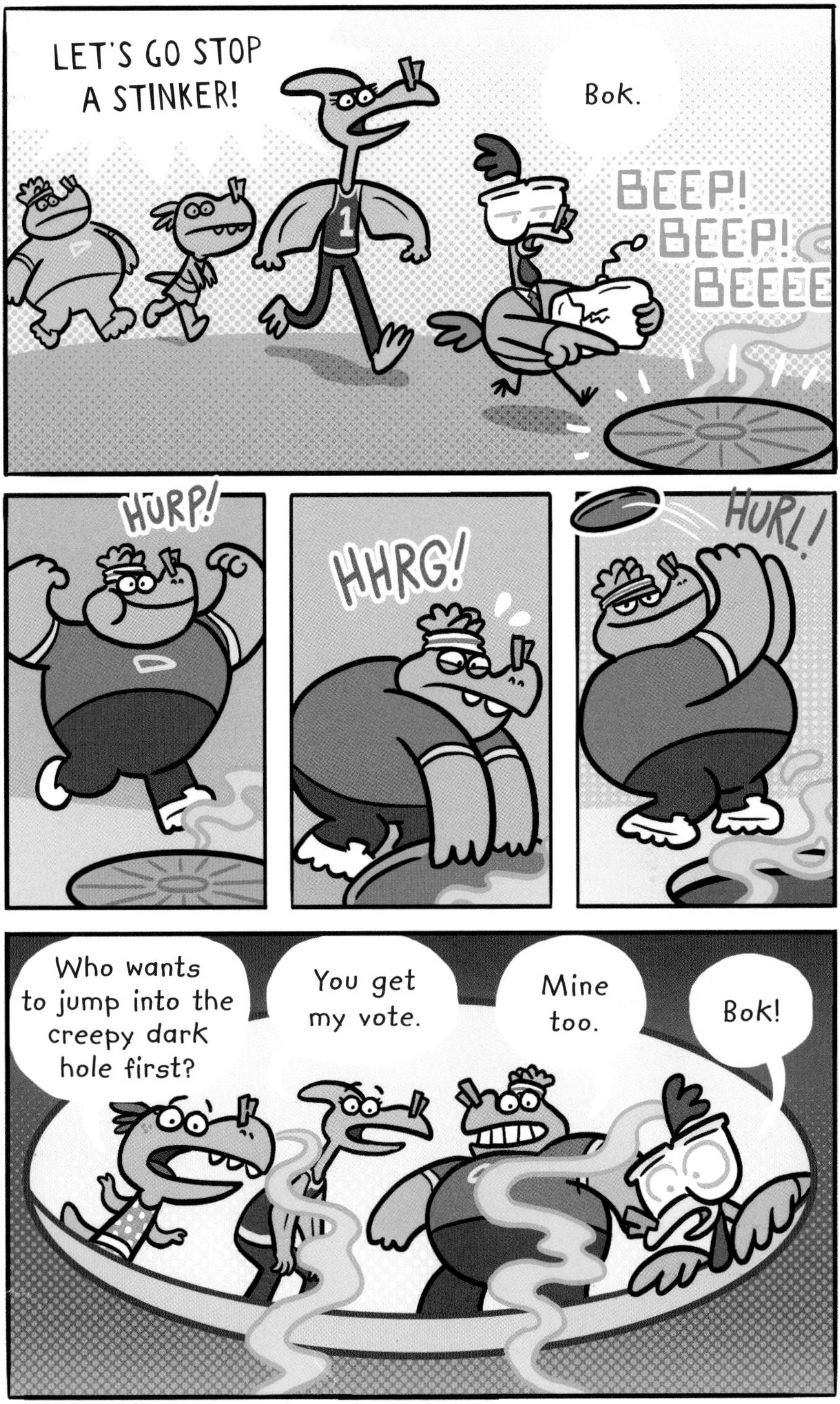
LET'S GO STOP A STINKER!
Bok.
BEEP! BEEP! BEEEE
HURP!
HHRG!
HURL!
Who wants to jump into the creepy dark hole first?
You get my vote.
Mine too.
Bok!

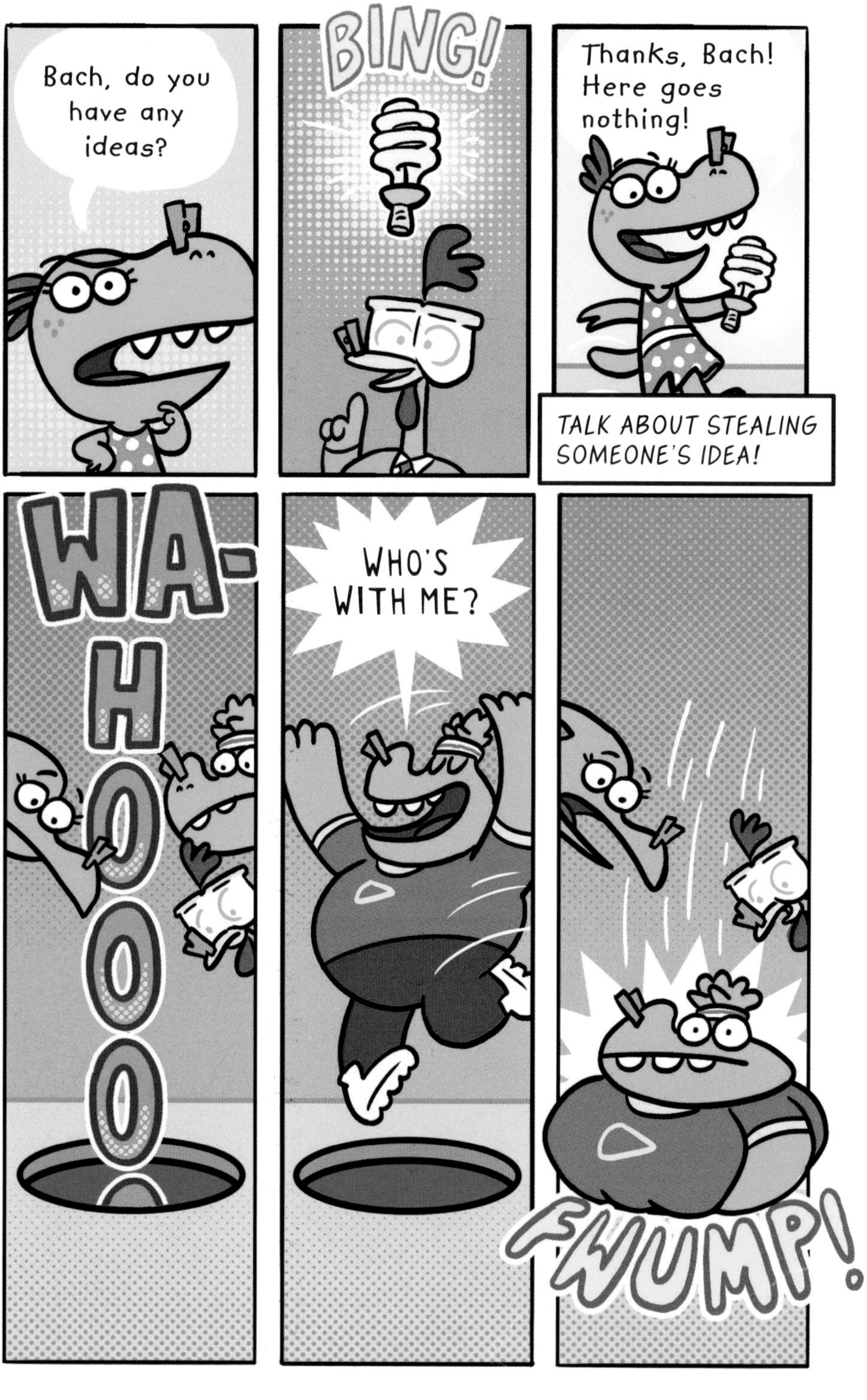
Bach, do you have any ideas?
BING!
Thanks, Bach! Here goes nothing!
TALK ABOUT STEALING SOMEONE'S IDEA!
WA-HOOOO
WHO'S WITH ME?
FWUMP!

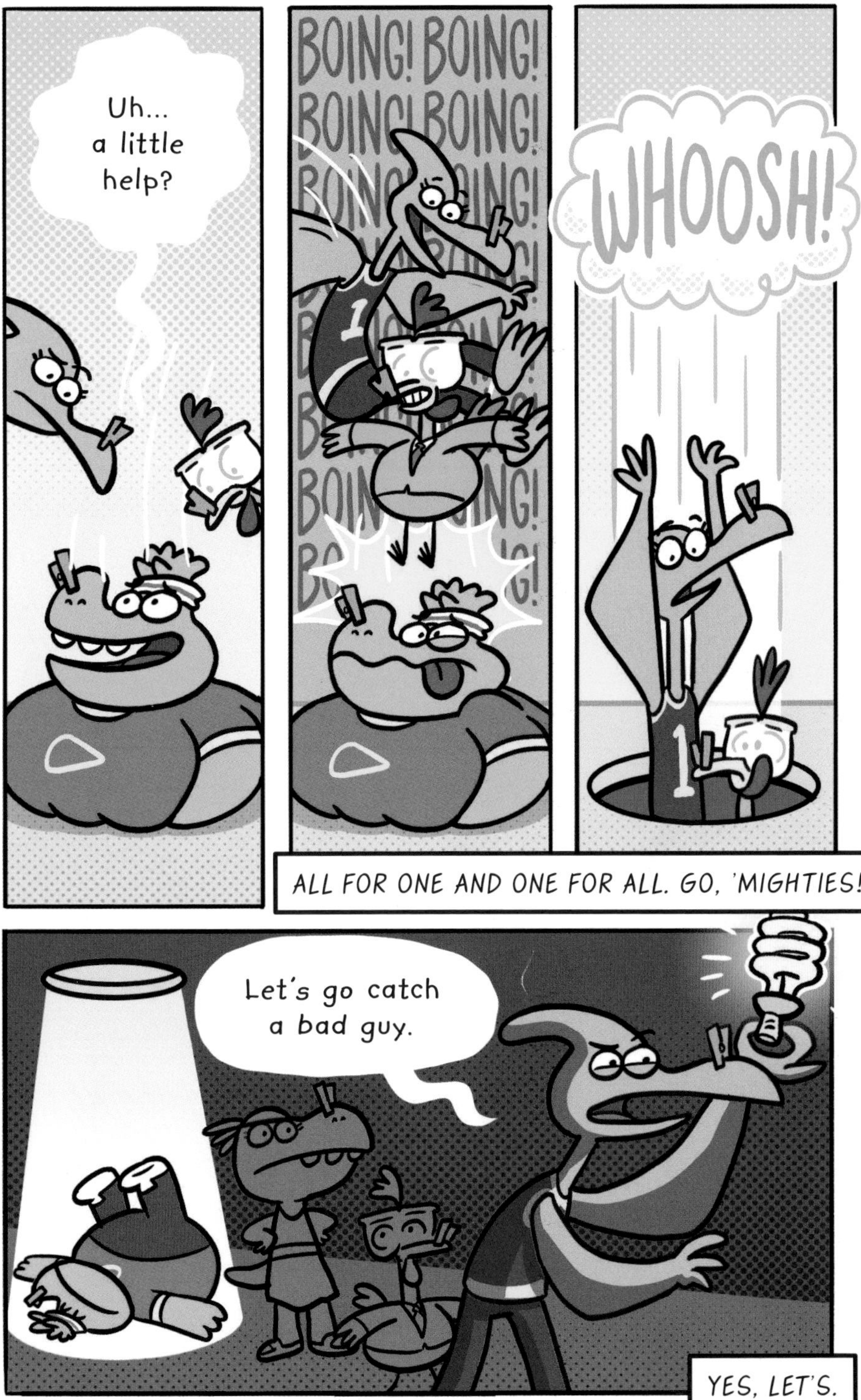
Uh... a little help?
BOING! BOING! BOING! BOING!
WHOOSH!
ALL FOR ONE AND ONE FOR ALL. GO, 'MIGHTIES!
Let's go catch a bad guy.
YES, LET'S.

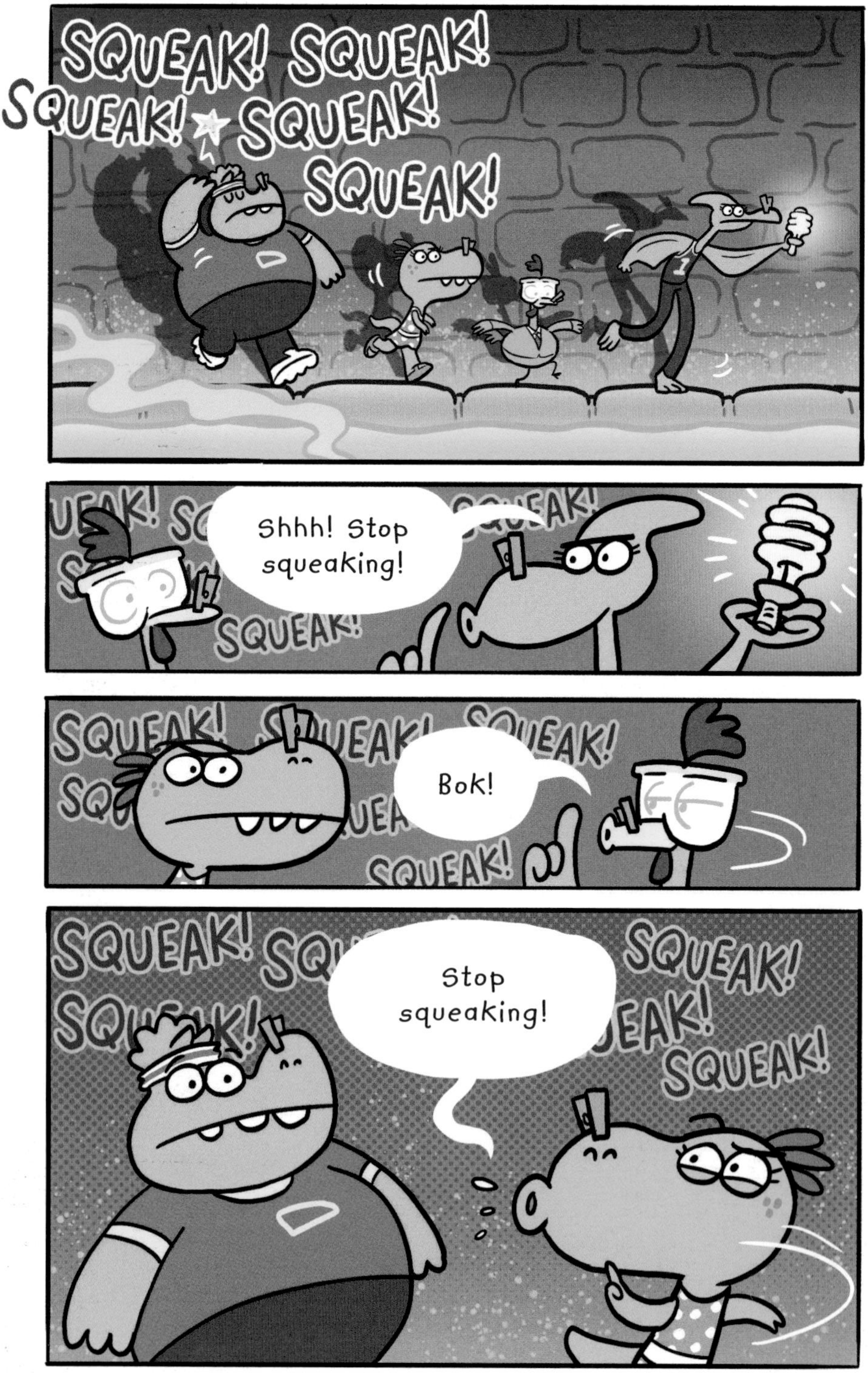
SQUEAK! SQUEAK!
SQUEAK! SQUEAK!
SQUEAK!
Shhh! Stop squeaking!
SQUEAK!
Bok!
SQUEAK!
SQUEAK!
Stop squeaking!
SQUEAK!
SQUEAK!

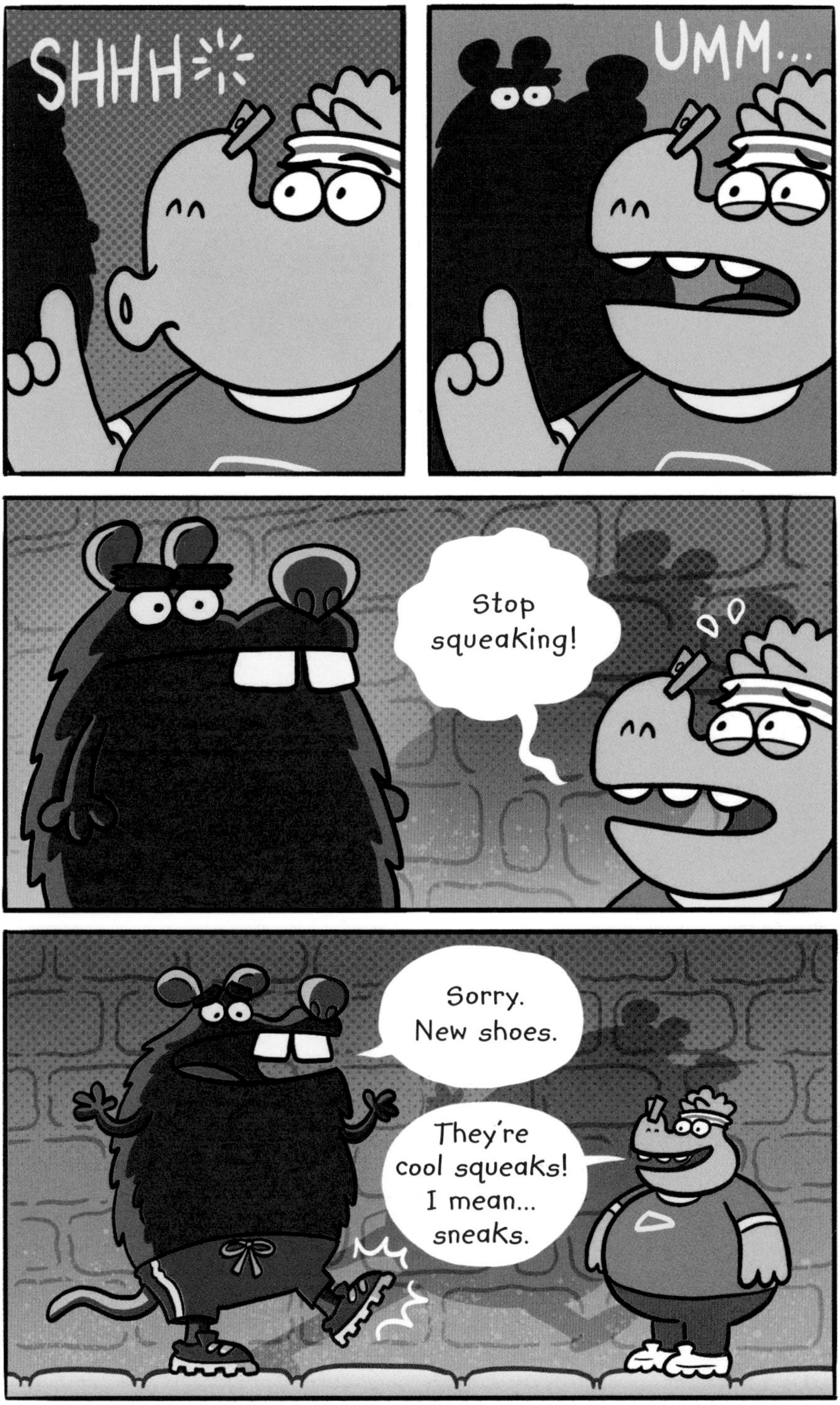
SHHH
UMM...
Stop squeaking!
Sorry. New shoes.
They're cool squeaks! I mean... sneaks.

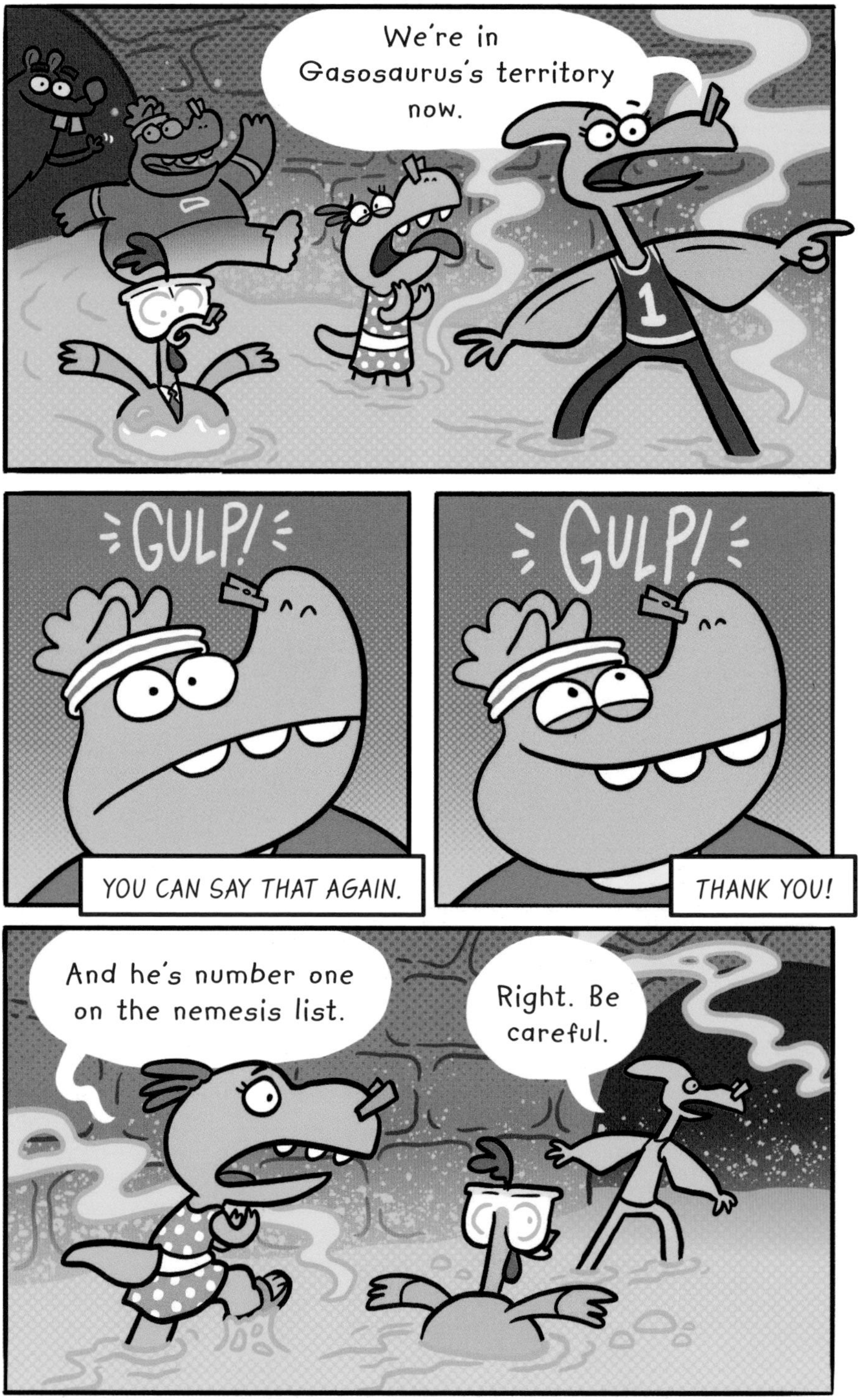
We're in Gasosaurus's territory now.
GULP!
YOU CAN SAY THAT AGAIN.
GULP!
THANK YOU!
And he's number one on the nemesis list.
Right. Be careful.

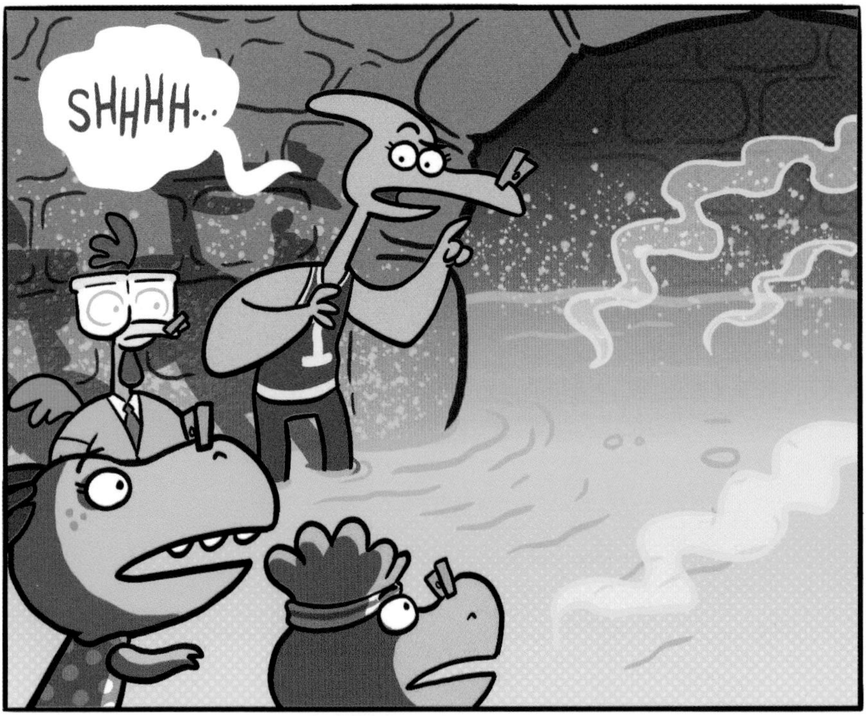
SHHHH...

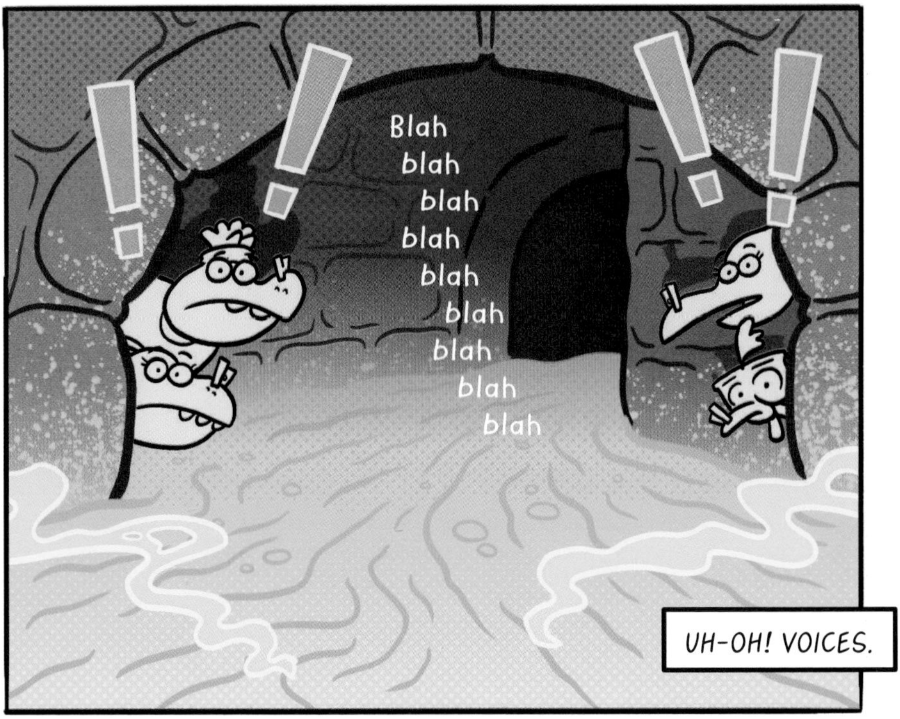
Blah
blah
blah
blah
blah
blah
blah
blah
blah
UH-OH! VOICES.

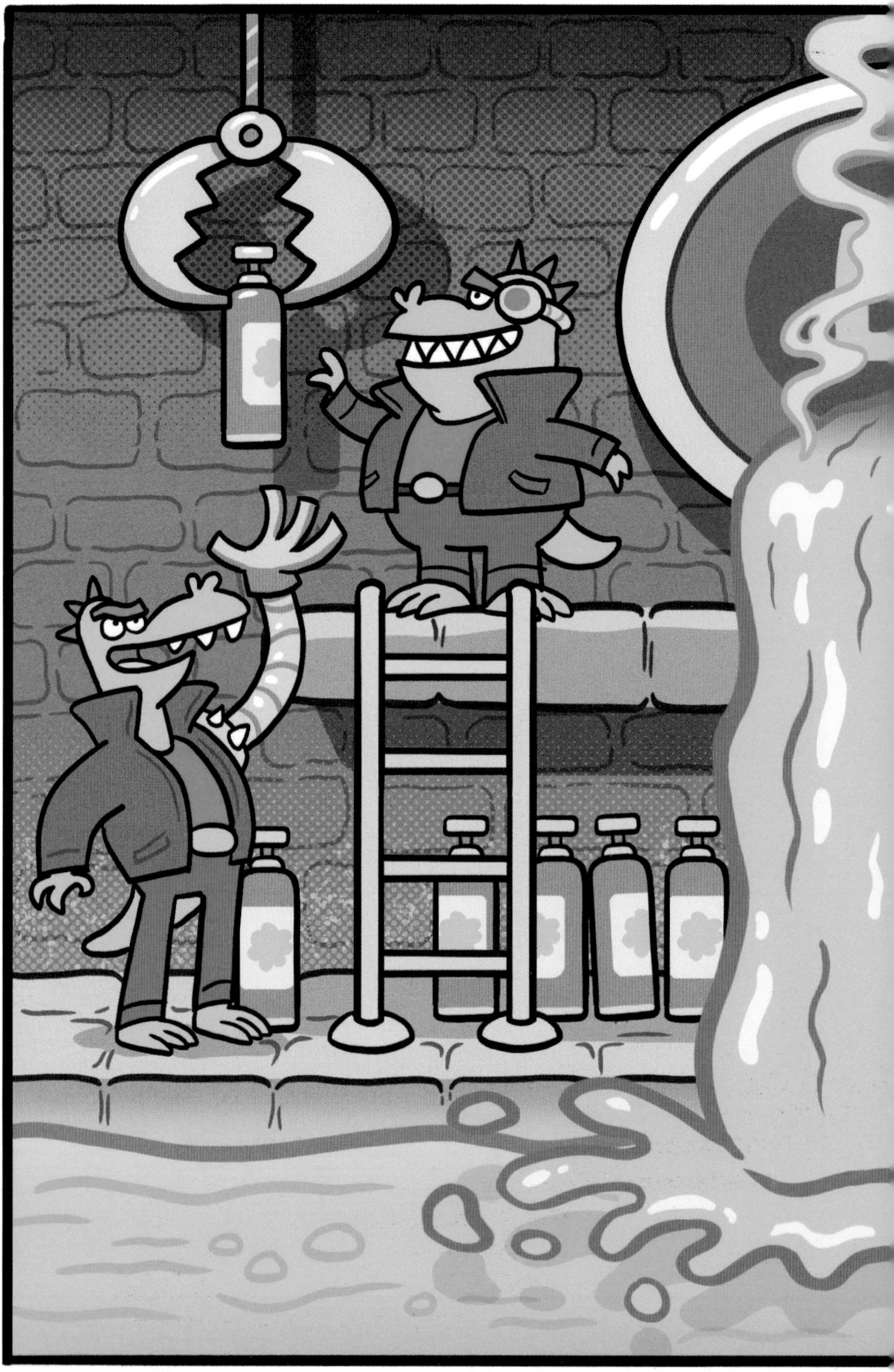

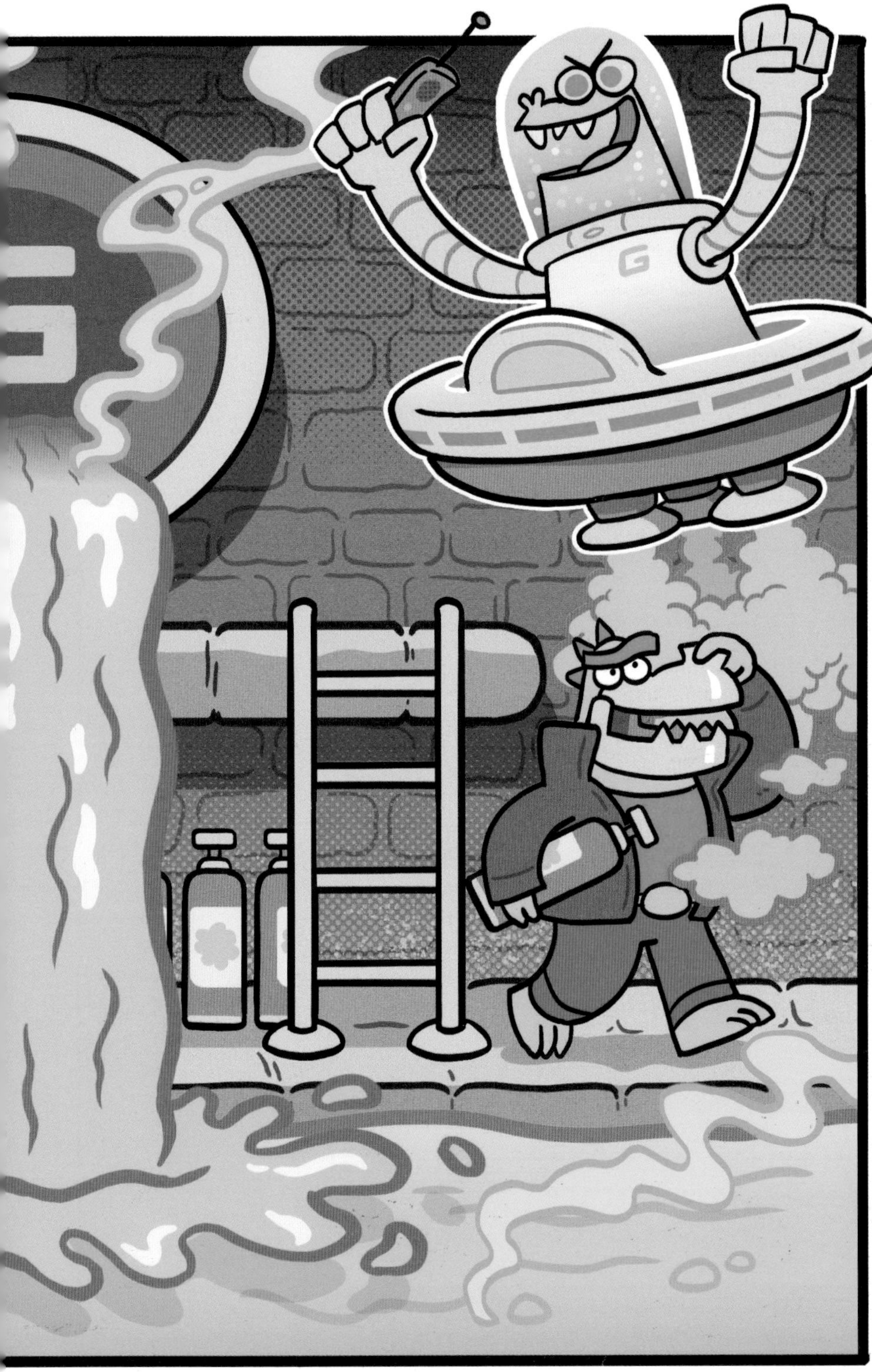
G

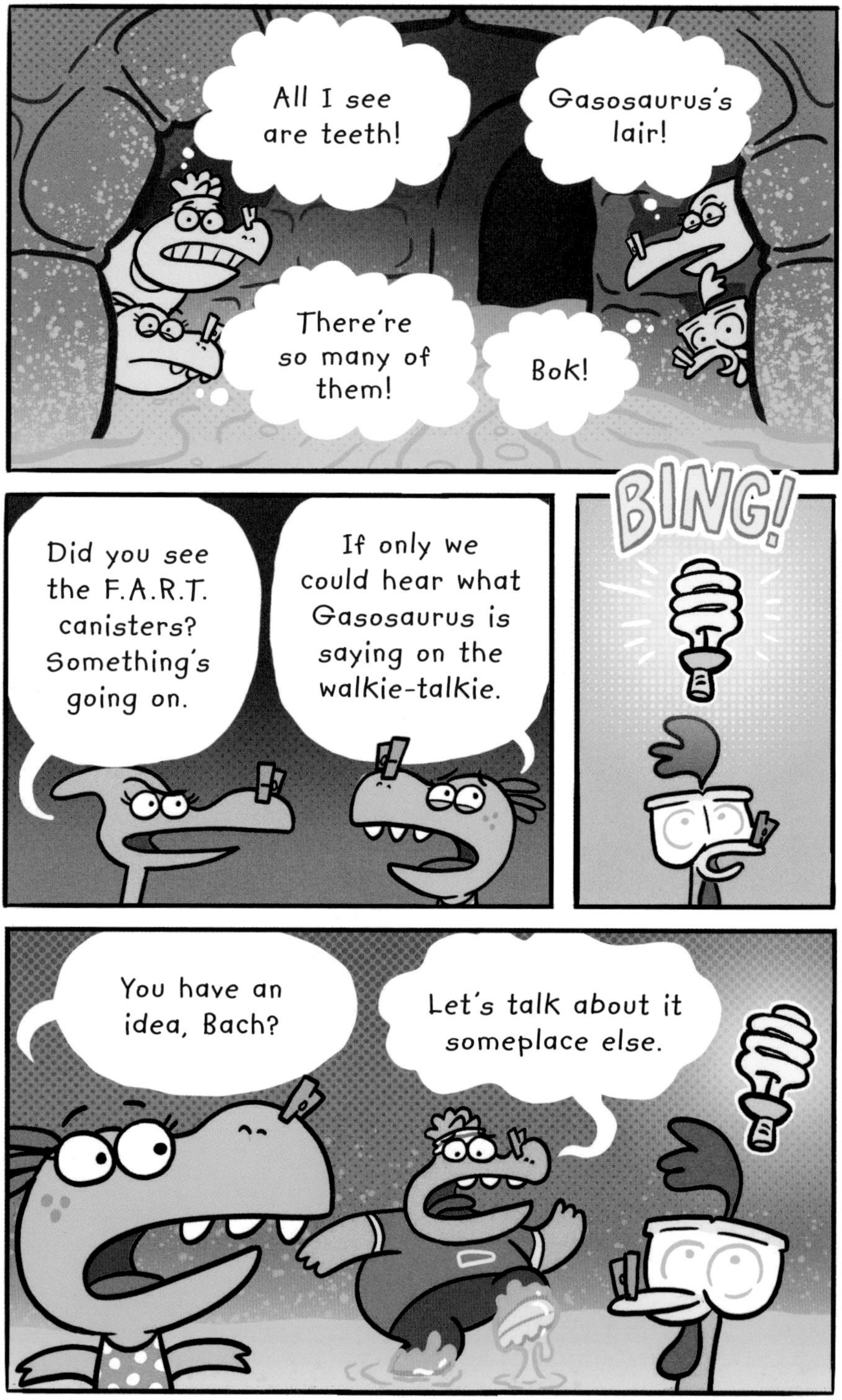
All I see are teeth!
Gasosaurus's lair!
There're so many of them!
Bok!
Did you see the F.A.R.T. canisters? Something's going on.
If only we could hear what Gasosaurus is saying on the walkie-talkie.
BING!
You have an idea, Bach?
Let's talk about it someplace else.

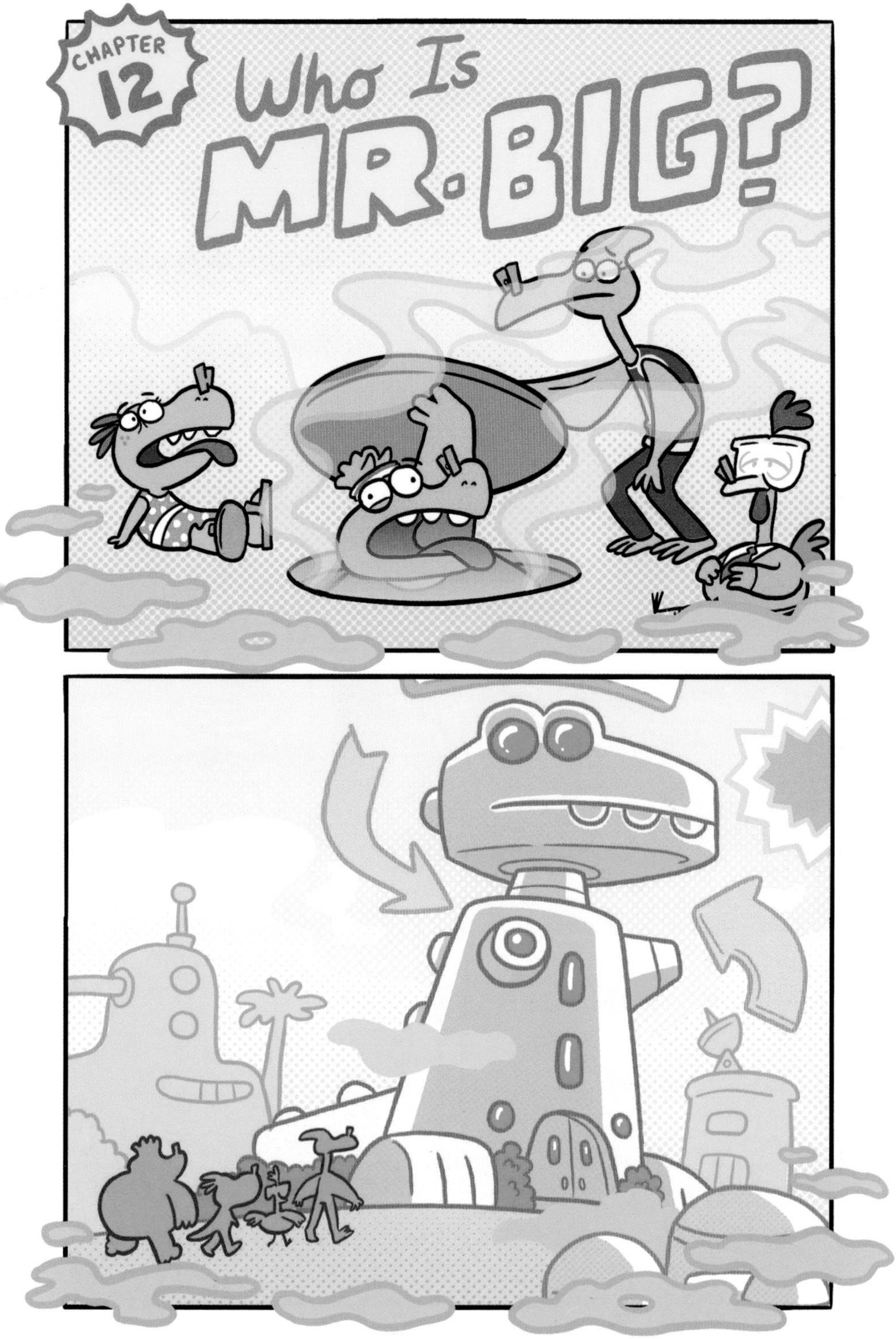
CHAPTER 12
Who Is MR. BIG?

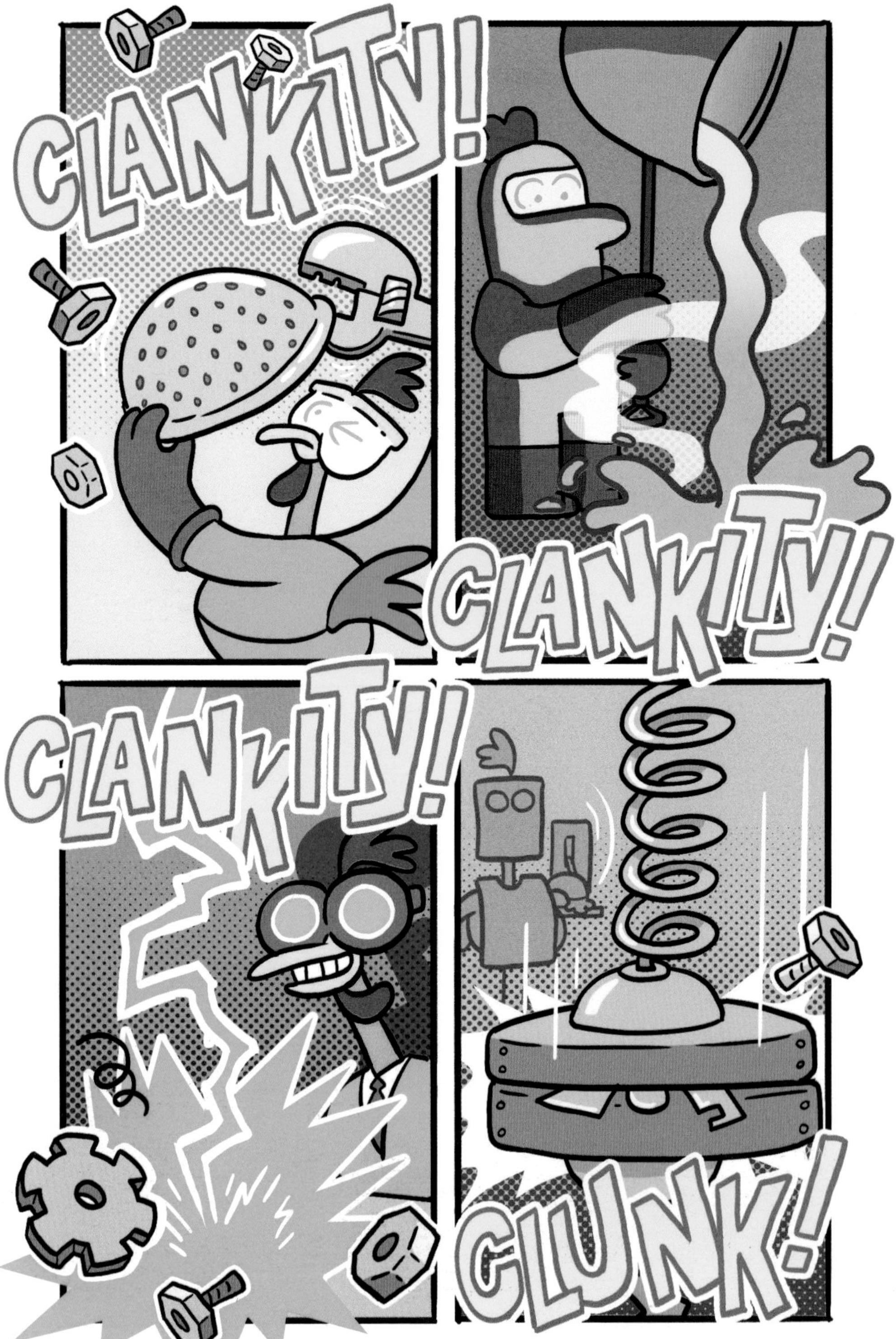
CLANKITY!
CLANKITY!
CLANKITY!
CLUNK!

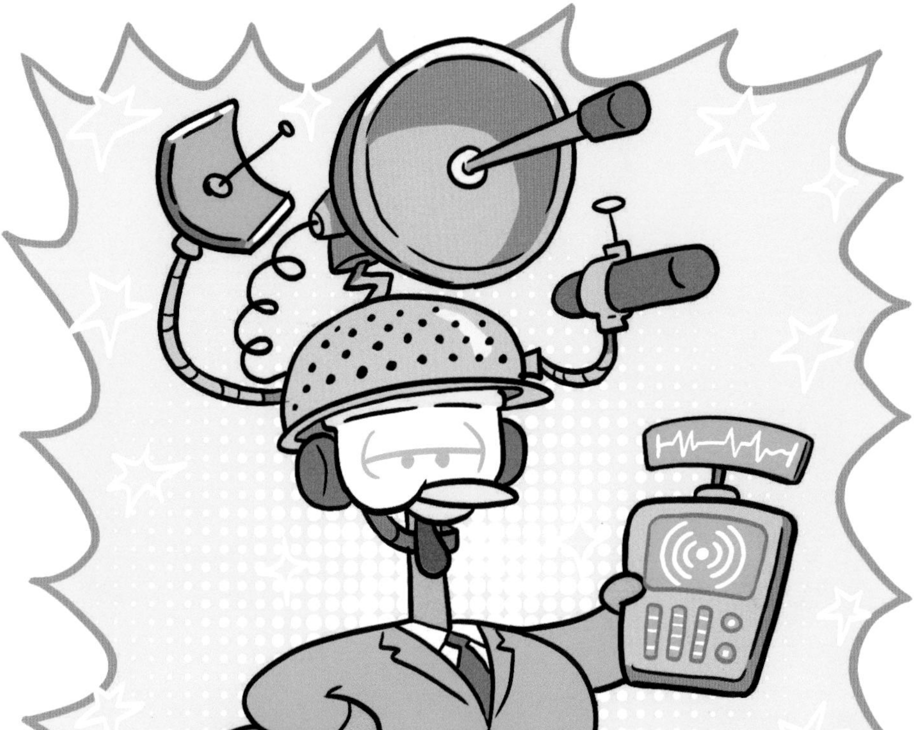

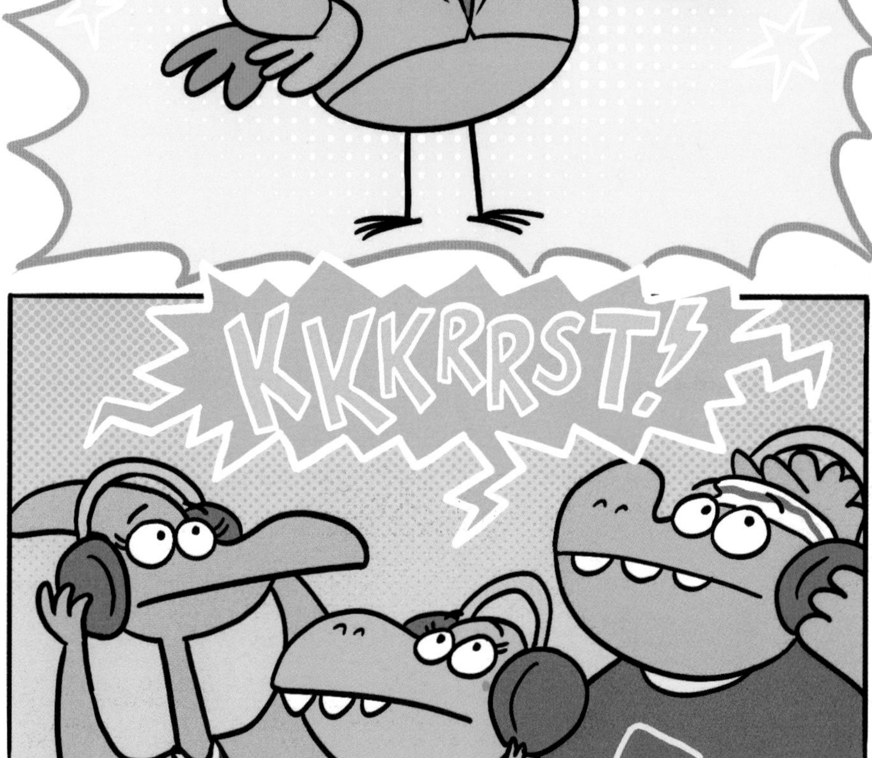
KKKRRST!

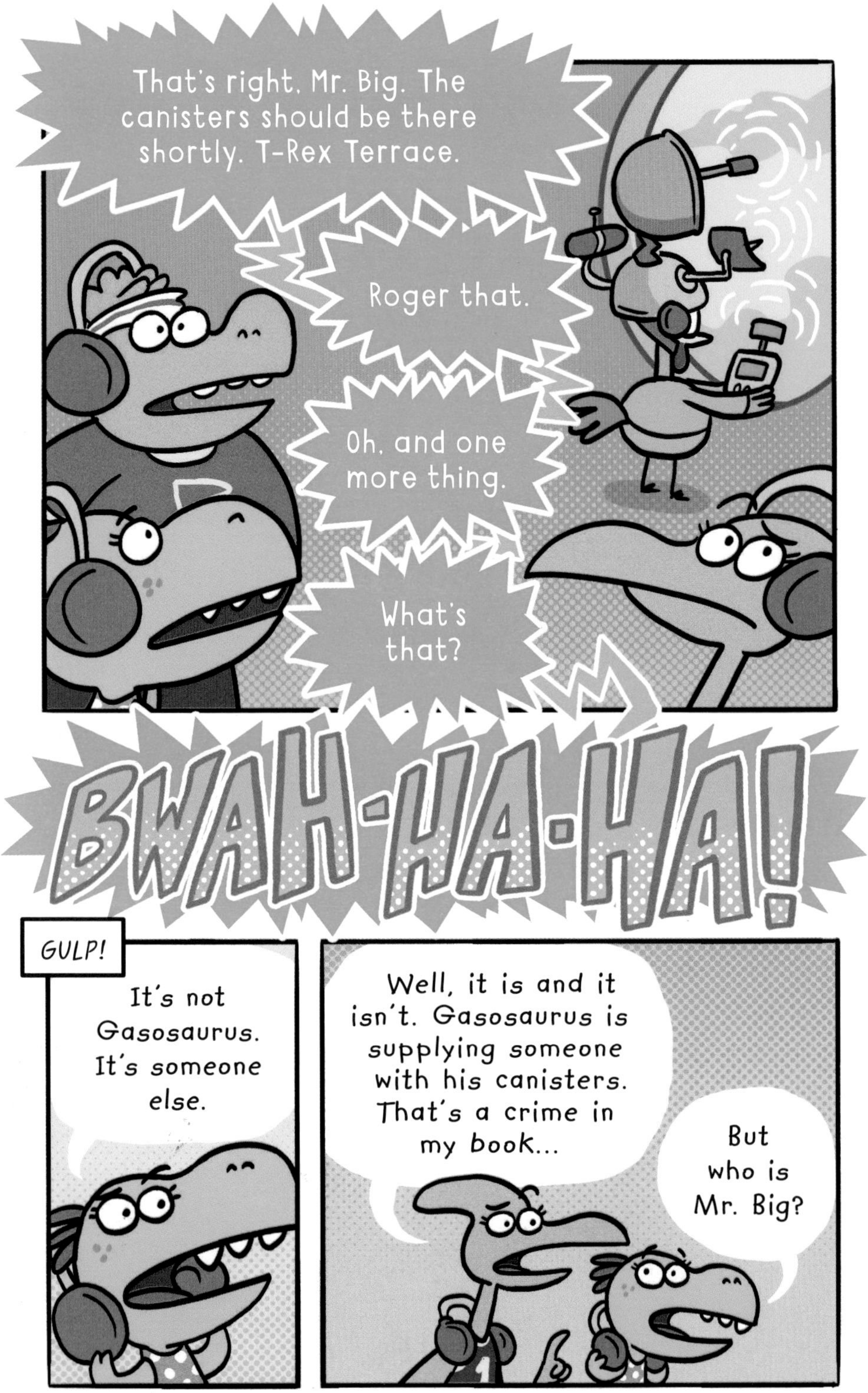
That's right, Mr. Big. The canisters should be there shortly. T-Rex Terrace.
Roger that.
Oh, and one more thing.
What's that?
BWAH-HA-HA!
GULP!
It's not Gasosaurus. It's someone else.
Well, it is and it isn't. Gasosaurus is supplying someone with his canisters. That's a crime in my book...
But who is Mr. Big?

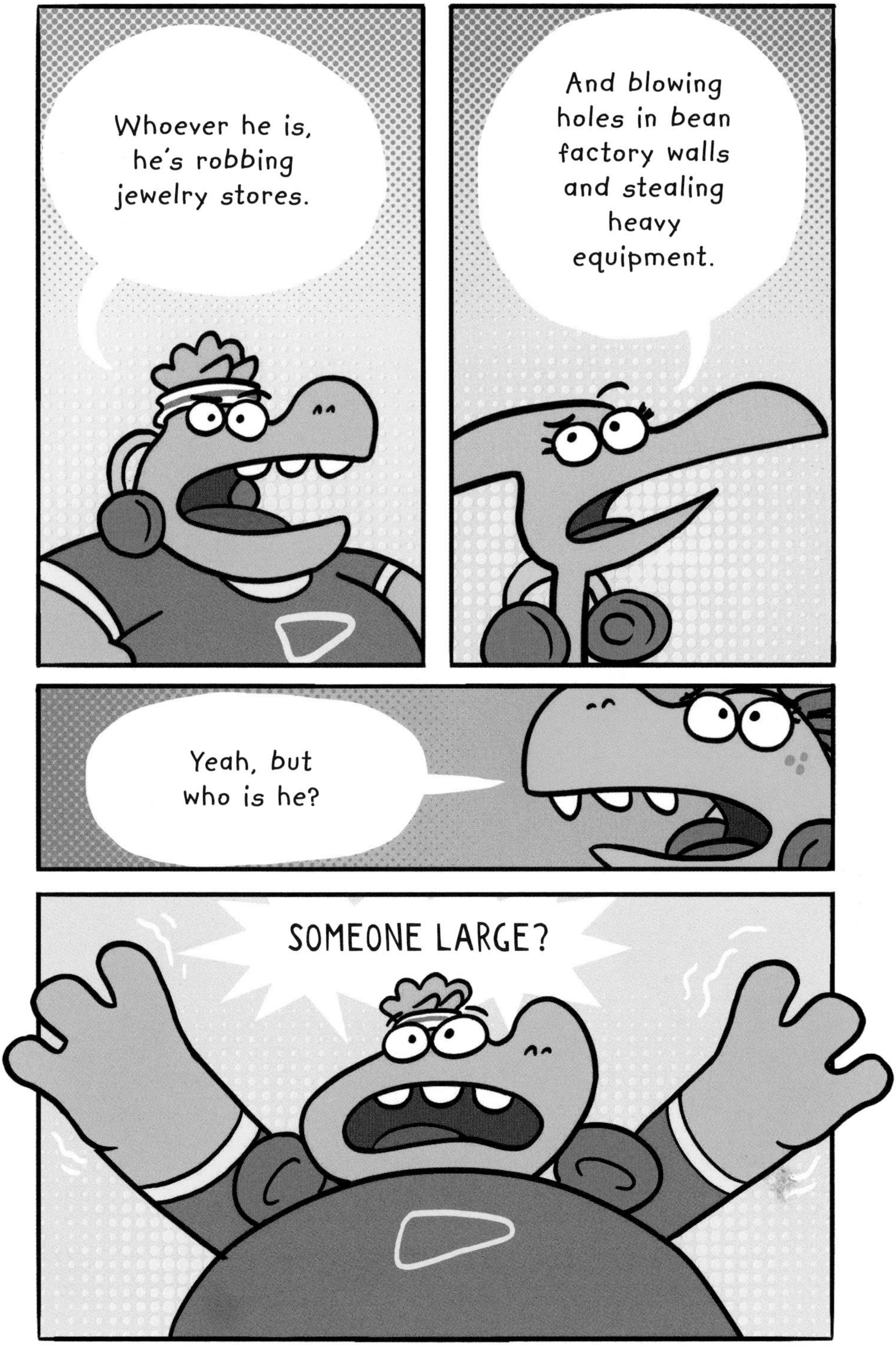
Whoever he is, he's robbing jewelry stores.
And blowing holes in bean factory walls and stealing heavy equipment.
Yeah, but who is he?
SOMEONE LARGE?

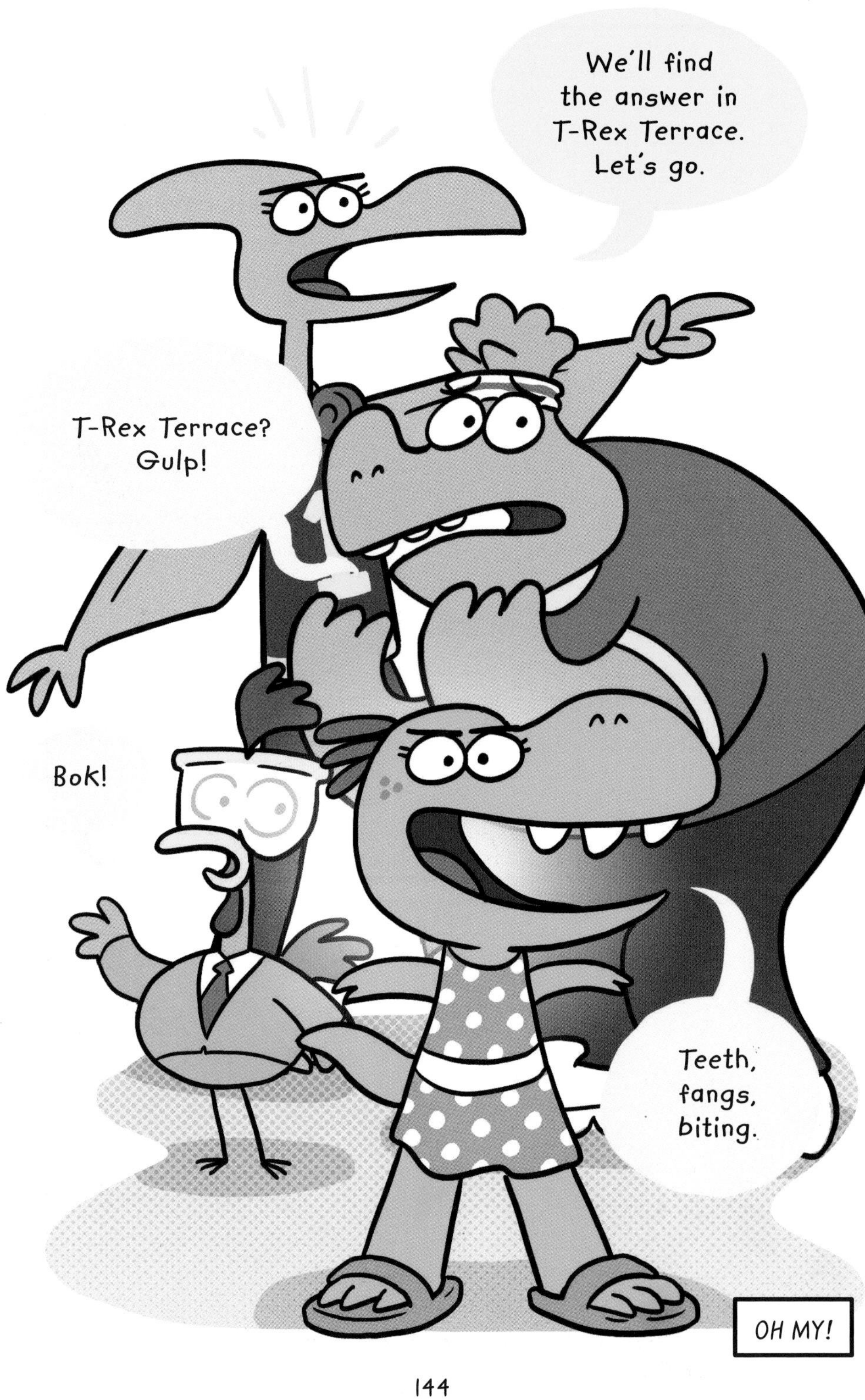
We'll find the answer in T-Rex Terrace. Let's go.
T-Rex Terrace? Gulp!
Bok!
Teeth, fangs, biting.
OH MY!

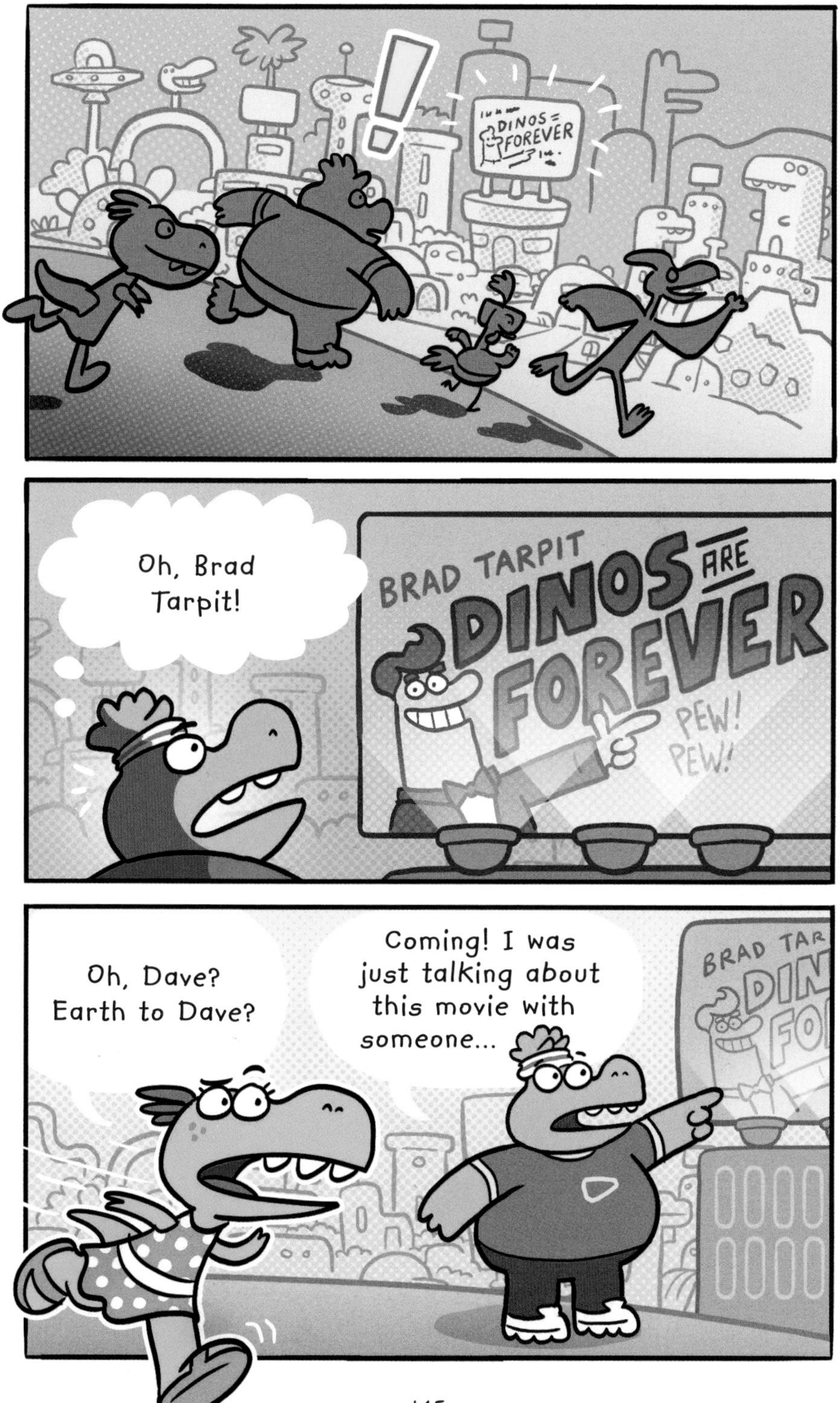
!
DINOS FOREVER
Oh, Brad Tarpit!
BRAD TARPIT
DINOS ARE FOREVER
PEW! PEW!
Oh, Dave? Earth to Dave?
Coming! I was just talking about this movie with someone...
BRAD TAR

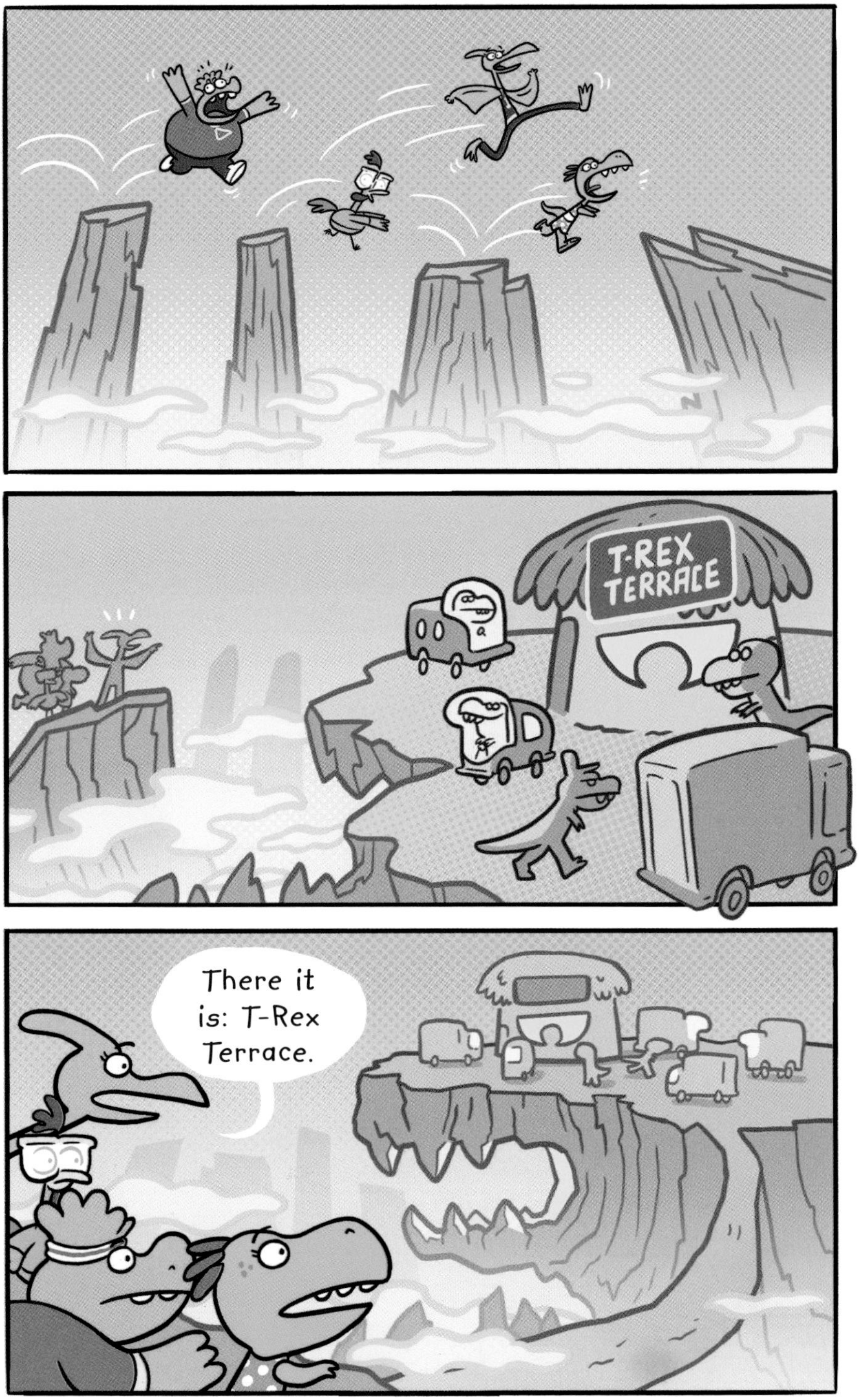
T-REX TERRACE
There it is: T-Rex Terrace.

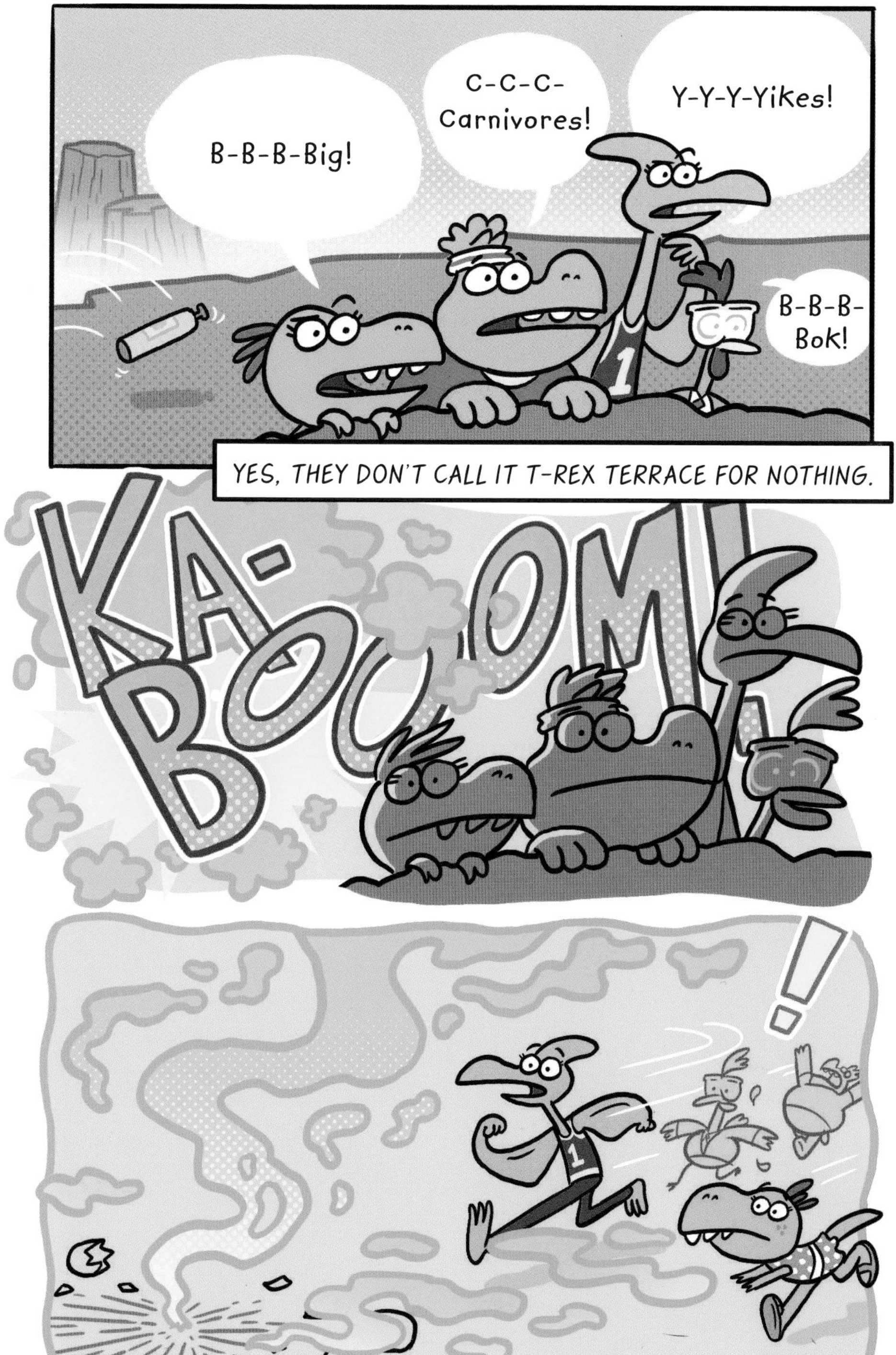
B-B-B-Big!
C-C-C-
Carnivores!
Y-Y-Y-Yikes!
B-B-B-
Bok!
YES, THEY DON'T CALL IT T-REX TERRACE FOR NOTHING.
KA-BOOOM!
!

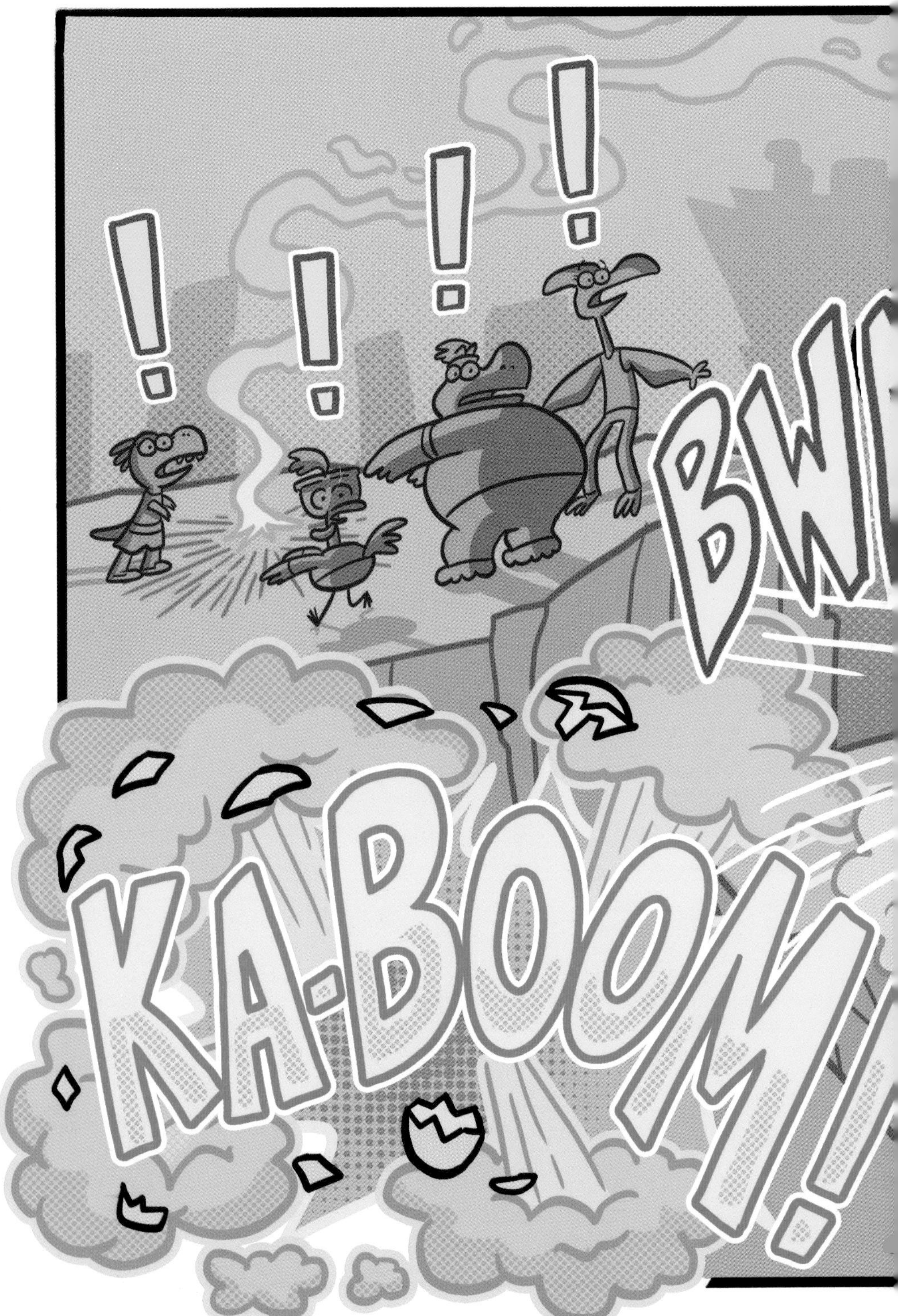
!
!
!
!
BW
KA-BOOM!!

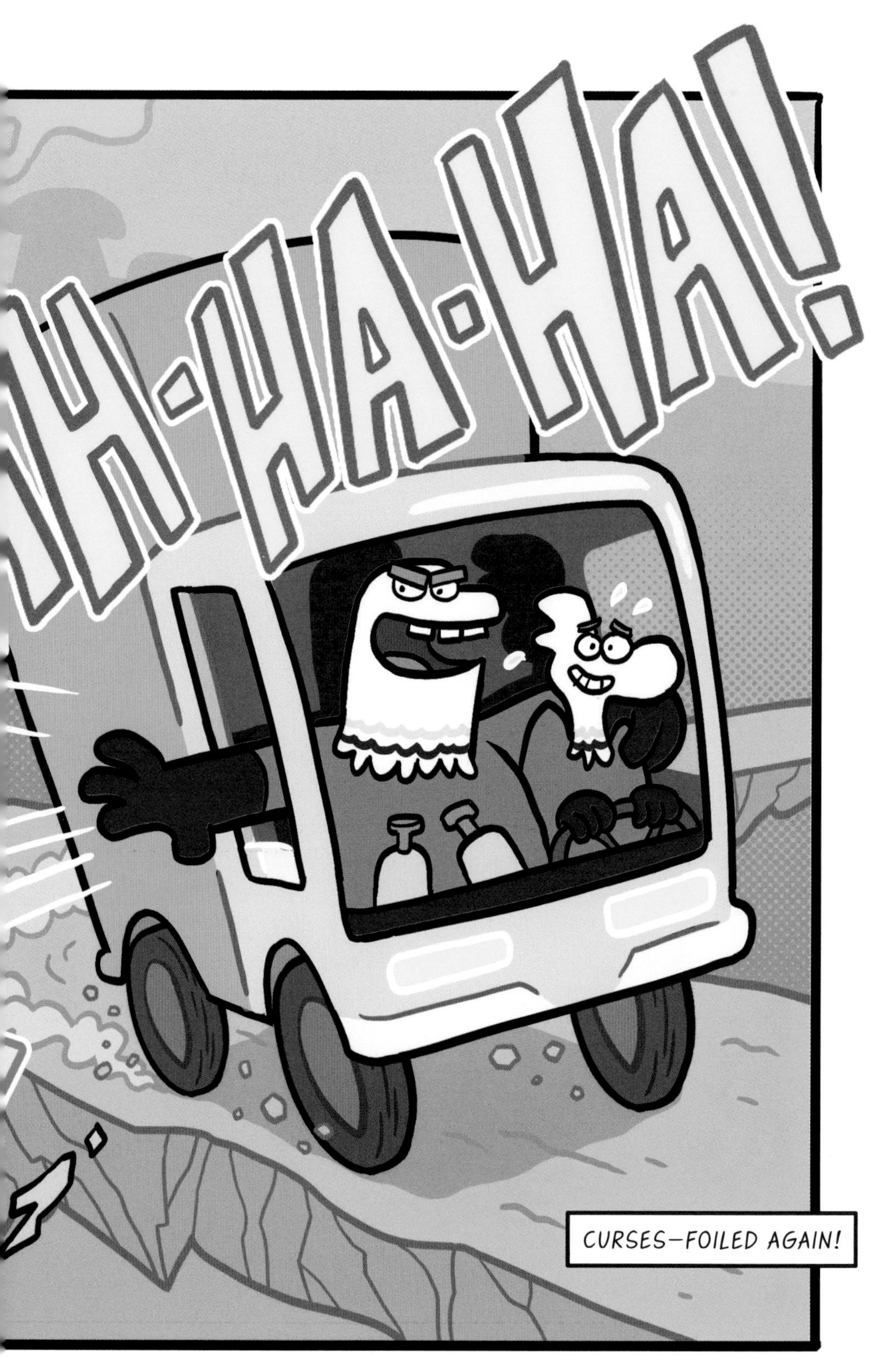
H-HA-HA-HA!
CURSES—FOILED AGAIN!

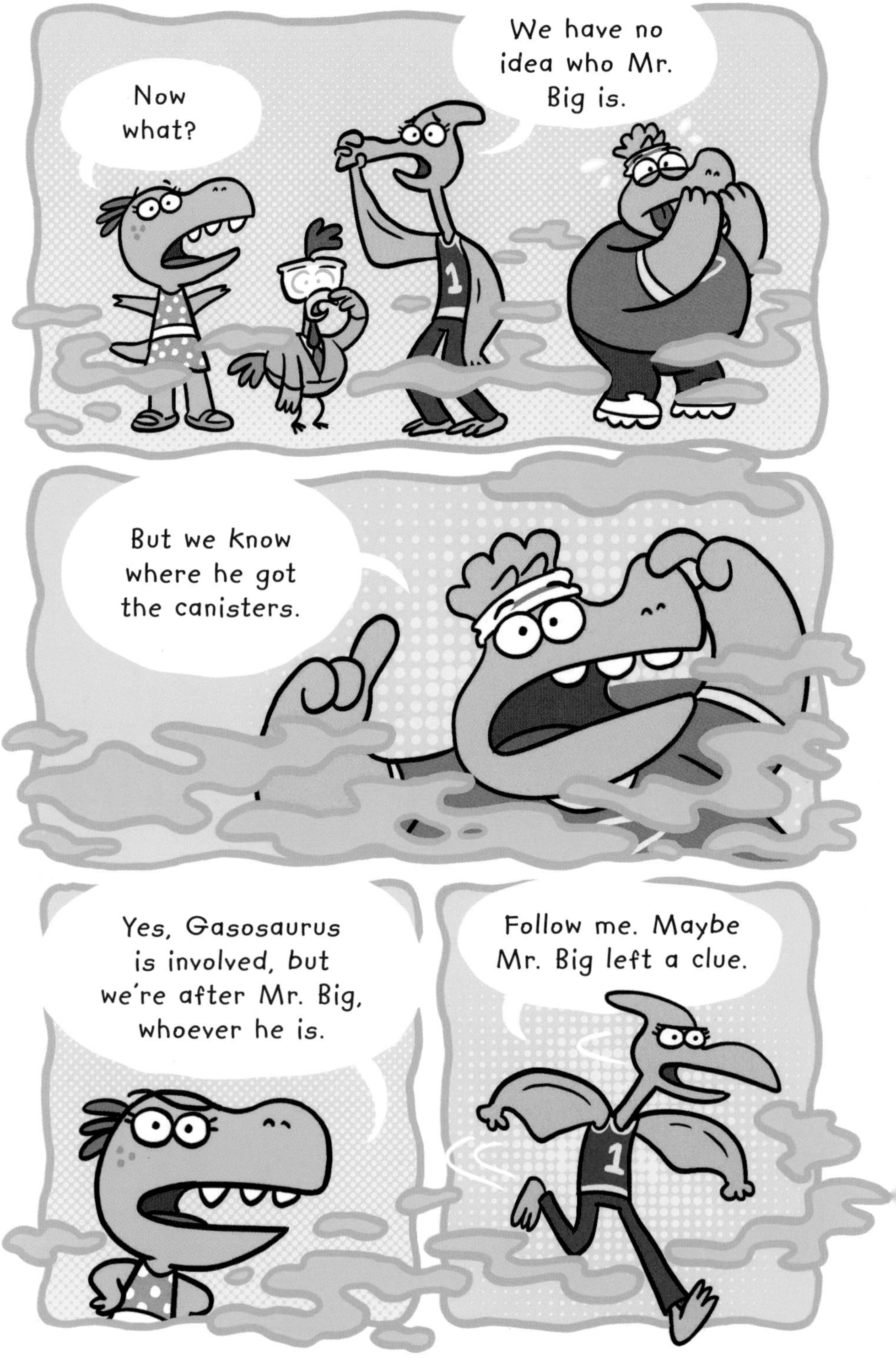
Now what?
We have no idea who Mr. Big is.
But we know where he got the canisters.
Yes, Gasosaurus is involved, but we're after Mr. Big, whoever he is.
Follow me. Maybe Mr. Big left a clue.

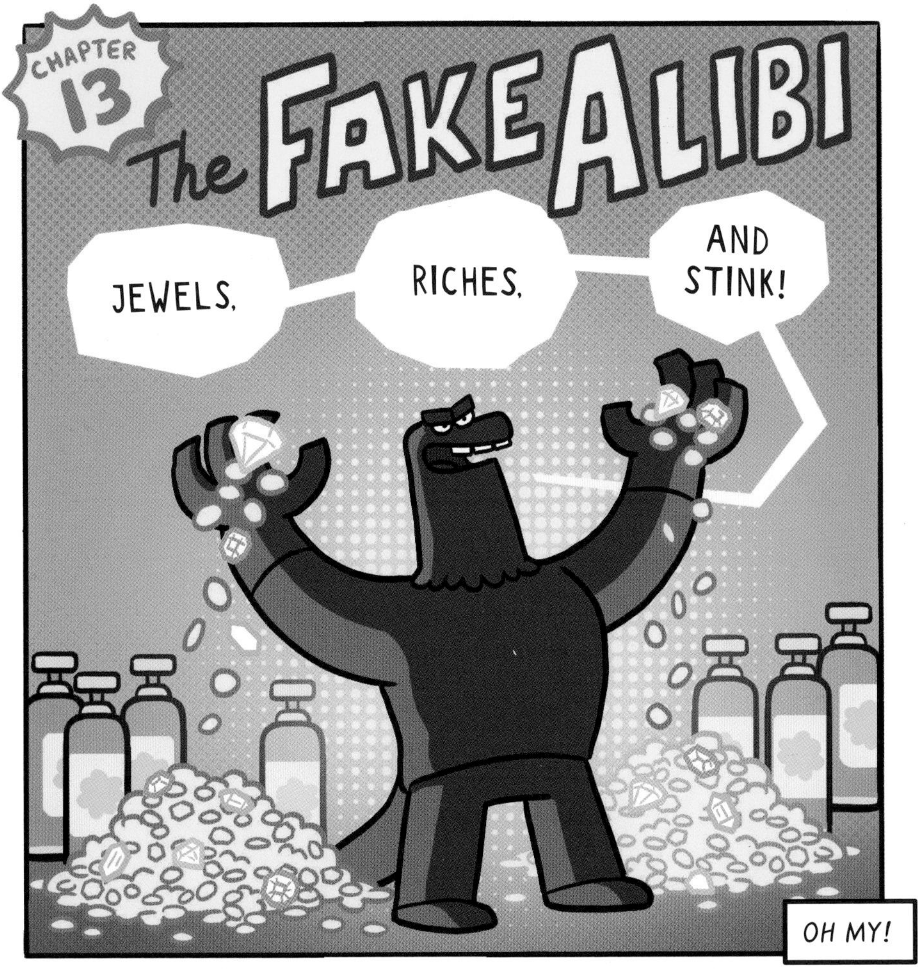
CHAPTER 13
The FAKE ALIBI
JEWELS,
RICHES,
AND STINK!
OH MY!

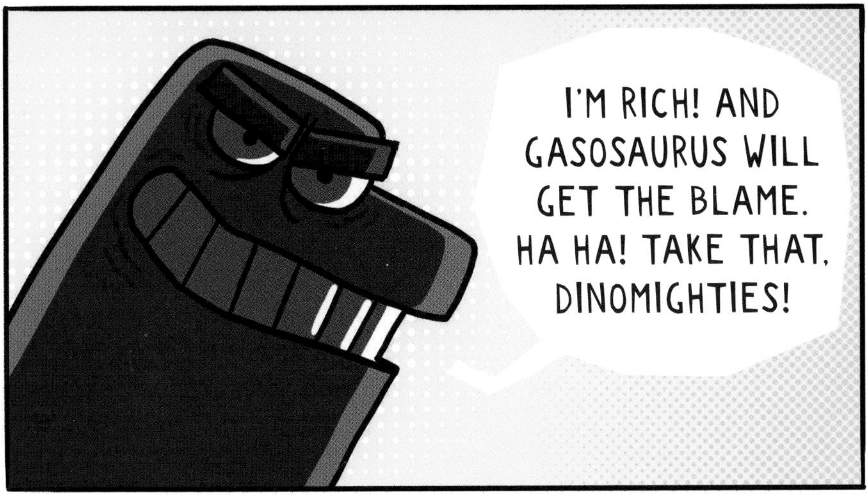
I'M RICH! AND GASOSAURUS WILL GET THE BLAME. HA HA! TAKE THAT, DINOMIGHTIES!

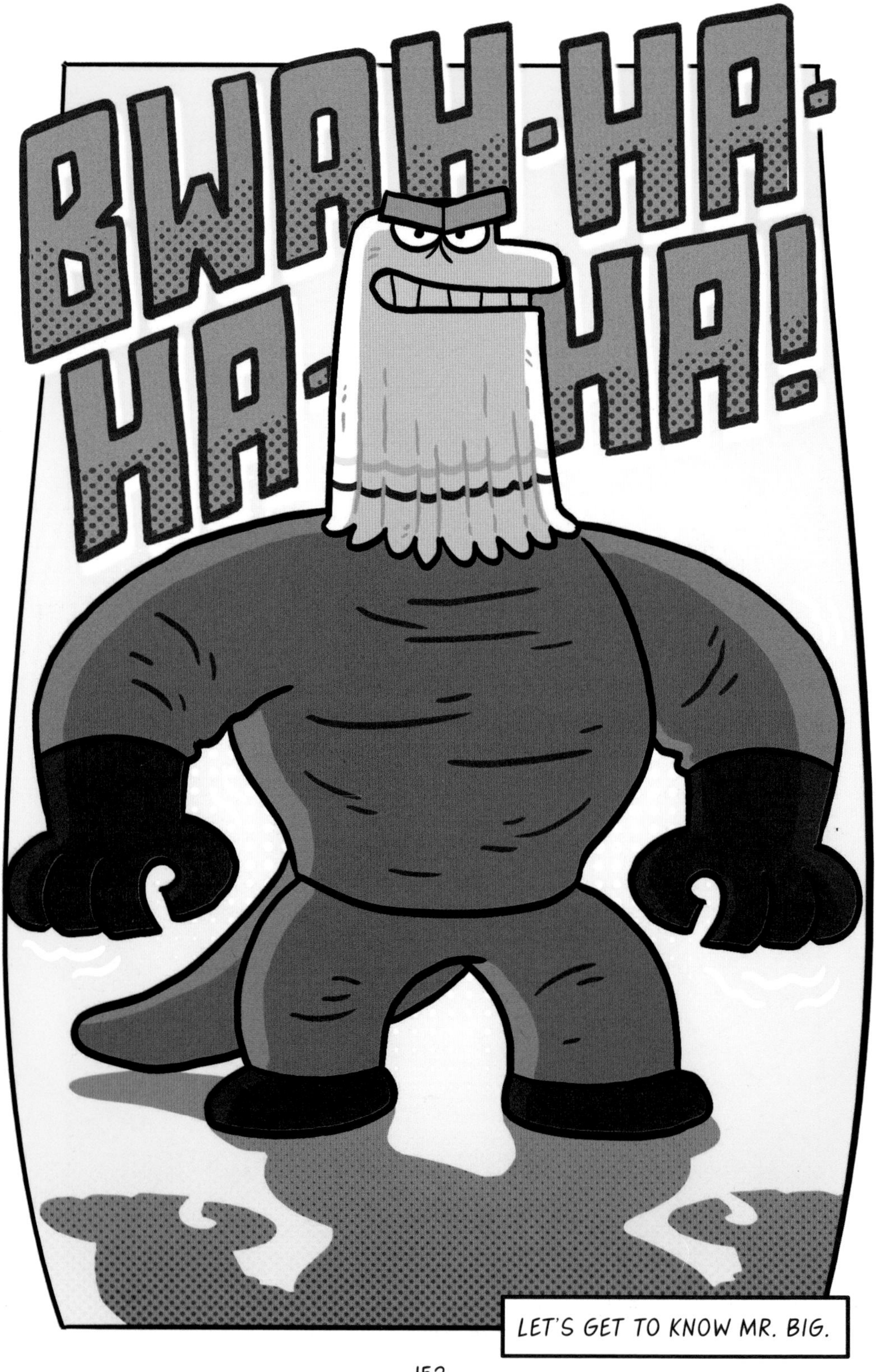
BWAH-HA-HA-HA-HA!
LET'S GET TO KNOW MR. BIG.

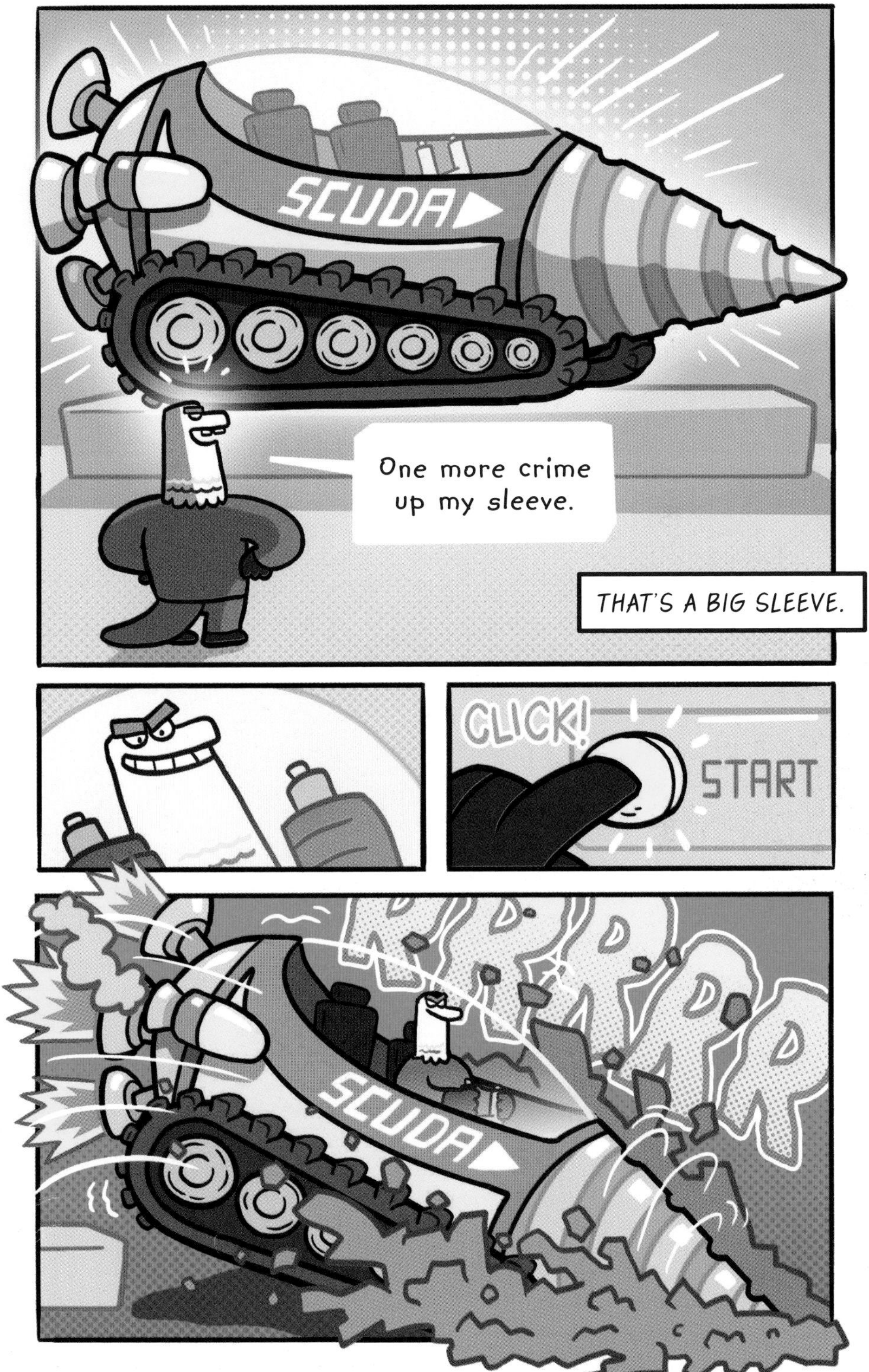

SCUDA
One more crime up my sleeve.
THAT'S A BIG SLEEVE.
CLICK!
START
SCUDA

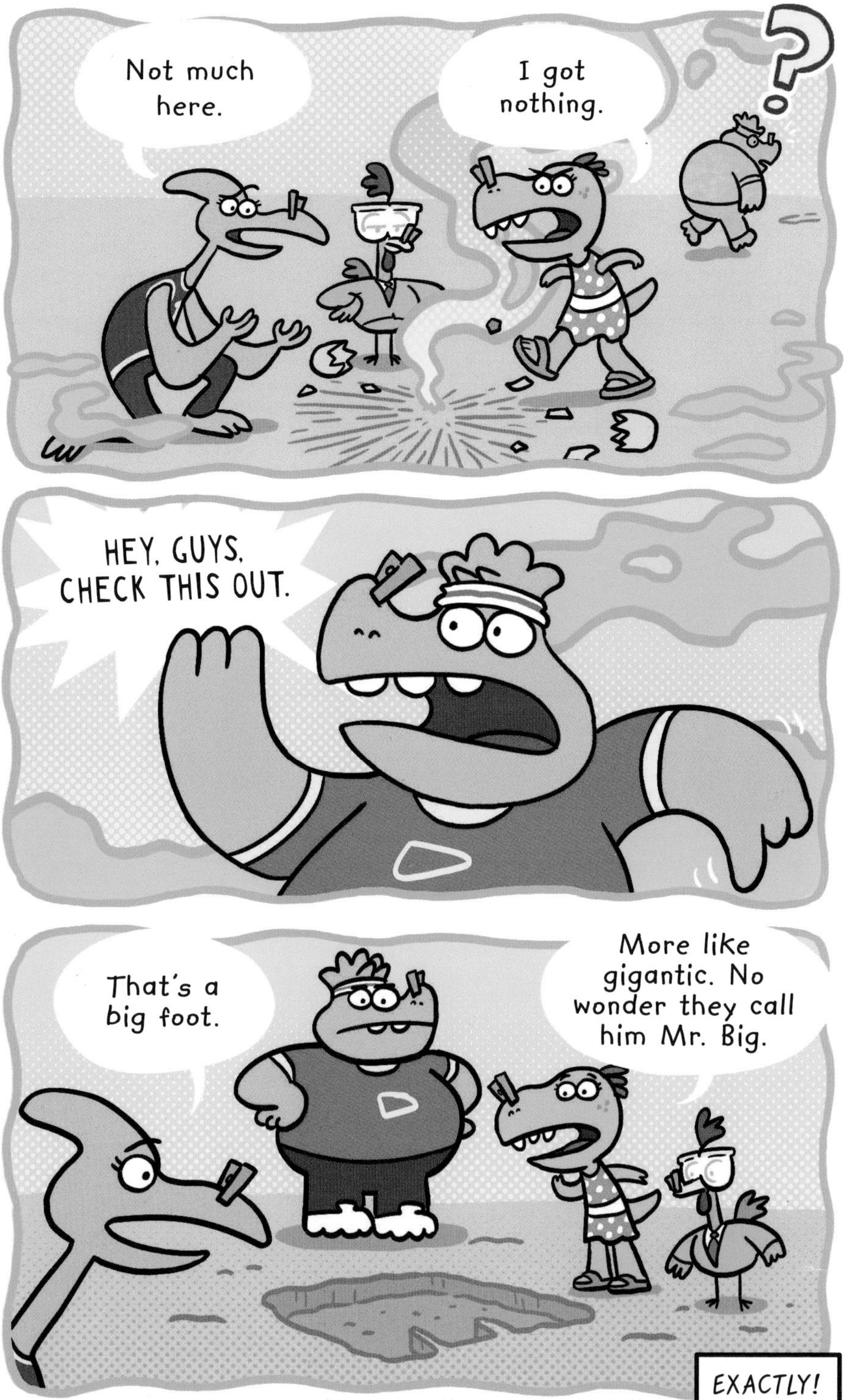
Not much here.
I got nothing.
?
HEY, GUYS, CHECK THIS OUT.
That's a big foot.
More like gigantic. No wonder they call him Mr. Big.
EXACTLY!

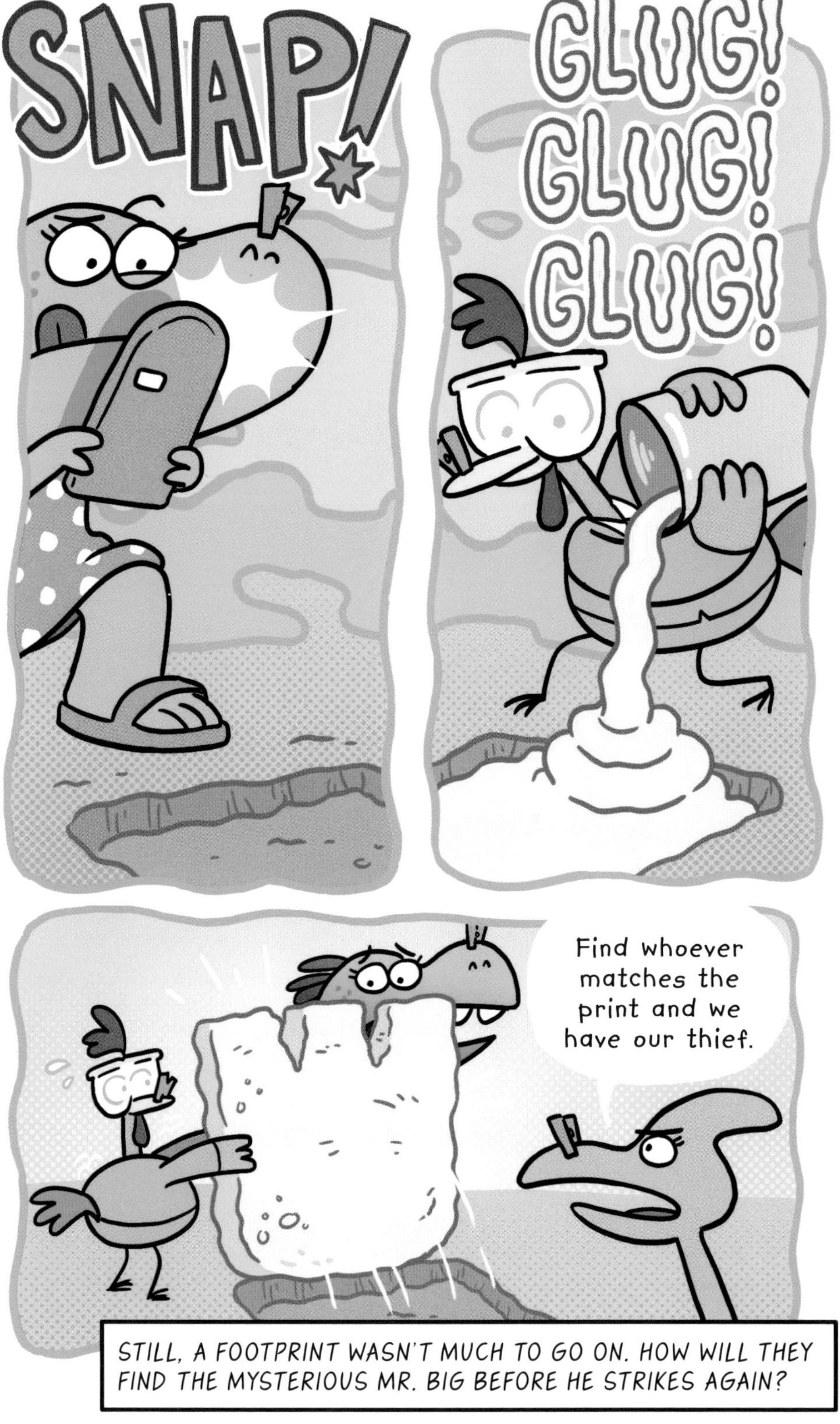
SNAP!
GLUG! GLUG! GLUG!
Find whoever matches the print and we have our thief.
STILL, A FOOTPRINT WASN'T MUCH TO GO ON. HOW WILL THEY FIND THE MYSTERIOUS MR. BIG BEFORE HE STRIKES AGAIN?

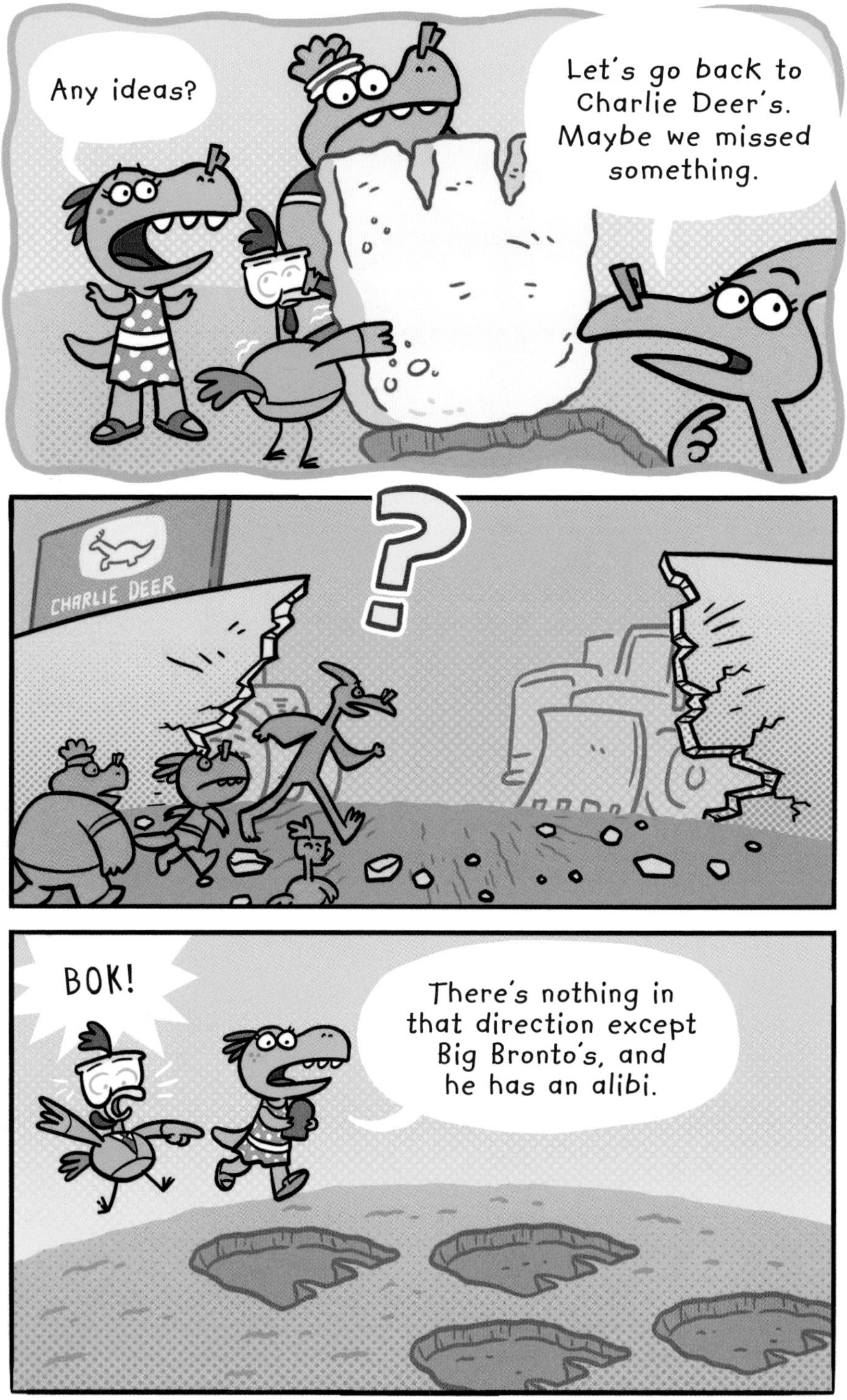
Any ideas?
Let's go back to Charlie Deer's. Maybe we missed something.
CHARLIE DEER
?
BOK!
There's nothing in that direction except Big Bronto's, and he has an alibi.

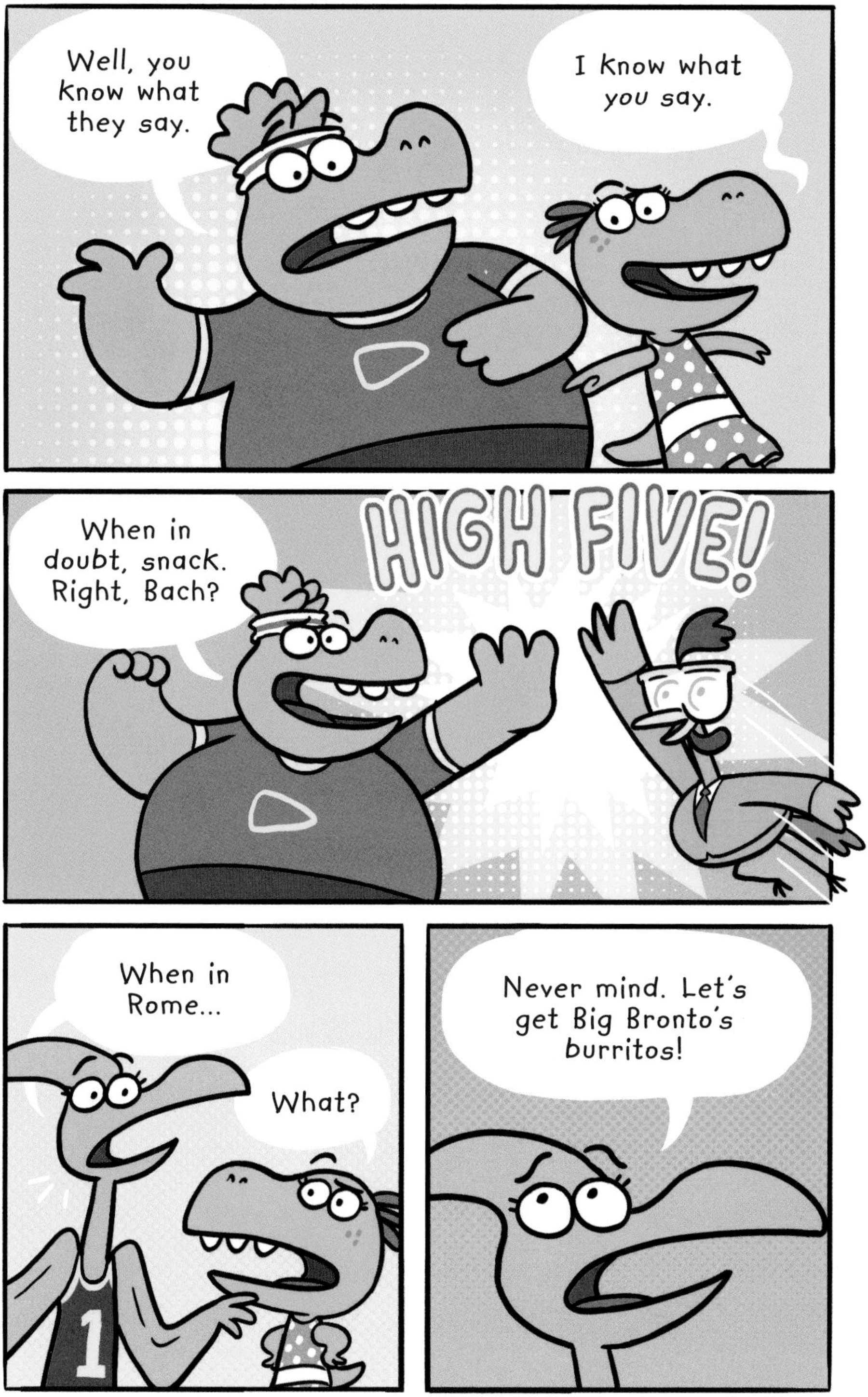

Well, you know what they say.
I know what *you* say.
When in doubt, snack. Right, Bach?
HIGH FIVE!
When in Rome...
What?
Never mind. Let's get Big Bronto's burritos!

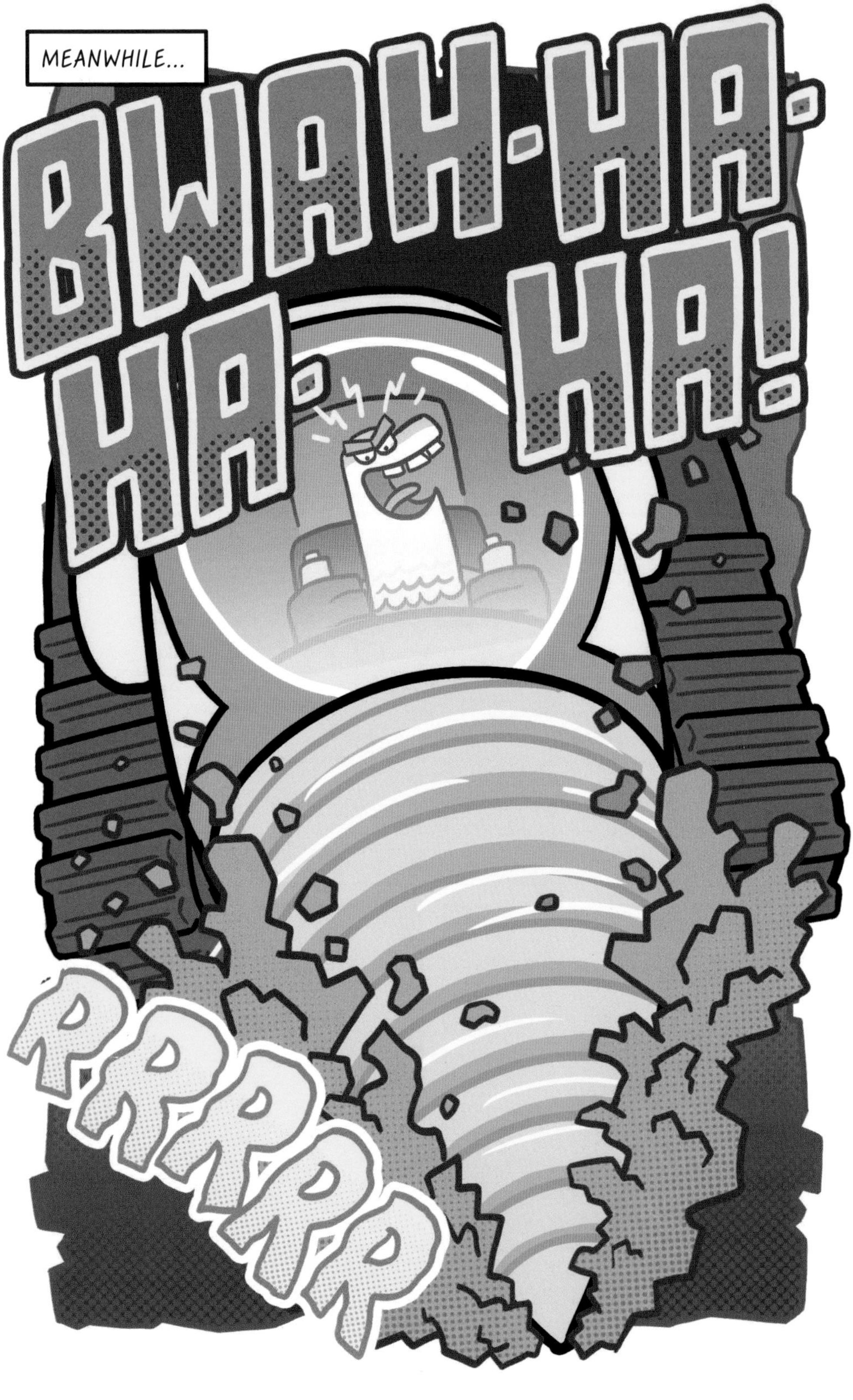
MEANWHILE...
BWAH-HA-HA-HA-HA!
RRRRRR

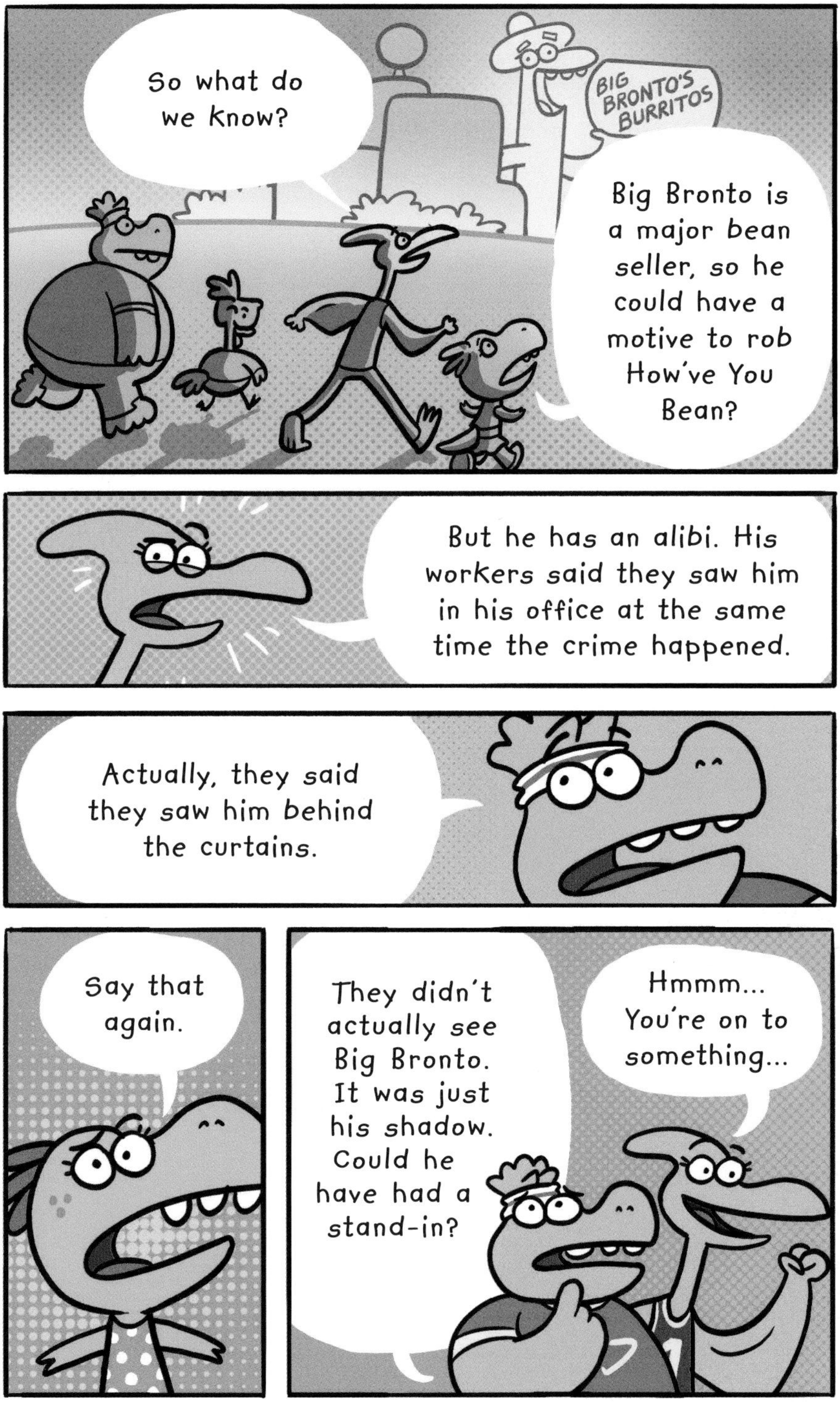

BIG BRONTO'S BURRITOS
So what do we know?
Big Bronto is a major bean seller, so he could have a motive to rob How've You Bean?
But he has an alibi. His workers said they saw him in his office at the same time the crime happened.
Actually, they said they saw him behind the curtains.
Say that again.
They didn't actually see Big Bronto. It was just his shadow. Could he have had a stand-in?
Hmmm... You're on to something...

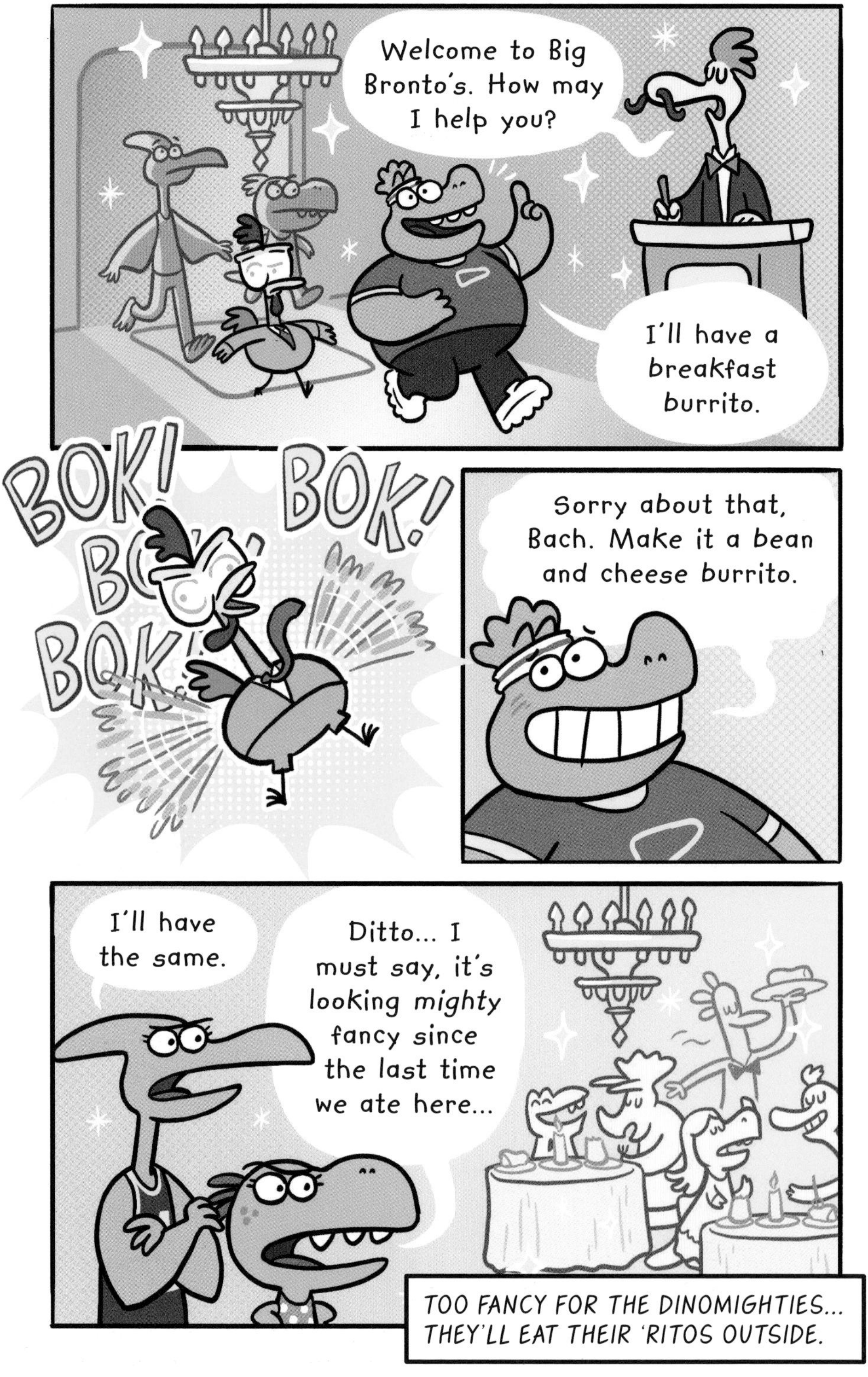
Welcome to Big Bronto's. How may I help you?
I'll have a *breakfast* burrito.
BOK! BOK! BOK! BOK!
Sorry about that, Bach. Make it a *bean and cheese* burrito.
I'll have the same.
Ditto... I must say, it's looking *mighty* fancy since the last time we ate here...
TOO FANCY FOR THE DINOMIGHTIES... THEY'LL EAT THEIR 'RITOS OUTSIDE.

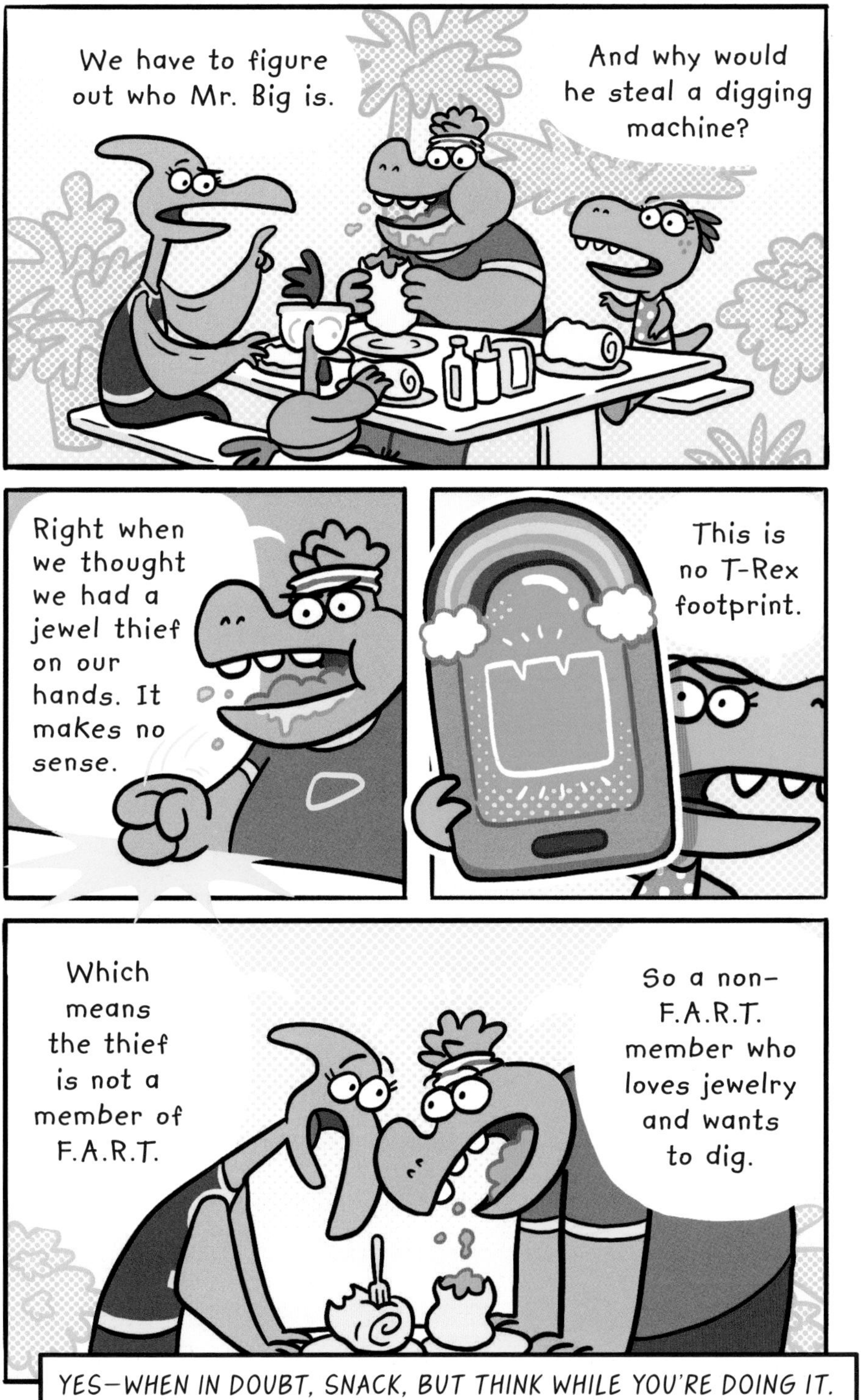
We have to figure out who Mr. Big is.
And why would he steal a digging machine?
Right when we thought we had a jewel thief on our hands. It makes no sense.
This is no T-Rex footprint.
Which means the thief is not a member of F.A.R.T.
So a non-F.A.R.T. member who loves jewelry and wants to dig.
YES—WHEN IN DOUBT, SNACK, BUT THINK WHILE YOU'RE DOING IT.

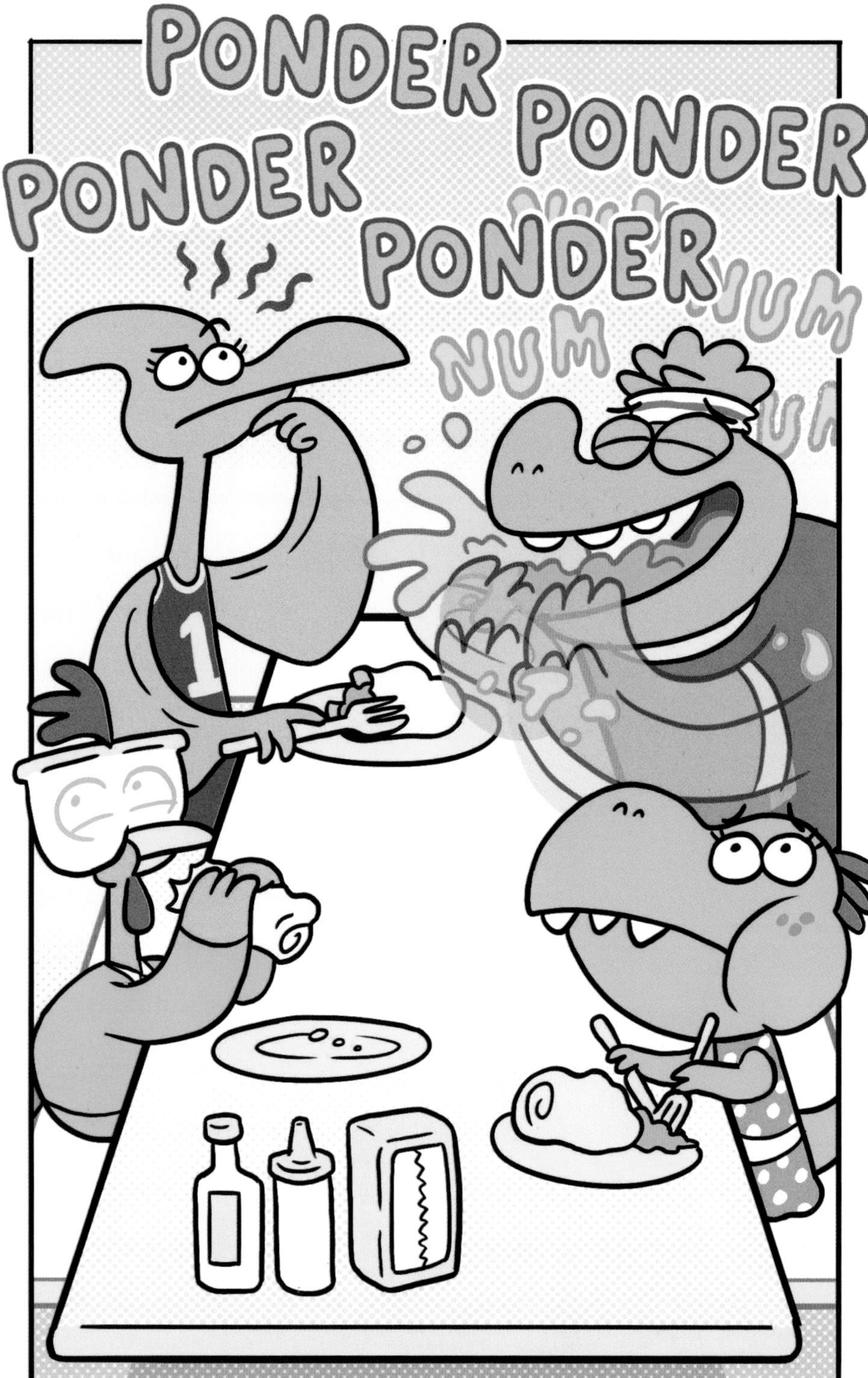
PONDER
PONDER
PONDER
PONDER
NUM
NUM

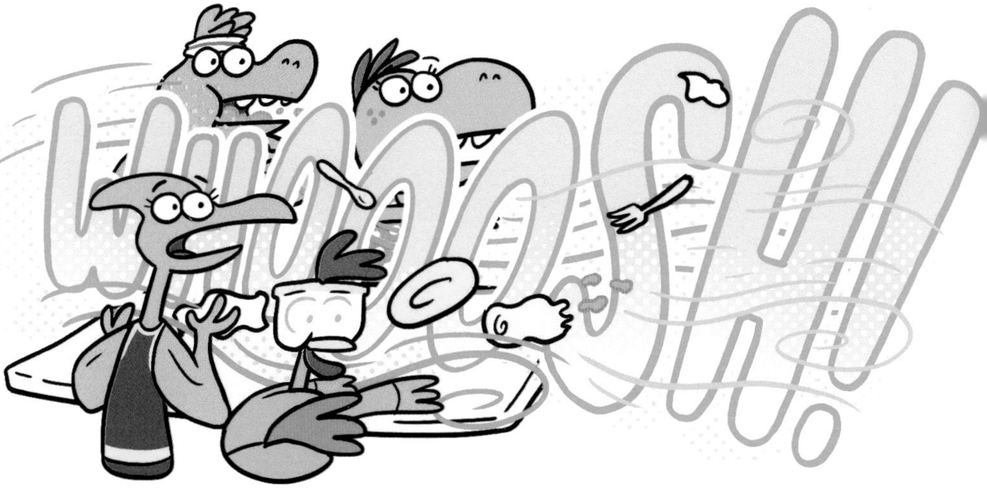
WHOOOSH!!
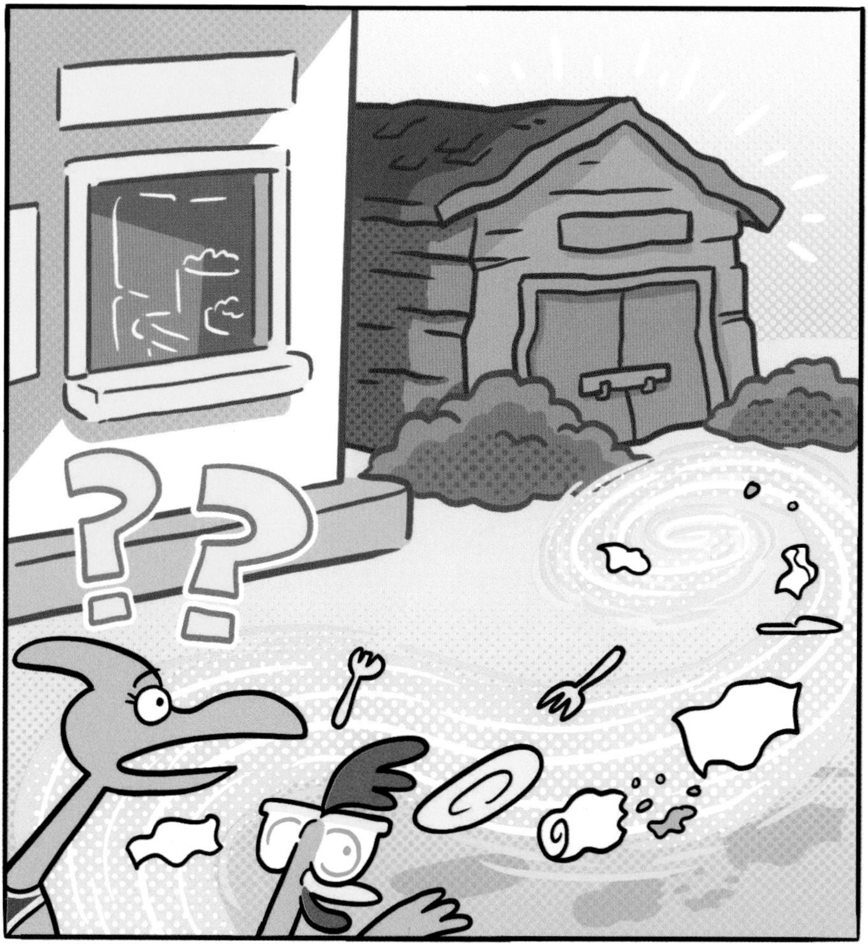
??

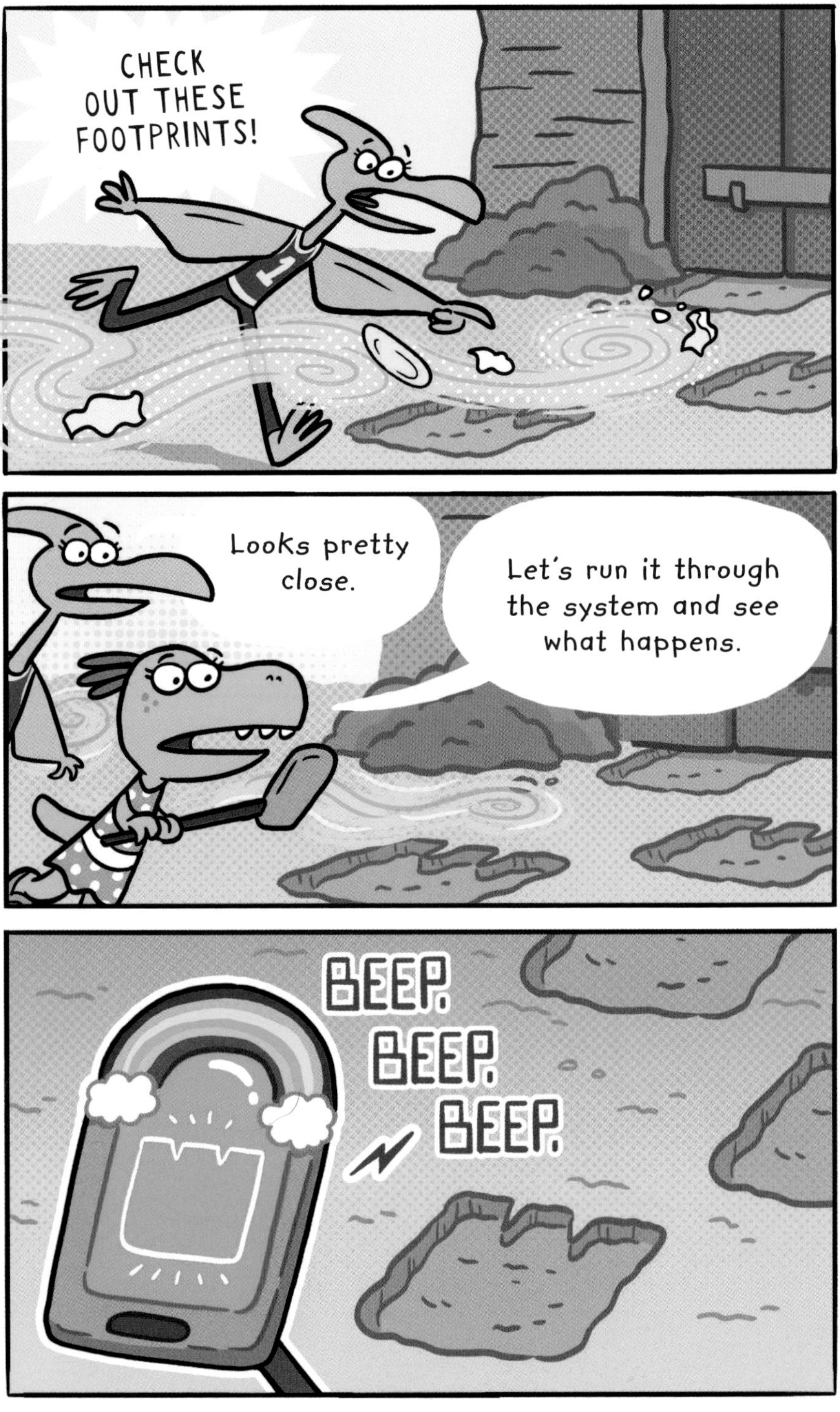
CHECK OUT THESE FOOTPRINTS!
Looks pretty close.
Let's run it through the system and see what happens.
BEEP. BEEP. BEEP.

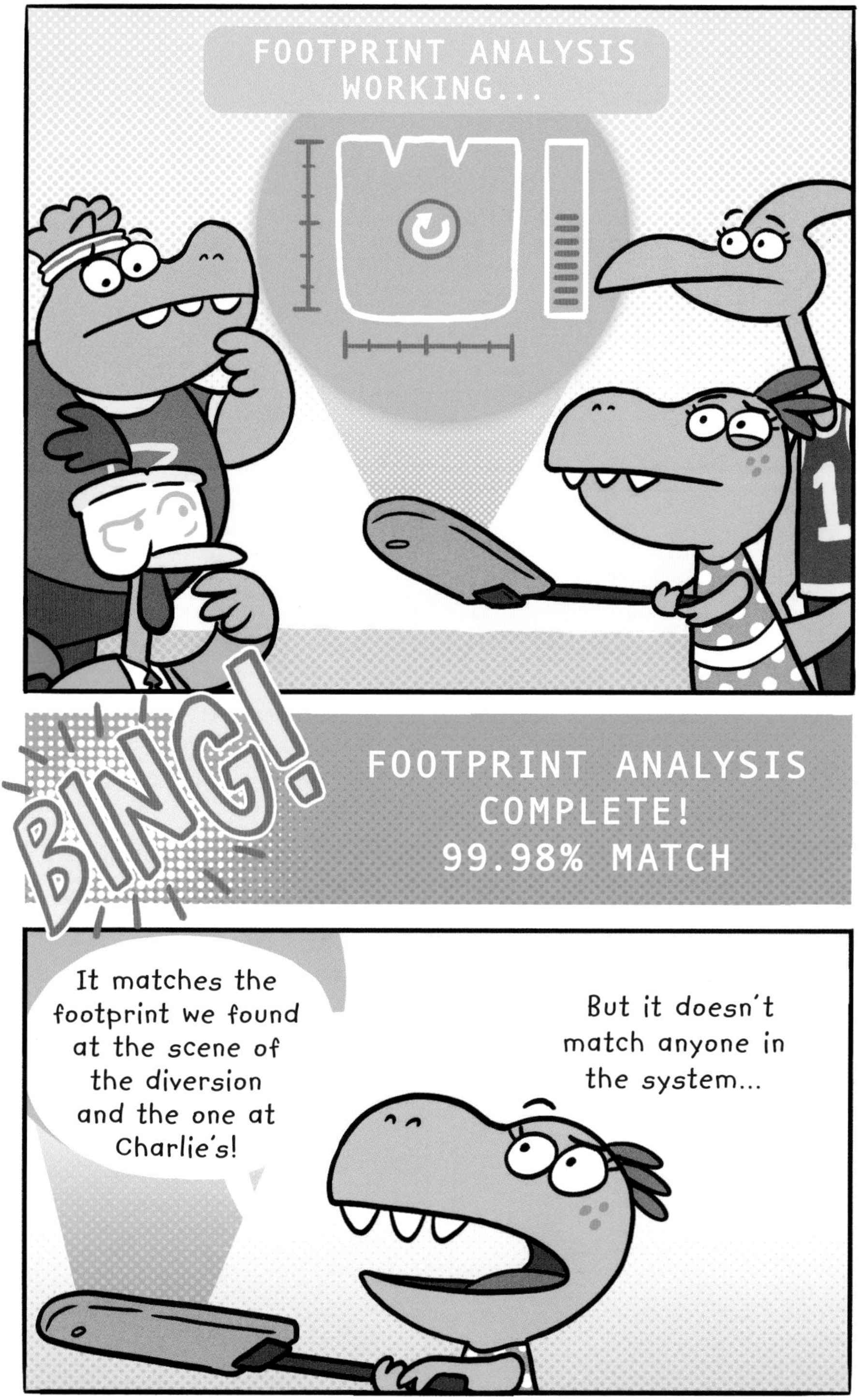
FOOTPRINT ANALYSIS WORKING...
BING!
FOOTPRINT ANALYSIS COMPLETE! 99.98% MATCH
It matches the footprint we found at the scene of the diversion and the one at Charlie's!
But it doesn't match anyone in the system...

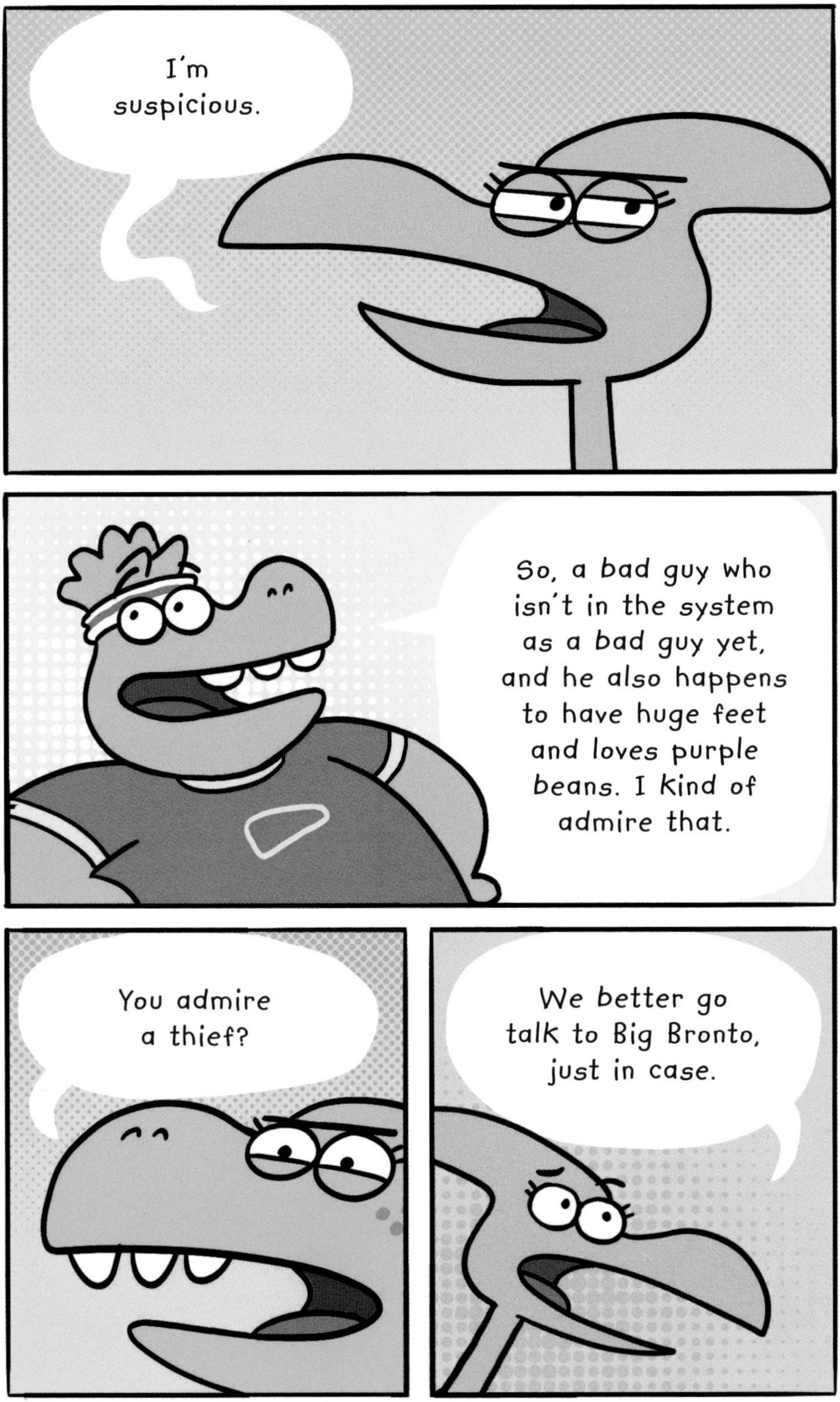
I'm suspicious.
So, a bad guy who isn't in the system as a bad guy yet, and he also happens to have huge feet and loves purple beans. I kind of admire that.
You admire a thief?
We better go talk to Big Bronto, just in case.

CHAPTER 14 LOOK OUT!

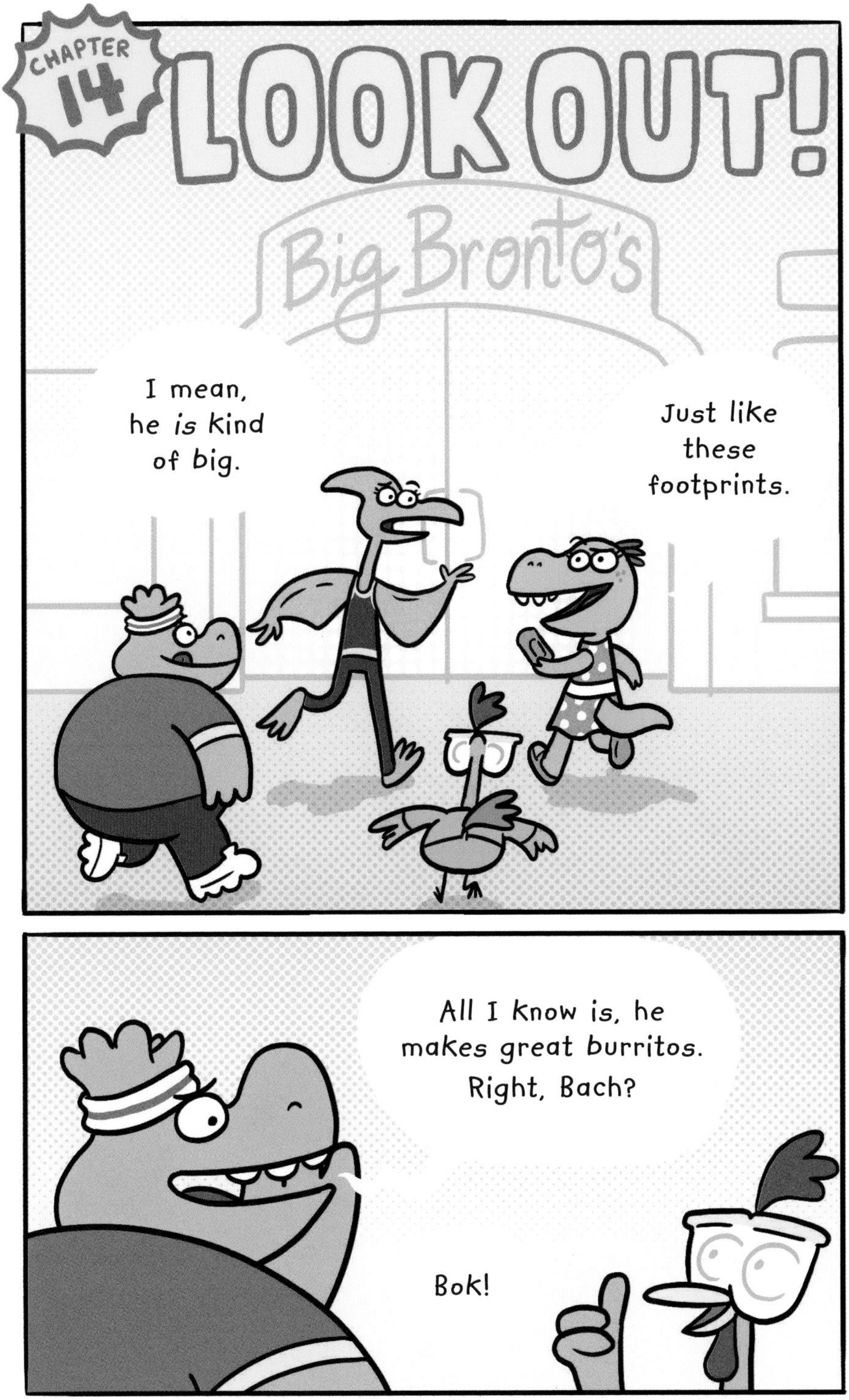
Big Bronto's
I mean, he *is* kind of big.
Just like these footprints.
All I know is, he makes great burritos. Right, Bach?
Bok!

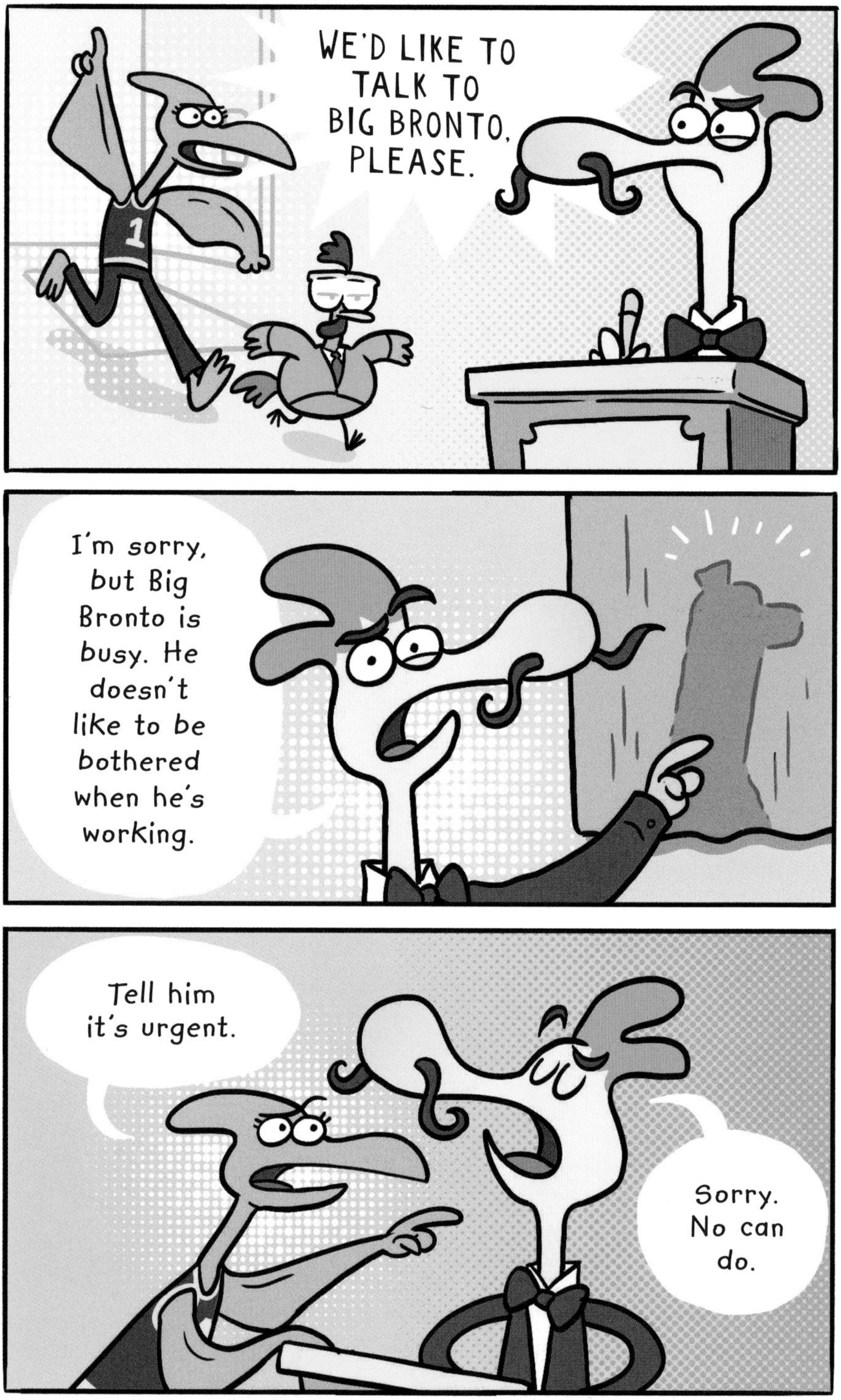
WE'D LIKE TO TALK TO BIG BRONTO, PLEASE.
I'm sorry, but Big Bronto is busy. He doesn't like to be bothered when he's working.
Tell him it's urgent.
Sorry. No can do.

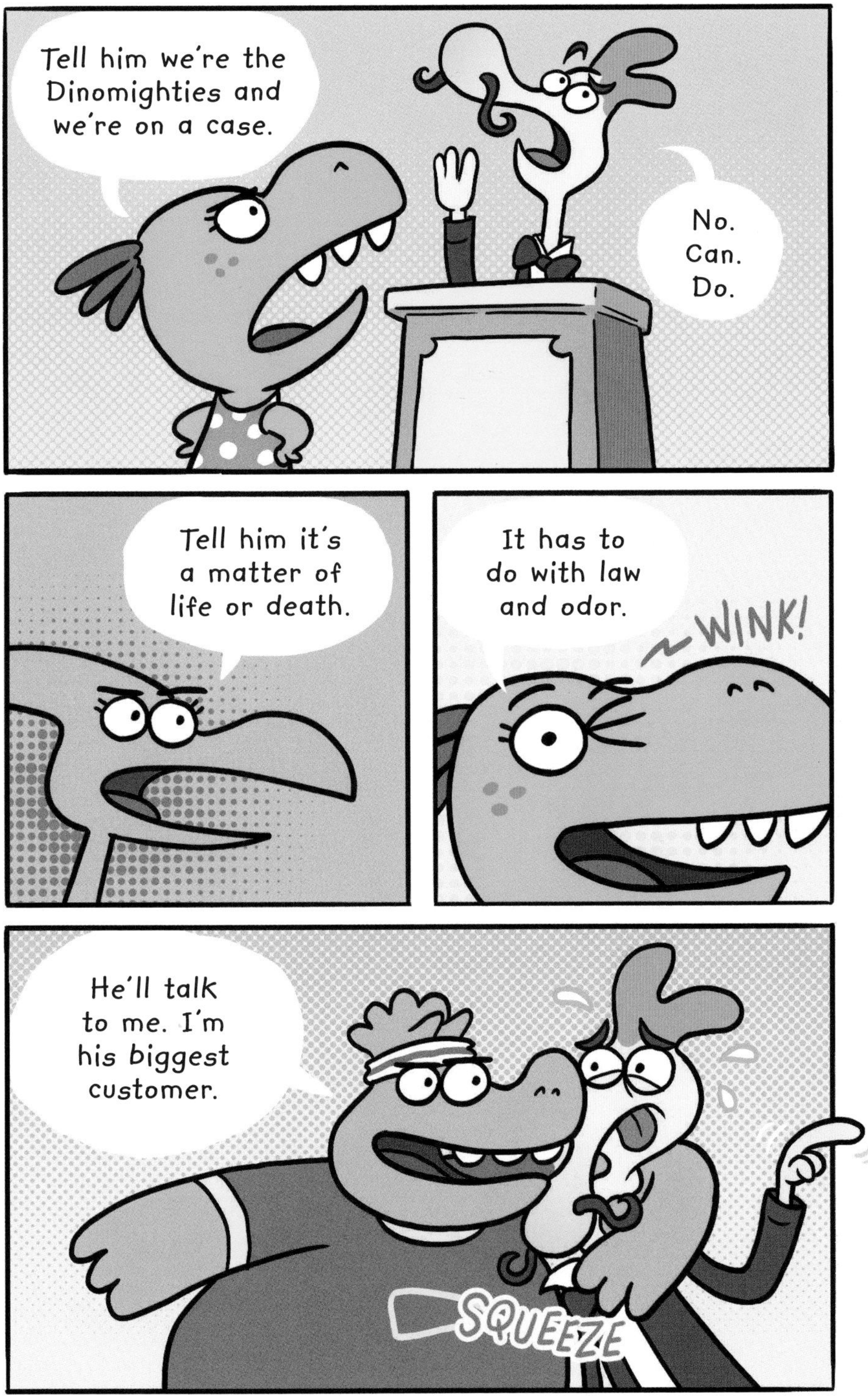
Tell him we're the Dinomighties and we're on a case.
No. Can. Do.
Tell him it's a matter of life or death.
It has to do with law and odor.
WINK!
He'll talk to me. I'm his biggest customer.
SQUEEZE

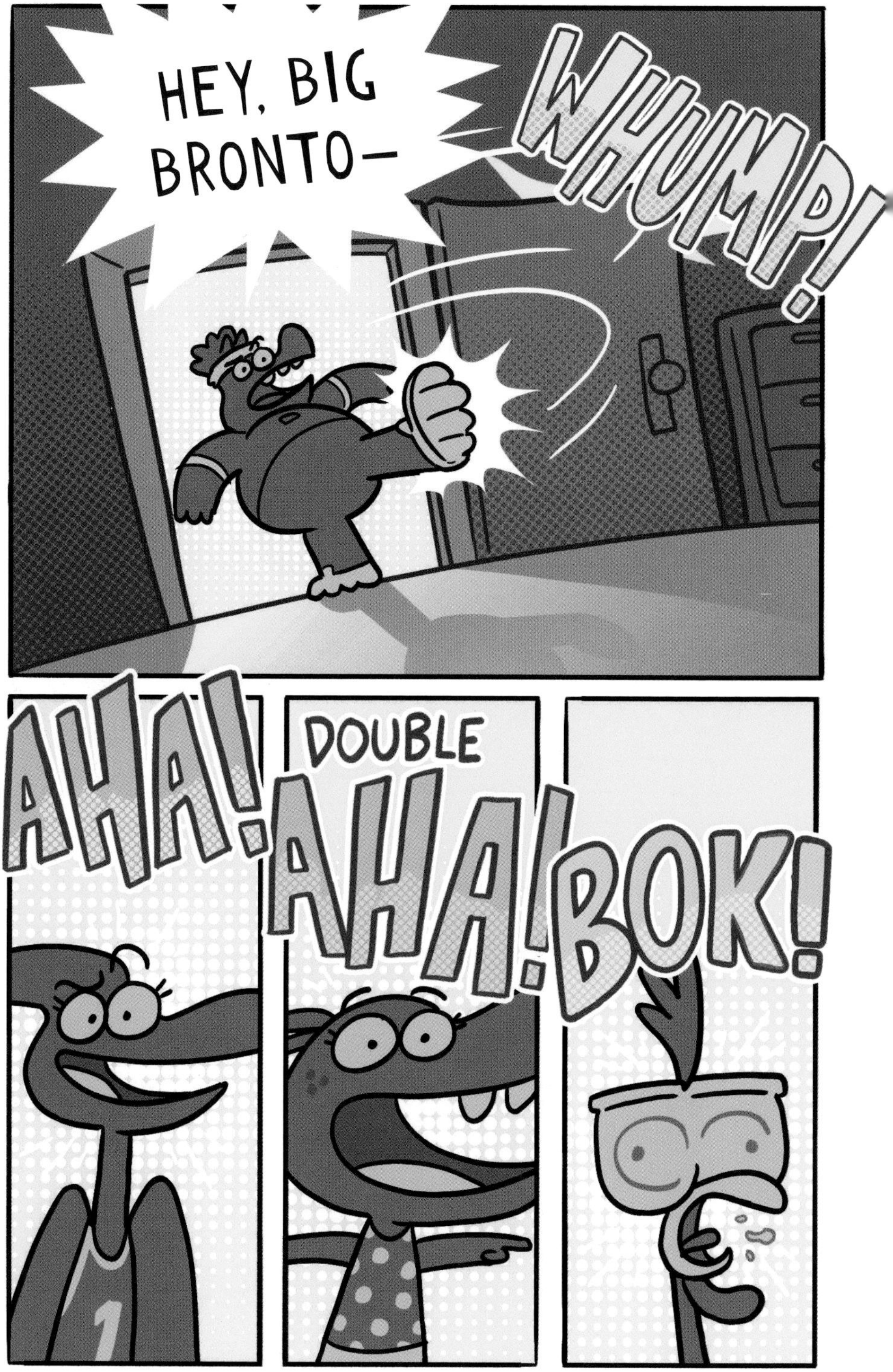
HEY, BIG BRONTO—
WHUMP!
AHA!
DOUBLE
AHA!
BOK!

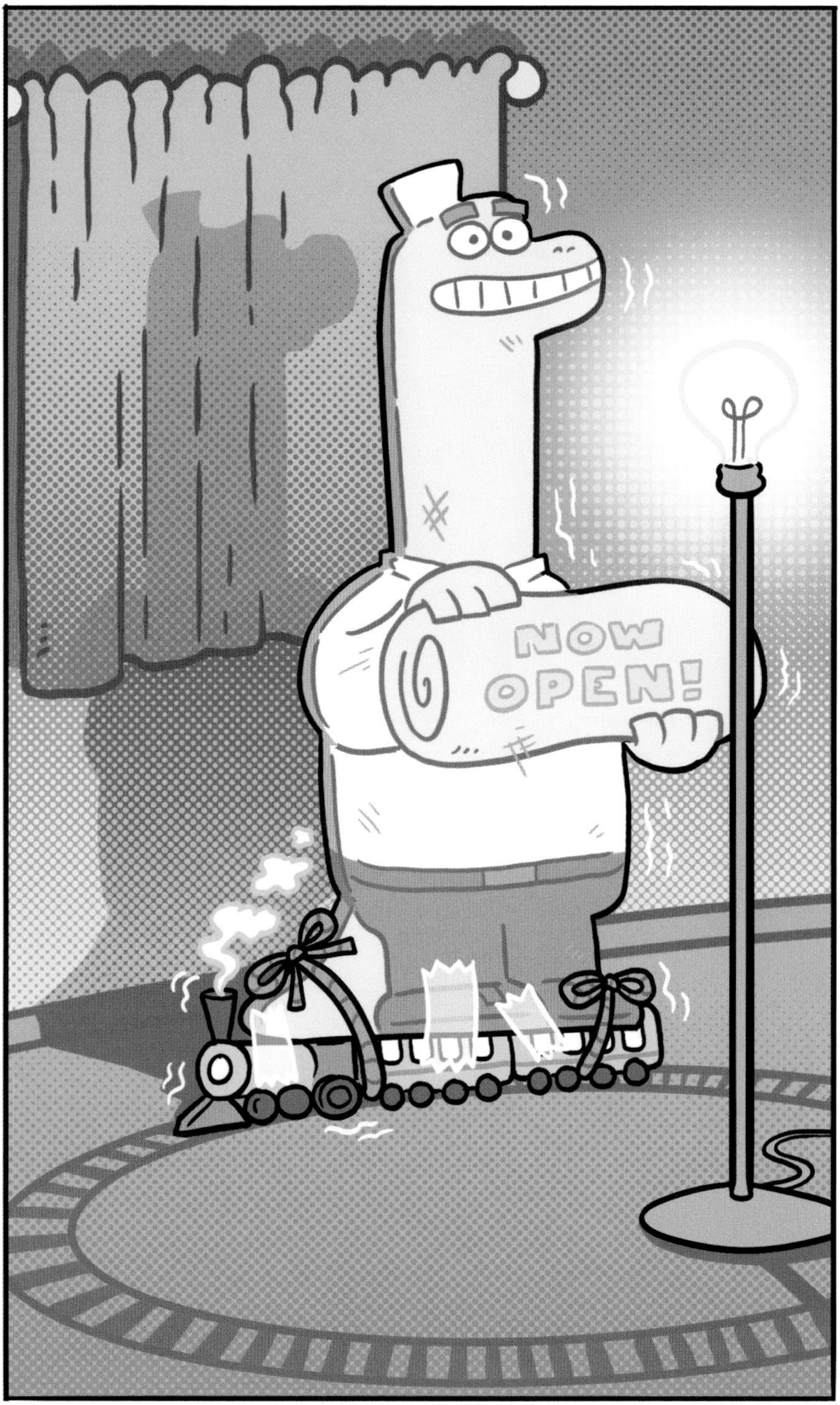
NOW OPEN!

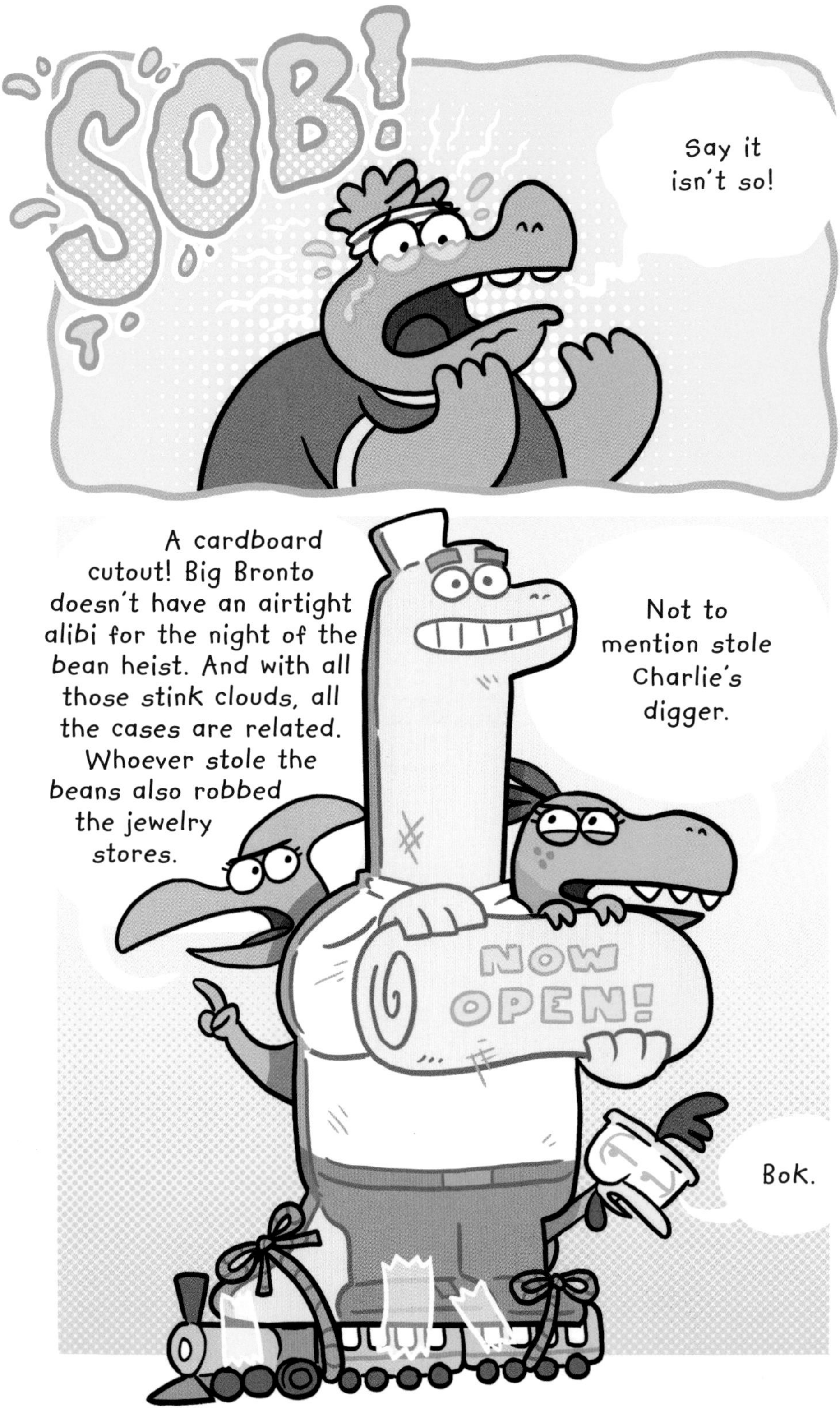
SOB!
Say it isn't so!
A cardboard cutout! Big Bronto doesn't have an airtight alibi for the night of the bean heist. And with all those stink clouds, all the cases are related. Whoever stole the beans also robbed the jewelry stores.
Not to mention stole Charlie's digger.
NOW OPEN!
Bok.

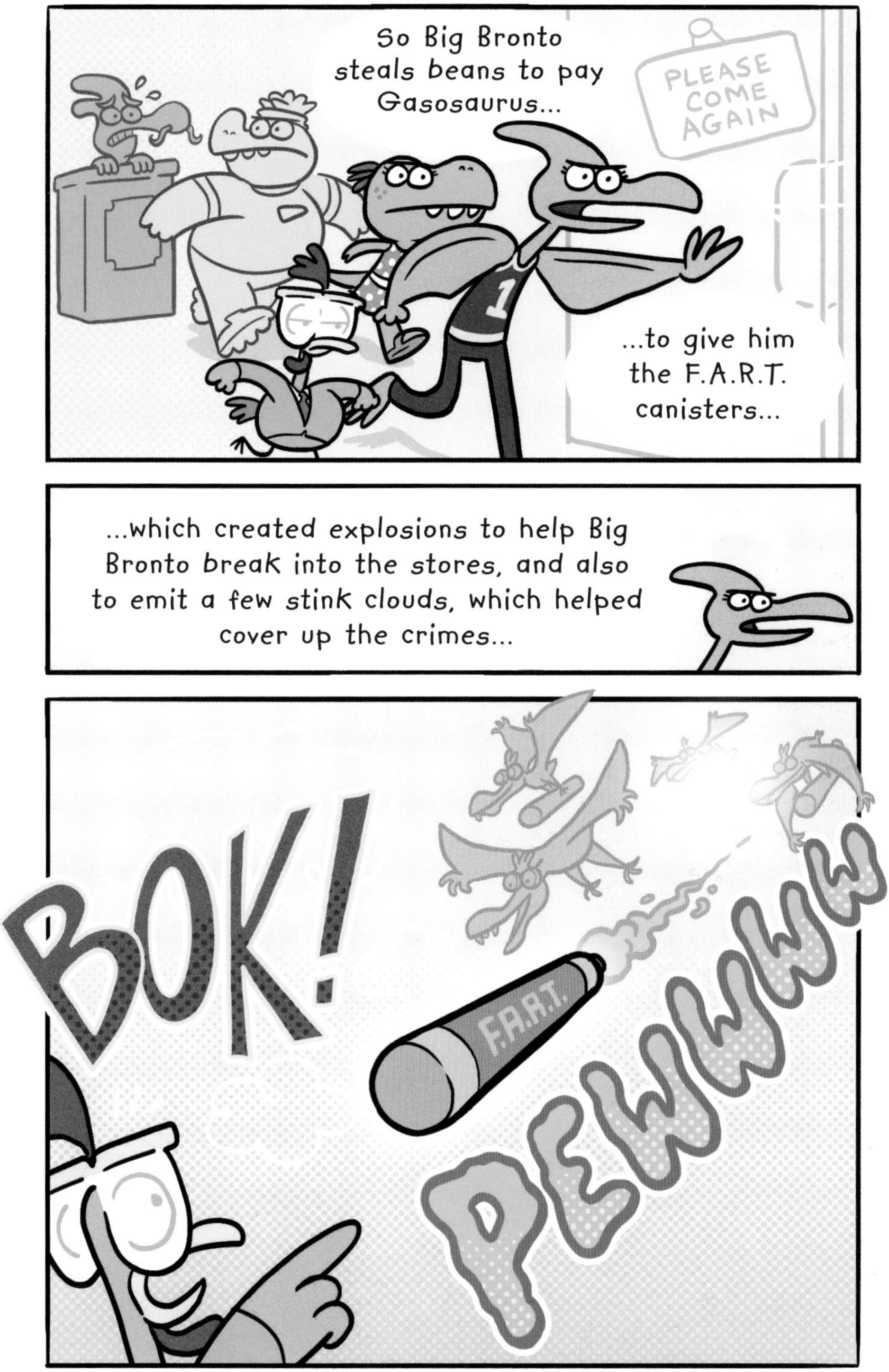
So Big Bronto steals beans to pay Gasosaurus...
PLEASE COME AGAIN
...to give him the F.A.R.T. canisters...
...which created explosions to help Big Bronto break into the stores, and also to emit a few stink clouds, which helped cover up the crimes...
BOK!
F.A.R.T.
PEWWWW

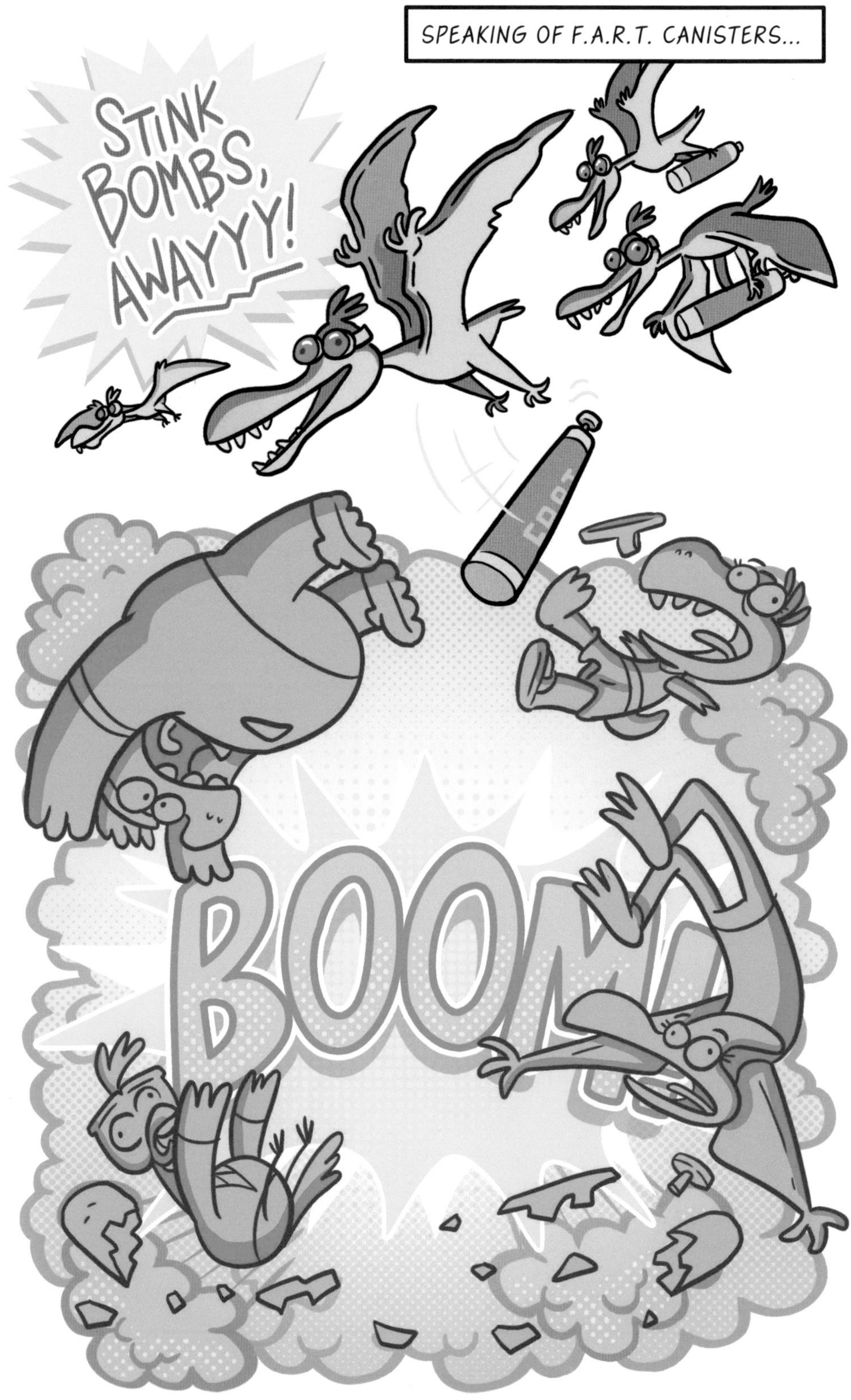
SPEAKING OF F.A.R.T. CANISTERS...
STINK BOMBS, AWAYYY!
BOOM!

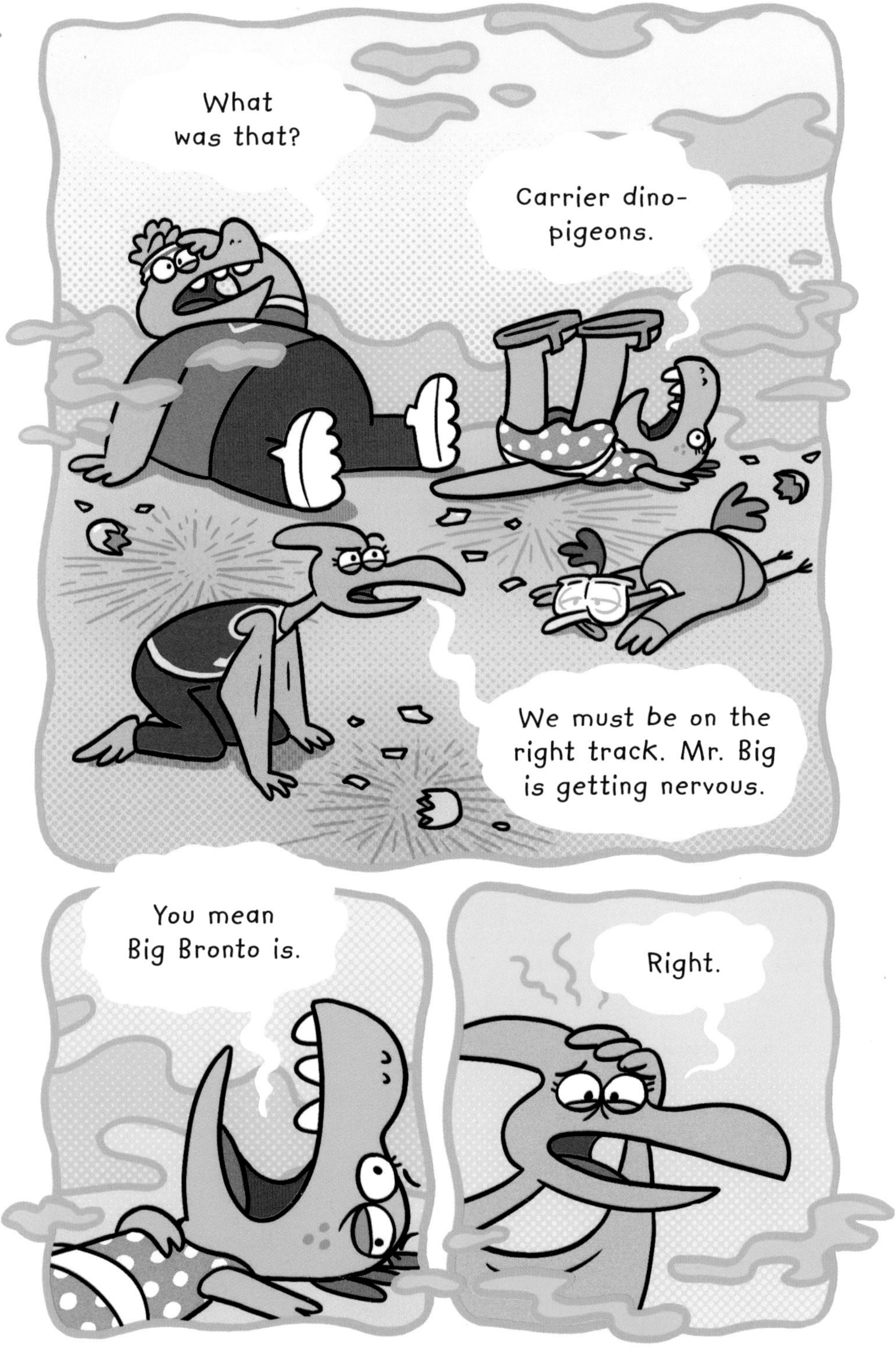
What was that?
Carrier dino-pigeons.
We must be on the right track. Mr. Big is getting nervous.
You mean Big Bronto is.
Right.

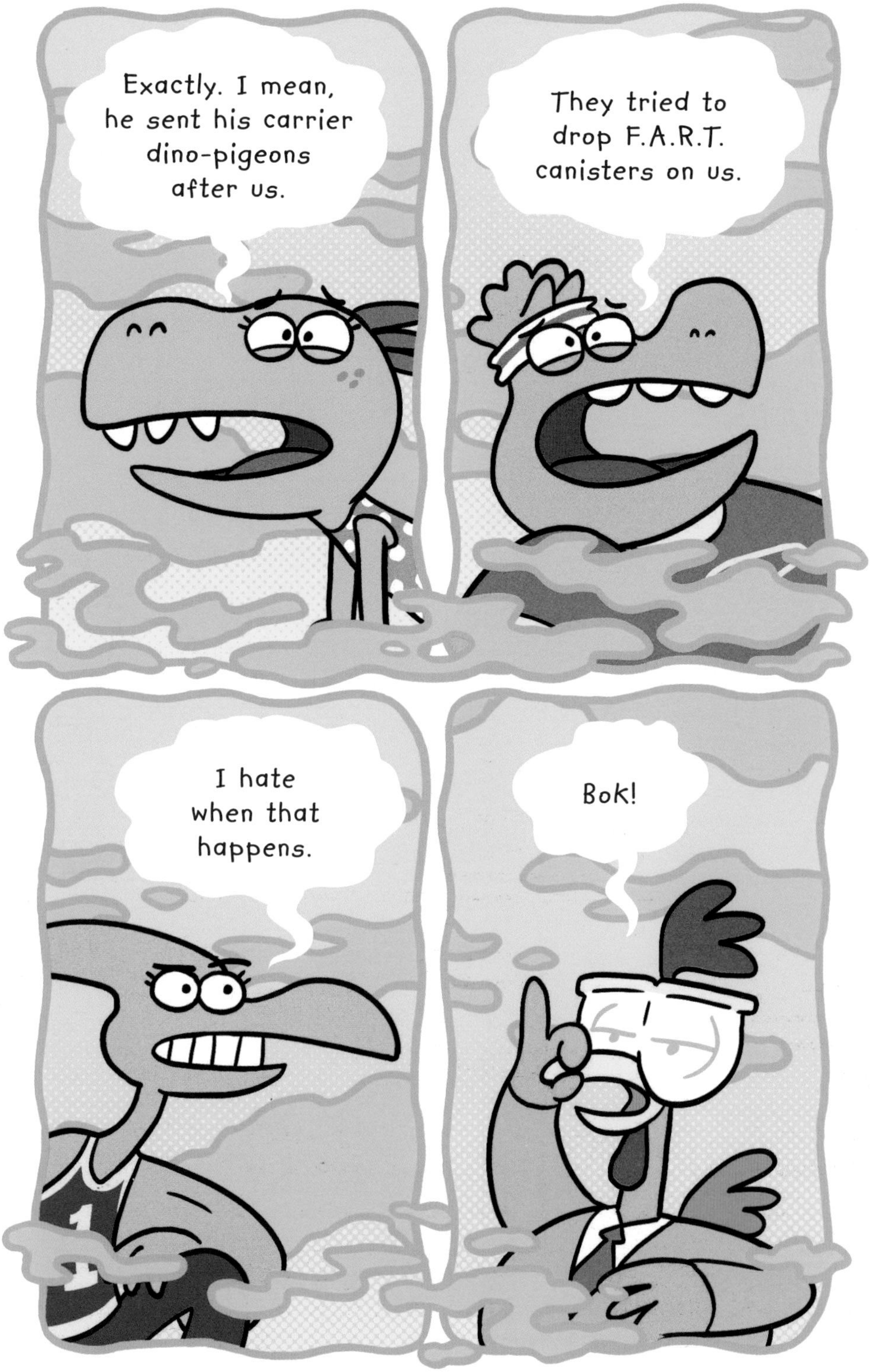
Exactly. I mean, he sent his carrier dino-pigeons after us.
They tried to drop F.A.R.T. canisters on us.
I hate when that happens.
Bok!

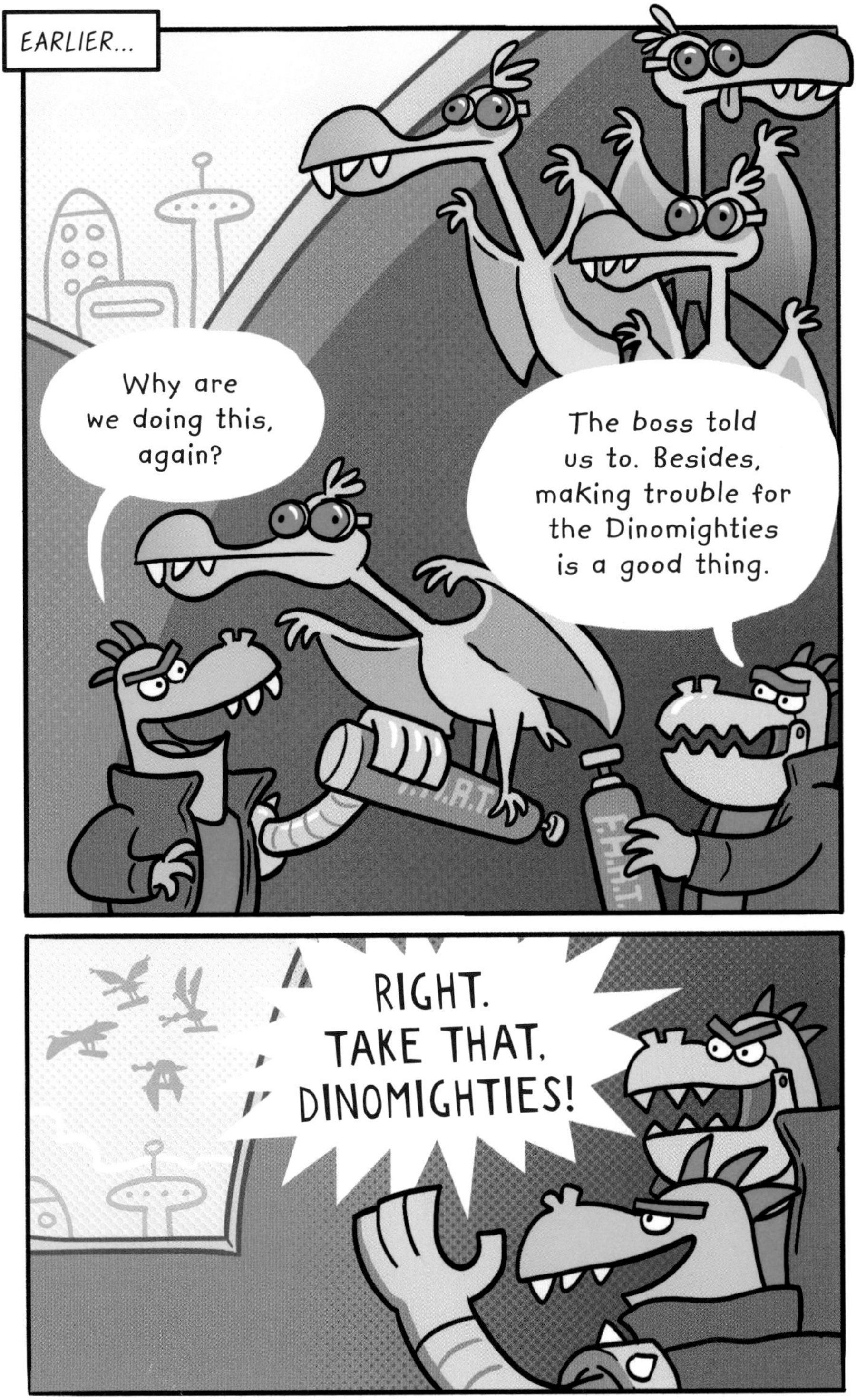
EARLIER...
Why are we doing this, again?
The boss told us to. Besides, making trouble for the Dinomighties is a good thing.
RIGHT. TAKE THAT, DINOMIGHTIES!

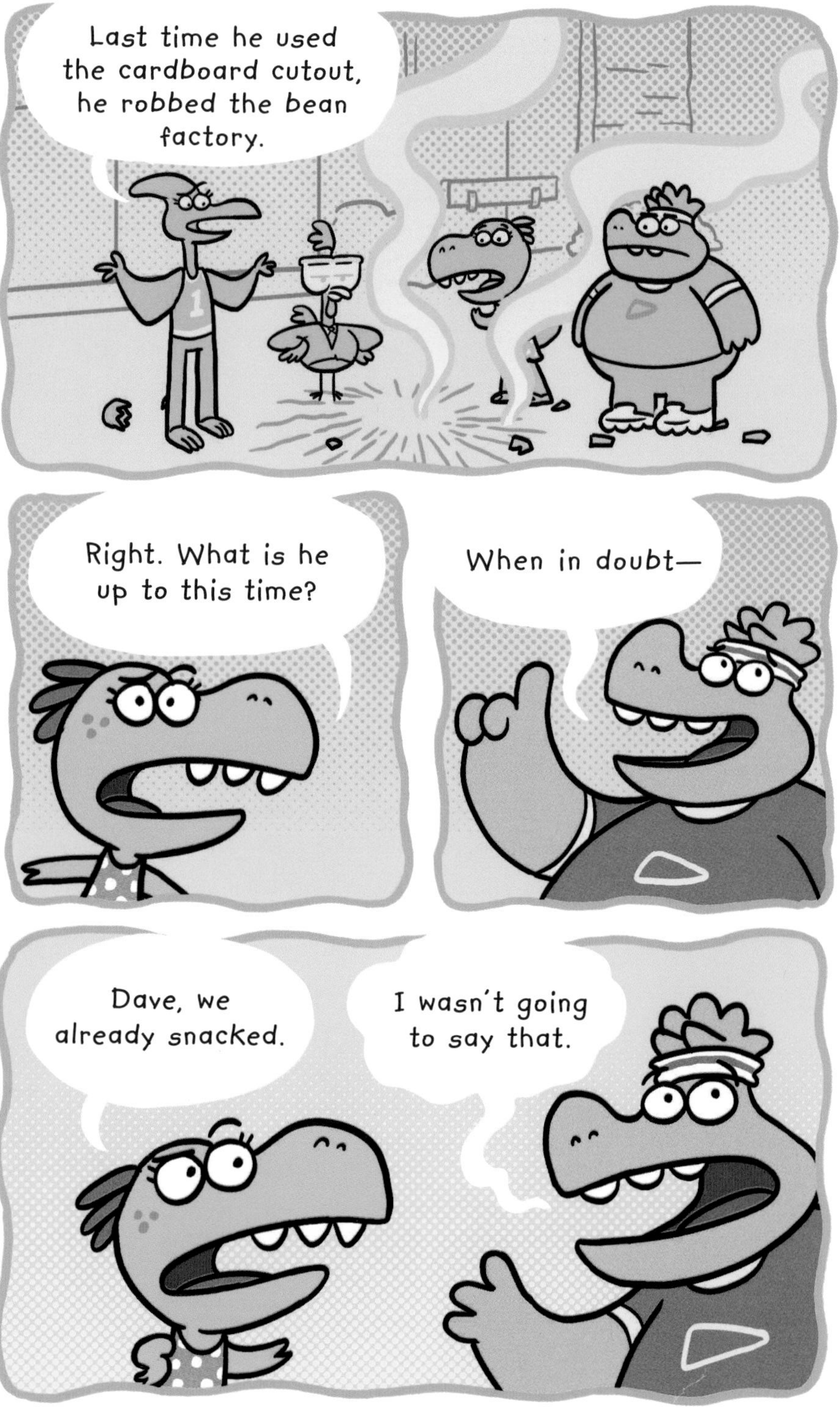
Last time he used the cardboard cutout, he robbed the bean factory.
Right. What is he up to this time?
When in doubt—
Dave, we already snacked.
I wasn't going to say that.

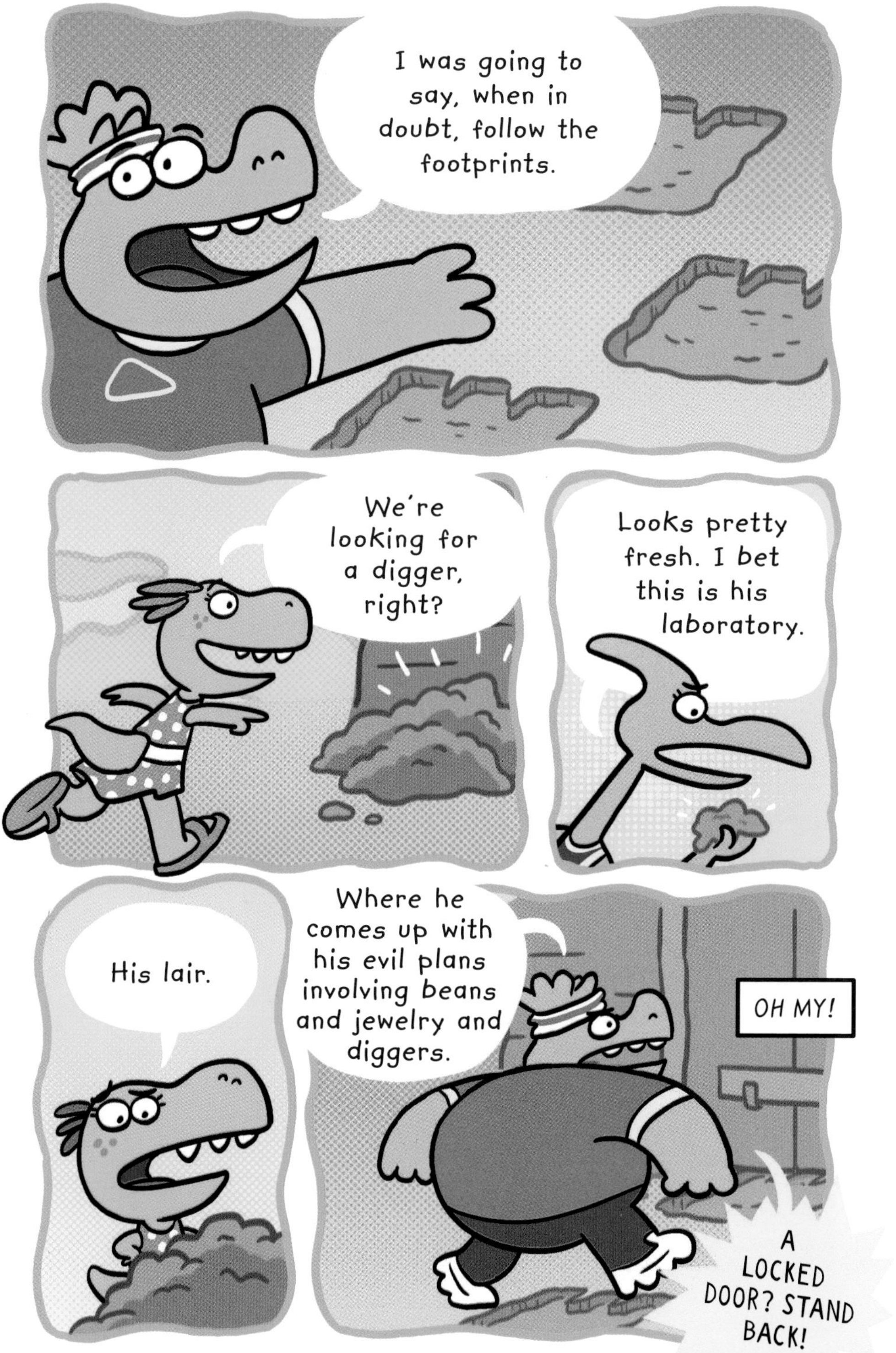
I was going to say, when in doubt, follow the footprints.
We're looking for a digger, right?
Looks pretty fresh. I bet this is his laboratory.
His lair.
Where he comes up with his evil plans involving beans and jewelry and diggers.
OH MY!
A LOCKED DOOR? STAND BACK!

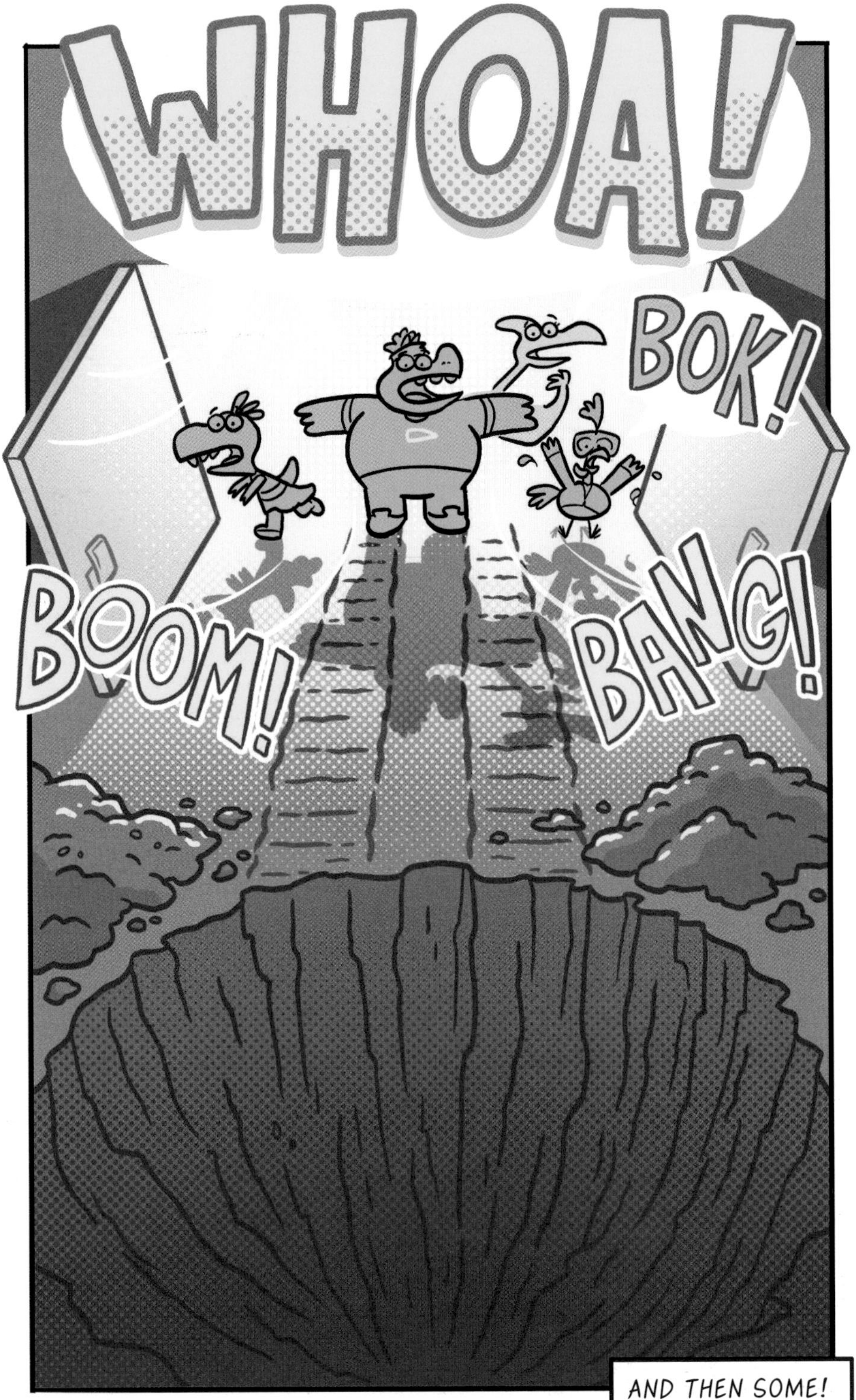
WHOA!
BOK!
BOOM!
BANG!
AND THEN SOME!

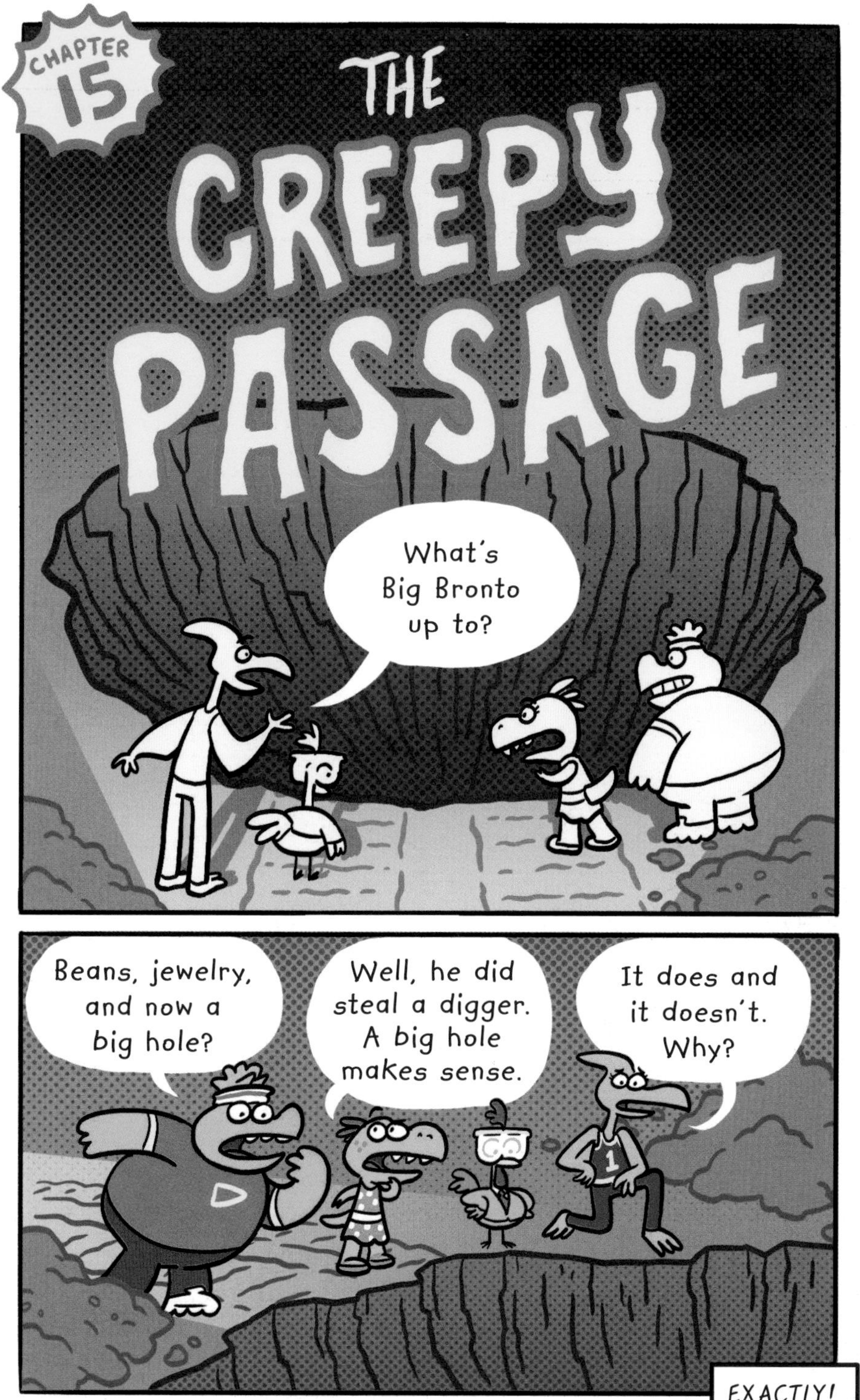
CHAPTER 15
THE CREEPY PASSAGE
What's Big Bronto up to?
Beans, jewelry, and now a big hole?
Well, he did steal a digger. A big hole makes sense.
It does and it doesn't. Why?
EXACTLY!

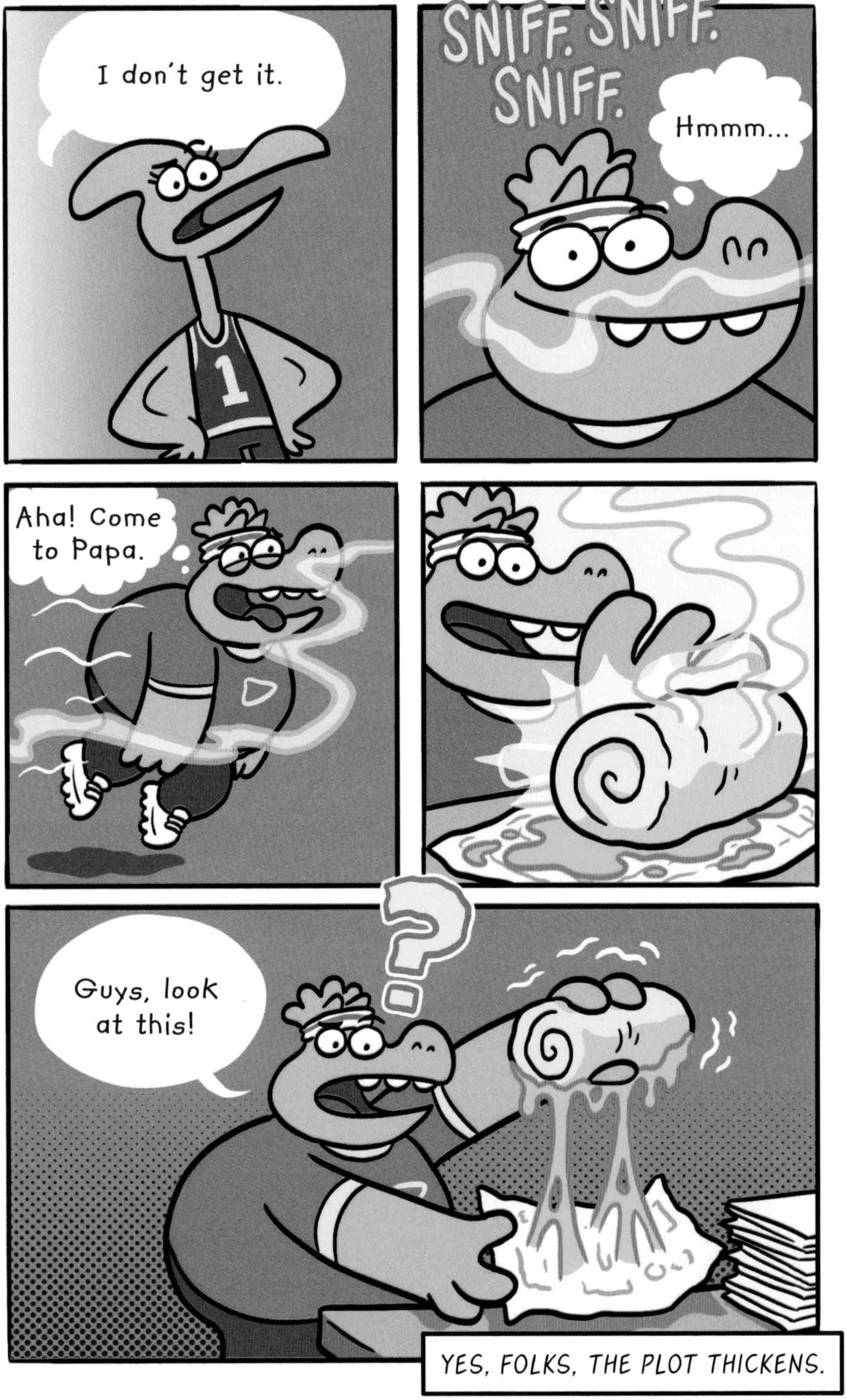
I don't get it.
SNIFF. SNIFF. SNIFF.
Hmmm...
Aha! Come to Papa.
Guys, look at this!
YES, FOLKS, THE PLOT THICKENS.

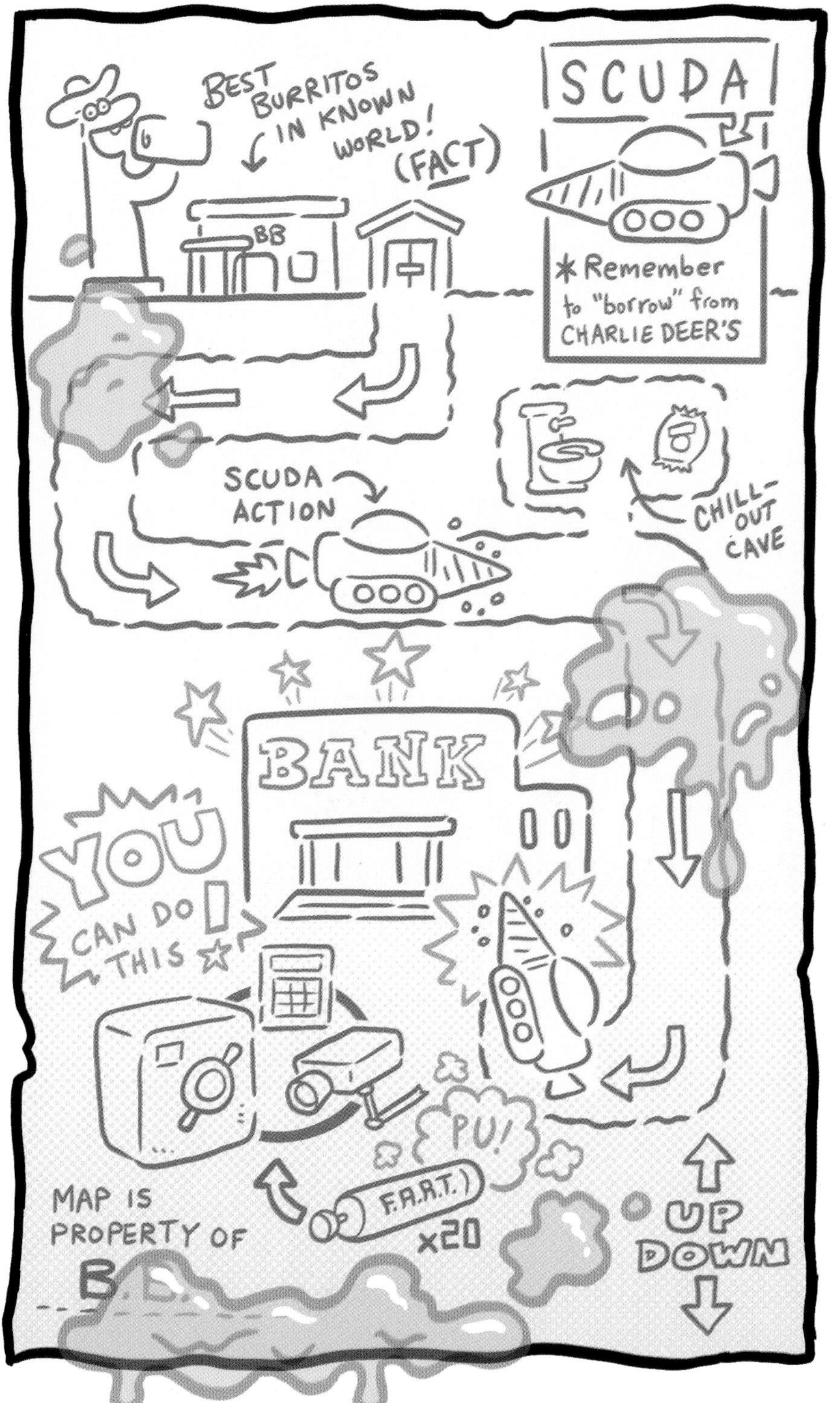

BEST BURRITOS IN KNOWN WORLD! (FACT)
BB
SCUDA
* Remember to "borrow" from CHARLIE DEER'S
SCUDA ACTION
CHILL-OUT CAVE
BANK
YOU CAN DO THIS!
P.U!
F.A.R.T.
x20
MAP IS PROPERTY OF
B
UP
DOWN

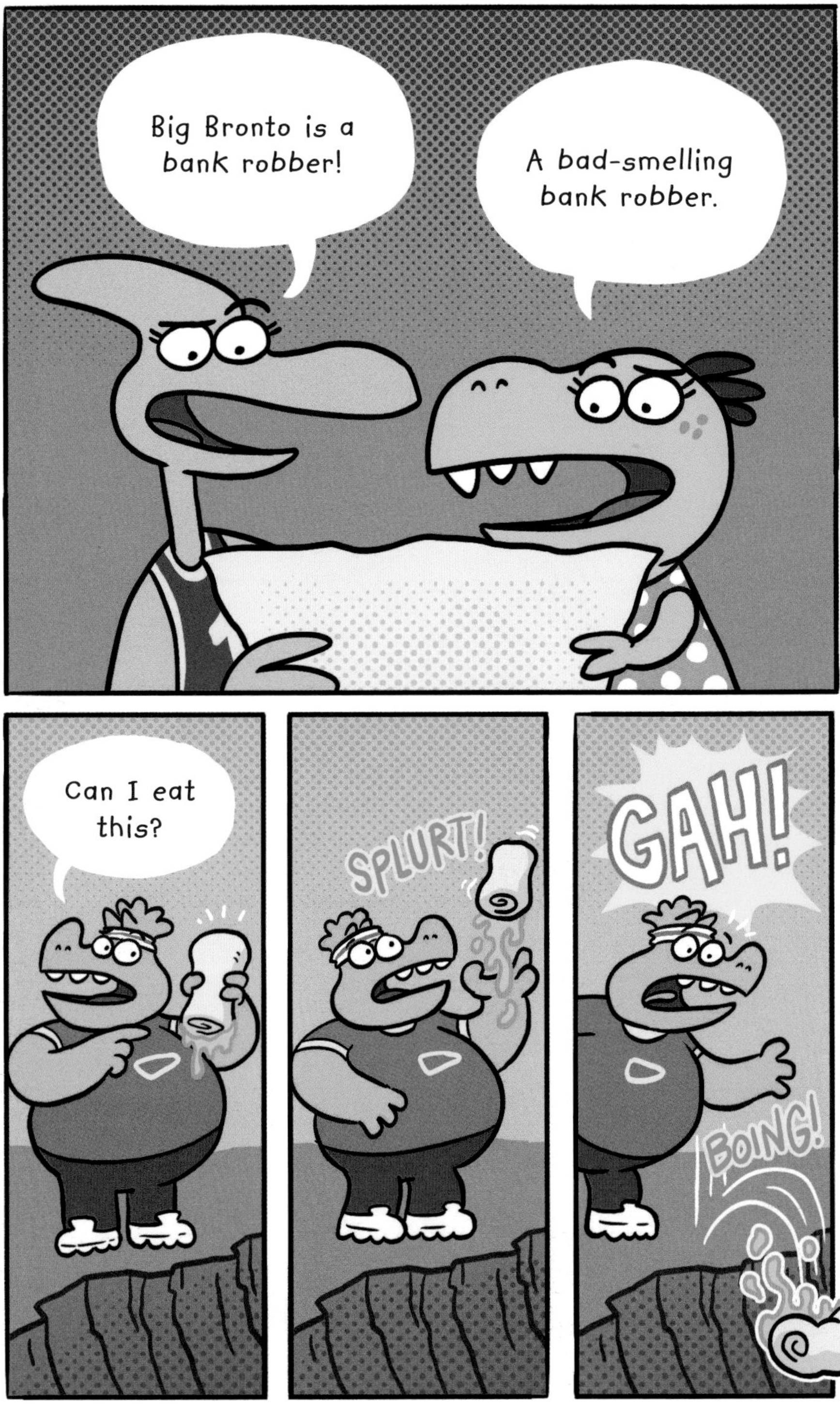
Big Bronto is a bank robber!
A bad-smelling bank robber.
Can I eat this?
SPLURT!
GAH!
BOING!

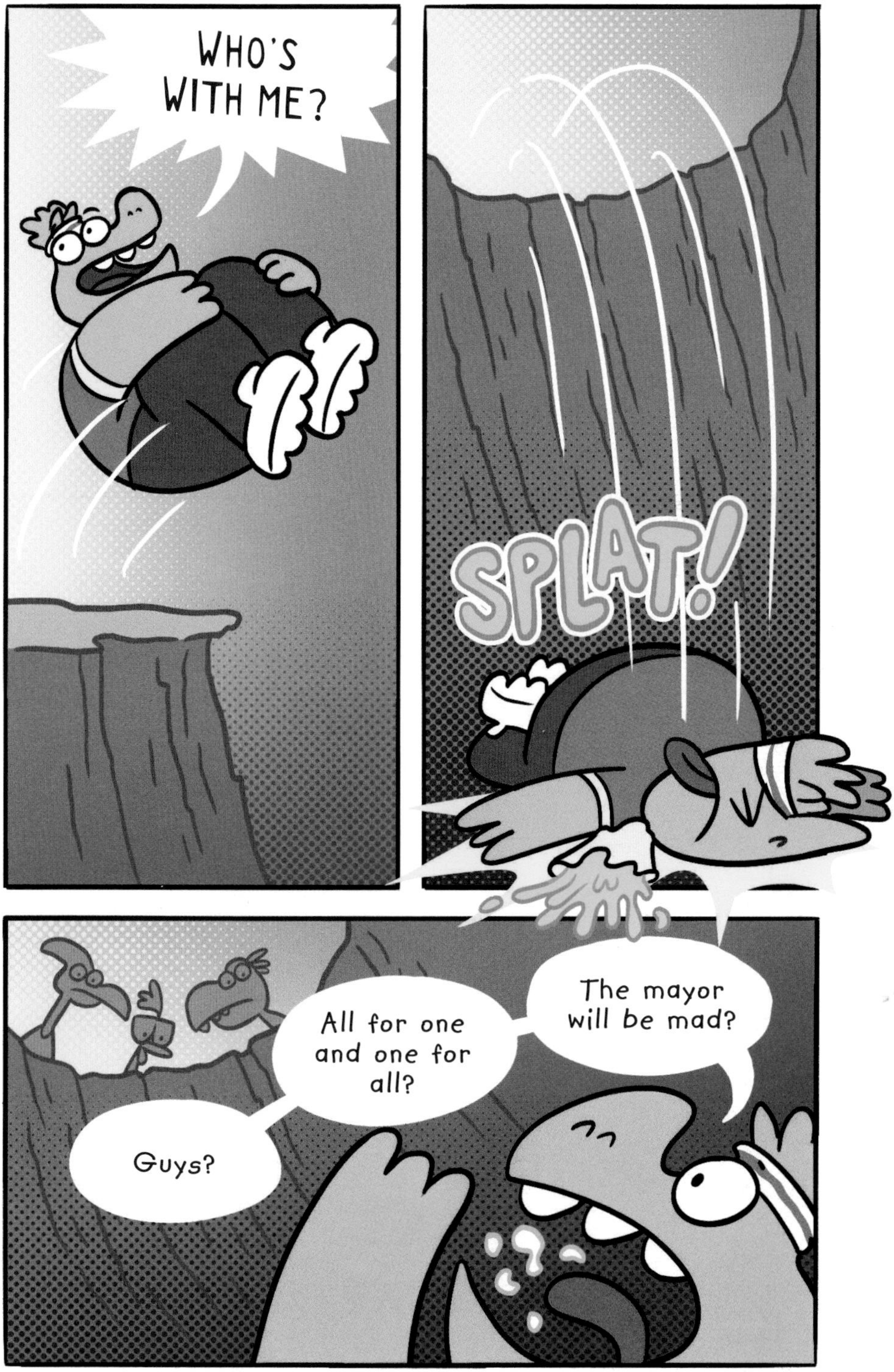
WHO'S WITH ME?
SPLAT!
Guys?
All for one and one for all?
The mayor will be mad?

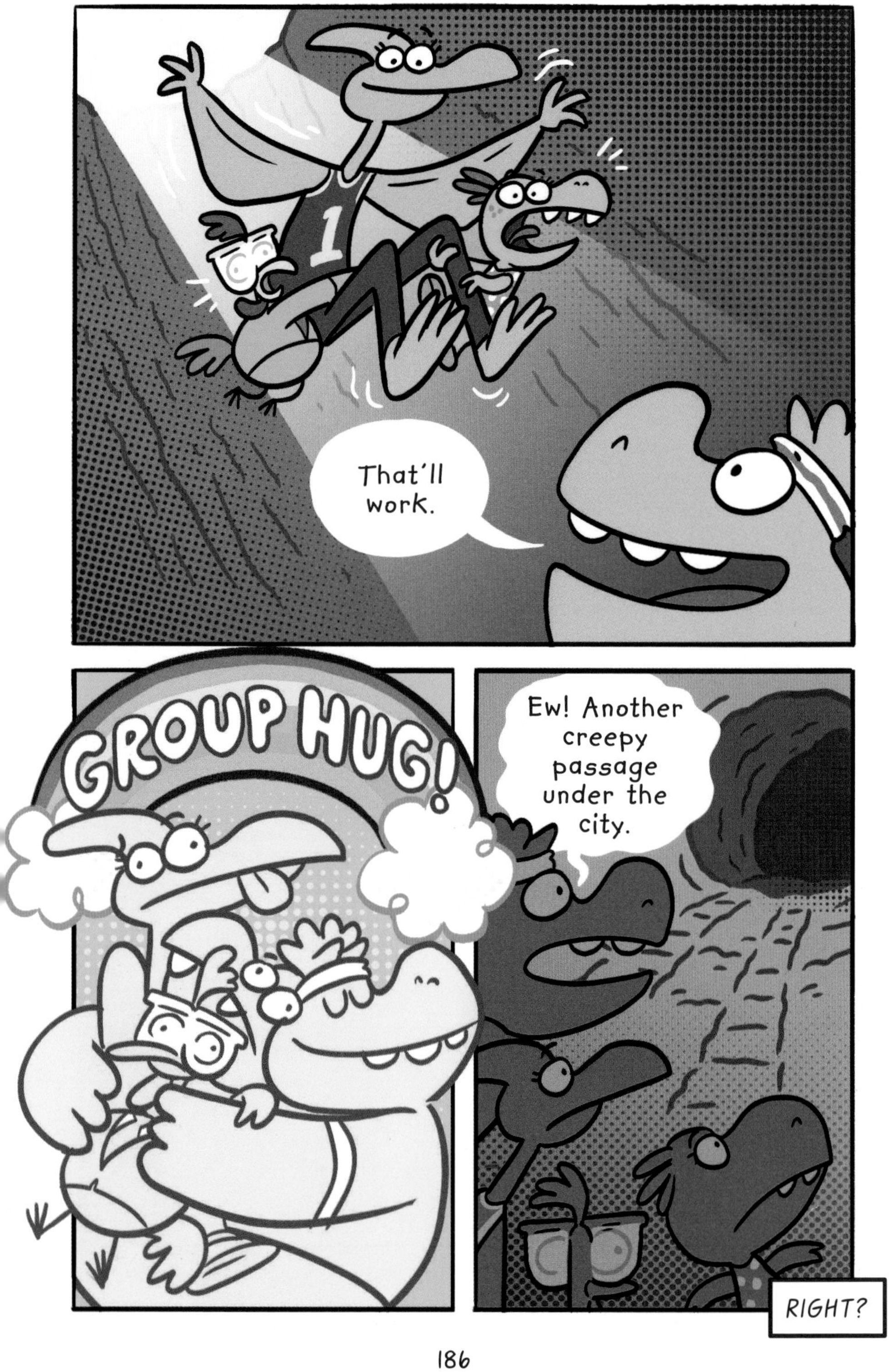
That'll work.
GROUP HUG!
Ew! Another creepy passage under the city.
RIGHT?

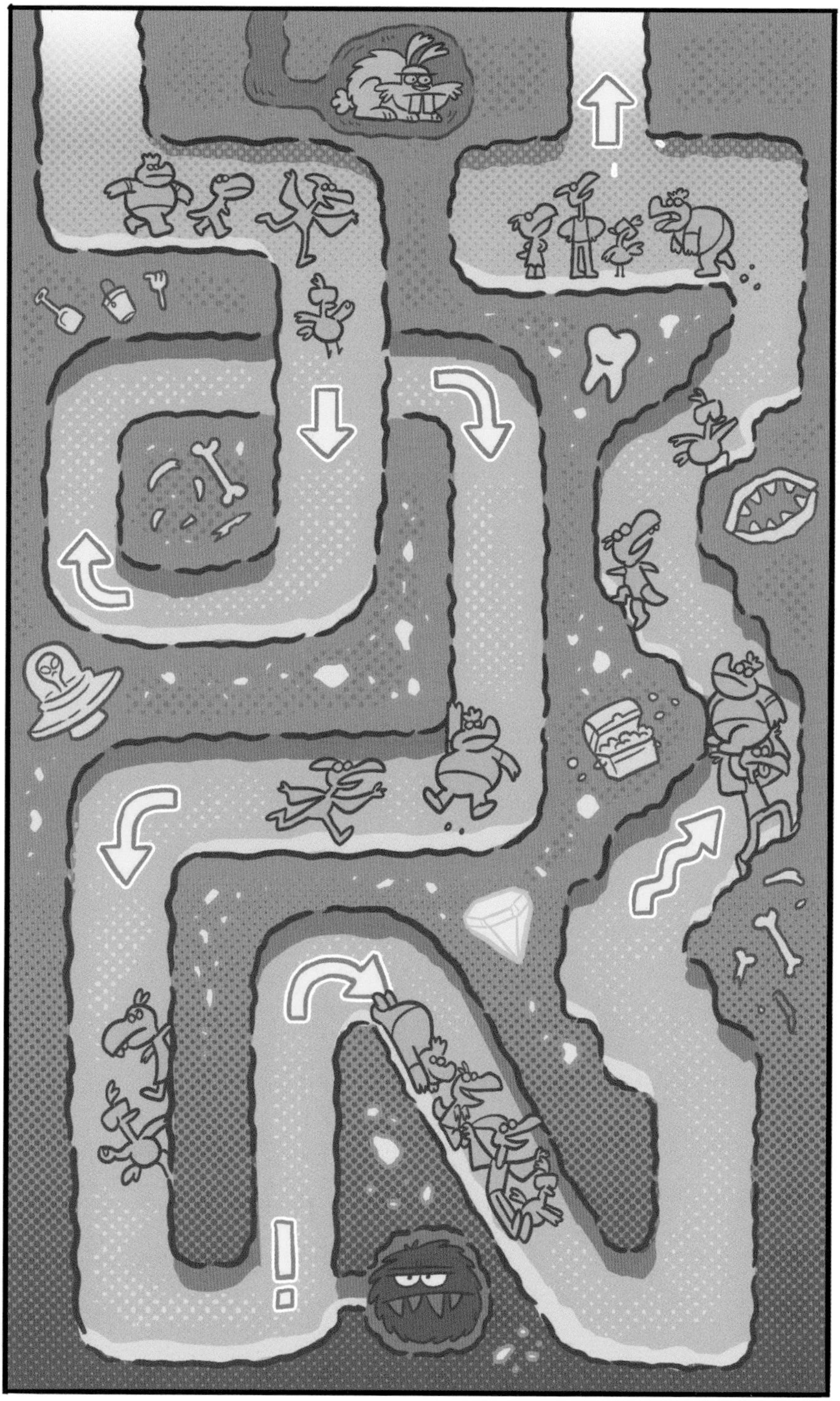

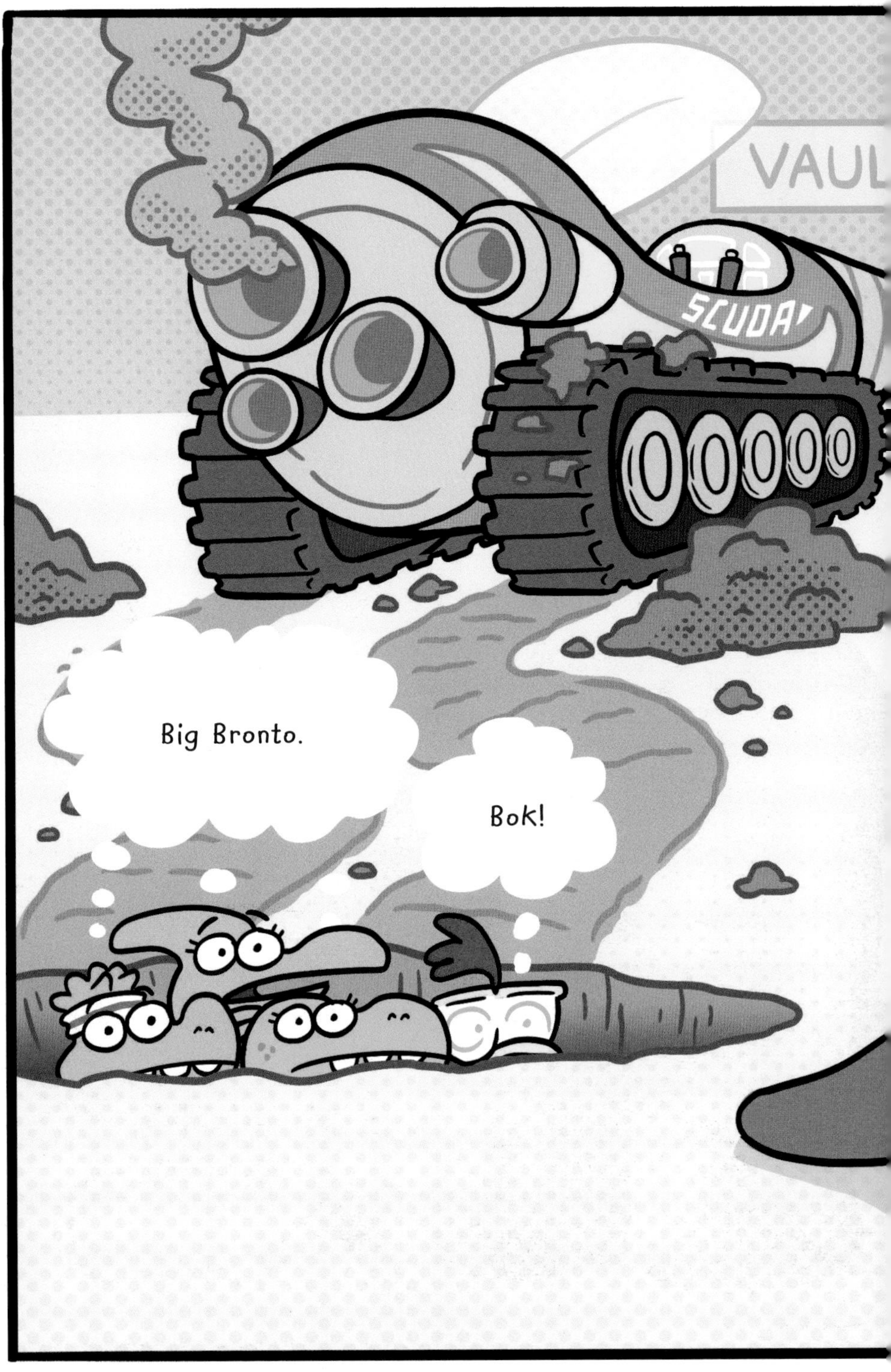
VAUL
SCUDA
Big Bronto.
Bok!

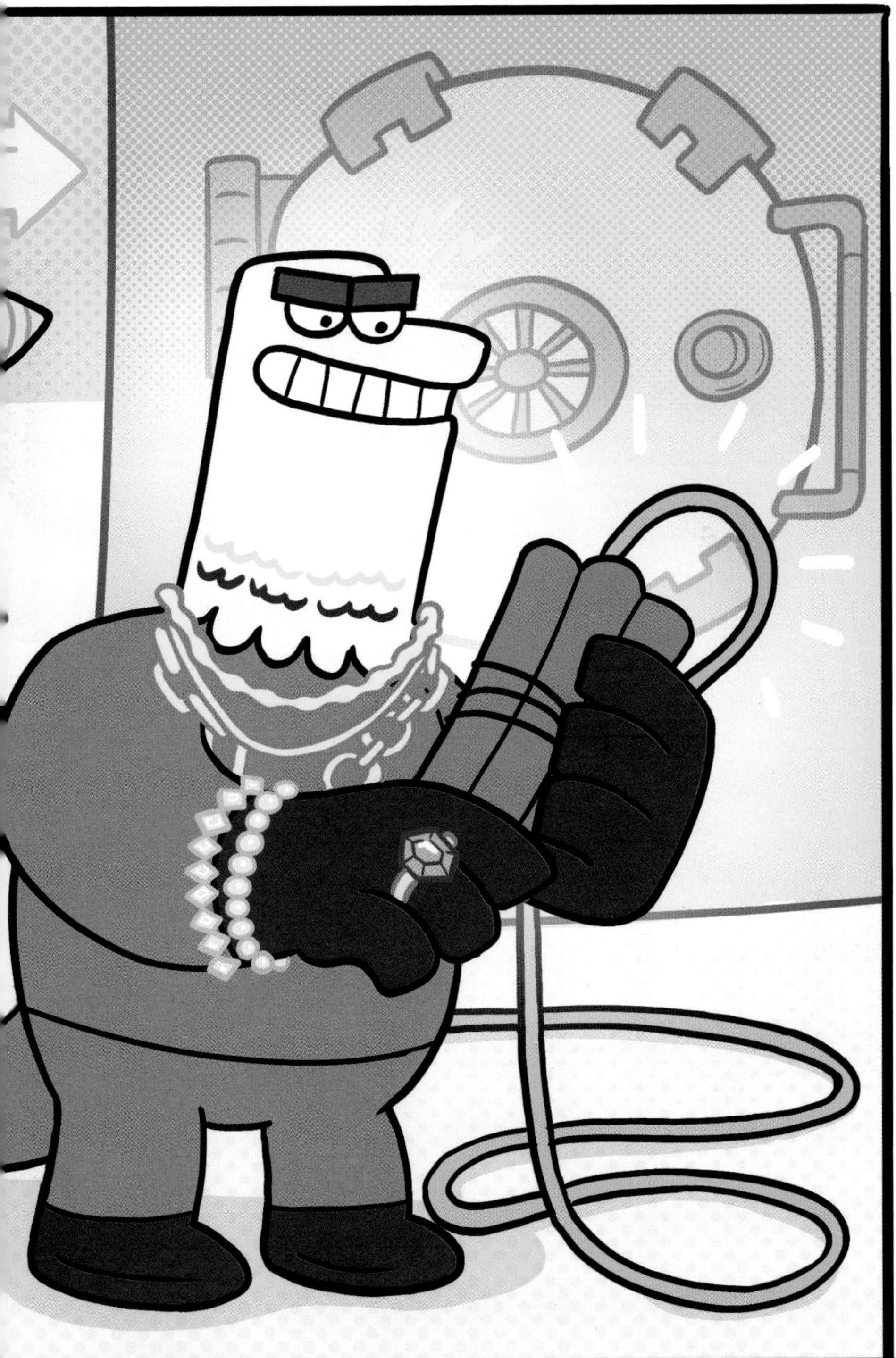

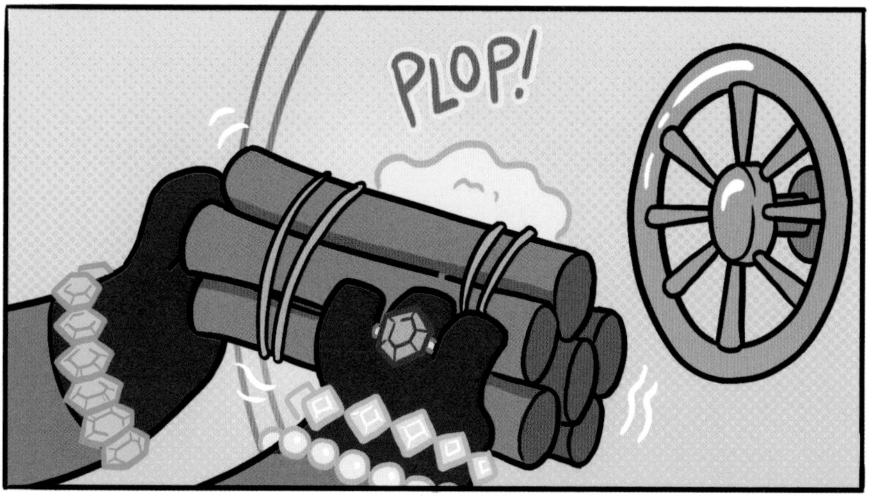
PLOP!

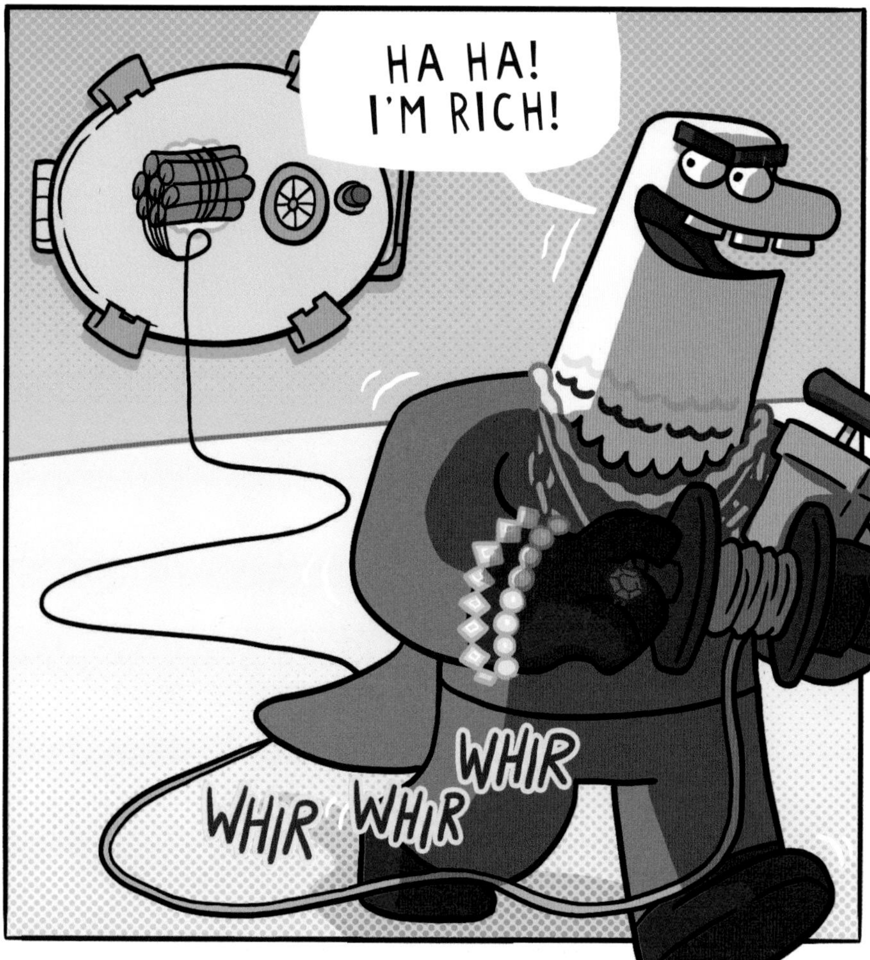
HA HA!
I'M RICH!
WHIR WHIR WHIR

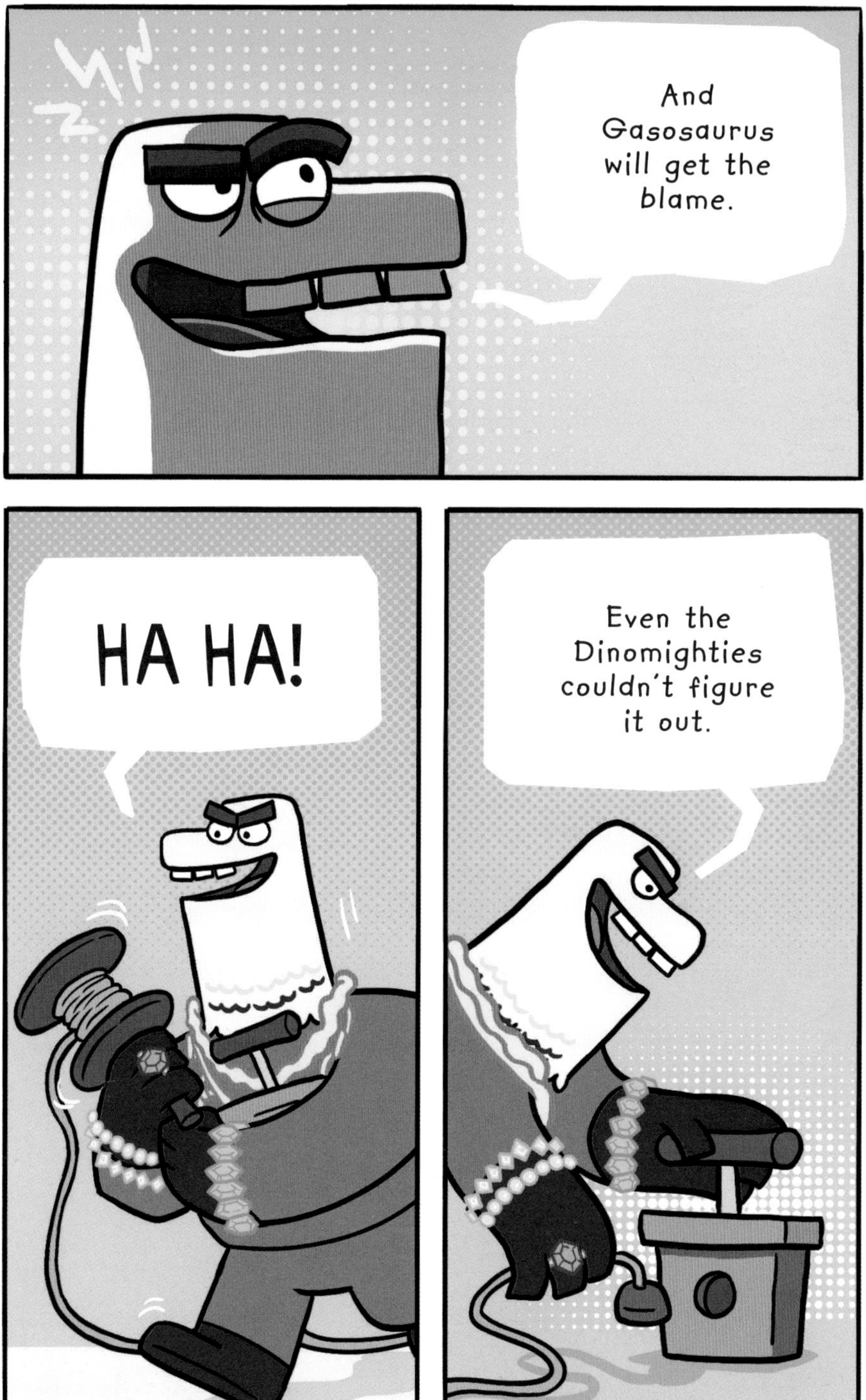
And Gasosaurus will get the blame.
HA HA!
Even the Dinomighties couldn't figure it out.

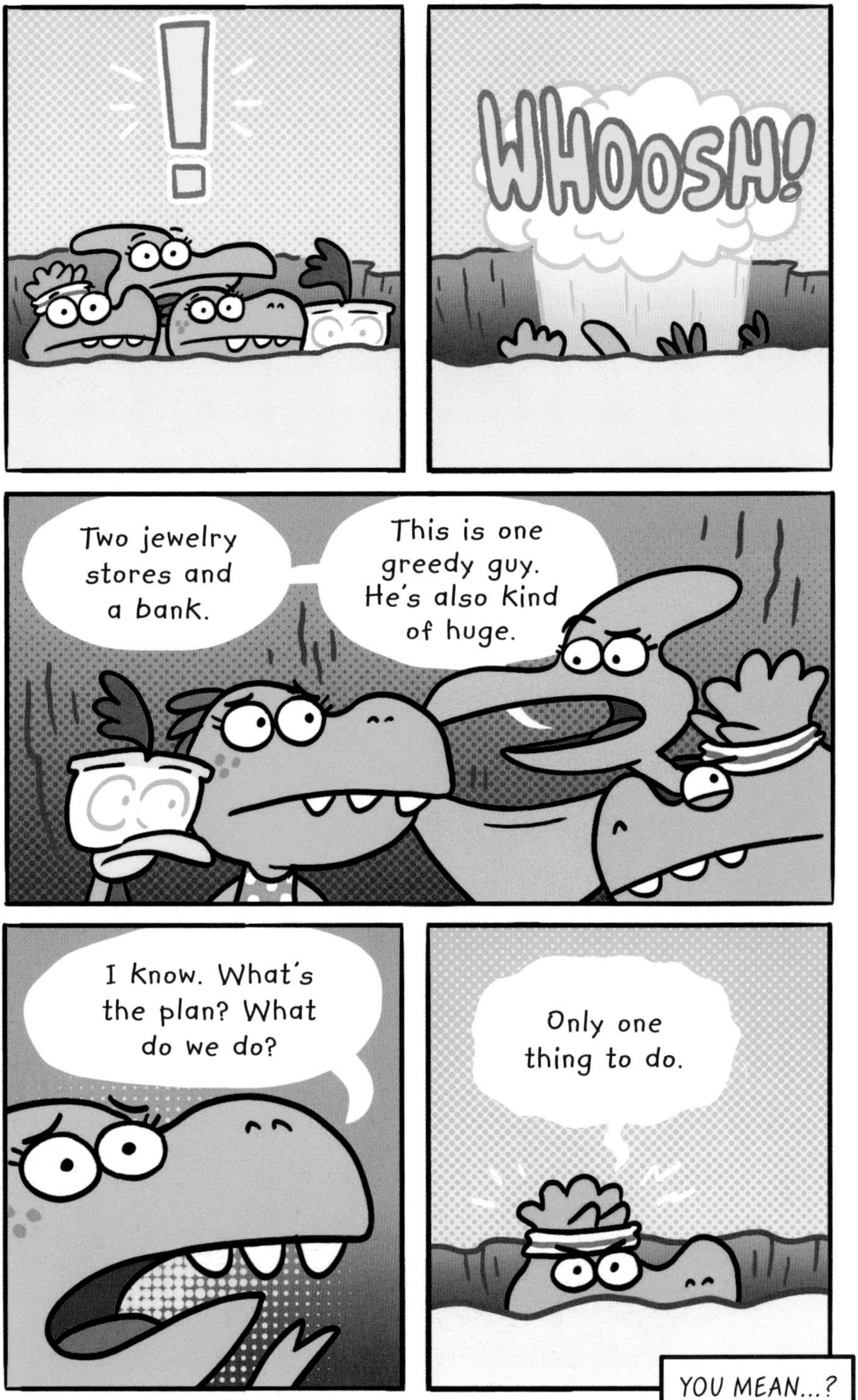
!
WHOOSH!
Two jewelry stores and a bank.
This is one greedy guy. He's also kind of huge.
I know. What's the plan? What do we do?
Only one thing to do.
YOU MEAN...?

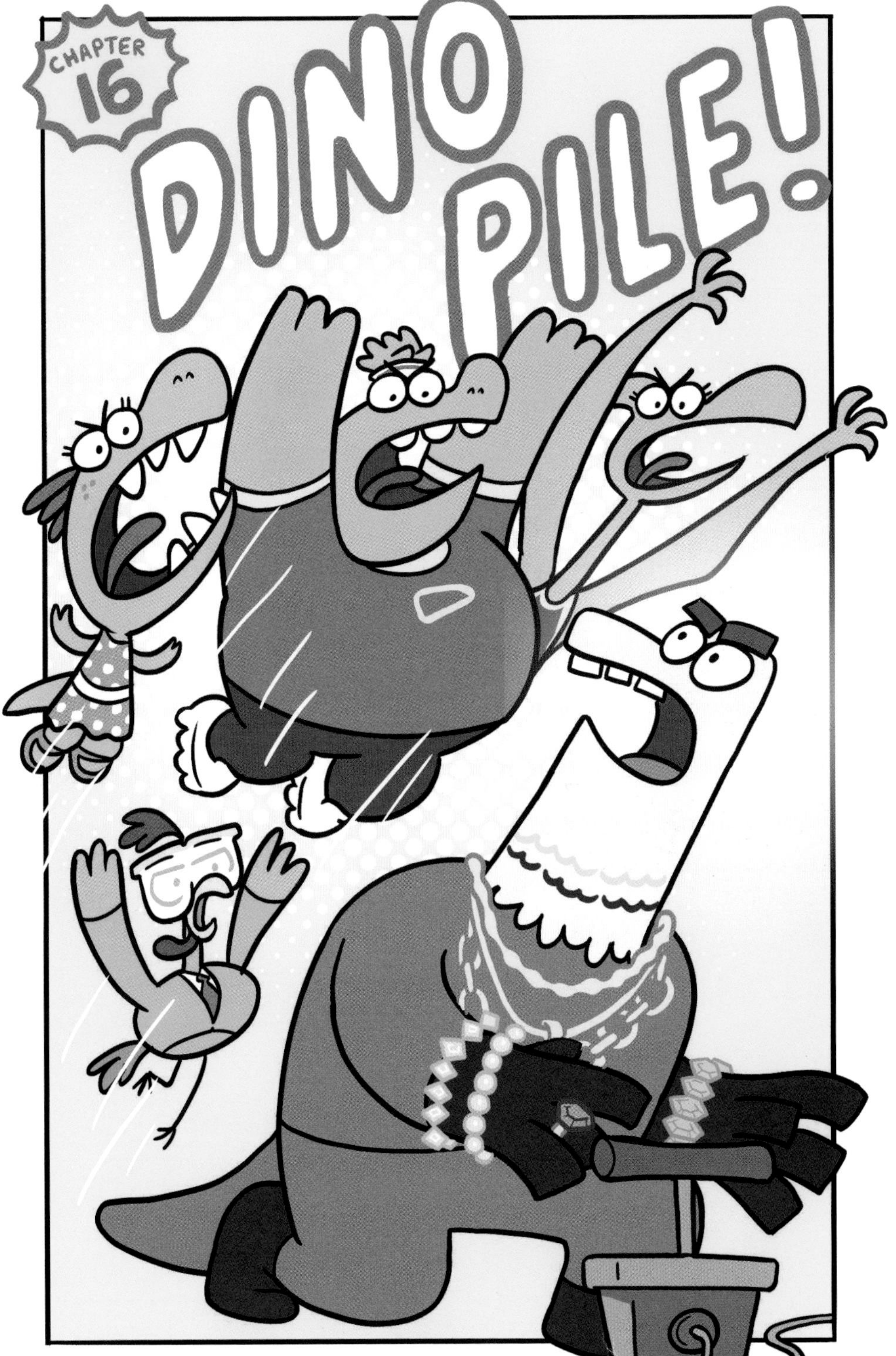
CHAPTER 16
DINO PILE!

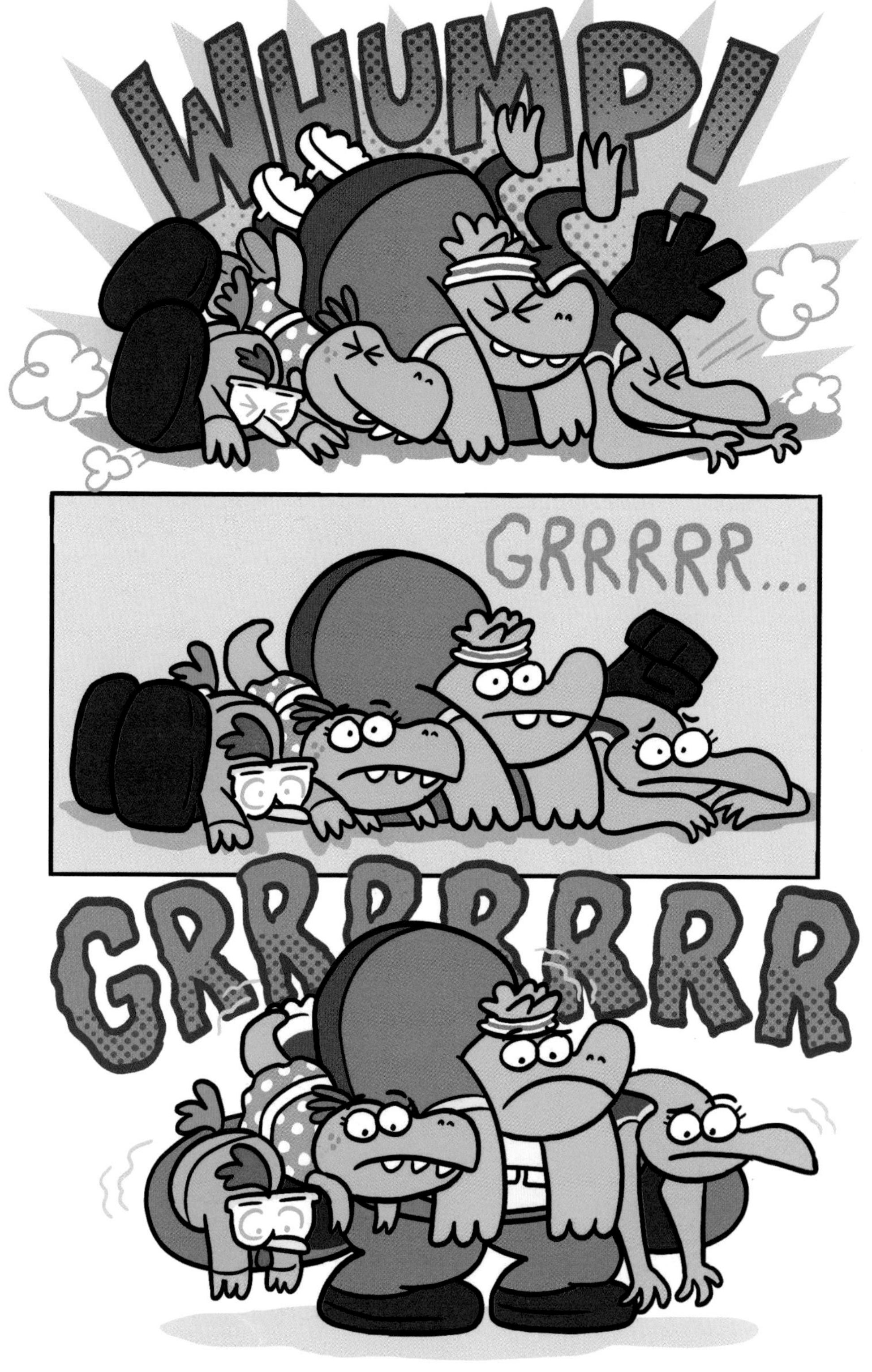
WHUMP!
GRRRRR...
GRRRRRRR

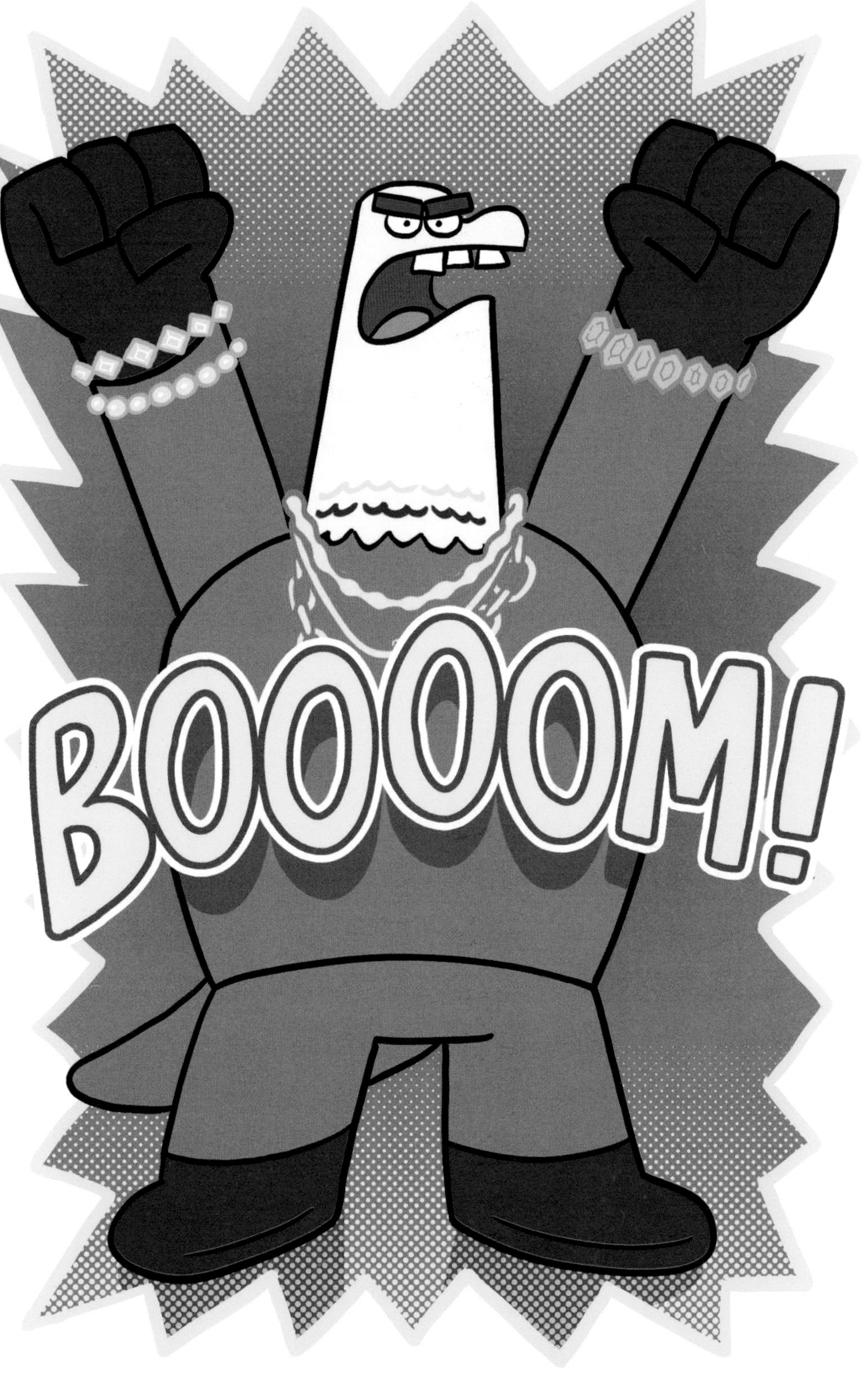
BOOOOM!

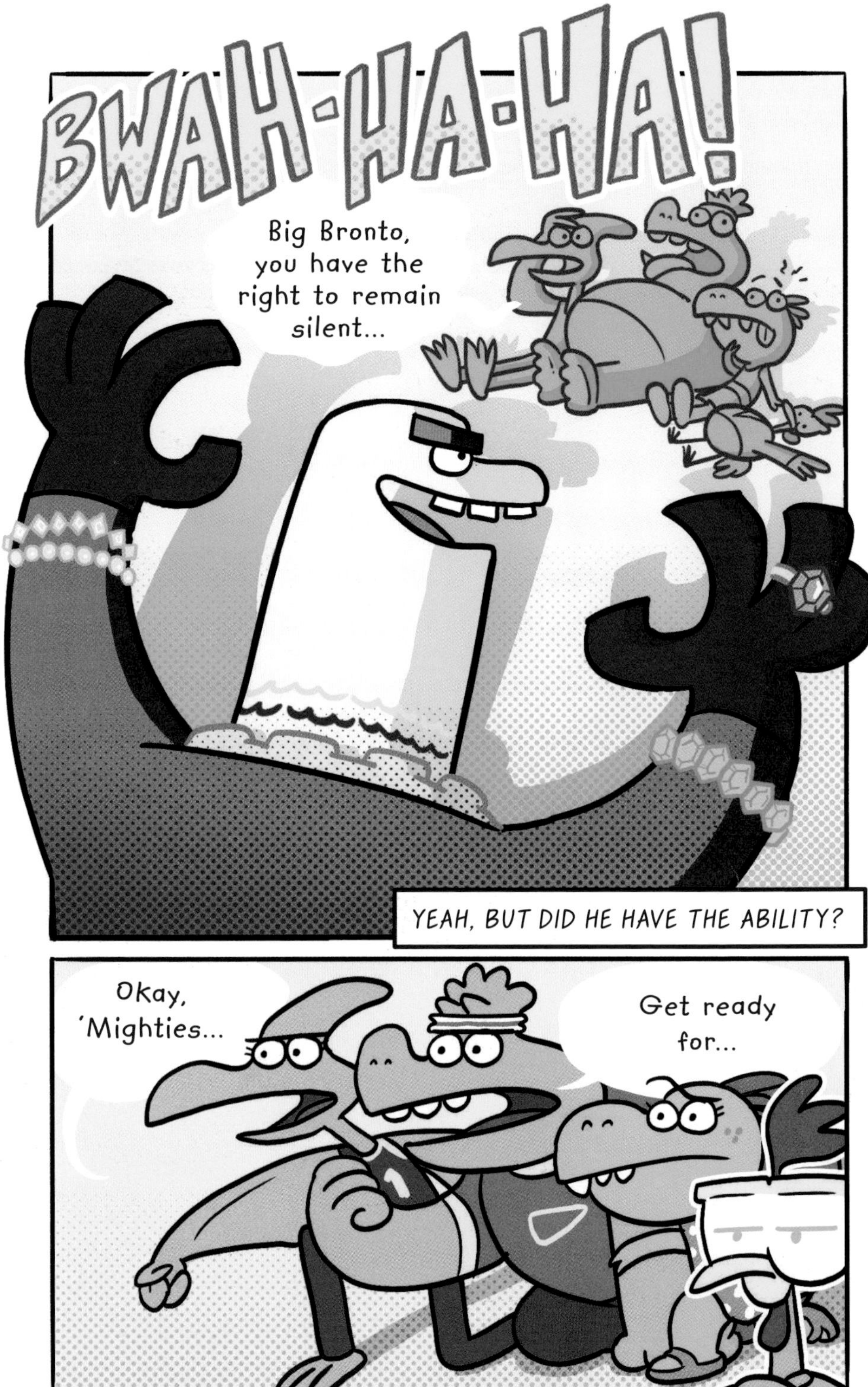
BWAH-HA-HA!
Big Bronto, you have the right to remain silent...
YEAH, BUT DID HE HAVE THE ABILITY?
Okay, 'Mighties...
Get ready for...

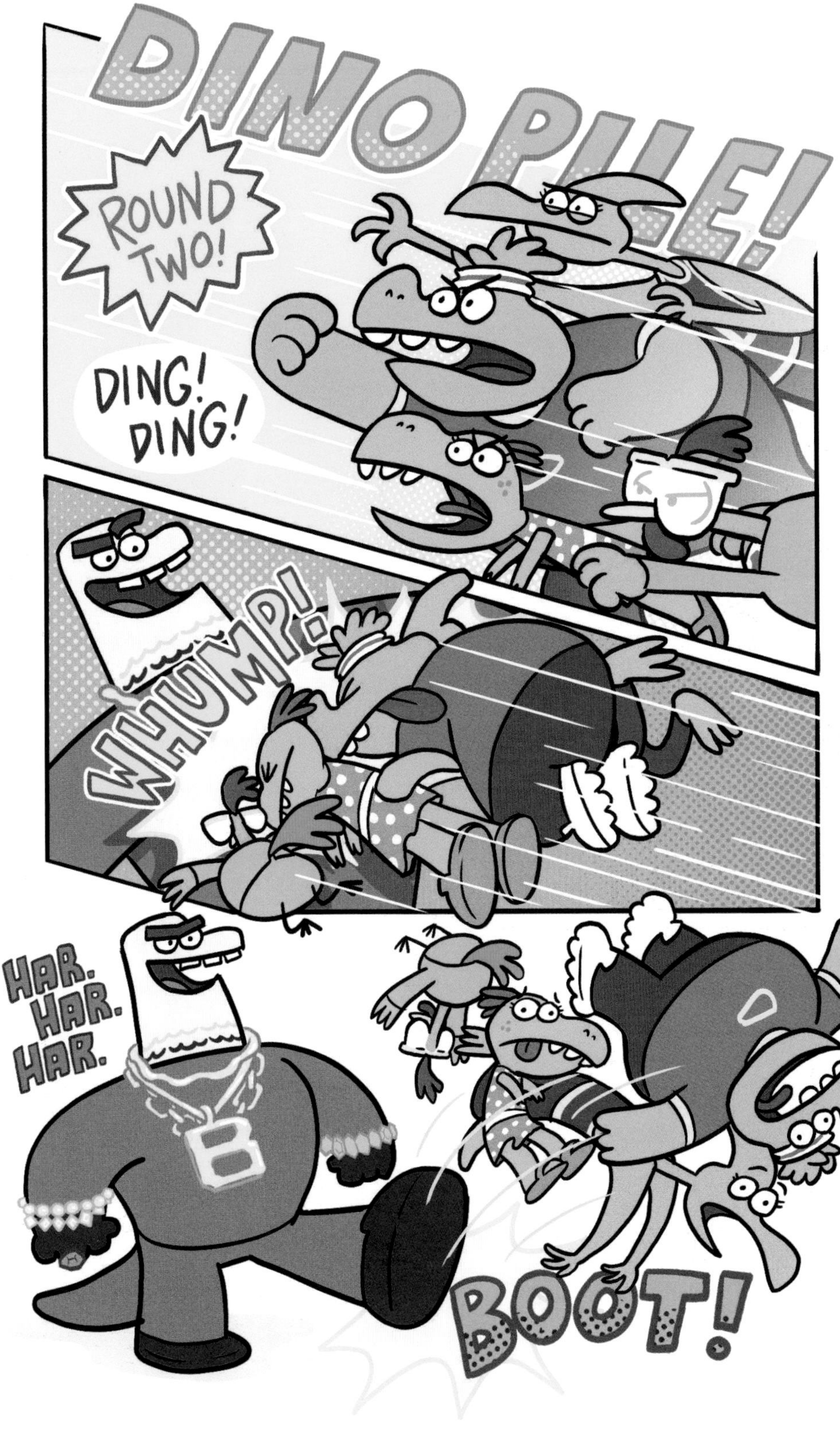
DINO PILE!
ROUND TWO!
DING! DING!
WHUMP!
HAR. HAR. HAR.
BOOT!

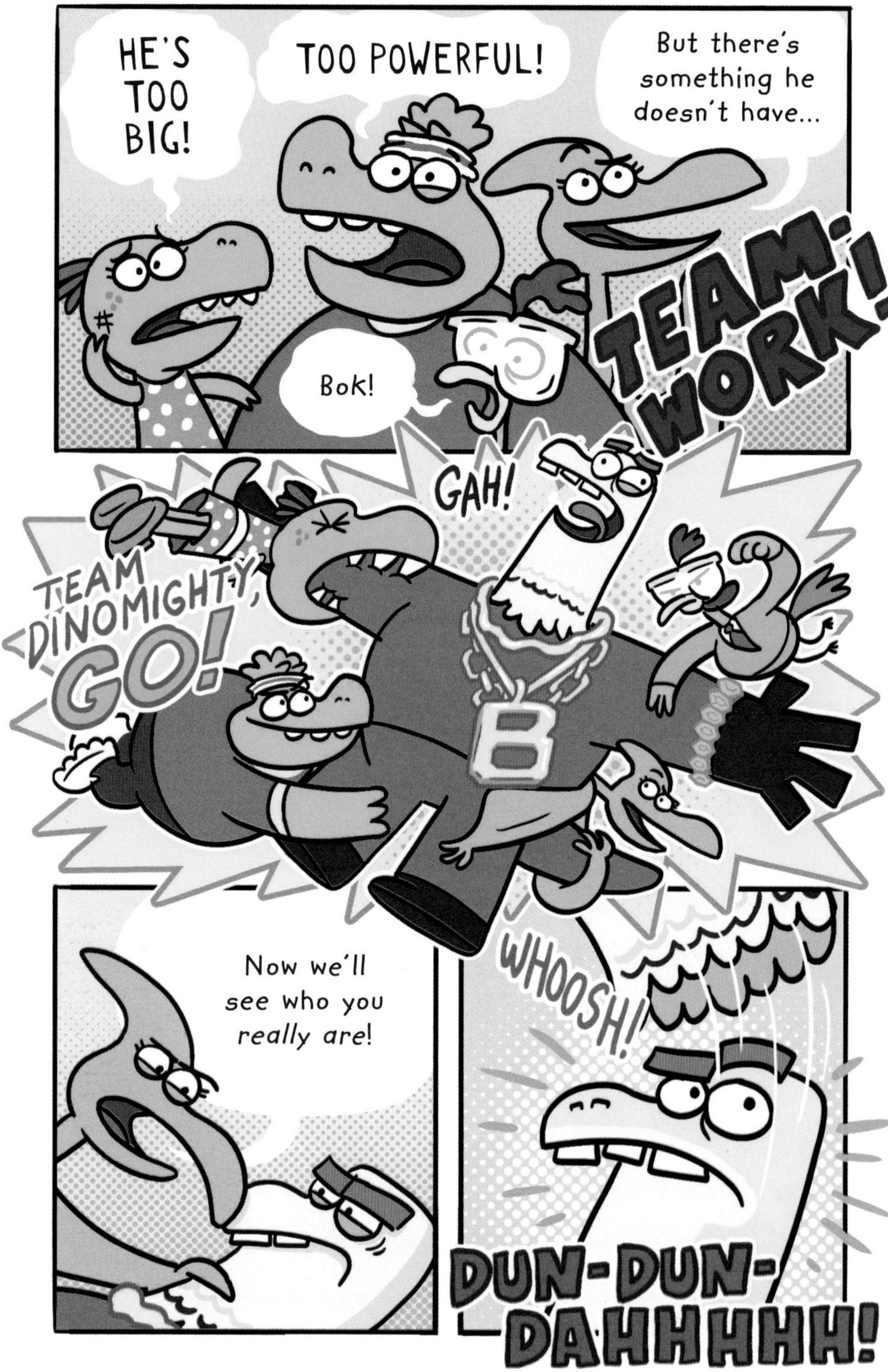
HE'S TOO BIG!
TOO POWERFUL!
But there's something he doesn't have...
Bok!
TEAM-WORK!
GAH!
TEAM DINOMIGHTY, GO!
Now we'll see who you really are!
WHOOSH!
DUN-DUN-DAHHHHH!

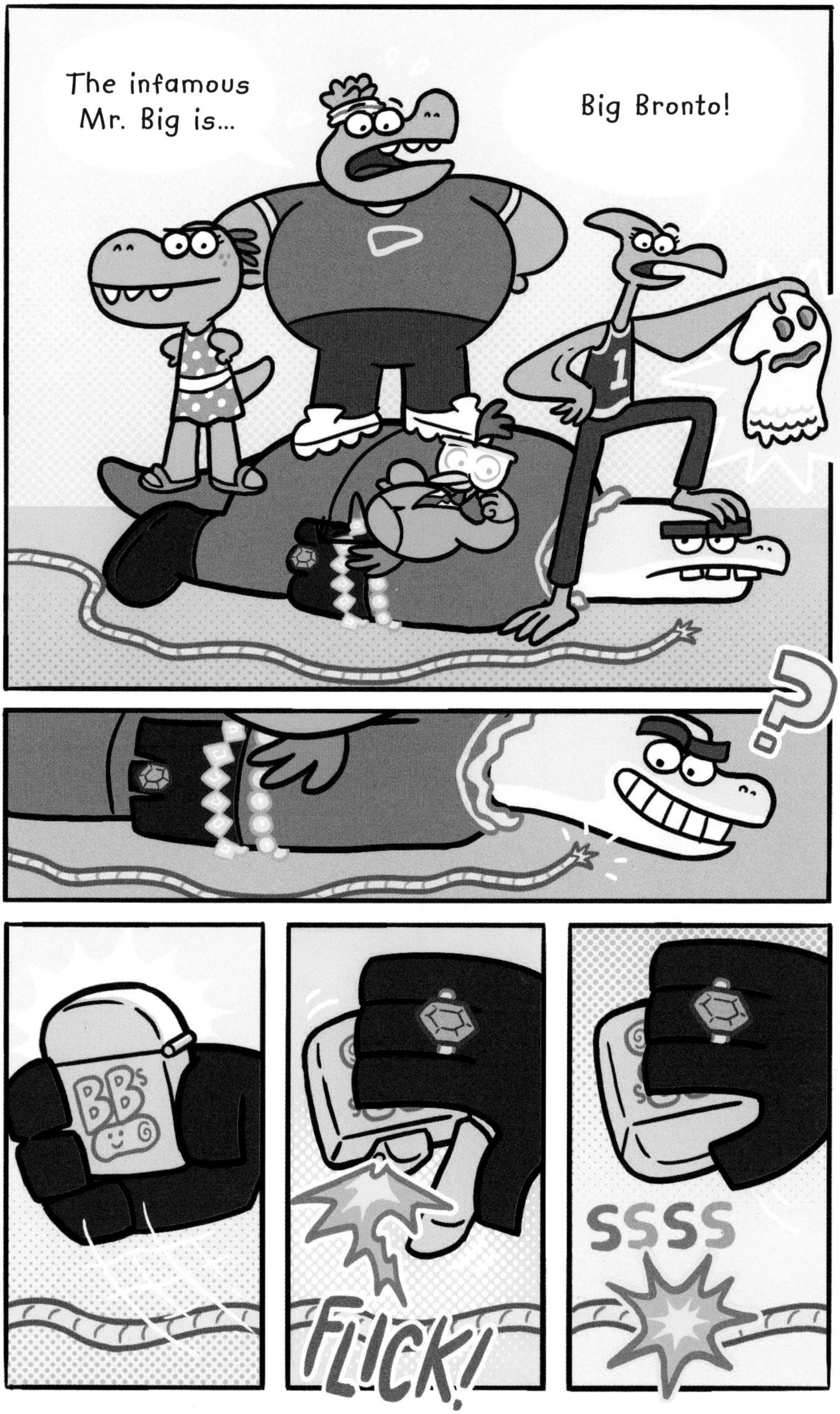

The infamous Mr. Big is...
Big Bronto!
?
BBs
SSSS
FLICK!
SSSS

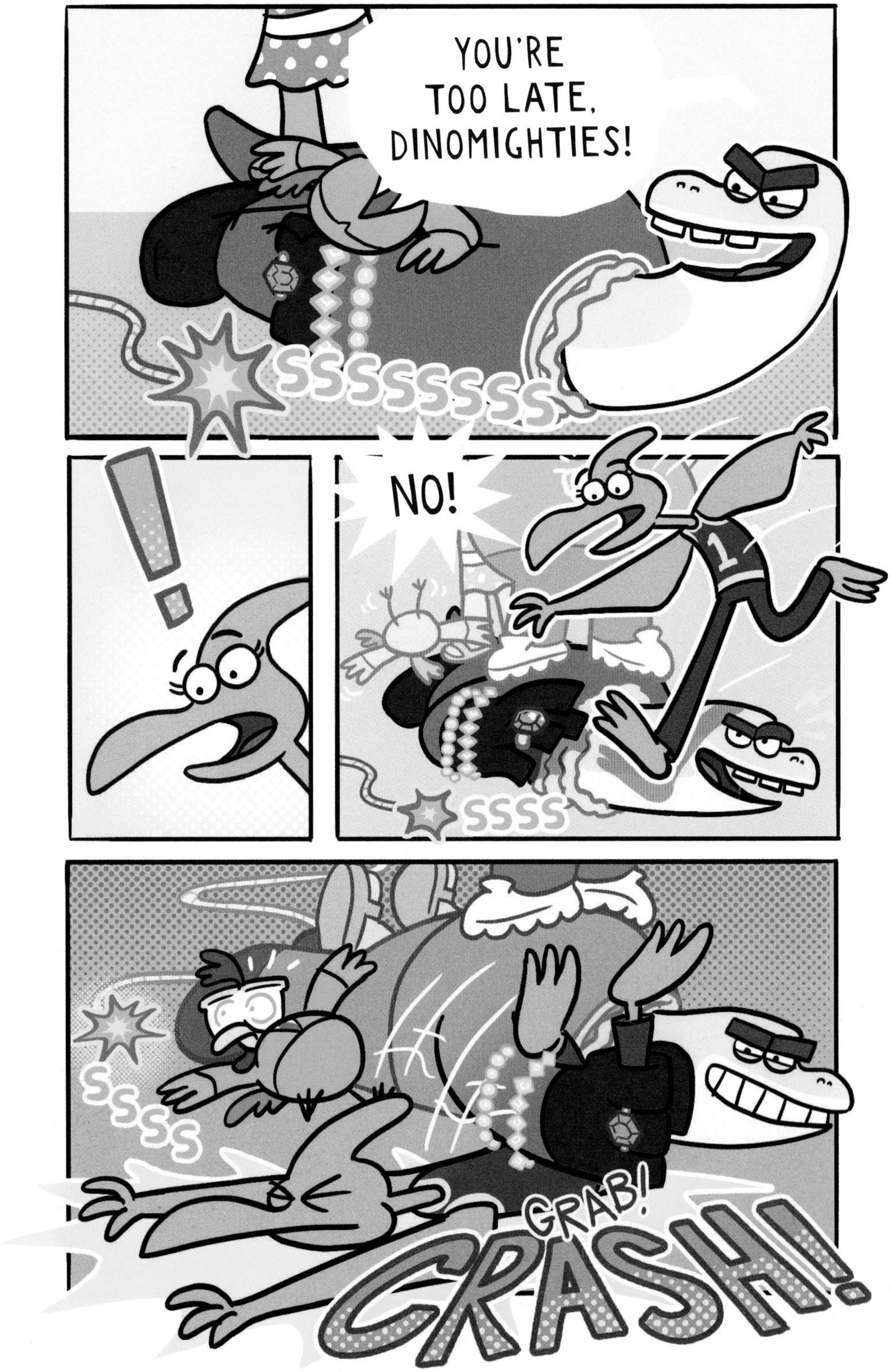
YOU'RE TOO LATE, DINOMIGHTIES!
SSSSSSSSS
!
NO!
SSSS
SSSS
GRAB!
CRASH!!

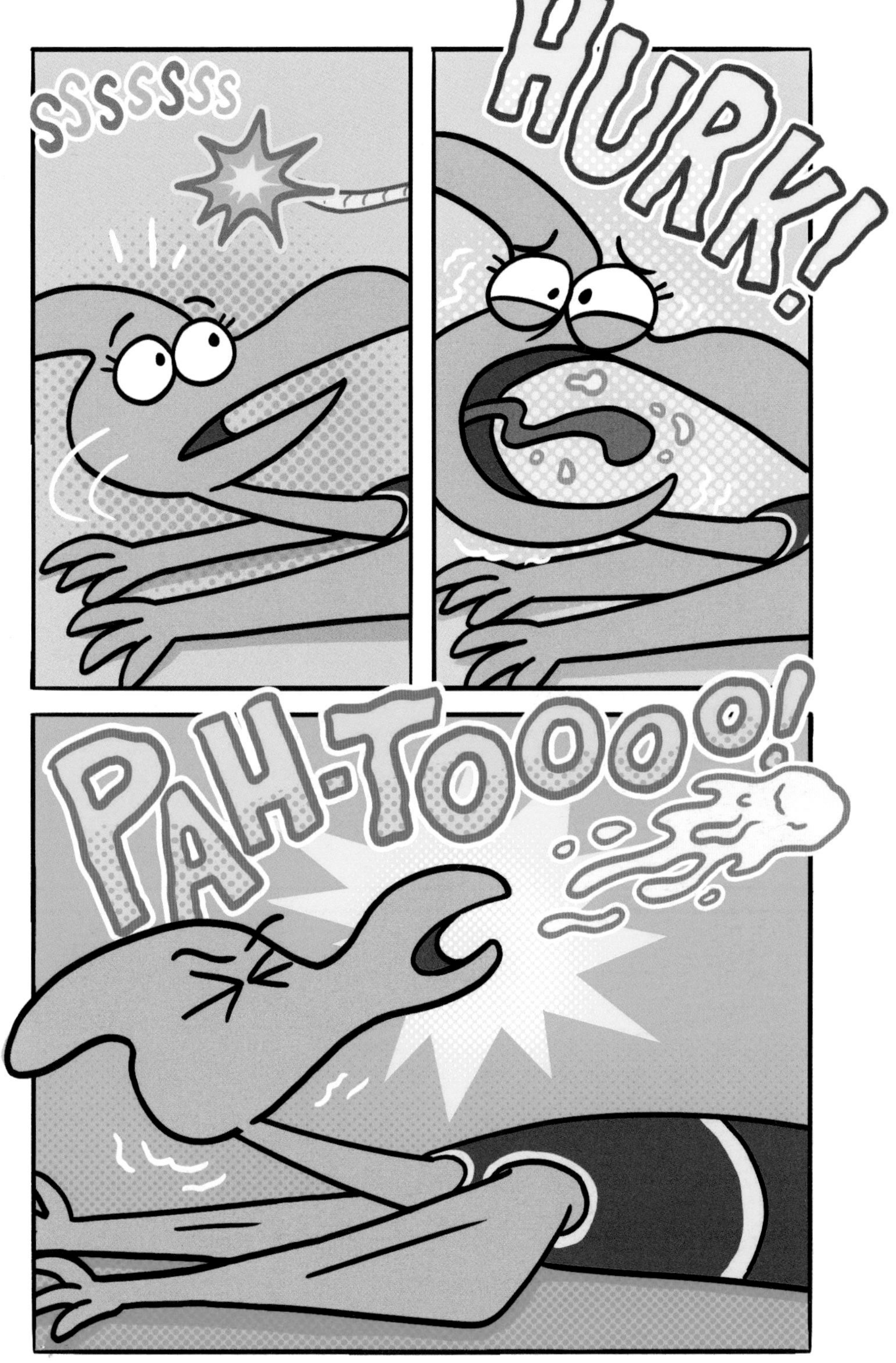
SSSSSS
HURK!
PAH-TOOOO!

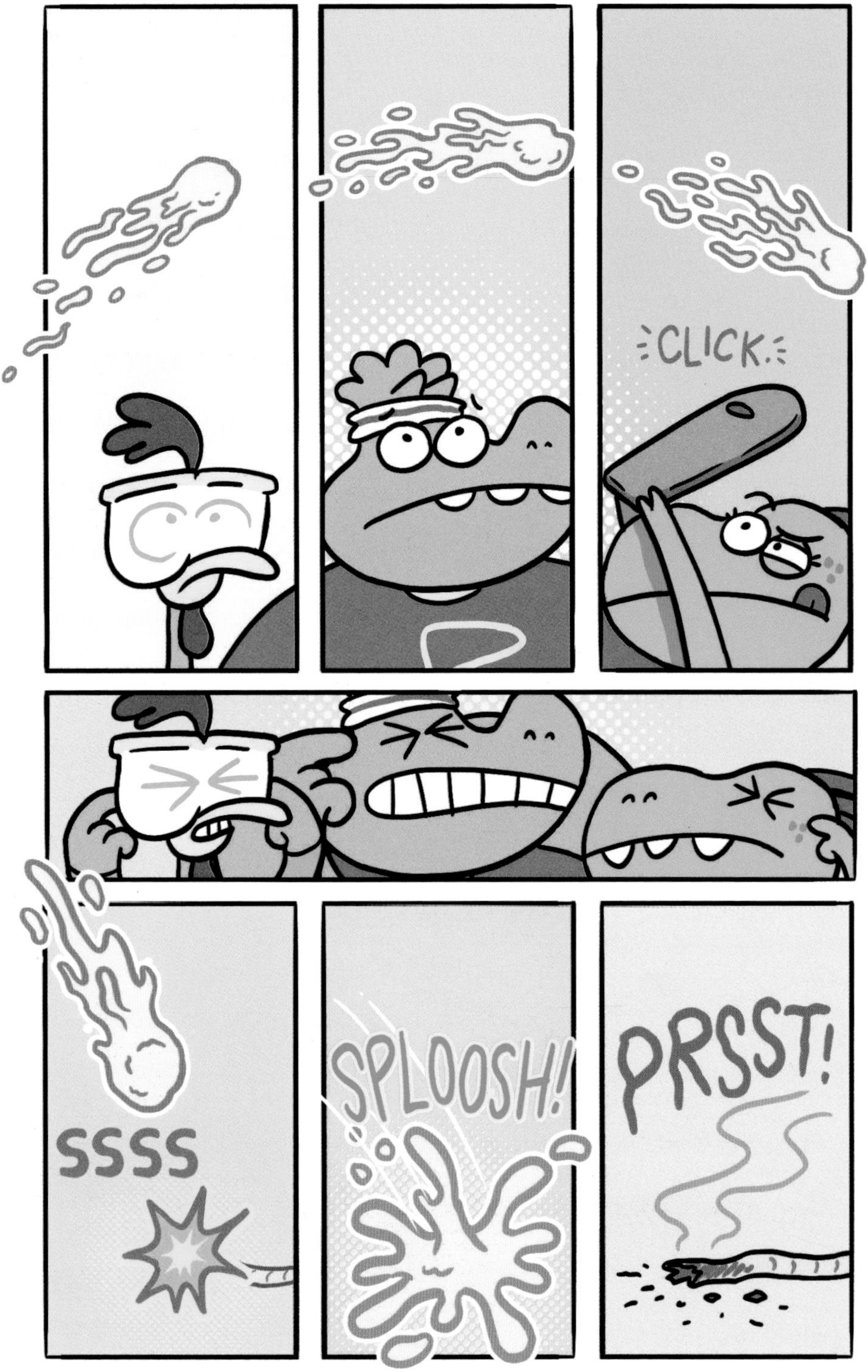
CLICK.
SSSS
SPLOOSH!
PRSST!

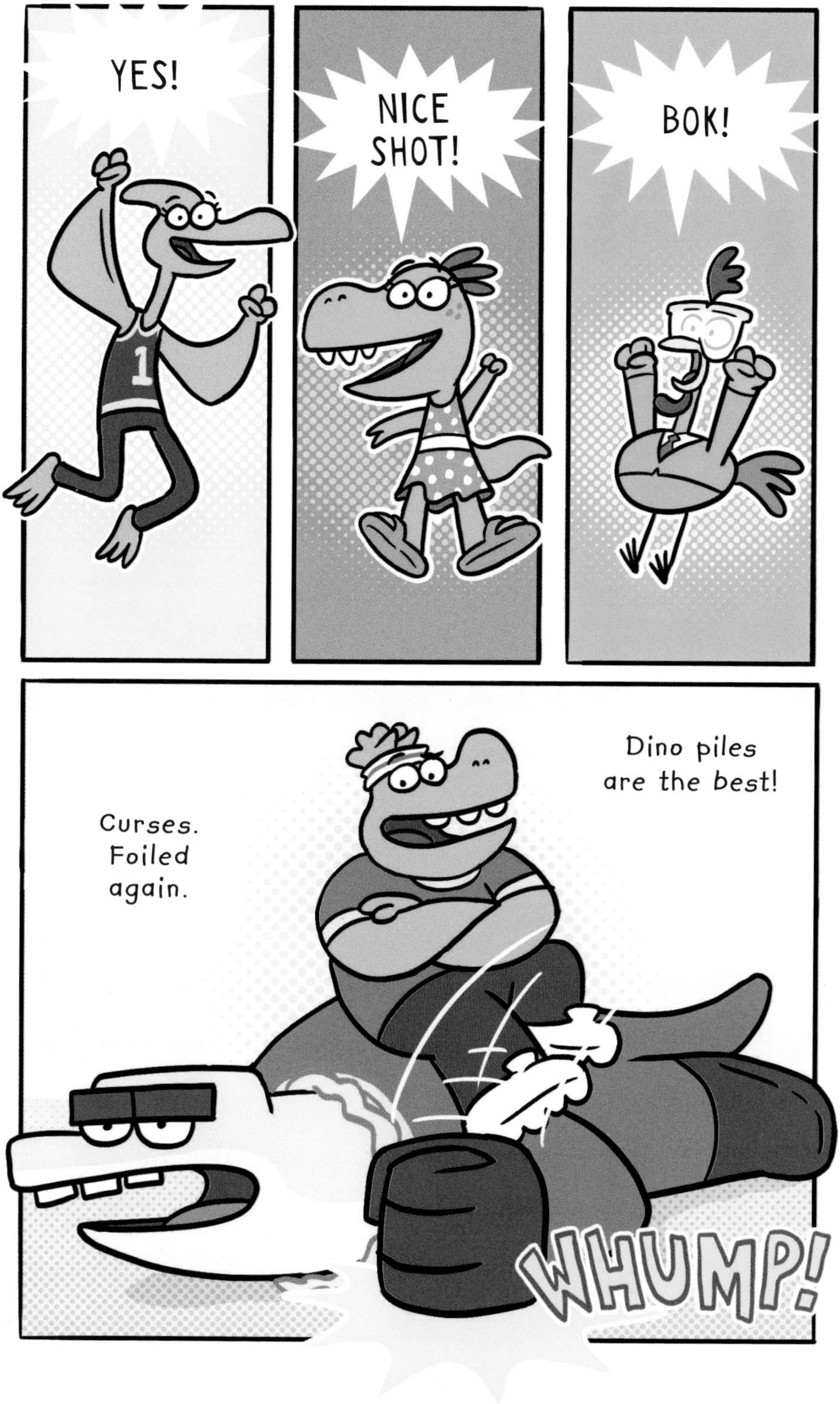
YES!
NICE SHOT!
BOK!
Curses. Foiled again.
Dino piles are the best!
WHUMP!

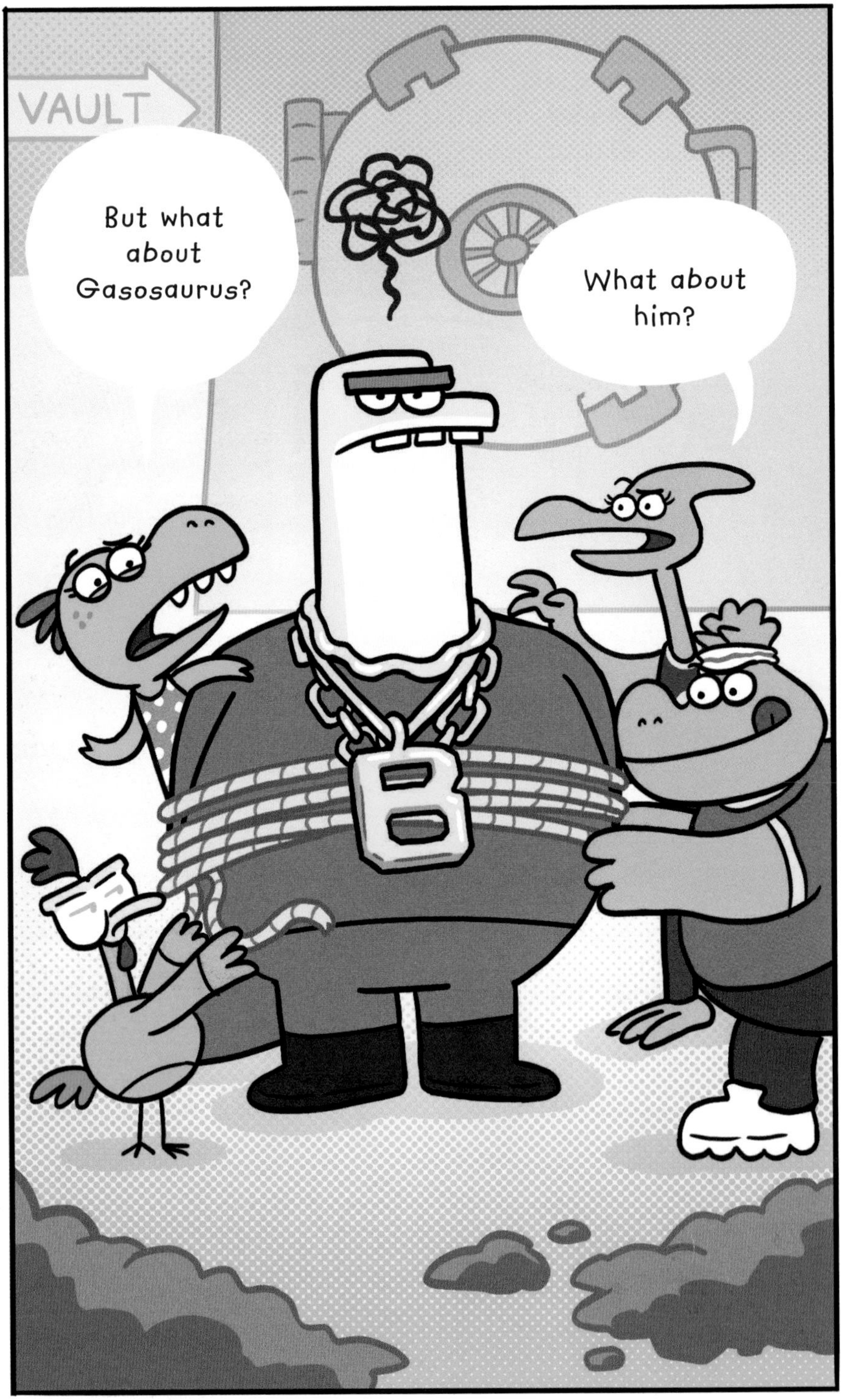
VAULT
But what about Gasosaurus?
What about him?

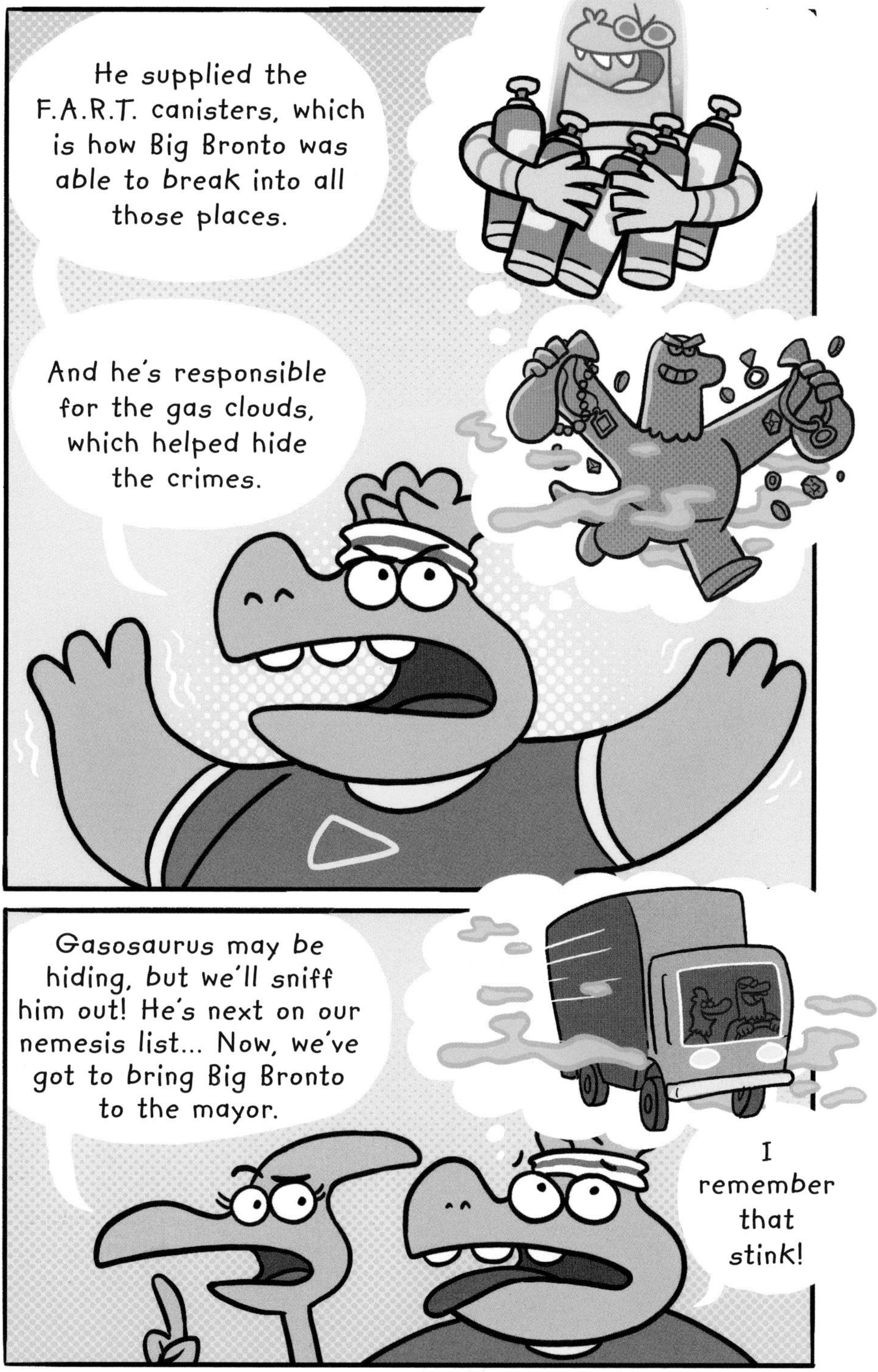
He supplied the F.A.R.T. canisters, which is how Big Bronto was able to break into all those places.
And he's responsible for the gas clouds, which helped hide the crimes.
Gasosaurus may be hiding, but we'll sniff him out! He's next on our nemesis list... Now, we've got to bring Big Bronto to the mayor.
I remember that stink!

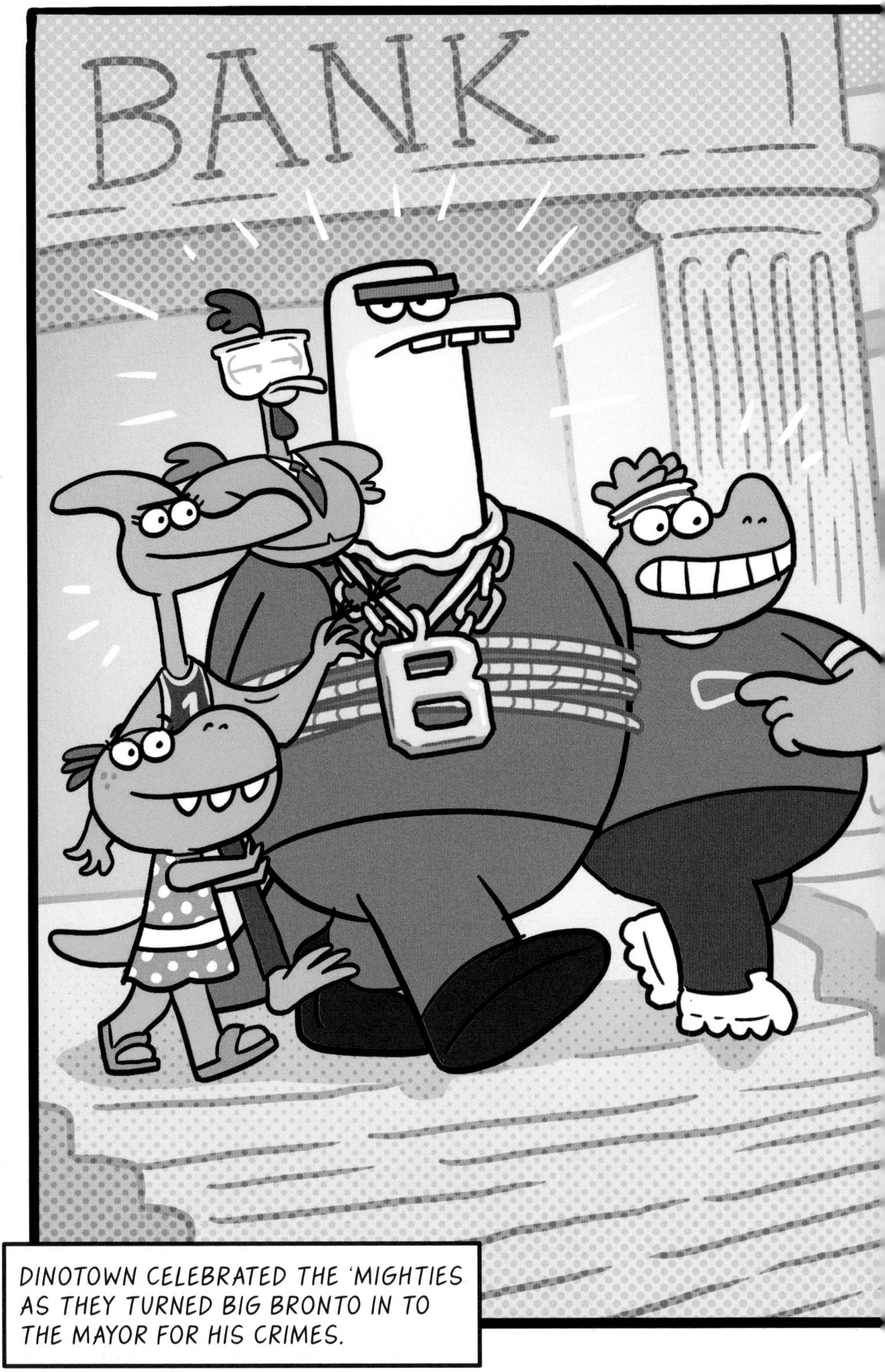
BANK
DINOTOWN CELEBRATED THE 'MIGHTIES AS THEY TURNED BIG BRONTO IN TO THE MAYOR FOR HIS CRIMES.

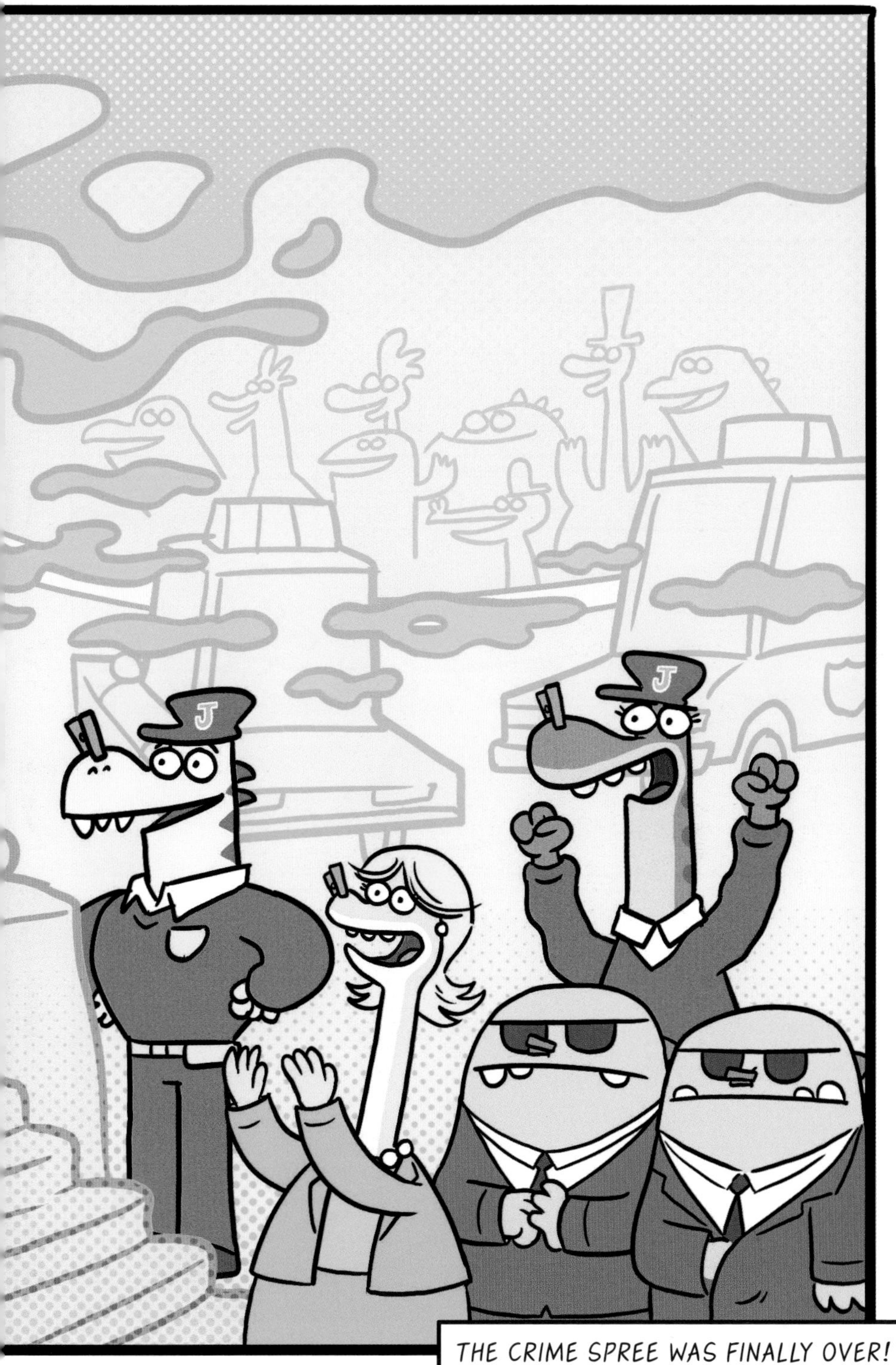
THE CRIME SPREE WAS FINALLY OVER!

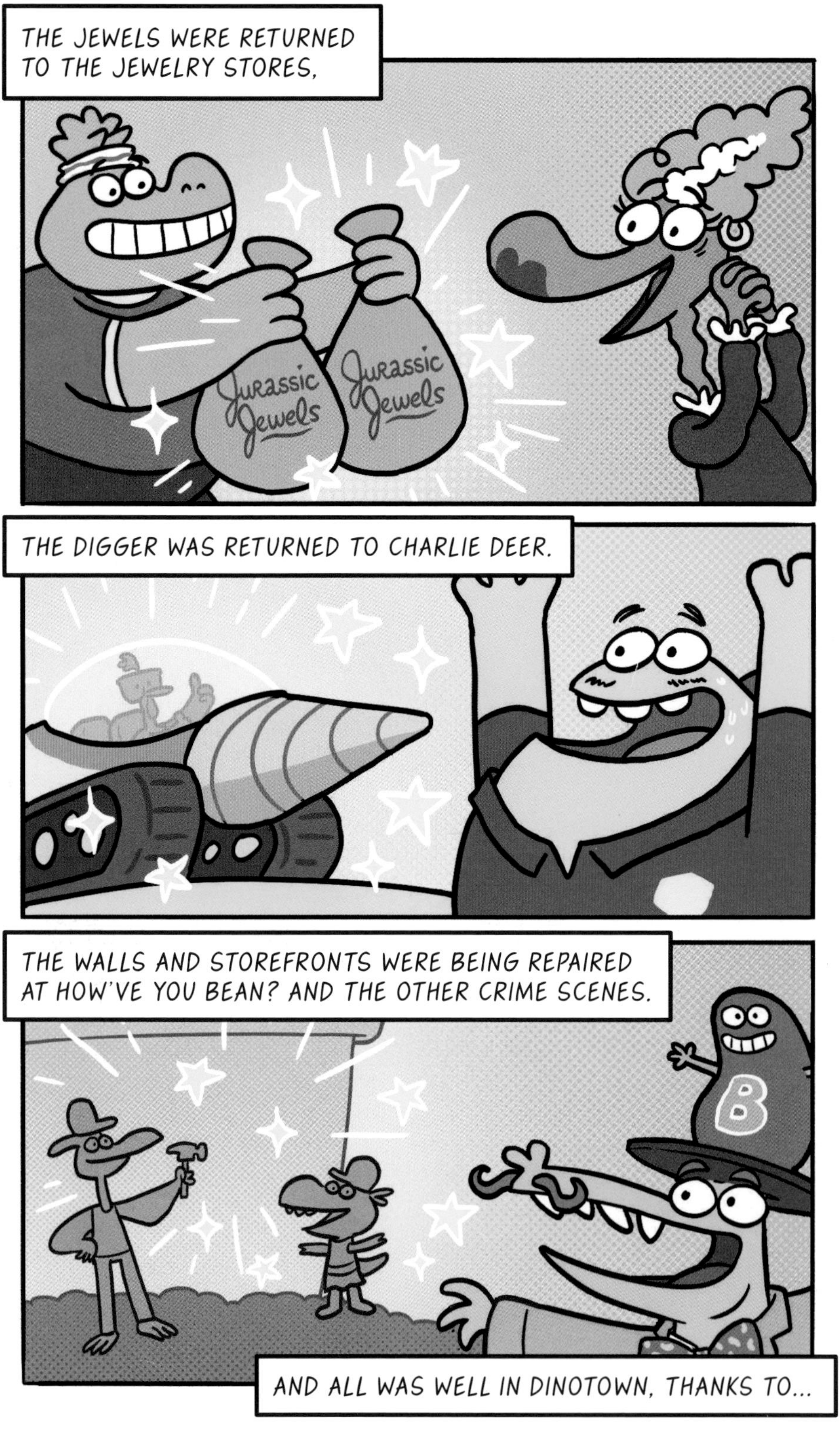
THE JEWELS WERE RETURNED TO THE JEWELRY STORES,
Jurassic Jewels
Jurassic Jewels
THE DIGGER WAS RETURNED TO CHARLIE DEER.
THE WALLS AND STOREFRONTS WERE BEING REPAIRED AT HOW'VE YOU BEAN? AND THE OTHER CRIME SCENES.
B
AND ALL WAS WELL IN DINOTOWN, THANKS TO...

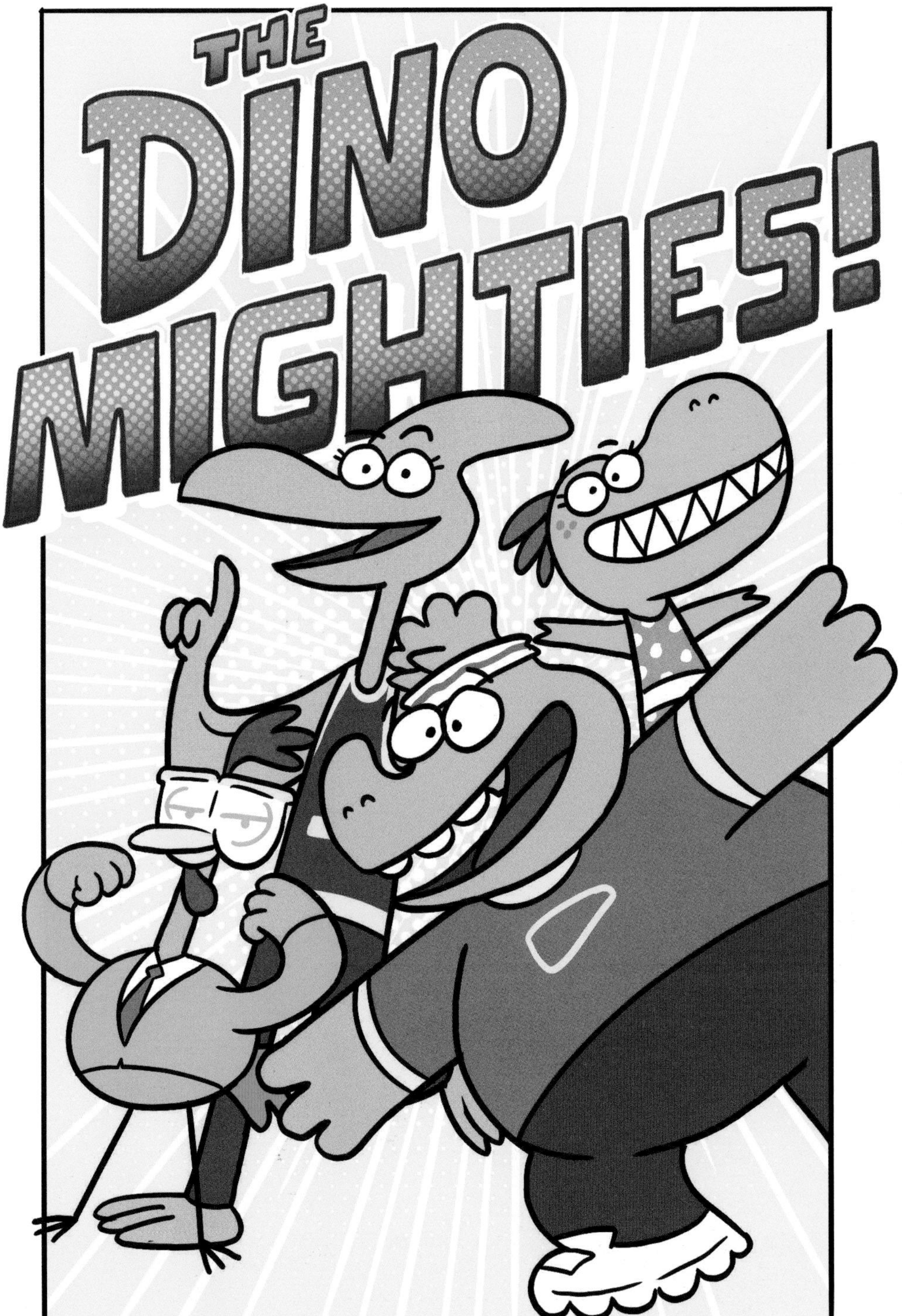
THE
DINO
MIGHTIES!

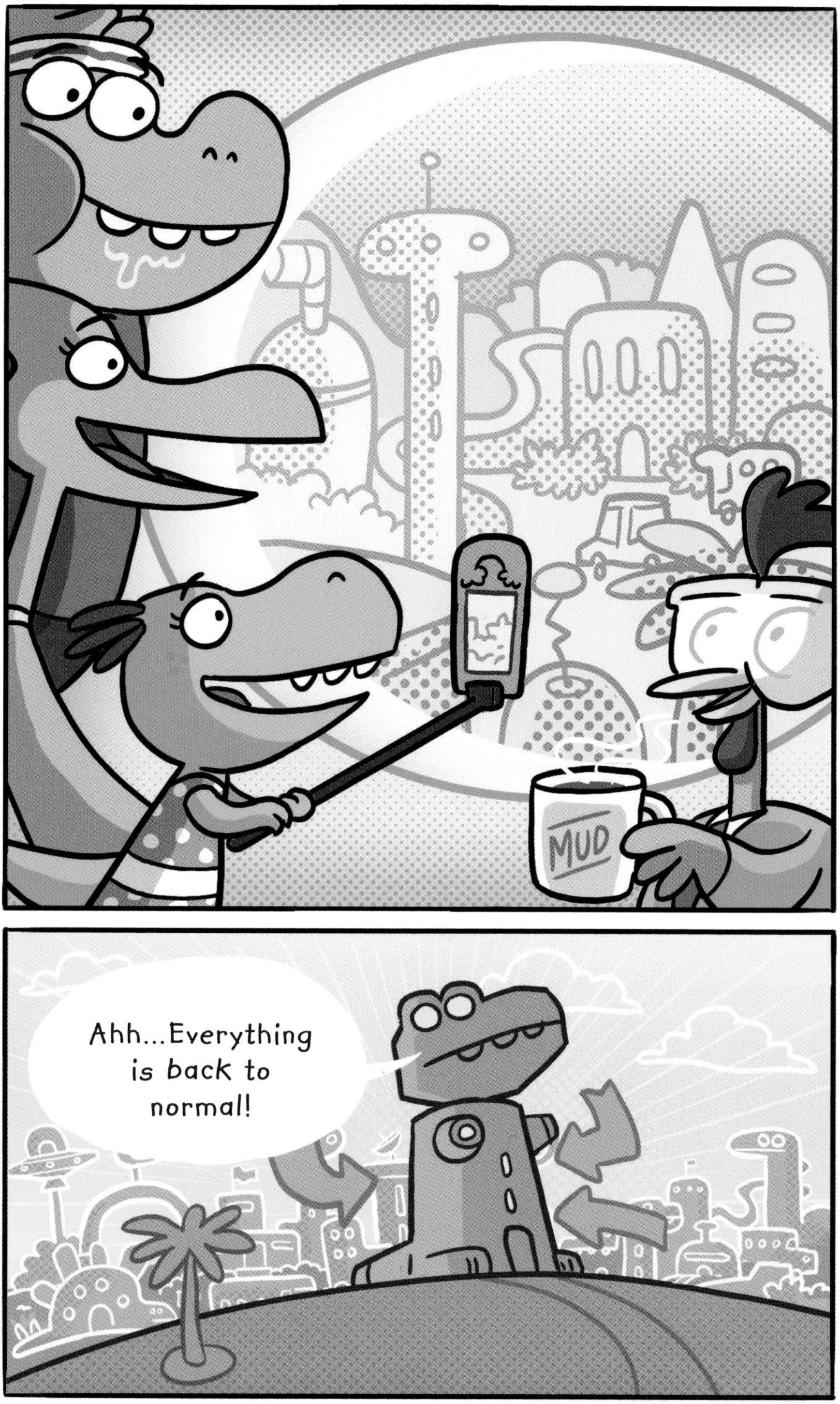
MUD
Ahh...Everything is back to normal!

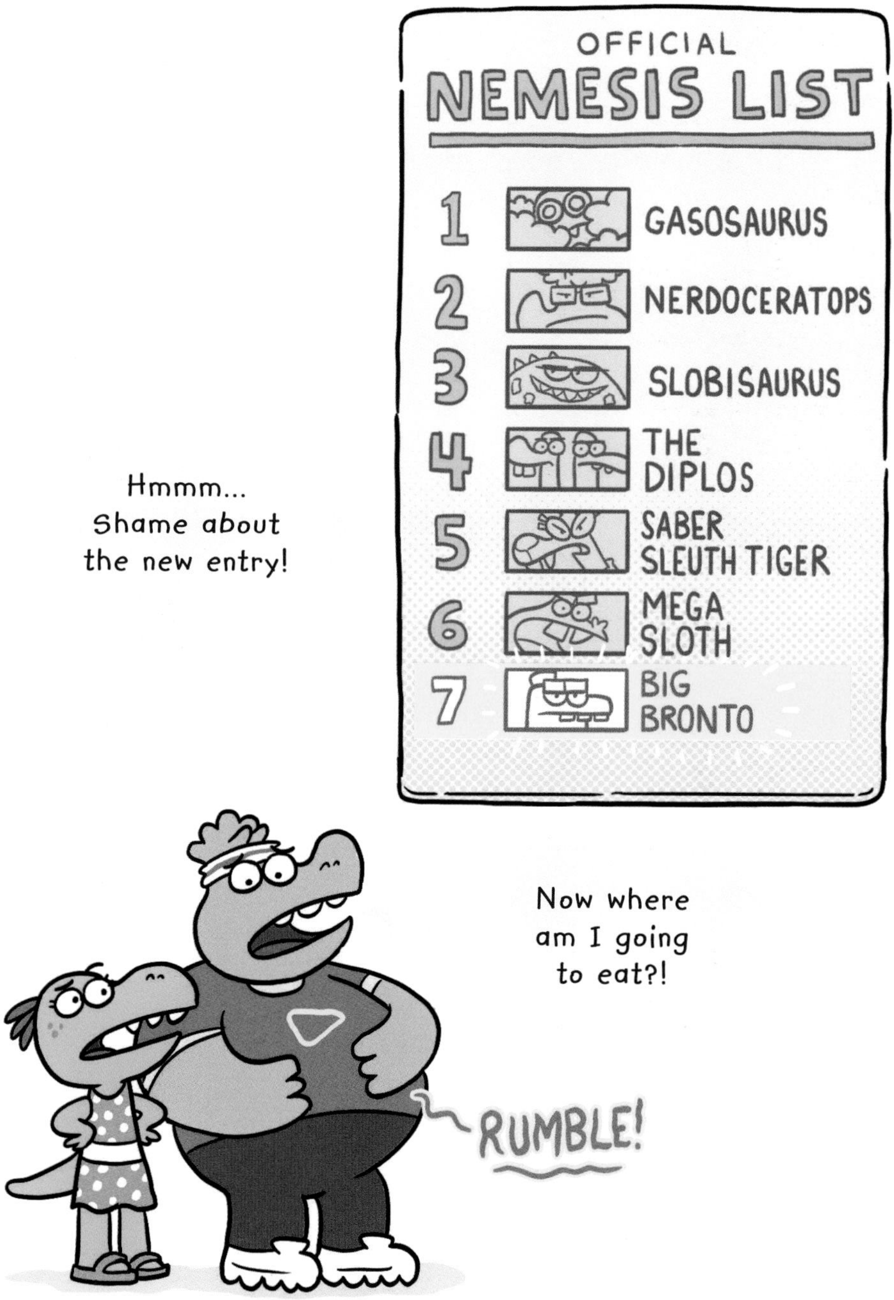
OFFICIAL
NEMESIS LIST
1 GASOSAURUS
2 NERDOCERATOPS
3 SLOBISAURUS
4 THE DIPLOS
5 SABER SLEUTH TIGER
6 MEGA SLOTH
7 BIG BRONTO
Hmmm... Shame about the new entry!
Now where am I going to eat?!
RUMBLE!

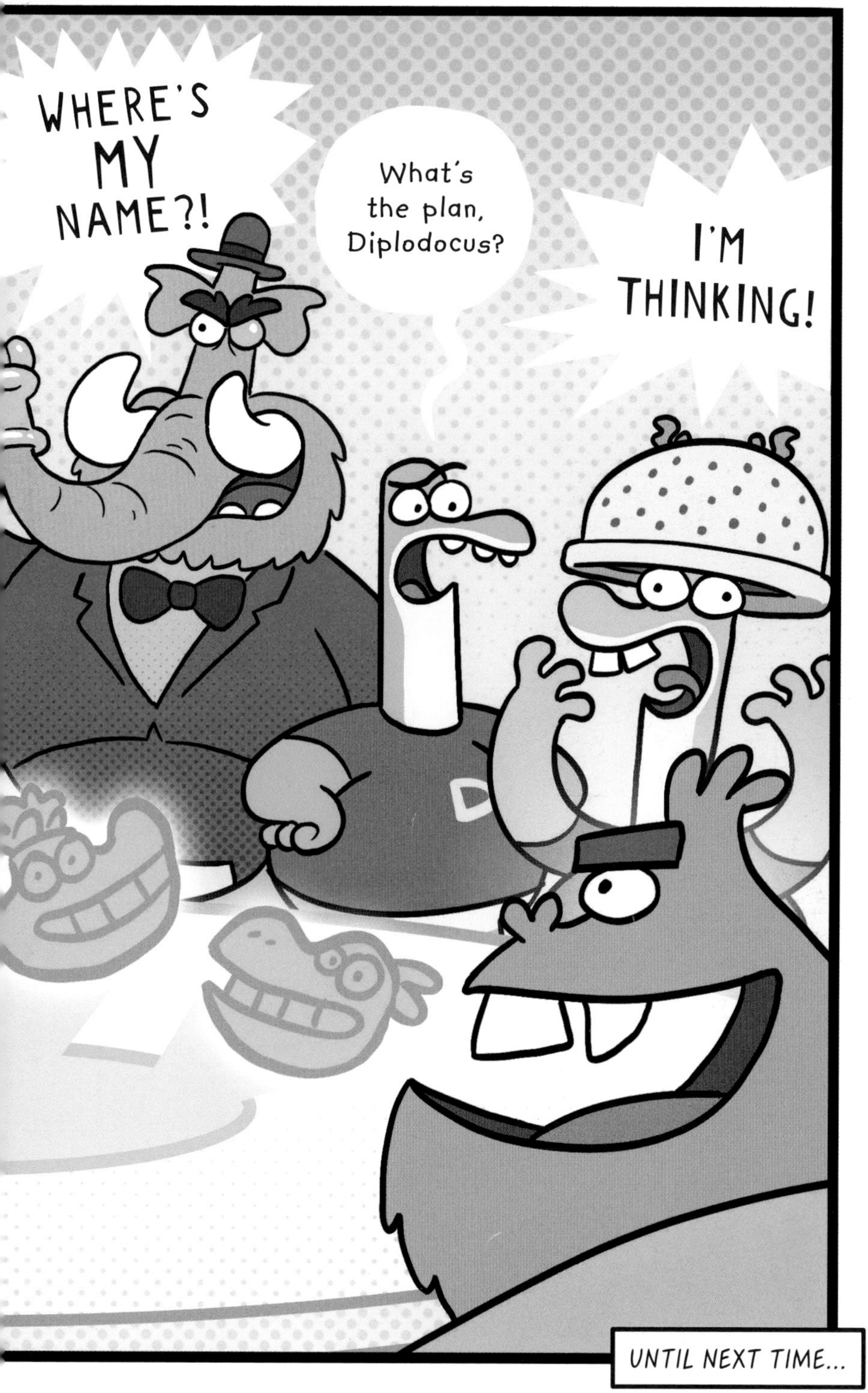
WHERE'S MY NAME?!
What's the plan, Diplodocus?
I'M THINKING!
UNTIL NEXT TIME...

DOUG PALEO IS A DINOMITE AUTHOR OF HILARIOUS BOOKS FOR YOUNG READERS. STONE IS HIS PREFERRED MEDIUM FOR ETCHING GRAPHIC NOVEL SCRIPTS. IN HIS FREE TIME, HE ENJOYS CAVE PAINTING, GOING ON LONG HIKES TO GATHER WILD BERRIES, AND OPEN-FIRE COOKING.

AARON BLECHA IS AN ARTIST AND AUTHOR WHO DESIGNS FUNNY CHARACTERS AND ILLUSTRATES HUMOROUS BOOKS. HIS INTERACTIVE ART EXHIBITION TITLED ALIENS, ZOMBIES & MONSTERS! IS CURRENTLY TOURING THE UK. AARON LIVES WITH HIS FAMILY ON THE SOUTH COAST OF ENGLAND. FIND HIM AT MONSTERSQUID.COM.

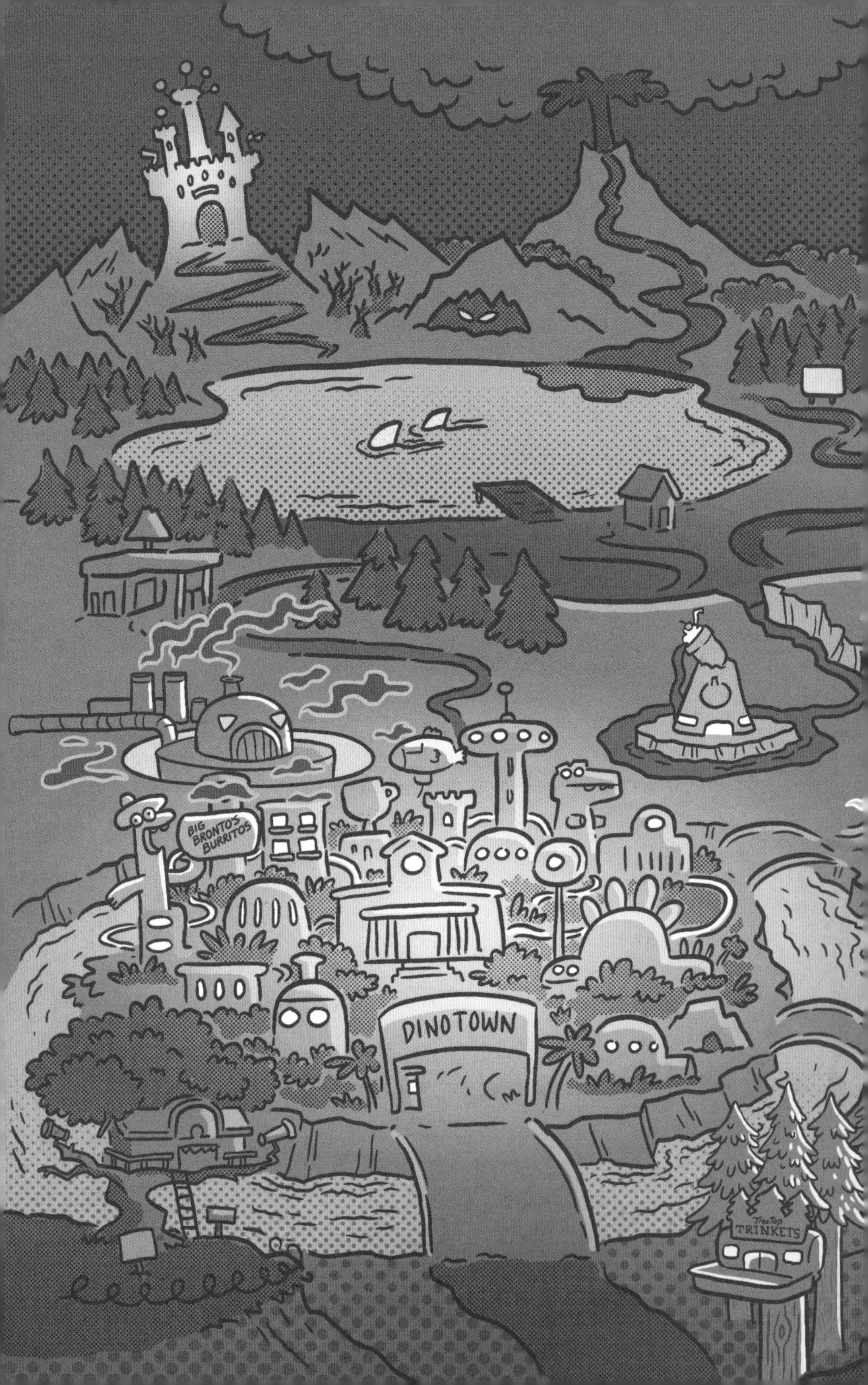
BIG BRONTO'S BURRITOS
DINOTOWN
TreeTop TRINKETS